Seemingly out ed into her, knock the windshield, then car sped away.

The speeding car turned sharply, tires screaming, and headed straight for the exit. It never slowed as it crashed through the barrier at the tollgate and sped off into the night.

Alvarez made for the terminal building. As luck would have it, he ran straight into Tory. After telling her to call 911, Alvarez headed toward the motionless Amy Cooper at a dead run.

He might as well have walked. She was most definitely dead, and it wasn't a pleasant sight. Alvarez had seen more than a few victims of car accidents and shootings during his career, but he had to swallow hard and take a few deep breaths to steady himself.

---- ★ ----

ROSEWOOD'S ASHES

ASHES

by
AILEEN SCHUMACHER

W🌐RLDWIDE®

TORONTO • NEW YORK • LONDON
AMSTERDAM • PARIS • SYDNEY • HAMBURG
STOCKHOLM • ATHENS • TOKYO • MILAN
MADRID • WARSAW • BUDAPEST • AUCKLAND

This book is dedicated to the memory of Rollie Steele.
You're the one who told me that this "writing thing"
would take me places I'd never imagined—
I just wish you would have stuck around to watch.
I'm trying to be grateful for the time we spent together,
but Rollie, damn it, it was way, way too short, and
wherever you are, I hope you know I'm still ticked.

ROSEWOOD'S ASHES

A Worldwide Mystery/May 2002

First published by Intrigue Press

ISBN 0-373-26419-4

Printed in U.S.A.

I'd like to thank the following people who helped make this book more factually correct: Ann Boyd, Jeff Buckholz, Bill Schumacher, Melba Schumacher, Tim Merrill, Lloyd Griffith, Liz Jenkins, Don Esry, Carole Kimberlin, Lucy Wayne and Suzanne Buth. I would like to be able to blame any factual errors on these aforementioned individuals, but I'm not certain that they're willing to be quite THAT helpful. Thanks to those who helped make this a better book: Sandie Herron, Bill Herron, Barbara Peters, Jane Rubino, Andi Shecter, Ann Henley and Jake Elwell. Thanks to those who cheered me on: Bobbye Straight, JoAnne Bowers, Janne Skipper, Pat Steele, Denise Stybr, Joe Forbes, Jan Franklin, Mickie Turett, Dina Willner, Patti Cheney, Arely Gonnering, Justo Vasco and Greg Smith. Thanks to Joanne Marshall for graciously lending me her late husband's name. Thanks to those who love me in spite of all my impossible deadlines: Nicky Blum-Schumacher, Kevin Blum-Schumacher and Richard Blum (who understands all about the dedications). I want to acknowledge the memory of Barbara Wood, Deb Whitney and Richard Marshall. Last but not least, I want to acknowledge the memory of every single person, now gone, who lost life, relatives, property and/or peace of mind because of the events that occurred in Rosewood, Florida, in the first week of January 1923.

MAP OF ROSEWOOD
AND SURROUNDING AREA

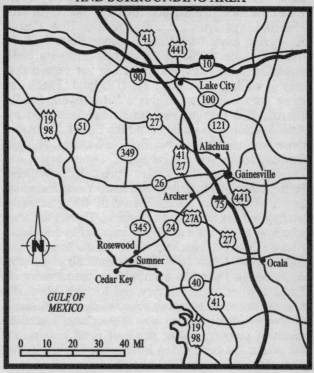

In 1923, the railroad track between Cedar Key,
Sumner, Rosewood, Archer and Gainesville ran
adjacent to the south side of State Road 24.

ROSEWOOD'S
ASHES

PROLOGUE

BLOOD TIES.

Tory Travers gripped the bathroom sink and confronted her reflection in the mirror.

Blood ties.

Those words kept going through her mind—not other words describing the unexpected, gut-wrenching discovery of a few minutes ago, or the devastating phone call that followed. Not even any words for how wretched she felt—the damp sheen on her pale skin and the dark circles under her eyes were witness enough to that.

Blood ties.

A person who had spent a lifetime knowing that one was never totally free of such ties should avoid making more of them.

But wait.

That kind of reasoning would cancel out Cody. Cody—her pride and joy, the one person Tory would die for without a second thought.

Other more realistic images followed the thought of her only son. Cody, the teenager rapidly turning into a man. Cody, who insisted on testing the maternal ties by getting himself a girlfriend—a serious girlfriend, first time out, at the tender age of fifteen. The only thing preventing Tory from calling it cradle robbing was the fact that the girl was only fifteen too.

She watched her reflection sigh. Nothing was ever simple, and as an engineer, Tory liked her answers simple. And accurate. And complete.

But future decisions were going to have to remain just that—decisions to be made in the future. For now, Tory needed to pull herself together and face the fact that she must return to Florida. She was going to have to return to the place she left at eighteen, so eager to put it all behind her that she never looked back. Never, that was, until the past seemed to hold the key to a threat to everything she held dear. Never, until the father she hadn't seen for over seventeen years decided to forge a bridge to the future via her only child.

There were those damn blood ties again.

Tory leaned her forehead against the cool, flat, solid surface of the mirror. She envied everyone who thought of Florida as Disney World and endless sandy beaches. She knew only too well that much of Florida was steeped in the Old South, as removed from high-rise resorts and amusement parks as gumbo and turnip greens from lobster and caviar. Just step off the beach or out the gate of the theme park and you could be there, suddenly wondering how you'd ever find your way back. Just take one tiny step into Tory's family history and you would be confronted with as many samples of the truth as a revisionist historian.

Get a grip. With an effort, Tory used that phrase to replace the endless chant of "blood ties" going round and round in her head. Logic had always been her saving grace. Logically, Tory knew that she needed to walk out of the bathroom, go into her bedroom, and open the phone book to the listings for airlines. It was just the shock and stress getting to her, making her think that that one action would be like opening a Bermuda Triangle window into the past, an opening that would consume her and everything she considered to constitute her future.

She shook herself into action, ignoring the echo still rattling around in her head. All her hard work, all her independence, all the years, miles, states, and cultures between her and her birthplace, and it still came down to this:

Blood ties.

ONE

The Visitors
November, Lake City, Florida

WHEN THE GAWKY young white woman first started coming around, hesitantly asking about other survivors, Lissy Hodden Garner had no more intention of talking to her than she had of talking to those other people. Those who came earlier had been full of themselves, a passel of black people Lissy had never seen before, excitedly claiming some kind of connection to her simply because of some relative who supposedly knew Lissy a lifetime ago. Then there were still others, black and white both, with their degrees and their book learning and their all-important mission, crowding into her room with tape recorders and notebooks and cameras.

It had sure set them back some, the fact that she had nothing to say. What did they expect? After all, *they'd* come looking for her, not the other way around. When they started talking about the possibility of money for her if she cooperated, Lissy would have laughed, except that she wanted them to remember her with lips pinched tight together, solemnly shaking her head, refusing to say a word.

The money, now that was a hoot, them thinking that the money would mean something to a shriveled up old black woman in a nursing home, with not one single blood relative left alive. She still had Andy's railroad pension, bless the man, and it was enough to keep Lissy in this place more days than she was interested in being here. Mind you, the place wasn't fancy, but here she could afford a room to herself.

But the others hadn't given up easy, she had to give them that. When they saw that talk of money had no effect in prying open her old clenched lips, they fell silent a while, blinking and staring at one another, puzzled as though some trusted family recipe had failed to produce a tasty dish.

Then one of them took a deep breath and started talking about justice and retribution, and soon the others were clamoring along just like a congregation switching hymns mid-song. So it went, from talk of money to talk of justice and retribution. Well, those were two words that Lissy Hodden Garner knew something about. She sure was looking forward to some of each in the next world, and she had no intention of tainting her chance of getting a peek at them by believing that justice and retribution could be granted by living, breathing people. At least not the kind of justice and retribution that Lissy had in mind.

We just want you to tell us your story, they kept at her. Tell us your story before it's too late, before it's lost forever.

Well, for all their book learning and degrees, and for all their claims of connection and community, those ignorant people didn't realize that that was the whole point. It was enough to make Lissy wonder whether they had been taught any common-sense manners while being so all-fired busy getting ahead in the world.

It was pure audacity, them thinking she would share her story with strangers. It was pure audacity to think she would share it with anyone. Lissy's story was the one thing that unquestionably belonged to her alone and to no one else. She hadn't chosen to share it with her parents or her sister, or with the actual acquaintances from that other time, who years ago would sometimes seek her out and wish to speak in low, furtive tones.

Lissy always hated chance encounters with those previous acquaintances, and not just because they were always after her, badgering her to tell them what she'd seen. They all had the same darting, seeking eyes, as though on the lookout for someone following close behind them. Some of them out-and-out claimed they were being stalked, that they had to move constantly, changing their names and occupations as often as the season. They talked about fearing for their lives—claimed that they had to whisper and talk behind their hands to avoid being sought out and punished.

Lissy was always devoutly grateful that regardless of whatever else had transpired, she hadn't turned into a ghost-person with darting, seeking eyes. Lissy didn't have to whisper and talk behind her hand, because she had nothing to say. More than that, she had nothing to fear. She had been to hell and back again, and it had burned the fear right out of her for a lifetime.

Tell us your story, they kept prodding her. Didn't they realize her parents had spent years of prodding before going to early deaths, and it had never made a difference? Lissy's sister Garland had prodded until it became an obstacle between them, a barrier neither one could reach over. When little Homer Marshall grew up and went off to fight Hitler, returning a ruined shell of a man, there was nothing left to bind the sisters, and they lived out the rest of their lives with minimal contact. But it hadn't been minimal enough, for had Lissy known that Garland would provide a trail between her and the people who crowded into her room, she would have forgone even the annual Christmas card.

No use frettin'—it was all water under the bridge now with Garland dead these past few years. Lissy heard that her sister had slipped away with no family member at her side to ease her journey from this world to the next. Well, there were worse things than dying alone, and one of them was a lack of peace.

That was the one thing that Lissy dreaded. Because although she had all the resolve in the world, all the resolve of an eighty-three-year-old woman worn out by a lifetime of hard work might not have been sufficient to the task. Tell us your story, they kept asking. Lord, she had more visitors in a week than the rest of the nursing home residents had in a month of Sundays.

Tell us your story, tell us your story—to Lissy's ears it started to sound like a chant. One single soul knew little Lissy Hodden's story, and that was sweet Andy Garner, who had been resting in his grave for nigh onto twenty years now. There wasn't a day came and went that Lissy didn't miss Andy, that sweet man-boy who held her night after night and wiped away her tears, but it was almost enough to make her glad he'd passed, so these prodding ones couldn't badger him along with her.

In the end, it was big, strapping Tazzy they didn't count on. Tazzy, with her pierced nose and tongue and Heaven-only-knew what else. Tazzy, with her bleached kinky hair and her coffee-colored skin crawling with snake tattoos. Tazzy might not be a nurse, she might not have a fancy title, and she might not have much book learning, but Tazzy sure did have something. Tazzy called it street smarts; Lissy called it gumption. Tazzy stood up to all those people and told them to leave an old woman alone. When one man asked if maybe Lissy was senile, and if that was the reason she wouldn't talk to them, Tazzy used language that made his lips turn whitish, all the while tugging on his sleeve, ushering him out of the room with the rest.

Lissy and Tazzy didn't have much in common besides their

distant African heritage. Lissy didn't approve of Tazzy's appearance or her language—except when it came in useful. Lissy didn't approve of the way Tazzy went through men like hair colors and had no ambition to settle down, and Lissy could only marvel at Tazzy's stories of growing up in the Bronx—it seemed to her to be a foreign land. It deeply pained Lissy that Tazzy claimed not to believe in God.

On top of all of this, Lissy couldn't fathom what it must be like to have a name like Tazzy—it sure didn't come from the Bible or any book Lissy had ever read, and it didn't stand for something else, like Lissy stood for Little Sister, once long ago. But despite their differences, one thing that Lissy and Tazzy had was an understanding, and that understanding included the fact that if a grown woman had achieved the ripe old age of eighty-three, she certainly had the right to decide whether she wanted to talk to people or not.

After Tazzy showed those others out three days in a row, they stopped coming around. A reporter would call up now and then, but since there was no one else who would be calling, Tazzy could be counted on to tell the caller that Mrs. Garner wasn't available. When Tazzy wasn't on duty and someone else brought the phone around, Lissy would hold it to her ear, shake her head in a puzzled fashion and then hang up, remarking with surprise how there was no one on the other end of the line.

Well, that was the truth, it just wasn't the complete truth. There was no one on the other end of the line that Lissy wanted to talk to.

So it was no wonder that when young Chloe Pitts showed up pale and awkward as a newborn calf almost a year later, Tazzy was in fighting form to show her out the door. But the homely white woman was quiet and respectful, and she came bringing flowers, which caught Lissy's interest right off the bat. She had always been a sucker for flowers, ever since Andrew Garner first came courting her, clenching a bunch of wilted lilies in his huge sweaty fist. Lissy told Tazzy that she would call if she needed her, then she told Chloe Pitts that she could sit and visit a spell if she was so inclined.

It was the very awkwardness of the woman that disarmed Lissy. Chloe haltingly explained how she was a graduate student in history at the university in Tallahassee, and how she worked for one of those others who had come earlier. Lissy never knew exactly which one, and she never wanted to know. She liked to think it was the man Tazzy gave a talking to. Chloe explained nice and respectful-like that she was working on her own, checking facts and stories and names before the sunsetting.

The talk of sunsetting confused Lissy. She didn't know how much fact and story-checking the young woman was going to get done in this out-of-the-way nursing home before the sun set that afternoon, especially with the days getting so short.

But then Chloe explained that she was talking about sunsetting on the mission of those people looking for survivors. And sunsetting didn't mean what Lissy thought it meant—it meant that there was a deadline. If all the survivors weren't identified by December 31, then those who hadn't been found wouldn't be survivors.

Lissy would have laughed out loud at this if the other woman hadn't been so serious and solemn. The very idea, that if someone's name wasn't on a list by a certain date, it meant they weren't who they were. That sounded just like something white folks and government would cook up together.

Chloe was polite and Chloe brought flowers, and Chloe didn't ask one single time for Lissy to tell her story. She just showed Lissy her list and asked her if she knew of anyone who should be added. Lissy didn't even put on her glasses to look at the list or to find her own name. She just pretended to study it for a while and then handed it back, saying she would think on it. Then she asked Chloe about her own family and upbringing, and the young woman answered shyly, but thoughtfully and in detail, not just as though she was humoring an old woman. After listening for a while, Lissy thought that despite their differences, Chloe's story of growing up poor and white in Micanopy, the offspring of two alcoholic parents, almost sounded similar to growing up poor and Negro in a Florida timber town.

Almost.

When Tazzy stuck her head in to say that supper was coming, Lissy was surprised that the afternoon had passed so quickly. She told Chloe Pitts that she could come back and visit again some time, and that Lissy sure did like flowers. Chloe came back five times during the next three weeks, always bringing flowers, always willing to talk about whatever subjects struck Lissy's fancy. But at some point during her visit she always asked if Lissy knew of anyone who should be added to the list, and Lissy always told her that she would think on it.

Lissy wasn't senile and she wasn't stupid, and she knew the visits wouldn't last forever. It was getting on to being Christmas, and after that would come the sunset, the sunset that a group of lawmakers had declared, as though they thought they could rival God. So Lissy thought on the matter, and at the end of the third week she decided that there were certain things she could tell Chloe Pitts that wouldn't compromise sweet Andy Garner's status as the only person who'd heard her story.

Lissy decided to tell Chloe Pitts about the Marshall boy, and the consequences be damned.

TWO

Bathroom Revelations
Saturday

FOR DAVID ALVAREZ, a seasoned member of the El Paso Police Department Special Case Force, remaining cool was a way of life. So when the plane he was on tipped suddenly and alarmingly in his direction, causing him to slide across his seat toward the window, he used the opportunity to look out and study the impressive nighttime thunderstorm raging over Tallahassee. This was his very first visit to Florida, and he didn't want to miss anything. Particularly not the runway.

The plane righted itself and Alvarez glanced at his seatmate to see if any potential distraction might be coming from that source. Not likely. Pale and silent, the woman next to him had her eyes closed. She might appear to be asleep, but Alvarez knew she wasn't. He saw the way her fingers gripped the armrests of her seat, and someone would have to be drugged to sleep through this ride.

Reading was no good—Alvarez had skimmed the in-flight magazine earlier, and he hadn't been charitably disposed toward it to begin with. It was a publication from a major airline, looking bright, glossy, reassuring—and out of place on this thirty-seat prop plane belonging to an affiliated commuter line. He wanted to get his mind on something other than the landing, so he thought about the woman next to him.

Alvarez knew from past experience that amazing things happened when Tory Travers was around—take, for example, the very sequence of events that caused him to be in this plane, hovering over Florida in the middle of the night, in the middle of a thunderstorm, waiting for clearance to land.

To be fair, there had been warning signs early on in the relationship that it was not to be a smooth one. Things first started to get dicey when Alvarez tried to rescue Tory from an unknown assailant and ended up being the one held at gunpoint. Alvarez wasn't dumb—after that he'd tried to stay away, but he hadn't been successful. Then one thing led to another in a rapid succession of events that made him grateful for health insurance.

Simply kissing Tory had been followed by a close encounter with a car bomb. Recovered, he finally managed to make love to her, only to be shot by a homicidal maniac the next day. It made Alvarez feel rather as though he'd won the jackpot in Monopoly and then immediately drawn the Go to Jail card. He'd landed back in the hospital for a longer stay, but even that paled in comparison to this morning. Pretty much everything paled in comparison to this morning.

Hours ago, a lifetime ago, it had been a regular boring medical-leave Saturday morning. Alvarez was at home, sporting clean jeans and a fresh arm sling, considering some training options proposed for his convalescence. Cotton, a dog that looked like some teenaged girl's white fluffy stuffed animal, was lying in a limp heap across his bare feet. Alvarez was thinking that hostage negotiation looked interesting, especially since it might give him some pointers in getting his partner's wife to lighten up about letting Scott attend weekly poker games. Alvarez thought it was a sad day, or evening, when a detective had to alibi himself.

Then the phone rang.

Getting a call from Cody Travers was a surprise. Cody and Tory had spent years as a family of two ever since the premature death of Cody's father. Tory was estranged from her own family, thus increasing their isolation. However, a recent chain of events had brought her father, a former politician, back into her life in an uneasy new alliance with much of the man's interest focused on his only grandchild.

It was this very grandfather Cody was calling about. "We got a call about an hour ago," he told Alvarez. The kid avoided calling Alvarez by any form of address, including plain old Hey You. "I thought you'd want to know—my grandfather has been in a car accident."

The accident had occurred in Gainesville, Florida, which raised a question in Alvarez's mind. He knew Tom Wheatley lived in Ocala—wherever that was, Alvarez's off-hand geographical knowledge of Florida was pretty well limited to Miami and Disney World—but before he asked, Cody explained that Ocala was about as far south of Gainesville as El Paso was south of the Travers residence in Las Cruces, New Mexico. Then something clicked, and Alvarez remembered that Gainesville was a place Cody visited when he stayed with his grandfather over Christmas break.

The accident had occurred late the previous evening—the exact time was impossible to determine, since the man hadn't been discovered until another driver came upon Wheatley's lone crumpled car, which had spun to a stop in the middle of an intersection. The local police deduced that one car had run a stoplight and struck another. Alvarez, hundreds of miles away and without benefit of viewing the scene of the accident, deduced that the driver at fault probably hadn't been Tory's father—guiltless drivers rarely fled the scene.

But guilt wasn't the issue. After Wheatley was identified and the police contacted his Ocala residence, it was finally sorted out that Tory was the victim's closest living relative. And so she got the call telling her that her father was in a coma in a Gainesville hospital.

Cody related all of this quickly, and Alvarez responded similarly. "Put your mother on the phone," he said.

"I can't," the kid replied. "She's being sick. She's had some kind of stomach flu for a while."

"She's being sick right now?" In Alvarez's past experience with Tory, she got through a crisis first and then threatened to throw up later.

"Yeah, she's been in the bathroom most of the morning. That's why I called. She comes out every few minutes to try to make plane reservations, then she gets sick and goes back to the bathroom." Cody paused for a moment. "You know, she's never been back there, not once, not since she was eighteen. She won't let me go with her and I'm worried about her. I don't want her to go by herself."

"Why won't she let you go with you?"

"She says she doesn't know how long she'll be gone, that I can't miss that much school. She's really stressed. I told her not to worry about me. I told her I could always stay with Kohli's family."

Alvarez could just imagine Tory's response to the idea of Cody staying with his girlfriend's family. "And?" he prompted anyhow.

"She flipped out," said Cody. "She said, over her dead body."

"Too bad—you were just trying to help," replied Alvarez. "What's the alternate plan?"

"Sylvia and Jazz."

Alvarez felt irrationally elated that Tory's rancher friend Lonnie Harper hadn't gotten tapped for kid-sitting duty. Then he thought of Sylvia and Jazz together, and wondered whether Tory's crusty foreman and her flamboyant secretary could live in the same household without killing each other. "Sylvia and Jazz," Alvarez said. "That's really interesting."

"Yeah, that was my response, too," the kid deadpanned.

"So that takes care of you," said Alvarez. "When is your mom leaving?" He felt like an idiot every time he called Tory "your mom," but what was he supposed to do? In his life up to this point, he had avoided not only marriage, but also contact with kids who weren't breaking the law. Did calling the kid's mother by her first name imply an assumed intimacy? Another part of his brain questioned whether anyone cared.

"That's the problem," said Cody. "She's upset and worried and sick on top of it all, and it turns out there's some big racing event in Gainesville and all the flights are booked."

"Horse racing is that big in Florida?" asked Alvarez blankly.

There was a pause. "Car racing," said Cody. "NHRA."

So what if the kid knew something he didn't? Alvarez always liked to end conversations on a positive note. He looked at his watch. "Tell her—tell your mother—" He stopped himself. "Tell Tory I'll be there in two hours, and I'll bring two plane tickets with me."

"You can really do that?" The kid's voice was filled with relief.

"I'm not a member of something called Special Case Force for nothing," said Alvarez. And then, because he really did want to make an effort to be honest with the kid, he added, "Also, I can be really persistent and obnoxious, but I have something going for me that's even more important than that."

"What?" asked Cody, right on cue.

"I just paid off the balance on my credit card."

THE PROMISE TO CODY Alvarez with an hour to get plane tickets, call his sister, pack, and make arrangements for Cotton. It took twenty-five minutes to book two seats on a circuitous route that would eventually end in Gainesville, Florida, and it took more of the remaining credit card balance than Alvarez would have thought possible. I must be in love, he thought, as he replaced the pillaged Visa in his wallet, and, as always since he'd first tried out the words in his mind, the notion brought him up short.

He paused to review the thought processes that had led him

to commit to traveling across the country with a woman who had the stomach flu and a gravely injured father. He figured he either hadn't had any thought processes, or that the image of a motel room with a double bed had figured in the decision-making. He shook his head, mentally chiding himself, and, like many of the individuals he came across in a professional capacity, searched for other justifications. This trip didn't sound like a lovers' getaway. On the other hand, he was tired of being at loose ends on medical-leave. Time spent with Tory was rarely, if ever, boring, and fortunately, the City covered his health care insurance.

Alvarez shrugged. This review of motives had taken a full minute; it took another nine to pack. Five minutes were allotted to making a collect call to his sister Anna at Horizon House in Las Cruces, a call that would never appear on any billing under her name.

Alvarez lived a life that was as hostage-free as he could make it. Any casual investigation would uncover a relationship between him and his retarded sister that merely consisted of the basics defined by decency. There were no records of weekly visits or frequent phone calls, and the sisters who ran Horizon House were only too happy to incorporate this small amount of intrigue into their daily record keeping.

Alvarez explained to Anna that he was leaving on a trip and might miss his weekly visit. Five more minutes were required to get his partner, Scott Faulkner, to agree to dog-sit, which was fitting, since it was Scott who had convinced Alvarez to take Cotton when the dog's wealthy owner became a casualty in one of their cases.

It took ten minutes to drive to Scott's house, and Alvarez was congratulating himself for being on schedule when he ran into a delay: Scott wanted custody of Cotton should Alvarez die while Cotton was in his care. And he wanted it in writing.

"You've got to be kidding," said Alvarez.

"It's the right thing to do," replied Scott in the slow, deliberate way of speaking he had recently adopted in an effort to overcome his stuttering. "If something happened to you, you wouldn't want her to end up with strangers, would you?" Since Cotton was a Hungarian sheep dog, a purebred Puli with hair covering her eyes, Alvarez wondered if Cotton would know the difference. Okay, that really wasn't fair, he and the dog had bonded and he'd want Scott to have her instead of some stranger, but that wasn't the issue.

"*Chíngate!*" Alvarez snarled at the man with whom he'd trust his life in a minute. "I'm in a hurry, *cabrón*. I always knew you were jealous of Cotton's money, but this is really low." A few days after Alvarez first took Cotton home, the two detectives had discovered that she was endowed with her own trust fund for her care and for the person who provided that care. Alvarez figured it evened out—Scott had his wealthy wife, and Alvarez had Cotton.

"Hey," Scott protested. "I'm just looking for a chance to p-p-potentially recover some of the money I've lost in bets over the years."

"This is a great time to get petty. What a pal you're turning out to be."

"'There are three faithful friends, an old wife, an old dog, and ready money,'" quoted Scott.

Alvarez frowned, thinking. "Shakespeare."

"Benjamin Franklin," said Scott. "And I want it in writing." The man had obviously planned ahead; he held out a notebook and pen.

Alvarez thrust a sack of dog chow and the end of Cotton's leash at Scott. He grabbed the notebook and started scribbling on it. He finished and held it up for approval.

"You need to date it," said Scott.

"You're the kind of person who thinks anal-retentive is a compliment," growled Alvarez. He put the date under his signature.

Scott looked thoughtful. "Maybe it needs to be notarized..." he began.

Alvarez didn't stay to listen. He gave Cotton a quick scratch behind the ears and climbed back in his car. Scott studied the scrawled custody agreement while Cotton sat next to him, politely wagging her tail as though in response to a joke she didn't really think was all that funny. Alvarez made a rude parting gesture and drove off. It was good to have friends you could count on.

ALVAREZ ARRIVED AT Tory's door forty-five minutes later. He didn't need to knock—the door was thrown wide open at his arrival and Sylvia Maestes launched herself at him, proclaiming "Dah-veed!" as though they hadn't seen each other in years. Alvarez moved his injured arm out of the way just in time.

It took at least three minutes to disentangle himself from Sylvia, and when he managed to set her aside, he was momentarily distracted by her shiny red leggings and oversized black shirt. The shirt was covered in gold bangles that looked like tiny mirrors. Sylvia wore earrings that matched the bangles, and her long fingernails were alternately painted red and black in the same shades as her shirt and leggings. Alvarez was impressed in spite of himself. "Cool outfit," he said.

"Oh, this?" Sylvia replied, looking down at her generous curves. "This is nothing. I just threw this on to go to the gym. Then Cody called, and I came right over." She raised one sculpted eyebrow. "Did you get plane tickets like you said you would? Are you really going with Tory back to Florida?"

When he said yes, they had to do the hugging routine all over again. Alvarez was falling behind schedule. "Where's Tory?" he asked.

Sylvia shook her head regretfully. "She's in the bathroom again. She's been sick lately—this was all she needed. Cody told you?" Alvarez nodded. "I'm packing for her, to save time," said Sylvia. Alvarez decided he definitely couldn't afford the time to think this over.

"I'm going to go talk to Tory, see when she thinks we can leave," he said, and Sylvia stepped aside.

In the living room Cody and Kohli were sitting side by side on the couch. When the boy saw Alvarez, he stood and offered his hand. "Thanks for coming and helping out, man. I really appreciate it." Damned if Alvarez didn't feel as though he'd passed some kind of test. He walked down the hall and through the master bedroom to knock on the bathroom door.

"Can I come in?"

"Is it really you?" This did not have the sound of someone grateful for his assistance. Cody and Sylvia must have used up the quota of enthusiasm for Alvarez's arrival.

"Your powers of deduction are amazing, as always. Can I come in?" he asked again.

"Oh, why not?" he got in return. "I don't see how things could get any worse."

Alvarez pushed open the door and walked into the bathroom. Tory was barefoot, in jeans and a sweatshirt, sitting cross-legged on the floor. Her forehead rested on arms draped over the toilet seat. Her dark hair fell forward, covering most of her face, but what was visible was pale.

"I'm really sorry to hear about your dad," he said.

Tory turned her head just enough to look up at him with one eye. "Thanks. I can't believe Cody called you and cooked up this whole deal. You really managed to get plane tickets?"

"Yes, ma'am. Plane tickets, ground transportation and escort, ready and waiting."

"Who do you think you are, Sir Galahad?"

"No. I'm someone with two plane tickets, ready to help out. And you look like you could use some help."

"You don't know the half of it."

It wasn't like Tory to admit to any misery. "Look, I know it's going to be tough, going back to Florida and dealing with all this. But it'll be okay, one way or another. I'll be there—I'll help. You can depend on me."

"Oh, brother." The words were muffled since Tory had rolled her head back to address the water level in the toilet.

"Sylvia's packed for you. We need to leave in thirty minutes to make the flight I've booked. Have you thrown up everything that can come up? Is this a trial run, or are we still doing the real thing?"

"If you use 'we' one more time, I'll kill you," she replied.

"We'll have to get up off our ass to do it," he told her.

"Come on, we'll take the wastebasket if we really think we're going to puke again. We'll thank Kohli for being around to comfort Cody, and we'll hint at practicing safe sex. We'll get our luggage from Sylvia, and we'll be on our way. If we're a good girl, we'll have a nice surprise down the line when we see what she's packed."

All he got in return was silence. "Hey, buck up," he said. "Here's some good news—according to reliable sources, there aren't any outstanding warrants for your arrest back in Florida. I checked that once, remember?"

More silence.

Alvarez knew Tory was sick and he knew she'd been broadsided with the news about her father's accident, but her behavior was so atypical that he was starting to get worried. He abandoned trying to bait her.

"Tory?"

"So you're going to help me?" she asked the toilet. "You're going to be *dependable?*" This wasn't the response he expected, and he didn't like the emphasis she gave the last word.

"What's going on?" Alvarez couldn't help it—he resorted to his cop voice. Tory looked sideways again to study him with one eye. He could see a faint sheen of perspiration on her face, and it wasn't warm in the bathroom. "What's wrong?" he asked, suddenly very concerned.

"I'm pregnant," she told the water in the toilet bowl.

THREE

The Telling
December, Lake City, Florida

LISSY HOLDEN GARNER looked out her small, smudged window as the day came to an end, looked out beyond the scraggly grass lawn that was winter-brown but sporting some sad-looking Christmas lights twinkling sparsely in the twilight. Lissy didn't much hold with trying to make some place like a nursing home look festive, but she had a grudging admiration for the useless repetitive effort that went into the annual decorating. The overall effect was sad and tacky and worn-out, which Lissy thought was probably a good bit more appropriate than ever intended by those in charge.

Beyond the brown grass and the sparse lights futilely proclaiming the joy of the season was a parking lot almost devoid of automobiles. Lissy could see Chloe Pitts hurrying toward her shapeless old hulk of a car, an uncharacteristic springiness in her step, an animation that was foreign to the woman on any other day. Well, Chloe Pitts thought she had something to hurry about, something to be excited over. She thought she had just been told something she understood.

Once Lissy started talking, no matter how careful she had been about the story she had to tell, the excitement had been contagious. Now even Tazzy was climbing on the bandwagon, getting all excited about a box full of faded old papers, saying how she was going to file the forms for Lissy's claim whether Lissy wanted her to or not.

Well, that was how things went sometimes, with one thing following another like a row of falling dominoes, until the effect was nothing like you'd ever imagined when first deciding on a course of action. Lissy sighed and leaned over and pulled on the rod that lowered institutional gray blinds over the window. The blinds sure were dusty. There was a time when that would have bothered Lissy something fierce, but that time was long past.

No matter how excited Chloe Pitts was, no matter how much she thought she knew, to Lissy she was just another outsider. Outsiders always pretended to be interested in what came after, that cause and effect they all talked about, but what they were really interested in was the story of the Now.

Every rape and murder and torture occurs at a specific time and place, fixed forever in the minds of those who hurt and those who were hurt and those who simply watched. Everyone involved would forever afterward divide their lives between the Now, the Now when something too horrible to be comprehended was only too-fully comprehended, and the After, when the memory of that knowledge could never be erased. That's what people like Chloe Pitts thought they understood, the Now of rape and murder and torture, and the After.

But that left a big something missing that an outsider could never fathom, though they might give it lip service. Outsiders could never understand that for every tale of the Now of rape and murder and torture, there was a tale of Before.

Days of Before, months of Before, years of Before—a lifetime of Innocence Before. But in the horror of the Now, maybe one realized that it wasn't really Innocence after all, that what might have been Innocence before the Now was really a kind of Knowing All Along. And that kind of Knowing meant Being Part Of, and that meant that the Before and the Now and the After were all just part of the same thing, World Without End, Amen.

Lissy blinked and shook her head to shake those thoughts right on out. It might be dark outside, but it was sure enough still light in her little room. She'd gotten all stirred up talking to that Chloe Pitts, but if she made the effort, she could stop the Before and the Now and the After from tumbling all together endlessly in her mind. It was an awfully big effort for a tired old woman, and it would take a while, a big while for someone who didn't have too much time left.

Try explaining all that to an outsider. Try telling all that to anyone in a single afternoon. That kind of knowledge took years for the telling, and sweet Andy Garner was the only one who ever had the time to listen to it all.

FOUR

The Journey
Saturday

ALTHOUGH ALVAREZ NEVER mentioned it, he always remained certain that after Tory spoke the words, "I'm pregnant," the room tilted for a moment. He decided to sit on the edge of the bathtub.

At the speed of a computer, his brain posed and discarded responses, including, "This is no time to be joking", "We used a condom—how could this happen?" And the trite but common, "You've got to be kidding". He had enough sense to realize that whatever he said next might be very, very important. He settled on posing a question that would surely seem reasonable to an engineer. Actually, he settled on posing two questions. "Are you sure? How do you know?"

"You're a detective—you figure it out."

Alvarez had questioned hardened criminals who were more forthcoming. "Indulge me." He tried not to let the words come out in his cop voice.

"Then you'd better listen close, because I'm only saying this once. First, I felt sick all the time. Then I was late. Then I started remembering how I felt when I was pregnant with Cody, so I bought one of those test kits. I worked up the nerve to use it just before I got the telephone call about my father."

Alvarez's mind was obviously no longer working at top speed—it apparently took him longer to think about what Tory had just told him than she thought was necessary. "I'm sorry it's not a more original story," she told the toilet bowl. She didn't sound sorry.

"*Querida,*" he tried to soften his next question, "how did this happen? There was only the one time, although I tried to convince you otherwise—"

"Actually, you only tried convincing me until some evidence turned up—evidence you needed to go running off and evaluate. Remember?"

Never argue facts with an engineer. "Whatever. We used a condom, so how did this happen?" That sounded like too much of an accusation. "Or have you had time to consider this?"

This seemed to effectively distract Tory from her nausea. She actually lifted her head to look at him. "That's all I've been thinking about—that and my father and having to go back to Florida. I have three theories."

"Three?"

"Three," she answered firmly. "One—you are so inept you don't know the proper use of a condom."

Alvarez was affronted. "You can rule that one out."

"Two, there is always a rare but statistically predictable failure rate of any chosen birth control method. Like they teach in the schools, abstinence is the only sure thing."

Abstinence didn't sound like Alvarez's definition of a sure thing. "And three?"

"Three. God has singled me out to punish me."

"For having sex twice in the last decade? I don't think so."

"It hasn't been the last decade." This sounded almost like the old Tory.

"So I rounded up."

"I hate you," she said vehemently. "I hate Lonnie. I hate my father. I even hate Jazz." She leaned her forehead on her arms again. "I hate all male engineers and all male architects and all male construction workers. I hate all men."

"What about Cody?"

"He's not a man yet," replied Tory. Alvarez thought about Cody letting an attractive young woman offer him solace and comfort at that very moment. "So, aren't you going to say something horrible and stereotypical?" Tory continued, "Aren't you going to ask me something about how I can be sure who the father is?"

"No," said Alvarez. He had a sudden vivid memory of Tory standing in a hospital room, holding an unidentified baby girl. At the time, he'd thought that having Tory turn all mushy on him wasn't on his agenda. Nothing about this day had been on his agenda, either.

Alvarez took a deep breath and squatted down next to her. He used his sound hand to hold Tory's hair back so he could see at least part of her face. "I have something else to ask you," he said, trying to ignore how completely wrong the ambiance was, squatting in a chilly bathroom next to a woman draped over a toilet. "Will you marry me?"

At first he thought she was laughing, then he realized that she was being sick in earnest. "I'm really sorry—" Tory gulped, then was too busy retching to say anything else.

He continued to hold her hair back, at least on one side. An arm in a sling was a damned pain in the ass. "Well," he said philosophically. "At least that wasn't a no."

WHEN ALVAREZ finally coaxed Tory out of the bathroom, looking too spent and drained to throw up again, she took a look at the suitcase lying on her bed and turned back to face him. "Listen, I appreciate you trying to help—getting the plane tickets and driving up here," she said. "But you don't need to come to Florida with me."

"Yes I do," Alvarez told her. He started looking in the closet for some shoes to put on her feet.

"What I told you in there, nobody else knows. I'd like to keep it that way."

He stood up and held out a pair of athletic shoes for her approval. "I think I already figured that out," he told her. "What I asked you in there, you didn't answer."

She wouldn't look at him. "I know you're trying to be a nice guy. But this is my deal, and I just can't talk about it any more right now, not with everything else going on."

Alvarez gave this the grave consideration it warranted. "Where do you keep your socks?" he asked.

THE SMALL PLANE took a steep nosedive, abruptly bringing Alvarez's thoughts back to the present. He tried for optimism. "Looks like we're going in for the landing," he observed.

Tory didn't open her eyes. "I can't believe we're going to Gainesville via Tallahassee," she said. "This trip feels like it's taking forever."

Alvarez didn't bother to reply. It had been a long, exhausting trip, plagued with delays and overcrowded flights. They barely missed the last flight from Atlanta into Gainesville, and a bored ticket agent assured them that diverting to Tallahassee or renting a car were their only two options. The car rental was looking better and better all the time, but it was a little late for that.

One steep rushing dive and four bone-crushing bumps later, they were actually on the ground. Alvarez kept expecting to hear someone from the cockpit say "Whoa, big fella" over the loud-speaker, but what he heard instead was the announcement that they would be on the ground in Tallahassee for thirty minutes.

Alvarez unfolded his six-foot-two-inch frame from the window seat, which he had taken in order to give Tory the aisle seat. The rain seemed to have abated for the moment, so if he disembarked maybe he could stretch his legs and inspect the aircraft for any obvious damage that the pilot and crew might choose to ignore. He was no aviation expert, but he wanted to cover the basics—make sure a wing or engine wasn't missing from the other side of the plane.

Tory didn't move as he climbed over her. In spite of being more subdued and withdrawn than usual, she hadn't thrown up again since his bathroom proposal. Alvarez didn't know whether to take that as a good or a bad sign.

It was good to be outside in the fresh air, along with the added advantage of being able to touch the ground. After Alvarez had walked around the small aircraft a couple of times, a scattering of people began to straggle out from the Tallahassee terminal toward their plane. Alvarez had already been through this drill at the Atlanta airport. It seemed that their plane was too small and fragile to attach a standard covered passenger walkway, so any passengers hoofed it from the terminal to the aircraft, bad weather notwithstanding.

Alvarez was also familiar with seeing an airline official guarding entry to the plane, confiscating everything larger than an oversized handbag. It seemed that in addition to not lending itself to automated covered walkways, their aircraft did not accommodate standard-sized carry-on luggage. Alvarez half expected the man guarding the door to whip out a bathroom scale and weigh each passenger and piece of luggage before letting them board. It looked as though only seven passengers were joining them for their journey to Gainesville. How much could seven passengers and their luggage weigh?

But perhaps there would only be six. The last passenger, a stocky young woman in a rumpled business suit, wasn't willing to acquiesce to the airline's last minute runway baggage policies.

She and the uniformed official were having a game of tug of war over a standard-sized piece of carry-on luggage.

"I'm sorry," said the airline employee. He looked tired and hassled, but not very sorry. "This won't fit under the seat or in the overhead bin. I'll tag it for you and you can collect it in Gainesville."

This was one determined young woman. Not only did she fail to let go of her bag, she gave it a hard enough yank that it was once more in her sole possession. "No way," she said. "My laptop computer is in here. Besides, I've carried this bag on countless airlines."

"Well, you can't carry it on this one." The baggage man was sounding less and less sorry. "If you take your computer out, you can carry it on the plane with you and I'll check the bag." The man made this sound as though it were a major concession on his part.

"It's locked and the keys are in my other luggage that I already checked," the young woman replied. The man raised an eyebrow at this lack of luggage logic, but the young woman didn't give an inch. "I'm not parting with my computer," she said. "It goes where I go."

Alvarez looked at his watch and sighed. He didn't see any more passengers straggling out to the plane, but he didn't think they'd be leaving any time soon at this rate.

He walked over to the dueling duo. "I couldn't help but overhear," he said. "I have some experience with luggage locks—sometimes they can be jimmied." He looked at the young woman hugging her carry-on bag to her chest. "With your permission?" He gave her his best smile and she surrendered her bag.

Alvarez put it on the ground and squatted down next to it, putting his body between the bag and his companions. There were three things that he never traveled without—cash, a credit card, and a set of basic lock picks.

This lock proved to be no challenge. Alvarez popped open the top of the case, extracted a laptop computer, handed it to the young woman, then closed and relocked the bag, which he handed to the airline employee. He was rewarded by a stunning smile from the young woman and a suspicious look from the man.

Alvarez shrugged at them both, then followed the owner of the laptop computer onto the plane and watched her settle into the seat across the aisle from Tory. Twenty minutes and some bump and grinds later, they were in the air once more.

Alvarez was looking out his window when someone called "Hey" over the drone of the engine.

Tory opened her eyes, looked at the young woman sitting across the aisle, and said, "Yes?"

"Not you." The young woman softened her words with a grin. "The guy sitting next to you."

Tory turned to Alvarez. "You make friends so quickly," she said. "It never ceases to amaze me."

Alvarez leaned forward and nodded to the young woman. "Hey," he said back. He could have sworn Tory rolled her eyes, which was more life than he'd seen her show for a while.

"That was a really cool thing you did back there," the young woman said, speaking loudly to be heard over the plane's engine.

"She says that you did a really cool thing back there," Tory translated for him.

"I heard," said Alvarez.

"I'm Amy Cooper," said the young woman, leaning forward to talk over Tory. "What takes you to Gainesville?"

"She wants to chat," Tory said.

"I figured that out on my own," Alvarez replied.

Tory unfastened her seat belt and stood up. Alvarez stood up too, forgot he was in the window seat and banged his head into the overhead bin.

"That makes two cool things you've done," murmured Tory, as they changed places. She refastened her seat belt, leaned her head back and closed her eyes again.

Alvarez introduced himself to Amy Cooper and shook hands across the aisle. Ms. Cooper was young and attractive and wanted to talk. She told him that she had been in Tallahassee doing research, and that she'd put all her notes on her laptop but hadn't had a chance to back up her files, so she would be eternally grateful to him for rescuing her computer.

"What type of research do you do?" asked Alvarez.

"Historical. I'm with the Center for State Heritage Studies."

"What's that?"

"We're a brand new division of the History Department at the University of Florida." Amy lowered her voice as though sharing a secret. "Actually, I'm a graduate student right now, but I got assigned to the Center as junior staff member while I finish my degree. Twenty-five graduate students applied for the position, and I got it."

"Good for you."

Amy flashed a brilliant smile and lowered her voice even more. "The assistant director happens to be my second cousin, but that didn't have anything to do with it. I was picked by a totally independent selection committee. Besides, it's not like I was ever close to that part of the family."

"What does this Center for Heritage Studies do?" asked Alvarez.

"We're rewriting the history of the State of Florida," said Amy.

Alvarez blinked. "Why?"

"Because of everything that's been left out," Amy told him. "It's the Center's mission to study the people who've been left out of history books to date—African Americans, Seminoles, women—even Cuban refugees. When was the last time you saw something in a museum exhibit about the contribution of Cuban refugees?"

Alvarez honestly couldn't recall. "Whose idea was it for you to rewrite Florida history?"

"We were initially funded as an academic response to the Rosewood Bill," Amy said, as though that explained everything.

"Rosewood Bill?" Damn, he was beginning to sound like an echo.

Amy frowned. "You didn't see the movie?"

Alvarez shook his head. "I'm from Texas," he said in way of explanation.

"It's just as well," said Amy. "There was the real Rosewood Massacre in 1923, then the movie, which a lot of people called the *second* Rosewood Massacre." Alvarez must have looked confused, because Amy explained: "Back then, there was this little black town called Rosewood, over by Cedar Key, and there was a white town two miles away called Sumner. A white woman from Sumner accused a black man of attacking her. The county sheriff let a mob run wild for a week. Innocent people were killed, and the whole community of Rosewood was burned out and destroyed. In 1993 the state legislature commissioned a study of what happened."

"Seventy years later?" asked Alvarez incredulously.

"There were extenuating circumstances," said Amy, waving away his question. "In the end, the state was found liable for payment of compensation to the survivors and the descendants of people who lost property. My cousin was a graduate student in Tallahassee when the movement for restitution was getting started. By the time the legislature passed the Rosewood Bill, there were only a handful of survivors left. Everyone was scrambling to identify them before any more died off—the professors who did the study, the people at the Attorney General's Office who were supposed to enforce the bill, and the descendants themselves. Chloe found the last survivor—can you imagine it? And now she's assistant director of the Center."

"Why didn't they make her the director?" Alvarez would bet ten dollars that the director of this Center was male. He'd been hanging around Tory too long.

Amy sighed. "Well, Chloe's still kind of young. She got tenure out of the work she did, but when she came to Gainesville, the University said she didn't have any experience in administration or fund-raising." Amy paused. "There was something else, too. Chloe went and married the son of the survivor she discovered. That didn't help her academic reputation any."

"I see," said Alvarez carefully, thinking that Scott would love to hear about this one. A job where you went hunting for people to receive government payments, and then married the son of the one you found. A real equal opportunity position—maybe he hadn't been hanging around Tory too much, after all.

"So they did a national search for a director," Amy continued. "They picked someone from the University of Chicago, but he's originally from Florida, so it worked out perfect. Right now, there's just the three of us, Dr. Reynolds, Chloe and me. But we're just about to land an independent endowment for an eminent scholar all by ourselves, and if we pull that off, the sky will be the limit as far as the budget we can request next year."

Tory had opened her eyes sometime during this conversation. "What's Reynolds's first name?" she asked.

"Rolland," said Amy, barely breaking her conversational stride. "He's a real go-getter, and politically connected to boot. Turns out he has ties to some wealthy families in Florida and he's been raising funds like you wouldn't believe. Like I said, we're right on the verge of closing the funding for an eminent scholar chair. Dr. Reynolds hooked up with some previous contacts, and presto, all of a sudden we're talking to a former state senator about a two-million-dollar endowment."

"I know Rolland Reynolds," said Tory, and Alvarez suddenly had a premonition of what was coming next. "What's the name of the former senator, the one who's making the contribution for this endowment you're talking about?"

"Wheatley," said Amy with a satisfaction reminiscent of a woman thinking about her sugar daddy. "Tom Wheatley."

FIVE

The Difference
May, 1915. Rosewood, Florida

LISSY HOLDEN WAS little more than five years old when she first decided she was Different from everyone else she knew. She spent the next seven years off and on trying to decide why this was so—after that, she had other things to think about.

At five, Lissy was already wise enough to know from Bible stories told at Church and at home that everyone was different, that everyone was unique in their own way. That was why Jesus loved every single person just the way they were, sinners and saints alike.

But Bible stories were one thing, and Knowing was something else, and Lissy knew she was Different.

It didn't have to do with being rich or poor, although her daddy would have laughed to know that Lissy looked around her and thought about such things. He would have told her that everyone in Rosewood was poor, at least everyone in Rosewood who was Negro. But it wasn't that simple. Almost all the families in Rosewood were Negroes, just like almost all the families in nearby Sumner were white. There were some white people in Sumner who Lissy's daddy would have called dirt poor, while there were some Negro families in Rosewood that had things Lissy much admired.

The Carriers for instance. They lived in a two-story house with lace curtains on the windows and a piano in the parlor. The Bradley family lived in a two-story house, too, and they had something that impressed Lissy even more than a piano—they had a bedroom no one lived in, a bedroom kept vacant and waiting for visiting ministers. Lissy felt certain that people with pianos and vacant bedrooms weren't poor.

The Hoddens didn't live in a two-story house and Lissy and her sister Garland had to share a room, much to Garland's regret. But their house was clean and neat and had glass windows, not like John Marshall's one-room shack next door. John Marshall must be poor, Lissy decided, but she liked him anyhow. He was cheerful and friendly and could whistle better than anyone she knew. Lissy decided that if the Carriers and the Bradleys were rich and John Marshall was poor, then the Hoddens were in between, and being in between rich and poor wasn't what made Lissy Different.

It was Garland's fifteenth birthday that really set Lissy to thinking about being Different. For one thing, almost everyone else in town had a passel of aunts and uncles and cousins and sisters and brothers, while Lissy just had her parents and Garland. Lissy didn't think it was really fair to call someone ten years older a sister. Someone ten years older was never a play-mate. Someone ten years older thought she was just the right age to act like a parent but didn't have the patience or the wisdom to carry through like one. Lissy didn't know exactly what Garland was, but the word sister just never seemed to fit.

Maybe Garland was a mirror sent by Jesus to show Lissy what she would never be. While Garland was short and slight and laughing and always on the move, Lissy was tall for her age and thin and silent and kept to herself. Wherever they went, it was Garland who drew everyone's eye and got all the attention. Garland even got the best name in the family. Lissy's real name was Ruth, and although Lissy's mother was quick to explain how special Ruth was in the Bible, Lissy felt as though her parents had used up every bit of their meager store of originality in naming her older sister.

She'd bet her parents didn't find the name Garland in the Bible, not that it mattered anyhow, since Lissy considered her name to be just one more thing in a long line of hand-me-downs. It appeared that the long-awaited baby Ruth Ann immediately became Sister Ruth, then Little Sister, and finally Lissy. At least this was what Lissy was told, as these events occurred before her earliest memories. She felt certain that she was the only one who remembered that her real name was Ruth Ann Hodden, except when she said something about it and her mother pretended to remember.

No matter how much Lissy studied on these things, well, Garland was Garland and Lissy was still just plain Lissy. Even with five-year-old logic, she knew her parents loved her regardless. She had to look no further than Garland's birthday celebration for proof. Josie Hodden had made sure that while there was plenty to eat and drink at the picnic for the young people at Garland's birthday celebration, there were also games for the younger children so that Lissy would feel included.

So while the young men and women eyed each other and exchanged short breathless phrases before darting off to the safety of their giggling companions, Lissy was supposed to play tag with those other children, those laughing, giggling, constantly talking brothers and sisters and cousins—even aunts and uncles that were five and six and seven years old.

In the midst of being pushed and shoved and pinched and chased, Lissy could see Garland a ways off, drawing handsome young Sylvester Carrier into the shadow of the trees beyond their house. Garland might not have Sylvester by the hand, but Lissy could see that she was drawing him along with her just as surely as if she had an invisible rope looped around his neck.

All the noisy, vivid interconnectedness of the running children and the constant talking of the adults and the silent drawing away of Garland and Sylvester made Lissy want to sit down and write out every detail. The only problem was that Lissy Hodden had absolutely no idea how to write.

That night, when she could hear Garland faintly snoring across the room, Lissy had a thought—a thought all her own, not one that she'd been taught or heard from her parents or been told in a Bible story. She thought that maybe, while everyone else got on with the business of living their lives, she just wanted to watch. Maybe she even just wanted to watch herself. Maybe that's why she was Different.

SIX

The Arrival
Saturday

TORY SHUT HER EYES and let her head fall back against her seat. From a seemingly great distance she heard the young woman ask, "Ma'am, are you all right? Is it something I said?"

Alvarez answered, turning the woman's attention away from Tory. "Tom Wheatley is her father," Alvarez said. "We're on our way to Gainesville because he was in an automobile accident last night."

"Oh, I'm so sorry," replied the young woman. "Is he seriously hurt? Will he be all right? Is there anything I can do?" After a pause, she added: "I don't remember anything about Senator Wheatley having a daughter."

Tory wasn't sure whether she wanted to break into tears or start laughing. This woman had probably been too young to read when Tory made headlines across the state as a scandalously immoral seventeen-year-old. She heard Alvarez give polite reassurances—he certainly came in handy sometimes, she had to give him that.

The very thought jolted her into another wave of shock—what the hell was she doing here with Alvarez? They were actually traveling together, to Florida of all places. And she was pregnant, pregnant with his child, the result of the one single impetuous action in her adult life.

What were the appropriate guidelines in this situation?

Before leaving her house that morning, there had been another phone call, this time from a man in charge of the Seagle Building, where Tory's father maintained a condo for his visits to Gainesville. The man had expressed shocked sympathy and told Tory that a key and directions would be waiting for her at the airport when she landed, that she was welcome to stay in her father's condo as long as necessary.

Cody had described the condo when he visited his grandfather, so Tory knew it had two bedrooms. What was she going to do about sleeping arrangements? Where was Miss Manners when you needed her? And assuming, just assuming, that Tory reverted to her purported wild ways after returning to the state of her birth and thus invited Alvarez into her bed. What if she started throwing up again?

As if sensing her dilemma, Alvarez turned and studied her carefully. *"Querida,"* he said in a tone that sounded anxious for him, "you look even whiter than before, if that's possible. Are you okay? Is there something bothering you about the business between Reynolds and your father?"

Bothering her? Everything going on around her was bothering her, so why not include Rolland Reynolds? Tory had more than enough reasons to despise the man. Tory thought there had always been something sneaky and sly about Rolland. Even his own parents, affluent, educated black people with political ambitions of their own, had seemed slightly put off by their only child. Rolland had had a talent for surrounding himself with people who could do something for him, and then abandoning them as soon as they had served their purpose.

Most of all, Tory remembered the girls giggling and breathless with their own brand of daring civil rights, flocking around Rolland Reynolds—girls who would have never given him a second look if his family hadn't possessed that greatest of all equalizers—money. As much as Tory had despised these members of her own sex for their unadmitted hypocrisy, not a one could hold a candle to Rolland for sheer cruelty when it came to playing the race card.

Barely on the verge of understanding what sex was all about, a young Tory had wandered upstairs searching for an unoccupied bathroom during one of her parents' many dinner parties. Suddenly the door to one of the upstairs bedrooms was flung open, and Tory saw a partially dressed teenaged Rolland standing in the doorway, backlit by the dim glow of a bed table lamp. He unhurriedly zipped his pants and tucked in his shirt, apparently untouched by the sound of sobbing coming from the room.

"I'll bet you'd fuck me faster than I can say Black Sambo, Cammie Blake," he said with a drawl, "if only I was white, honey-chile." As Rolland turned from the room, Tory glimpsed a young girl in an evening gown sitting on the bed, naked to the waist, sobbing into her hands. Then suddenly Rolland and Tory confronted each other in an empty hallway.

Rolland quickly rearranged his face into an expression of concern. "Why, where did you come from, all of a sudden?" he asked.

"Did you make Cammie Blake cry?" Tory asked.

Rolland's smile never wavered as he reached behind him and shut the bedroom door. "No, honey, you're mistaken."

"I don't think so," said Tory stubbornly. Rolland gave her a look as though she'd just become interesting.

"Honey, if you go telling tales about Cammie and I say it's not true, you're going to look pretty foolish, aren't you?"

Tory considered the logic of this. She could tell her older brother Tommy, and he'd believe her, because he always believed everything she told him. But Tommy liked everybody, and Rolland was his friend, and Tory would just as soon eat glass as hurt Tommy. She turned to retreat but fired one final shot to save her dignity.

"I don't like you," she told Rolland Reynolds.

He grinned at her. "I don't like you either. Not old enough to bleed, not old enough to breed." Even years later, when she could fully understand the meaning of his words, they still had the power to shock her.

But what did it matter? Really, what did it all matter?

Tory had disowned her surviving Florida family long ago, and so her father could consort with whomever he chose. Still, it was a shock to hear that he was making a contribution to something called a Center for State Heritage Studies. Tom Wheatley was a Democrat, but he had aligned himself much closer with his right-wing counterparts than with many members of his own party. He had opposed civil rights legislation, not exactly embracing a defined separatist policy, but claiming that progress in race relations should happen through private channels, not through government action and regulation. If some recent discussions with her father seemed to reflect a softening on these issues, well, Tory needed to remember that he was first and foremost a political animal—a political animal that had steadfastly supported the military intervention in Vietnam. The moment this thought entered her head, Tory closed the door on her recollections.

She could choose to ignore certain memories, but it didn't change the fact that nothing in her entire experience with her family could lead her to believe that her own father was funding some group charged with rewriting history. This must be an insane function of her return to Florida. Home, where nothing was ever like it seemed. Home, where outward appearances were of the utmost importance, and hidden currents ran so deep and contradictory that it would take an entire center devoted to studying her family to figure it all out. Home, where five-foot-ten outspoken Victoria had never fit in.

But Florida wasn't home. It was chilling how soon she could forget that.

Tory realized that Alvarez had picked up one of her hands and was rubbing it softly. "You haven't answered my questions," he chided her. "Talk to me, Tory."

Alvarez could play at being solicitous when it suited him, but Tory knew just how persistent he could be when he was after information. She made her head move side to side.

"That's a no?"

Of course Alvarez wouldn't be satisfied with a mere shaking of her head. The trick was to talk about the past without getting all caught up in it, without looking at it as a catastrophe of pain and loss. "Rolland Reynolds is a thoroughly despicable person, or at least he was back when I knew him. He's black, and he never lets you forget it, especially if you don't agree with him. He'd be a great person to rewrite history, since he always had his own personal version of everything."

"How well did you know him?"

How well did she know him? How well did she know anyone back then, including her own parents? Tory swallowed, forced herself to think of a rational answer to the question. "Well enough. His parents had money and they were politically active, so they made my parents' list of desirable acquaintances. Rolland was my brother's age, so there were a couple years he hung around our house a lot."

"Keeping your brother company?" Alvarez asked.

"At first. Tommy got along with everyone, so he was too nice to tell Rolland to take a hike." There, she'd said Tommy's name and lived through it. It shouldn't be any worse than speaking of her dead husband, but she had always felt that Tommy had died needlessly, that someone should have done something...

"And how about you, did you tell him to take a hike?"

This was one specific trip down memory lane that Tory didn't want to take in Alvarez's presence; the man was just too damned observant. "Let's just say the dislike was mutual." She needed to change the subject, tried desperately to think of something else to say.

"There any reason to think that this Reynolds would have

something to do with your father's accident?" Alvarez asked. God, the questions cops came up with.

"Would Rolland Reynolds run into my father with a car?" Tory tried to lighten her tone. "Not likely, not with two million dollars at stake."

"Then why the big reaction?"

"No big reaction." Alvarez didn't look as though he believed her. "It was just surprising, hearing Rolland's name, then hearing that he's hooked up with my father." Tory said. "But I don't know why anything should surprise me now. I'm fine."

Alvarez held up Tory's hand for a moment and looked at it. He didn't comment on the fact it was shaking. He placed it on her knee and covered it with his own. Tory felt as though she'd been granted a reprieve, but it didn't last long.

"Let me ask another question then. Does your father really have so much money that he can go around donating two million dollars to a group that spends their time rewriting history?"

Tory nodded.

"Wow," said Alvarez. "That's even better than Carumba Cotton Candy's trust fund. This makes me view you and our relationship in a whole new light. Maybe we should get married and start a family."

Tory stared at him. "That was incredibly tasteless," she said finally. "Even for you."

Alvarez shook his head at her. "I'm disappointed. The Tory I know would have said, not without a prenup, we don't."

Tory felt a little calmer now, but she didn't want to give Alvarez credit for it.

He leaned back, took his ticket out of his pocket and looked at it. "Well, it's been a long, hard trip, but we're in luck. This says we're coming in at Gate One—that should be close to baggage claim and the rental cars."

"There're only two gates, and they're really just two different doors off the same big room," Amy Cooper said.

"Piece of cake," Alvarez told them both.

THE HANDFUL OF PASSENGERS who had braved the trip from Tallahassee to Gainesville trooped to the baggage claim area, and Amy Cooper kept telling Tory how sorry she was about the accident while Alvarez gathered their luggage. Then Amy suddenly realized that her checked bags hadn't shown up and went charging off to look for someone in the deserted airport to help her, muttering how she'd known all along that she couldn't trust the man who'd tried to get her computer from her.

As soon as she left, Alvarez and Tory got into an argument. It started when Tory said, "I have to get a map." She pulled a crumpled paper out of her pocket. "They said my father is in a hospital called North Florida Regional Medical Center."

"Original name for a hospital," commented Alvarez. "We'll get a map at the rental car counter, figure it out tomorrow morning."

"I have to go there tonight," insisted Tory. She felt as though she were in a grueling marathon and someone was standing between her and the finish line.

"We'll call tonight, find out his status. You can go tomorrow."

"Don't tell me what to do," said Tory. It sounded childish even to her.

"Goddamn it, Tory," he said in his cop voice. "Why do you always have to make everything harder than it is? It's after midnight—you look like death warmed over, you haven't eaten a thing all day, and I'm not taking you anywhere tonight but to bed."

"Ha," she said, and he got even angrier.

"You know what I mean. If your father regained consciousness and saw you now, it would be enough to put him back in the hospital."

"So you've finally stopped being Mr. Nice Guy," Tory snapped. "I knew it couldn't last."

Alvarez glared at her. "I *am* being Mr. Nice Guy," He pointed at some chairs and said, "Go sit over there."

"I'm not your dog," Tory muttered.

"No, you're not," Alvarez agreed. "Cotton has more sense."

Tory picked up her bags with as much dignity as she could

muster while Alvarez headed over to the rental car counters. He returned almost immediately, shaking his head in disgust. "This place must be a real one-pony town. The whole damn airport is shut down. There's a sign at the rental car place with my name on it, saying to pick up the keys at the ticket counter. Why didn't they just take out an advertisement? So much for the right to privacy."

"What's the problem?" sniped Tory, still smarting from the comment about Cotton. "Plan on doing some undercover work while we're here?"

Alvarez looked at her, thought a moment, then grinned. "You've cheered me right up," he said, heading off in the other direction and making Tory feel as though she'd just lost another round.

Tory could see Amy Cooper at the ticket counter, waving her hands at the lone agent left to hold down the fort. The other few passengers had collected their bags and melted away, waiting for rides or getting their vehicles in the parking lot. Amy finally yielded her place at the counter to Alvarez and started walking in Tory's direction.

"Can you believe it?" she called. "They take my damn bag right out of my hands to put in the baggage hold, and somewhere between now and then they claim it's disappeared, along with the suitcase I checked. Now they say the baggage handlers have shut down the holding area and gone home, so nothing can be done until tomorrow. It's fucking tomorrow already—" she caught herself and grimaced. "Sorry. Missing luggage isn't anything like your problem."

"It's okay," said Tory.

"God, just think what would have happened if I'd given them my computer…" Amy shivered at the thought, then seemed to remember once more who she was talking to. "Listen, Miss Wheatley—"

"Travers," said Tory. "Tory Travers."

"Ms. Travers, then. I'm really sorry about your father. If there's anything I can do, I'd be happy to help. Do you need a ride somewhere?"

"No," said Tory. "My friend is getting a rental car." She remembered her own manners. "You're kind to offer. Can we give you a ride?"

"No, my car's in long-term parking—a little bit of a hike, but nothing's too far away at an airport as small as this one." Amy paused. "I've been gone for a week. I had just a couple days of work, but I stayed longer to give myself some space. My husband and I are having some problems."

"I'm sorry to hear that," said Tory, wondering why she was having this conversation. What was taking Alvarez so long?

"Well, it's good news, really, at least for him," said Amy. "He runs a field office for an engineering firm, and he's been offered a project manager position at their headquarters in Atlanta. The problem is, I have two years left here before I finish up."

Tory just skipped the part where she told Amy that she was an engineer and asked about her husband's job. "I hope it works out for you," she said simply.

"Yeah, I guess. Funny how things change, and don't turn out the way you think. Sometimes they don't turn out the way anybody thinks." Amy looked off into space for a moment, then seemed to shake off any gloomy thoughts about her matrimonial future and gave Tory another one of her bright smiles. "Anyhow, I wish you the best. I'll come see how your father's doing if you tell me where he is."

"That's very kind," Tory replied and gave her the name of the hospital.

Then there was nothing left for them to say. Amy Cooper walked out through the automatic sliding glass doors, still clutching her computer. Alvarez followed fast on her heels.

"Got the key to the condo, key to the car, and a map," he said without breaking his stride. "I'll pick you up in a minute. Stay there."

"Woof," said Tory dispiritedly.

"You made a joke—you must be feeling better," replied Alvarez, and then he too was gone, leaving Tory and the ticket agent as the sole occupants of the terminal.

Almost immediately there was the sound of a roaring engine, screeching tires, and a woman screaming. Then Tory heard a man yell, "Oh my God," and she was on her feet headed out the door herself, unconsciously waiting for the sound of an explosion, thinking, hurry, hurry, hurry, without any idea why she was hurrying. She ran headlong into Alvarez, who, even with one arm in a sling, somehow managed to steady her and turn her back toward the terminal building.

The screaming continued without pause, but Alvarez ignored it. "Go back inside," he told her. "Call 911. Tell them to send an ambulance and the police." Then he was gone. Tory took one look back through the sliding glass doors and saw a screaming woman standing next to a lone yellow cab. A black taxi driver held her as he looked out toward the parking lot, shaking his head in disbelief. Tory noted that Alvarez was running, but not in their direction. She also realized that this was not the time to argue with what he was telling her to do.

SEVEN

The Brother
November, 1916. Rosewood, Florida

"WHAT YOU LOOKING so solemn for, Lissy Hodden?"

Lissy nearly jumped out of her skin where she was sitting next to the road, playing with a stick. Sylvester Carrier had come up so quietly that she had no warning until he was suddenly standing right behind her, so tall he blocked out the sun when she turned to look at him. He was as proud and handsome as anyone Lissy had ever seen, dressed in his trademark black clothes. People in Rosewood didn't call Sylvester The Man for nothing. Even though he'd spoken her name, Lissy was so surprised by the idea of The Man stopping to talk to her that she turned to look back at the road, to see if maybe someone else had appeared there and she just hadn't noticed.

"What you looking 'round for, like some kind of rabbit or something? I be talking to you, girl." This mild rebuke was given in a kind tone of voice, and Sylvester squatted down next to Lissy as he spoke so she didn't have to get a crick in her neck looking up at him. "What you be doing out here in the road all by yourself?"

"I be *by* the road, not in it," said Lissy carefully. "Mamma'd smack me something fierce, she found me in the road."

This defense earned a wide smile. "I can't hardly argue with a fact, girl. So what you be doing, out here *by* the road?"

"I'm practicing the letters Mizz Mahulda taught us in school today," Lissy told him.

Sylvester took a closer look at the dirt in front of Lissy. "Looks like you be doing a good job of it, too," he said. A wave of pleasure washed over Lissy, but she wasn't allowed to bask in it for long. "Why you always by yourself, girl, and not with other children?"

Lissy went back to drawing in the dirt. "'Cause I get tired of them," she said, slanting a look up at The Man to see how he would react to this answer. He seemed to give it serious thought.

"If you don't be playing with other children, what you spend your time doing, Lissy Hodden?"

"Thinking. Studying." Lissy found the courage to say what she really wanted to say. "Wishing," she added in a rush. "I spend lots of time wishing."

"Wishing? Now ain't that something? I wonder what a little girl like you be wishing for."

"A brother," Lissy said tentatively, drawing out the word.

"You got a sister."

Lissy was disappointed with the obviousness of his answer. "I know I got a sister."

"I sure do know it, too," said The Man, and gave such a laugh that it took all the sting out of his words.

Lissy gathered up her courage again. "I'd like a brother like you," she said in a rush.

"Like me?" The Man looked at Lissy with surprise. "What you be wanting with a brother like me?"

"You could show me things. Secret things," said Lissy.

The Man was no longer smiling. "What kinda secret things

you be talking about, little girl? Someone been messing with you?''

Lissy didn't know what he meant. "You know, secret things. You could take me to the Lodge and show me what happens there,'' she suggested slyly.

"I see,'' Sylvester said. He looked relieved. "You mean the Masonic Lodge?'' Lissy nodded. "Baby, you maybe know all the letters Mizz Mahulda been teaching you, but you not thinking clear in the head. Only men-folk allowed in meetings there.''

This ruined Lissy's fantasy, but The Man told the truth. Her daddy had flat-out forbidden Lissy to ask any more about what went on at his meetings. Garland laughed and said she didn't care, and Lissy's mamma said she wished she knew just so she could tell Lissy to keep her from asking about it again.

"If I had a brother like you, you could tell me other secrets,'' said Lissy stubbornly.

"Like what, baby?'' The Man was still smiling, and Lissy took his words as a challenge.

"Like 'bout fireball,'' said Lissy, issuing a challenge of her own.

The Man frowned. "How you be knowing 'bout fireball, Lissy Hodden?''

"I saw one night,'' she told him.

The Man shook his head in disbelief. "How a baby like you see fireball?''

"I couldn't sleep. Sometimes Garland makes sounds and it keeps me awake.''

"Does she now?'' The Man was smiling again, and Lissy hurried with her explanation before his attention turned back to her sister.

"I sat up in bed and I looked out the window, and I saw fire go 'cross the sky.'' It worked—The Man was listening to her every word. "So I climbed out the window and followed it to the ball field. That's where I saw you and other boys—some white mens, too. At first I couldn't figure what was going on— then I saw you do it.''

"Saw me do what?'' The Man sounded as though he still needed convincing.

"Soak a baseball in turpentine and light a match to it. You tossed it up in the air and you hit it with a bat and one of the white mens caught it. Then he dropped it and everyone laughed, then someone said, 'Light me up one, Man,' and you did it all over again. 'Cept this time, it didn't get dropped, it got tossed 'round 'til the fire went out."

"Then what happened?"

"I went back to my house and climbed in the window and went to sleep."

The Man shook his head in wonder at her story. "So you saw me out in the ball field in the middle of the night, playing fireball with some white mens there?" he asked. Suddenly Lissy was afraid she had made him mad, but she'd been brought up to tell the truth and it was too late to take back her words anyway, so she just nodded. "Who you told?"

"Nobody. I knows how to keep a secret."

"Whoeeeeee." The Man let out a long exhaled breath, looking up at the sky as though searching there for his next words. Then he looked back at her. "You a strange child, Lissy Hodden, and that be the truth. You understand how some people would get all upset, the notion of white mens playing ball with us on our ball field?"

Lissy nodded. Of course she understood. She couldn't remember a time that she wouldn't have understood.

"Well," said The Man slowly, "this what I think. I think you best not be telling anyone else what you told me. I think you best not be crawling out your window at night anymore." Lissy hung her head, not with shame, but with disappointment that The Man was saying the very things that her mamma or daddy or Garland would have said. But she had given up too soon—Sylvester Carrier wasn't called The Man for nothing.

"Don't you be looking sad, Lissy Hodden. You tole me a secret, so I'll tell you one back."

"What?" asked Lissy, her disappointment a thing of the past.

"The best secret you can think of," said the Man, smiling widely. "A secret brother. Me."

Lissy was speechless for a moment. "You promise?" she asked.

"Of course I promise," said the Man sternly. "You think I be telling a secret and then taking it back?" Lissy shook her head hard so he would know that she had faith in him. "Put that little hand up here," he told her, and Lissy put her hand up against his, thrilled with this implication of ceremony. "I, Sylvester Carrier, do say that Lissy Hodden be my secret sister from now on, and I be her secret brother and teach her such things as is good for strange solemn little girls to know."

Lissy frowned. There was something vaguely disappointing in the words, but she couldn't quite put her finger on what it was. "Ruth Ann," she said.

"What?" asked the Man, puzzled.

"Ruth Ann. That be my real name, not Lissy."

This earned another smile. "Ruth Ann, then."

"You my secret brother now, for real? You won't forget?"

"I won't forget."

"Not even if you make Garland mad and she cries and calls you names and slaps your face?"

The Man threw back his head and laughed long and loud. "Sister," he said finally, "you be one strange baby child, wandering 'round on your lonesome too much. You climb on my shoulders and I carry you home. Your new brother be scared 'bout leaving you out here on your own. Good Lord only knows what you be seeing next."

And that was how Lissy Hodden returned home on the day that she sat by the road and found a brother, on the broad tall shoulders of Sylvester Carrier, then and forever afterward known as The Man.

EIGHT

Witness
Early Sunday Morning

ALMOST SIMULTANEOUS with hearing an engine roar into life and seeing motion out of the corner of his eye, Alvarez sensed that there was something wrong. He was already reaching for his missing gun as he turned toward the airport parking lot, away from the row of rental cars parked near the terminal. The lot was deserted except for Amy Cooper, standing a good distance away, frozen between two rows of sparsely parked cars. Seemingly out of nowhere, a dark vehicle crashed into her, knocking her momentarily up onto the windshield, then dumping her to one side as the car sped away.

The speeding car turned sharply, tires screaming, and headed straight for the exit. It never slowed as it crashed through the barrier at the tollgate and sped off into the night.

Alvarez made for the terminal building. As luck would have it, he ran straight into Tory. After telling her to call 911, Alvarez headed toward the motionless Amy Cooper at a dead run.

He might as well have walked. She was most definitely dead, and it wasn't a pleasant sight. Alvarez had seen more than a few victims of car accidents and shootings during his career, but he had to swallow hard and take a few deep breaths to steady himself.

Alvarez took off his coat and covered as much of Amy Cooper as he could, but not before getting his notebook out of his inside pocket. He hunkered down by Amy's body and started writing down everything he could remember.

Part of his mind noted that the screaming had stopped. The black taxi driver approached, and Alvarez waved him back, briefly glancing toward the terminal to see who else might be coming. He saw Tory come through the sliding glass doors, take a long look at him and the covered body in the parking lot, then lead the woman who had been screaming back inside. That left a ticket agent hovering outside the terminal doors and the parking attendant who had been inside the tollbooth when the car crashed through the barrier. The parking attendant jogged up from his post and said, "Man, the way that car was heading for me, I thought I was a goner."

Alvarez told the man to wait inside for the police to come and take his statement. This left the ticket agent, who had made his way out to the scene of the accident and seemed to feel duty-bound to join Alvarez in his vigil. "Is she dead?" he asked hesitantly, standing a cautious three car-lengths away.

"Yes, she's dead."

"There's usually a police officer on duty here, but only during regular hours. Your flight came in so late that…" The man cleared his throat, abandoned that statement and opted for another. "We've called 911. Help should be on the way."

"Thank you," said Alvarez. "That's very helpful. Please go wait inside with the others."

"Uh, are you sure you're all right out here by yourself?"

"I don't think that vehicle is coming back any time soon," Alvarez told the ticket agent. The man started to say something else, then changed his mind and headed for the terminal building.

Alvarez and Amy Cooper kept solitary company until the arrival of a police car a few moments later. The driver cut the siren as he pulled up, but the lights were still flashing and Alvarez corrected himself. This was a sheriff's vehicle.

A lone deputy stepped out of the car. He seemed relaxed enough, but still, Alvarez stood up slowly, letting his hands spread open so the deputy could see that the object he was holding was a notebook. "I'm David Alvarez," he said. "I witnessed the accident."

"George Nelson, Sheriff's Office," said the deputy. Alvarez noted that George Nelson was a big man who still carried both his age and his weight well, but little remaining hair seemed to be included in the package deal.

Nelson had his priorities clearly in mind. He walked over to the jacket-covered body, squatted down, and lifted a corner to take a look. "Not much sense causing another accident then, rushing an ambulance here," said Nelson. He spoke into a crackling radio microphone while stepping carefully to avoid pieces of broken computer and picked up a purse that had been thrown to the side of the body. "Know who she is?"

"Her name is Amy Cooper. She flew in from Tallahassee, where she was doing research. She worked for something called the Center for State Heritage Studies. It's associated with the History Department of your university here."

Nelson shot Alvarez a sharp look, but only asked, "So, Mr. Alvarez, what did you see?"

Alvarez consulted his notebook. "The hit and run happened at approximately twelve thirty-five a.m. I was over there," he gestured toward the rental vehicles. "I heard an engine and the car seemed to come out of nowhere, no lights on. It must have been waiting out here in the parking lot, an old Chevy Impala, I'd say late '80s or early '90s. Dark color, maybe faded since I don't remember any light reflecting off the car. My guess would be black or dark blue. It didn't appear to have a vinyl top or different color roof. I can't tell you anything about the driver. There was no attempt to brake when approaching the victim, and after impact, the car exited the parking lot at a high rate of speed, driving through the toll barrier."

Alvarez looked up in time to see Nelson reach in his jacket and extract a toothpick to chew. "You sure about all this?"

"Yes."

"Who the hell are you, Mr. Alvarez?" Nelson asked.

"I'm a detective with the El Paso Police Department. That's in Texas," Alvarez added for clarification.

"I suppose you have some ID to show me." Nelson didn't make it a question, and Alvarez didn't make it a problem.

"I'm here with a friend, on personal business," he told the deputy. "I'd like to keep it that way," Alvarez said, replacing his wallet in his pocket.

"I don't see a problem with that," replied Nelson, chewing his toothpick. "You've been quite helpful, Mr. Alvarez, but you need to know up front that I won't be involved in the actual investigation of this case." Alvarez noted the use of the word "mister" instead of "detective."

"Why is that?"

"The airport's on city property, so it's the jurisdiction of the Gainesville Police Department. It's also out in the boonies, as we say around here, so after hours, whoever is closest takes the call."

"I see," said Alvarez.

Nelson looked down at Amy Cooper's body. "This is bad business. Sure hope we get the fucking bastard who did it," he said in the same conversational tone he'd used since introducing himself.

"So do I. If there's anything I can do to help—"

"Never know," said Nelson. "Here's one of my cards—it's got my cell phone number on it." As he handed Alvarez a card, an ambulance pulled up.

"Okay if I take my coat?" asked Alvarez. He hoped for laundry facilities sometime in the immediate future.

"Fine with me," said Nelson, "and thanks for asking." Two police cars rolled up and Nelson conferred briefly with the officers. "I'll stay and help out for a bit if nothing else comes up," he told them. He nodded in Alvarez's direction. "Let's head back to the terminal. I'm going to stick around, help take statements, so let's go see if your friend has anything to add."

"She won't," said Alvarez flatly. "She was inside the terminal when it happened."

Nelson gave him a look. "Let's go talk to her anyhow."

Alvarez, Nelson, and the two police officers walked together to the terminal building, leaving Amy Cooper with medics who had no medical help to give her. As the policemen approached the huddled group of witnesses, Alvarez motioned Tory aside.

"This is Deputy Nelson," he told her. "He needs to take your statement. Then we can get out of here."

George Nelson had come to a full stop. He was staring at Tory, and not in an admiring way. "Jesus H. Christ with bells on," he said, and Alvarez filed the phrase away as one he didn't want to add to his collection. "It's Vicky Wheatley, as I live and breathe, gone and growed up. My god, what stroke of rotten luck brought you into my county?"

Tory met Nelson's stare. "George," she said flatly. "Where has all your hair gone?"

"That's Deputy Nelson to you, Vicky."

Alvarez's visions of a waiting condo rapidly faded.

IT TURNED OUT that Tory did have some information to add. She remembered to point out that Amy's luggage had been lost, and she related the reference Amy had made about having a personal conflict with her husband's potential promotion. The third time Nelson took her over her conversation with Amy, Tory lost her temper. "I've told you three times," she snapped. "That's all I know."

"Never were at a loss for words before, whole time I knew you," Nelson said, but he closed his notebook.

Alvarez had also thought of something to add during Nelson's conversation with Tory. "I don't think there's any connection, but we're here because her father, Tom—"

"I know who Vicky's father is, don't I?" Nelson asked Tory. "Vicky or Tory, it don't change who your father is, does it? Just like it don't change our history, either, does it, Vicky?"

Alvarez thought about Amy Cooper's mission to rewrite history, and how she wouldn't be rewriting anything now.

"My father's been in an accident," said Tory coldly. "He's in a coma."

"I know," said Nelson. "And I'm sorry about that, although I can't say I'm happy to see it's brought you back to these parts."

"What do you know about the accident?" Alvarez asked quickly, before Tory could say anything.

"Not much, especially since GPD caught the call. Hit and run, late at night collision at an intersection with a stoplight. Sounds like the violator fled the scene." Nelson stopped and regarded Tory thoughtfully. "I'm starting to remember how the most amazing things happened whenever you were around, Vicky. Why, there was that parade—"

"I was halfway across the country when the accident happened, George," Tory snapped.

"That's Deputy Nelson to you—"

"What I wanted to tell you," interjected Alvarez, "is that it turns out the victim knew Tory's father. He's supposedly funding part of the research she was involved with."

Nelson thought that over. "I'll keep it in mind," he said, "but if there's a connection, I don't see it right off. Using cars to kill people isn't too smart. Guns are a lot more efficient."

"Thanks for sharing that," said Tory. "We'll try to keep it in mind."

Nelson didn't rise to the bait. "I'm sorry to hear about your dad, Vicky. You tell me where y'all are staying, and you can be on your way."

"Try Ms. Travers, Deputy," said Tory.

Alvarez pulled out his map and told Nelson the address of the Seagle Building. Nelson took down the information and then motioned for Alvarez to walk outside with him.

"Just a friendly piece of advice," said Nelson. "I haven't seen that one in there for almost twenty years, but she's not the kind to change her stripes. She spells trouble, and you'd be well advised to know it up front, you being a detective and all."

"I already know it; it's too late," sighed Alvarez.

"She was a hellion in her teens," Nelson continued, "down in Marion County, where I was a deputy then. Not really mean-spirited, but wild, and with a mouth on her that could just about drive you to smack her. And her old man, hell, she taunted us about him to our face. Every time she got picked up for something, she told us her father would get her off, and damned if that didn't turn out to be true. Every time. You better hope the sheriff here don't run across her—he goes back as long as I do, and Vicky Wheatley isn't someone who's easy to forget." Nelson gave Alvarez an assessing glance. "She married now?"

"Widowed," said Alvarez, hoping that one-word responses would end the conversation.

"He die a natural death?"

"Listen," said Alvarez, deciding to go for full disclosure before the deputy said something that made Alvarez want to hit him. "I know you mean well, but it's pointless. I'm in love with her."

Nelson still had more to say. "Something you should know then. Her daddy was still in office when she was a senior in high school. There was talk of him runnin' for governor, and he probably could have pulled it off. Your friend there," Nelson heavily emphasized the word friend, "she got caught at a motel with her daddy's top aide, and him a married man. The press had a field day, and her daddy never ran for nothin' again. She must have been all of seventeen, eighteen at the time.''

Alvarez could count on one hand the number of people who knew the true version of that particular story, and he was certain Deputy Nelson wasn't one of them. ''She was seventeen,'' said Alvarez shortly.

Nelson shook his head, finally admitting defeat. ''Good luck, buddy. You're going to need it.''

ALVAREZ WAS PRACTICALLY dragging Tory along by the time they got to the door of her father's condo, inside what looked to be Gainesville's only skyscraper at a whopping eleven stories. As horrified as Tory had been by the accident, the adrenaline rush had long given out, and she looked ready to keel over.

''Hang on,'' Alvarez said, propping her up against the wall. ''Let me get this door unlocked and we can go inside and get you to bed.''

''I have to call the hospital, have to call Cody.'' Tory sounded like a zombie. Then Alvarez saw the last thing they needed, signs of vandalism. R-A-H-O-W-A was spray-painted in big red letters on the door. He thought maybe he could get Tory inside before she saw the graffiti, but she wasn't that tired.

''What's that?'' she asked, as he unlocked the door.

''Probably the name of some jerk's girlfriend,'' he said, pulling the door open and sticking his head in for a quick look. ''Don't worry about it—everything looks fine. Come on, let's get you inside.''

Tory followed him into the condo as Alvarez went along switching on lights. She seemed immune to her surroundings, but Alvarez couldn't help but wonder if some of the paintings hanging on the walls were originals. He pushed Tory down into a chair, found a telephone directory and called the hospital. There was no change in Wheatley's medical status. ''We'll go see him first thing tomorrow,'' he told her. ''How are you feeling? Shouldn't you eat something? I read somewhere that keeping something in your stomach helps with morning sickness—''

''It's night,'' said Tory stonily. ''I have to call Cody.''

She got up and walked into a bedroom, closing the door behind her. Alvarez gave her plenty of time to make her call while he checked out the rest of the place. It wasn't lacking for anything, including food or laundry facilities. He put his coat in the washing machine, found some milk in the refrigerator that tasted good, poured a bowl of dry cereal and went off with both in hand to court his surly companion.

Alvarez knocked repeatedly on the bedroom door to no avail, but it opened when he pushed on it. Tory was lying on her stomach on the bed, fully clothed, out cold.

Alvarez put down the food and studied her a moment. She didn't look great, but she didn't look that bad, either. He firmly throttled this line of thought, and carefully and professionally removed her shoes and jeans, easing her under the covers. Then he ate the cereal, put his coat in the dryer, checked the doors, and brushed his teeth. Out of consideration for Tory's mood swings, he undressed only down to his briefs, then climbed into bed with her.

Maybe this was good practice for marriage, Alvarez thought, lying in the dark next to someone who was sick and exhausted and disgusted with you, someone who was wearing a sweater and knee socks, someone who was sleeping so deeply as to be almost comatose. Maybe he was getting domesticated.

He missed Cotton.

NINE

The Wedding
November, 1917. Rosewood, Florida

THERE WAS NOTHING LIKE a wedding to make your sister treat you nice. One day Garland was her regular old self, complaining about having to share a room and about how Lissy didn't do her share of chores. Then Garland rode the train with a church group to a picnic in Archer, outside of Gainesville, and everything changed. She came back sweet and dreamy and every other word was Lester Grant this and Lester Grant that, and pretty soon

Lester Grant himself started showing up regular at the Hoddens', and it was downright amazing how Garland introduced Lissy as her darling little sister.

Lissy frowned at Lester. She couldn't understand why Garland would want to spend time with him when she could spend time with The Man. It got even more confusing when Sylvester showed up one evening while Lester was sitting in the living room with Garland, because The Man shook hands with Lester right away and then acted real friendly. Lissy took a second look at Lester and noticed how he followed Garland around with his eyes every minute. Lissy thought maybe she understood something then, for The Man never acted like that with anyone.

Sylvester might be willing to act friendly with Garland's new boyfriend, but Lissy's daddy didn't like him from the moment he set eyes on him. Jim Hodden couldn't hardly stand to be in the same room with Lester, it seemed, no matter how many times Lissy's mamma scolded him for being rude. It was Lissy's mamma who started to seem like Garland's sister then. Lissy would walk up all quiet-like, as was her way, and she would come upon the two of them sitting and giggling like two school-girls.

So Lissy's daddy fumed and Lissy's mamma giggled, and then there was Garland acting all along like some stranger who took natural to being nice. Lissy wasn't quite sure what was going on, but whatever it was, she knew it couldn't last.

One night Lissy woke up to hear her parents arguing in the next room, and she wasted no time in pressing her ear to the wall. Josie Hodden was a sweet and loving wife, but once or twice a year she got to fighting with her husband, and those were the times when she said things that were real interesting.

"She's too young. I won't hear of it, Josephine, and that's the end of it." Lissy thought her daddy would have more sense by now than to tell his wife what was what, especially when she'd got her back up about something.

"Jim Hodden," Lissy's mamma said loud and clear, "you remember how old I be when you first start coming 'round?"

"Seventeen, eighteen," said Lissy's daddy, but this didn't sound quite as certain as his previous statement.

"Your memory be that bad, you need start looking for someone to take care of you in your old age," said Lissy's mamma.

"That be your job, Josie."

"Not if you a silly old man already. You know well as I do I be fifteen when you first start coming over, scared to meet my daddy."

"That be different—" started Lissy's daddy, but his wife didn't let him finish.

"That be different, Jim Hodden? You tell me how well you remember this, else I know you a silly old man afore your time. How old I be when—" Her mamma's voice turned low and husky and Lissy couldn't make out the rest of the question being posed.

Lissy was startled to hear her daddy laugh out loud in reply. Then there was more talk between the two of them that was so quiet Lissy couldn't understand, but she was beginning to lose interest anyway. Right before she fell asleep, she clearly heard her daddy say, "You sure do know how to fight, Josephine."

It wasn't but a week later that Garland started telling everyone that she was getting married, and then she and Lissy's mamma were together all the time, planning and giggling and talking. They tried to be nice about it and invite Lissy to join in, but she just wasn't much interested. The thing that fascinated her was the thought of what it would be like to have a room all to herself.

So that was how Lissy ended up sitting in the Hoddens' living room one early Sunday morning, in a new church dress that felt so stiff it seemed as though it could stand all by itself at the wedding while Lissy went somewhere else.

Garland and Lissy's mamma were in the kitchen getting the food ready to carry over to the church. Lissy wasn't allowed in there in case she got something on her new dress, because Garland kept talking about how the day had to be perfect, perfect, perfect. What was the point of a perfect day if you used it to marry someone like Lester?

Then all of a sudden there was Sylvester standing on the

porch, dressed up in a black suit and a black hat, with a white shirt as his only concession to the occasion. He looked like the handsomest man Lissy had ever seen, and she wondered how Garland could be so stupid. "Ain't you gonna open the door, Lissy Hodden?" Sylvester called.

Lissy stood up and opened the door. Maybe The Man had come to talk some sense into Garland. "What you be here for?" asked Lissy.

"I come to help carry the food over to the church, baby sister. How come you look so solemn on Garland's wedding day? You gonna be lonely, honey?"

Lissy adored Sylvester. She would give her life for him without out a second thought, but he sure did say some silly things sometimes. "I ain't worried I be lonely no ways."

"Then why you ain't got a smile on your face?"

"I want Garland to marry you," said Lissy flatly.

"Oh, baby child." Sylvester let out his laugh, the one that could cover you all over and roll you up in silky waves. "Garland be happy with Lester Grant, and he be a good man for her. Why you go on 'bout wanting Garland to marry me?"

"Because then we be truly brother and sister," said Lissy, wondering why someone as wonderful as The Man couldn't figure this out on his own. She knew what marriage was all about— forging permanent ties between two people. She'd heard Garland recite her wedding vows about a hundred times. "Forever," Lissy added for emphasis.

"I already told you once, we be secret brother and sister. Marrying Garland ain't got nothing to do with that." The Man winked at Lissy. "'Sides, I tell you a sister-secret. I got my eye on some other girl, no one but you knows this now. I tell you her name, too—it be something like yours—it be Gussie."

Lissy felt a sharp pang of jealousy; her heart fell like a rock. The Man didn't even remember that her real name was Ruth Ann.

"What you be looking like that for?" Sylvester asked.

"Garland be getting married, you be getting a new girl, you gonna go and forget me right quick," Lissy said forlornly.

"Stop talking nonsense, baby sister," said The Man. "Didn't I just tell you a secret, one nobody else 'round here knows?" Lissy nodded her head. "I ain't never gonna forget you, Lissy Hodden. You be my secret sister forever, no matter what."

"Really? You promise?"

"No."

Lissy felt her heart break, as sure as Garland claimed her heart had broken when she and Lester had a fight and didn't see each other for a week. "I done already promise," said Sylvester, grinning again. "You remember, girl? Once The Man promise, that be it. So you don' need go asking 'bout it no more, you hear?"

Lissy nodded her understanding, and gave her first wedding-day smile. Later on, when Lissy's mother told her how brave she was being about her only sister moving away to Archer, Lissy gave her second wedding-day smile.

TEN

Beginning The Vigil
Sunday

ALVAREZ DIDN'T SLEEP WELL. He dreamed about a wild-looking Amy Cooper trying to run him over in a hospital parking lot while Tory hailed a cab. It was a strange bed and a strange experience to share it with someone else. So at first light, he gave up trying to go back to sleep, took a shower, pulled on some jeans and wandered into the kitchen. He drank some orange juice and ate six slices of cold lunchmeat straight from the package.

Alvarez returned to the bedroom and stretched out on the bed, lying on his side so he could study the still-sleeping Tory. He didn't want to wake her up before she woke up on her own, but she must have heard his thoughts, for she opened her blue eyes and looked into his.

"It's you."

"Good morning." He gave her his best smile.

"I haven't brushed my teeth," she said immediately.

"Last night there were mitigating circumstances."

Still no answering smile. "You slept here last night." She didn't make it a question.

"It wasn't as much fun as it could have been. I generally like my women conscious."

The more he tried for a lighter tone, the more serious she became. "I don't know what to do," she said.

Alvarez sighed and rolled over onto his back. He'd made a career out of forcing people's hands, but if he was going to hear answers he didn't want to hear from this particular woman, he also didn't want to be looking straight at her while he heard them. "The questions may seem difficult," Alvarez told Tory, "but all the possible answers are simple. You go see your father, try to get through the day, see what decisions have to be made, or you go back out to the airport and get on the next plane to go home." He took a deep breath. "You have the baby or you don't."

"What do I tell Cody?"

"You tell him that he's going to have a baby sister or a baby brother. That's what people generally do."

"What do I tell him about you?"

"You tell him that you're going to marry me, or you don't."

"We can't get married."

"Is that a fact?" Alvarez rolled back onto his side to look at her.

"Where would we live?" Tory asked. It was an inane question, but it was still preferable to a "no."

"Somewhere. Anywhere. Hell, we could split the difference and live at the Shady Lady Motel in Anthony."

He'd said the first thing that came into his mind, referencing a run-down motel where Tory had once set up a meeting that was supposed to be out of EPPD's jurisdiction.

"We couldn't," she said immediately. "The Shady Lady is on the New Mexico side of Anthony, and Texas cops have to live in Texas."

Tory was off and running with her favorite diversion, an analysis of the most minute, unimportant facts. "It could still work," he told her.

"What do you mean? You set up a meeting there on purpose, when I told you that it had to be out of your jurisdiction." Tory narrowed her eyes. "Did you lie to me?"

"No. The office and *most* of the building are on the New Mexico side, and that's where the Shady Lady shows up on the tax maps. But a few of the rooms are actually over the border, in Texas."

"How about the one you used for the interview?"

"In Texas," Alvarez confessed.

"You're horrible." Tory punched him in his good arm, hard. "You are so bad," she added for emphasis.

"No," Alvarez replied, watching her, "like I told you once before, I'm very good. And as I recall, it's one of the few things you didn't argue about."

There was a pause; Alvarez restrained from thinking of it as a pregnant pause. "Yeah, well, look where it's gotten me," she said finally.

"Look where it's gotten us," he corrected.

"Us? What us? You're the one who doesn't even let people know that you visit your sister. It makes you feel superior to everyone else, even Scott, that you're out there on your own, with no one to worry about if things go bad. Tell me if I'm wrong. Tell me the truth."

There was so much unexpected accuracy in her statements that Alvarez had to think carefully before he replied. "I love you," he said finally. "That's the truth. And there's something I haven't told you. It's not a sure thing, that I'll be able to go back to the kind of stuff I've been doing."

Tory stared at him. While Alvarez was in the hospital, she'd probed about the long-term prognosis of his most recent injury, but he'd effectively deflected her questions and she'd gradually stopped asking. "I'm sorry," she said. "What will you do?"

"Life is full of options, *querida*—how does hostage negotiator grab you? Don't be sorry. But you need to know that if I can go back, I will. You wanted to hear the truth, so there it is. I love you.''

Tory closed her eyes. Now was the time to kiss her to force the issue. Now was the time to entice her to make love again, to bind her to him through shared passion and ensure her decision.

"Marry me, Tory. You getting pregnant may not be what we would have planned, but it could be the best thing that ever happened to us. Can you stop all your analyzing for just a minute to think about how good we would be together? Really, really good together?''

She glanced up, and he saw the shuttered look that came into her eyes and he sensed her draw away from him. It took all his resolve to make himself stay perfectly still, instead of getting up and breaking everything in sight.

Then it occurred to him that Tory was back in the place where she'd been faced with only bad choices, back with the father who had been part of a situation no young girl should ever have to face alone, back where she'd lived with a mother who'd let her own teenaged daughter take the fall for someone else's scandalous behavior. And Tory's plan, the best plan that she could come up with, the plan that had worked so well for her, was to run like hell and never look back. Alvarez knew he needed to wait.

"Listen to me," he said. He reached out with his good hand and shook Tory gently. "I want you to have the baby, and I want to marry you. But it's your choice. I may not like the decisions you make, but it's your choice.''

"I get to choose?''

"You get to choose.'' Then Alvarez thought about what he was saying, and to whom. "You get to choose some things," he amended. "About the baby, about getting married.''

Tory took a deep breath. "Okay," she said. "For right now, I choose to stop talking about it. I choose to get up, take a shower, put on some clean clothes, and just get through this day, try to deal with my father's accident.''

"Fair enough," said Alvarez. "And I get to choose some

things, too. I choose that before we go anywhere, you eat breakfast."

WITH THE LATE START, another call to Cody, and Tory making some threats to lose the breakfast Alvarez cooked for her, it was almost noon before they made it to the desk of the ICU at North Florida Regional Medical Center. In spite of the delay, there was still a welcoming committee of sorts.

When Tory identified herself, the male nurse on duty asked her to show some ID. Immediately, an attractive woman who looked to be in her sixties got up from a chair in the waiting area and walked up to Tory.

"So it's you, is it? You're finally here then, the ungrateful daughter who left her father on his own all these years. How does it feel, knowing that you're the next of kin and that you get to make all the decisions?"

"Lady, if you're hoping for an organ transplant, you better be nicer to Wheatley's daughter than this." Alvarez didn't know who was more surprised at his words, the nurse, Tory, the woman, or him. Well hell, he'd had a stressful last two days, and he was feeling protective.

The woman recovered first, and Alvarez watched in mild surprise as she swung up her hand to slap him. Tory was faster. She reached out and caught the woman's hand mid-swing, and Alvarez decided on the spot that she was the ideal mother for any child of his. "Don't hit a man with an arm in a sling." Tory said indignantly.

"Who the hell are you?" Alvarez asked the woman.

She shot him a look of pure venom. "I'm Dana Halloran," she said. "I'm Tom Wheatley's fiancée."

SIX HOURS LATER, Alvarez coaxed Tory from her father's bedside to eat some dinner in the hospital cafeteria. A few things had been sorted out—Wheatley's condition, for example. Indeterminate. The doctor in charge of Tory's father and Randy Sosa, the ICU nurse, saw no reason why Wheatley should not make a full recovery. If he regained consciousness.

Then there was the status of Dana Halloran. Indeterminate. The hospital staff could verify that she'd been constantly present at the ICU since Saturday morning, but their policy precluded visitors who weren't next of kin or allowed by next of kin. Since both Wheatley and Ms. Halloran were from Ocala, and since Tory had no remaining contact with any family friends, it was currently impossible to verify the woman's claim that she was Wheatley's fiancée.

Alvarez did ask Ms. Halloran why Cody Travers wasn't aware of his grandfather's engagement. The woman spat out that the boy's grandfather hadn't thought his grandson was ready for such news on his very first visit, so she'd been asked to keep out of sight. She complied out of respect for Wheatley's wishes, she told Alvarez. She also told him without being asked that if she had it to do over again, she would do it very differently.

"I never thought about the possibility of my father getting married again," said Tory, pushing some anemic-looking macaroni and cheese around on her plate. "I mean, it makes sense, my mother literally dropped out of sight after she left him, but somehow I never pictured him with someone else."

"You're named as his next of kin," mused Alvarez. "That means you get to make all the decisions, about who gets to visit him in ICU, what kind of medical treatment he gets—"

"Whether we put him on life support if things get worse, whether we take him off."

"We're not at that point yet," said Alvarez. "It makes me wonder though, who inherits if your father dies."

Tory put down her fork and stared at Alvarez. "Do you always think like this?"

"All the time," he said. "It's a gift, the ability to think nasty thoughts about any subject. We can talk about you, you and me together, or money."

"Money," Tory said immediately.

"How much do you think your father is worth?"

Tory shrugged.

He continued. "You're the engineer, the one who's always saying just tell me, is it bigger than a breadbox or smaller than a pony? Give me an educated guess."

"An educated guess," repeated Tory. "Okay. Fifteen, twenty million. Maybe more." Alvarez stared at her. She shrugged again. "People in my family had money to begin with, and they always married money—kind of like in-breeding." Alvarez continued to stare. "Money in my family is just a fact of life," Tory explained, "like—I don't know—like how some families have acres of farmland and marry people who have more acres of farmland."

"I'd rather have fifteen, twenty million dollars than acres of farmland," said Alvarez.

"Well, it depends," replied Tory thoughtfully, "on how many acres of farmland you're talking about, and how much it's worth—"

"Okay," Alvarez quickly cut her off. "You gave me a guess about how much your father's worth. Give me a guess about who's named in his will."

Tory ate a forkful of macaroni and cheese while she considered the question. "I guess it comes down to me, Cody, and my mom, if he still has any feelings for her. Maybe some charities. Maybe that woman out there with her nose pressed to the ICU window, I don't know."

After the initial contact with Ms. Halloran, Tory and Alvarez tried to ignore her, but it was impossible not to be constantly reminded that while they were granted access to the injured Wheatley, this forlorn and angry woman was separated from the man she claimed to love.

"Tory, don't take this wrong, but I need to know." Alvarez paused, trying to think of a tactful way to phrase his question. There wasn't one. "Are you worth something like fifteen, twenty million?"

Tory had been drinking milk and she choked. She held a hand up to ward him off from thumping her on the back. "Thinking about withdrawing your marriage proposal if I don't give the right answer?'' she asked when she had recovered sufficiently to be able to speak.

"Carumba Cotton Candy and I are creatures of independent means," Alvarez reminded her.

"My grandmother left me a trust fund," said Tory. "You know that, you know everything about me, remember? But it wasn't a lot. It was enough to pay my way through school, and pay for the house. Carl didn't want me to use my money, but I insisted. I wanted to provide something tangible for both of us, something we could count on to always be there." Tory put her glass of milk back down on the table so hard that some of it sloshed out. "God, I hate hospitals," she said vehemently.

Alvarez mopped up the milk with a paper napkin. He hadn't thought about the memories this hospital vigil must bring up for Tory, memories of her deceased husband's long and unsuccessful fight against cancer. "Must be different, growing up around money like that. Do you ever miss it?"

"No. Money is nice, but it's a tool, and too much money can be a trap. The best money of all is the money you earn yourself. I don't have original Monets and Picassos hanging on the wall, which means I don't have to spend my time worrying about someone stealing my precious possessions. I don't miss the money, and I sure don't miss my family's motto."

"What motto?"

"'Nothing's too good for the Wheatleys or the Hoddens,'" she quoted. "If I had a dollar for every time I heard that, I'd have more money than your Carumba Cotton Candy."

"Who are the Hoddens?" Alvarez asked blankly, feeling that he'd missed a step somewhere.

"You don't know?" Tory perked up. "Superstar detective does deep background investigation of innocent suspect, but doesn't even know the maiden name of subject's mother?"

"Her first name was LaBelle," he said defensively, then added, "And I remember exactly how tall she was."

"Before she married my father, her name was LaBelle Hodden," Tory said. "That was my grandmother's married name, the grandmother who left me the trust fund. Hodden," she repeated. The look of triumph faded from Tory's face. "Why are you asking these things? You only ask things for two reasons— to irritate people, or because you're working on a case." Her words came faster. "I should have known you wouldn't be able to leave well enough alone, leave the investigation of last night's accident to the local police. What is it you know that you're not telling me? Where did you go when you disappeared this afternoon?"

"I went to a bookstore," Alvarez said, "and I bought some books about this area." He'd also bought a book about what to expect during the three trimesters of pregnancy. He'd felt surprisingly foolish as the bookstore clerk rang up this purchase, but he didn't feel a need to mention any of this to Tory. "I need something to occupy my time, especially if you're not going to provide entertainment. Travel can be so educational. Did you know that Tom Petty and the Heartbreakers are from Gainesville?"

"Actually, they're not," said Tory. "Tom Petty is, and some of the others, but he didn't form the Heartbreakers until he moved out to California."

Alvarez was impressed. "Did you know that the Seagle Building, the very place where we're staying, was originally intended to be a luxury hotel? But it got donated to the University and was used as a museum before it was sold back into private ownership. Don't you think that's interesting?"

"Did you know that there's a huge sinkhole on the outskirts of town that goes all the way down to the aquifer, and that it's named Devil's Millhopper?" Tory countered.

"I haven't gotten to that yet," Alvarez said, but this game of Gainesville Trivial Pursuit had not distracted Tory from her original questions.

"What is it that you're not telling me?"

Alvarez sighed. "I checked in with your friend Deputy Nelson today."

"He's not my friend."

"I wanted to see if they'd made any progress in finding the driver from last night," Alvarez continued. "Seems that when they got around to checking out Amy Cooper's car last night, they found something spray-painted on it.''

"What?"

Alvarez knew just from looking at her that Tory already knew, but he told her anyhow. "The same thing that was spray painted on the door of the condo. R-A-H-O-W-A.''

"How strange," Tory said. "I wonder what it means."

Alvarez cleared his throat. "Nelson and his buddies already know what it means. It stands for something."

"What?"

"It's an abbreviation for the term Racial Holy War."

Tory looked at him in disbelief for a moment, then closed her eyes. "This is too much," she said. "I can't believe it. I refuse to believe it. What else can possibly go wrong?"

Alvarez winced. He and Scott had total faith that there were some things that were never ever said out loud, and Tory had just uttered one of them.

Like magic, someone approached their table. Alvarez looked up to see a tall, distinguished-looking black man in an impeccably tailored suit. The man acted as though Alvarez didn't exist.

"Hi, Vicky," he said. "It's been a long time, and I'm sorry to meet again under such tragic circumstances. But you and I need to talk."

Alvarez preferred Ms. Halloran's attempted assault to being ignored. He stood up and offered his hand. "You must be Rolland Reynolds," he said. "I'm David Alvarez."

ELEVEN

The Parting
March, 1918. Rosewood, Florida

LISSY WAS INCONSOLABLE.

The Man and his father were going away. Even worse, they were going away to prison. Lissy couldn't get her mind around it; it sounded more final than any marriage vows, and Garland said marriage vows were the very definition of forever. Lissy mourned and worried and couldn't even hardly eat. Then her mother finally wormed it out of her, what was bothering Lissy so.

"Sit down and let me talk to you 'bout this." Josie Hodden spoke in the tone she reserved for serious discussions. "Hayward and Sylvester be going away for while, but it could be a lot worse."

"Worse than *prison?*" Lissy couldn't imagine anything worse than the idea of going to prison, unless it was being dead.

"You hush now, that talk 'bout prison. They being punished for who they be, 'specially that Sylvester Carrier."

"Mr. Herrington in Sumner say they being punished for changing marks," said Lissy carefully, wanting to make sure that she got the words just right. "Then Mr. Wilkerson laughed and say that just a fancy name for cattle rustling." Lissy was puzzled. "The Man and his daddy, they don't have no cattle."

Josie Hodden's lips pressed into a thin line. "The Carriers don't have no cattle, that a fact. You come ask me afore you be going with your daddy to Sumner again, listening to Poly Wilkerson and his kind, don't matter whether he run the sawmill or not. Baby, you know the Carriers gots a fancy house. And you know how Sylvester be, dressing all fancy in black all the time, walking and talking proud. Some white folks don't like that much, what with him not working 'round here much, there's talk 'bout how he earns his money."

"He hunts good and traps good," said Lissy.

Lissy's mamma shook her head. "No matter. People be calling Sylvester uppity, and white folks don't like that in a black man. They like it even less, his family living in a house fancier than theirs, so they gonna send Hayward and Sylvester away for a while. But not a long while, baby child. Jesus be willing, they be back afore you know it."

"How you know?" asked Lissy. "I ain't never known no one go to prison, much less come back from there."

"They in prison just to start," said Lissy's mamma. "Then they get sent somewheres to work on roads, or maybe to the turpentine camps."

For once, Lissy didn't really care about the details. "But how you know they come back?" she persisted.

Lissy's mamma gave her a considering look. "You getting to be a big girl, maybe big enough to hear some growed up people things. But I better not hear you say a word 'bout what I be telling you, Lissy, or I'll switch you, I swear I will."

Lissy didn't mind the threat—this sounded even more interesting than her parents' infrequent arguments. "I won't tell nobody," she said solemnly.

"You know Mr. Carter?"

"The blacksmith?" Lissy's mamma nodded. Sam Carter was a big, quiet man. The most interesting thing about him was that he washed and bleached his overalls until they looked white instead of dirty blue.

"Fourteen, fifteen years ago," said Lissy's mamma, "Sam got sent to prison. He be there a year, now he be back, big as life and looking just fine."

"What he sent to prison for?" asked Lissy.

Lissy's mamma sighed. "I reckon I might be sorry I told you this. Ain't none of this your business, but you know half it already, so I might as well tell you the rest. They said Sam Carter threatened a man with a shotgun."

"*Our* Mr. Carter?" It was hard for Lissy to believe what she was hearing.

"The same Sam Carter you knowed ever since you was born," Lissy's mamma confirmed. "They couldn't prove nothing so they sent him home, and he's got along fine ever since. Now we talked 'bout all this long enough. You come sit down, eat some food and stop worrying 'bout these things."

Lissy obeyed part of what her mamma told her to do. She was still worrying when The Man made a special trip to her house to tell her goodbye. He said the same things that Lissy's mamma had said, that he would be just fine, and that it wouldn't be any time at all before he was back in Rosewood, just as free as any other man in the State of Florida.

Lissy didn't agree. "You gonna be gone a long time." She tried to suppress the wail in her voice.

"It be like no time at all," said The Man, "and there be plenty you can do to help me out while I'm gone."

"Like what?" asked Lissy eagerly.

"Like visiting my mamma and sisters. They be lonely with me and my daddy gone."

Lissy was a little afraid of The Man's mamma. She was so well known and respected in Rosewood that everyone called her Aunt Sarah, and everyone went to her for advice. But Lissy could visit Aunt Sarah if The Man asked her to. "What else?" she asked.

The Man gave her one of his best smiles. "What else? You know that little three-legged dog named Git, that one nobody ever pays much mind to 'cause he so ugly? I be partial to that dog. Git needs someone to scratch his ears and sneak him some scraps now and then."

"What else?"

The Man had to think now. "Well," he said slowly, "there be your neighbor, John Marshall, and his new wife." Lissy nodded, even though she was uncertain what the Marshalls had to do with The Man. "John's wife be sickly," Sylvester continued, "and it be hard for John, working and trying to take care of her. He might get tempted sometime to go looking for some cow wandering off, even if it belong to someone else. We don't want that happening to John Marshall, do we, baby sister?" Lissy shook her head. "So maybe you go over there sometimes and help John's new wife. You think you could do that for me, Lissy-sister?"

"I'd do anything for you," said Lissy.

"Then come here and give me a big goodbye hug," said The Man. "One that will last me a while."

Lissy did everything Sylvester asked her to do. She thought on the knowledge gleaned from her conversation with her mamma, and carefully watched the prison gangs that she and her daddy sometimes came across on the rare occasions that she was allowed to ride with him on errands. She never saw The Man or Haywood Carrier, but she started to recognize some of the prisoners and the men in charge of them.

There was one man who stood out from the others. He was in charge of a road gang working outside of Cedar Key, the fishing town west of Sumner. This particular man was different from the other guards in that he was younger and wore a yellow bandanna around his neck. Lissy had seen lots of red bandannas, but never a yellow one.

The other way he stood out was that he carried himself just like the Man, even with him being white and all.

TWELVE

The Pitch
Sunday

THE MAN STANDING at their table turned his gaze from Tory to Alvarez. "How do you know my name?" he asked. "Who are you?"

Before Alvarez could respond, Tory intervened. "Rolland. Imagine meeting you here." Her voice was expressionless. "This is David Alvarez, a family friend."

Alvarez liked the sound of that. It occurred to him, standing there, that it wasn't too much of a stretch from being a family friend to being the family solicitor.

Reynolds shook Alvarez's outstretched hand. "May I sit down?" He grabbed an empty chair from a neighboring table without waiting for a reply. "I want to express my sincere sympathy regarding your father's unfortunate accident. Has Tom's condition changed?"

"No," said Tory shortly. "You're on a first name basis with my father now?"

Reynolds smiled. "Things change, Vicky. People grow up. You have to admit, it's been a long time."

Alvarez wondered if Tory could tell him how long to the day.

"Some things change," she told Reynolds. "My name is Tory Travers now. Some things don't change—you wouldn't be here unless you wanted something."

Reynolds shook his head. "You never liked me much, did you?" he asked.

"No," said Tory, "and I recall every single reason why. How about you, Rolland? How good is your memory?"

Alvarez decided that if Tory pissed this guy off too early, he might leave without telling them what he was after. It seemed a good time to try out the role of family solicitor. "Ms. Travers is understandably under a great deal of stress," he said. "We should be offering our condolences also—it's Dr. Reynolds, isn't it? I'm sorry about the tragic death of your assistant. I only met Amy Cooper briefly, but she seemed to be a dedicated young woman. Her death must be a great loss to you professionally, as well as personally."

Reynolds eyes widened briefly, but he was a cool one; he recovered his composure quickly. "Yes, it's Dr. Reynolds, but why stand on formality? Please, call me Rolland, Mr.—"

"Alvarez," Alvarez supplied for him. "Just call me Alvarez, Rolland."

"Alvarez, then," said Reynolds, trying it out. "You knew Amy? I don't understand—"

"She sat by us on the flight from Tallahassee," said Alvarez. "We started talking and she told us about her work at, what is it, the Center for State Heritage Studies?" Reynolds nodded, his eyes narrowing now. "Your name came up, Tom Wheatley's name came up, one thing led to another." Alvarez spread his hands, or spread them as well as he could with one arm in a sling.

"I see," said Reynolds. It was obvious he didn't, but that he was trying hard to. "The police said there was a man in the parking lot when it happened," he said slowly. "A man who tried to help, who stayed with her body until the police came."

"We all tried to help," said Alvarez, closing this road of inquiry. "There was nothing anyone could do. It was tragic."

"Yes, tragic. That's certainly the word for it." Reynolds had latched onto an approach now. "Amy was so young and talented, and because the Center is so new and there are only three of us, we were like family. Actually, our assistant director, Chloe Marshall, was Amy's second cousin.''

"Yes, Amy mentioned that," said Alvarez.

"It's all so unbelievable," continued Reynolds. "Amy left behind a husband, but at least there weren't any children." There was a pause. "They say her luggage was lost—that on top of everything else. Do you know anything about it?"

"Nothing," said Alvarez flatly. If Reynolds wanted to go on a fishing trip, Alvarez could throw out a line of his own. "What seems even more disquieting is that Ms. Cooper's car was spray-painted with a racist term—Rahowa. That might have more to do with her death than missing luggage."

"I hope not," said Reynolds. "In our line of work, controversy and harassment are constants. One tends not to take them seriously, otherwise it would be impossible to get any work done."

"Controversy and harassment are constants in historical research?" asked Alvarez.

"Our center came into existence because of the Rosewood Bill, which was the first legislation requiring a state to pay victims of mass racial violence. That's taxpayer money, so you better believe there's controversy attached. On top of that, our mission is to correct historical omissions and misinformation. That in itself is intolerable to certain groups." Reynolds frowned. "Did Amy seem particularly upset, or fearful when you talked to her on the plane?"

"No. We mostly talked about her work."

"Then perhaps you already know why I'm here."

"No, we don't know why you're here," Tory said. "Why don't you tell us?"

Reynolds turned to address Tory. "A lot has changed since I've seen you, so why don't I catch you up on what I've been doing since we last saw each other?" He kept one flickering eye on Alvarez as he spoke. "I got two degrees in history at UF, then got my doctorate at the University of Chicago. I stayed on, got tenure, and would probably be there still, but UF formed the Center for State Heritage Studies. When they conducted a search to fill the directorship, I just had to apply. With my contacts at the University and in the community, it was a natural fit." Somehow Reynolds managed to make the statement sound modest. "It felt good to come home," he added.

"How did your wife feel about the move?" asked Alvarez.

"My wife?" Reynolds looked blank. "Oh, you must have noticed my wedding ring. Yes, I'm married. Carla and I have three children."

"So how did they feel about moving here?" asked Alvarez again.

"Carla loves being in Florida—she's from Puerto Rico. As a matter of fact, she and the children are visiting there right now." Reynolds paused. "You were asking about controversy and harassment. Out of the three of us, Amy was the only staff member not in a racially mixed marriage." Reynolds paused, but neither Tory nor Alvarez accepted the invitation to make a comment, so Reynolds continued with his discussion of family matters. "My parents sold their land, Vicky. They live in Miami now."

"I live in New Mexico now," she said, "and my name is Tory."

"Yes, of course. Tory. In any case, it was only natural that I renew some old family acquaintances upon my return."

"And my father was the only one left in my family for you to renew an acquaintance with," Tory replied.

Reynolds at least had the grace to look uncomfortable. "I never had a chance to tell you I was sorry about what happened—how you ended up leaving and all. In any case, it's all in the past now, isn't it, Vicky? And it's really none of my business."

"Tory," she said. "What do you want, Rolland?"

"This is rather awkward." Tory continued to gaze at Reynolds, not helping. He continued after a pause. "Well, maybe Amy told you about your father's plans. He's a big supporter of UF, and it's only natural that as he grows older, his interests turn to history." Tory looked incredulous but she didn't say anything. "About six months ago your father started talking about ensuring his legacy here—making a significant contribution to education and his beloved state of Florida. An endowment earmarked for historical research seemed just the right instrument to realize his goals."

Well, of course, thought Alvarez. That's just the thing I'd think of if I had a spare two million dollars sitting around. "Perhaps you could explain some of the details to us."

Reynolds was happy to oblige. "Are either of you involved in academia?" he asked. "I wouldn't want to bore you with things you already know." Tory and Alvarez shook their heads. "Endowments like the one your father had in mind are used to entice the best and the brightest to various institutions. An eminent scholar endowment must be self-supporting from the interest generated by investment of the principal funds."

"So someone gives enough money that the investment interest pays off the guy who fills the position?" Follow-the-money-trail: Scott would have loved this. Reynolds frowned, and Alvarez mentally kicked himself for using the term "pays off." If he was going to impersonate an attorney, he needed to drop the cop talk.

"The money is invested and the interest is used to provide a salary and support funding for the scholar," Reynolds explained more delicately. "The state matches any donations over a million, dollar for dollar, so Tom's proposed contribution is very generous indeed—it will result in a four-million-dollar endowment."

Tory didn't thank Reynolds for doing the math for them. "Proposed contribution," she repeated. "So it's not a done deal?"

"No," said Reynolds, drawing out the word. "But it was supposed to be. Your father met with my assistant director the evening of his accident to execute the agreement. For some reason, Chloe didn't leave with the signed papers. I imagine they got to visiting, it got late, and your father didn't want to keep Chloe while he went over the final paperwork—he was always very thoughtful about things like that."

"I'd be thoughtful, too, signing over two million dollars,"

said Alvarez. Reynolds shot him a sharp look, but Alvarez thought it sounded like a damn good lawyer-thing to say.

"Your father told Chloe that he would get everything to her on Monday. The endowment is something your father wanted to do—intended to do," continued Reynolds. "The papers were all drawn up, everything was resolved—it was just a matter of crossing the t's and dotting the i's. Then this horrible accident occurred, and everything changed in a split second."

"Like it changed for Amy Cooper," observed Alvarez.

"Exactly. In part, as macabre as it seems, I'm here because of Amy's accident. It brought home how we take things for granted. Amy's work is at an untimely end, but what your father intended can go on as planned."

"How?" Tory asked.

Reynolds cleared his throat. "If it doesn't sound too horrible, I'd like to give you copies of the papers your father planned to sign. If he regains consciousness—"

"And if he doesn't?" Tory countered.

Reynolds looked at her a moment. "Well, then, I'm hoping you'll respect his wishes."

"That's good, Rolland. You, depending on me to respect my father's wishes. Well, I could respect them all I want, and it could end up doing zilch for you." Tory paused for breath. "Unless you know something I don't. About his will, that is. You always did know the most amazing things about people, Rolland."

Reynolds finally looked affronted. "I don't know anything about your father's will. I just assumed that you would be in charge of his affairs, should the undesired outcome happen—"

"There's no reason for you to assume that," Tory shot back.

Alvarez held up his good hand. "How do you benefit from the endowment?" he asked.

"I don't. The beneficiary of Tom Wheatley's generosity is the history department, thus the University, thus the state of Florida."

"You wouldn't by any chance be filling the eminent chair position yourself?"

"Of course not. I wouldn't consider leaving my current position."

Alvarez felt certain there was a catch somewhere. "I don't mean to be impolite," he said, "but I need the name of someone who can verify what you've just told us." Tory shot him a look of pure amazement, but Alvarez ignored her.

"Of course," said Reynolds. Alvarez's request appeared to make perfect sense to him. "You need to talk to Marilyn Mortenson, head of the History Department." Alvarez wrote the name and phone number down in his notebook.

"If you would mention to her that I'll be—"

"I'll call her tonight," said Reynolds. It was amazing, the doors that a potential two million dollars could open. "And I'll make sure she has copies of the endowment agreement for you to look over." Alvarez nodded his thanks, mentally telegraphing Tory a message to close her mouth.

"Is there anything else I can do for you?" Reynolds asked Alvarez.

"I think you've done quite enough. Don't you agree, Tory?"

Like a good collaborator, she nodded her head.

Both Alvarez and Reynolds made more noises of sympathy about the various accidents suffered in the preceding two days, and then Reynolds was gone.

"What do you think you're doing?" asked Tory.

"Impersonating your attorney."

"My attorney is blond, five foot two, and named Marsha."

Alvarez shrugged. "I do the best I can. I'm used to winging it."

"Can't you go anywhere without being a cop?"

"No," said Alvarez honestly, and there was a short meaningful silence.

"Okay," Tory said finally. "What is this supposed to do for me?"

"Maybe provide some information we wouldn't get otherwise. And while I'm at it, I can check out Lady Love in the ICU, see if she's really who she claims she is."

Tory groaned. "This is like stepping into a soap opera."

"Scott says that hospital linen closets are sexy places on soap operas."

"I'm not going to ask about you and Scott discussing soap operas. Can you get into trouble?"

"Is that an invitation? You feeling better?"

"Can you get into trouble impersonating an attorney?"

"Not if I don't actually tell someone that I'm an attorney," replied Alvarez. "Want to tell me why you hate Rolland Reynolds so much?"

"No."

"I love working with cooperative clients," said Alvarez.

LATER, AFTER HE persuaded Tory that remaining in the ICU around the clock wouldn't be wise, after he got her to return to the condo and after he walked into the bedroom to tell her something without thinking to knock, he forgot all about client-attorney relationships.

Tory stood in front of the dresser mirror, dressed in a shimmering black nightgown with a plunging neckline. A scattering of rhinestones adorned the bodice. When she turned toward him, he could see that the gown was slit up to her thigh.

"Wow," he said simply. He was kind of shocked; Tory had never seemed like a rhinestone kind of woman.

"I've never seen this nightgown before in my life," said Tory.

Alvarez had heard more outrageous statements than that from people caught red-handed. "I doubt it belongs to your father."

"It's Sylvia's," said Tory. "And it's the only nightgown she packed."

"Good for Sylvia." Alvarez crossed the room and kissed Tory, gently, tentatively, not rushing anything, pleased when she kissed him back. He laid her down on the king-sized bed they shared last night, and things were just starting to get interesting when Tory stiffened in his arms. Alvarez didn't open his eyes. Whatever was going on, if he didn't see it, maybe he could ignore it.

"Tory," he whispered, "don't tell me you're having another intimacy crisis. It's okay. It's me. I love you. I'm not going to tell anyone, I'm not going to write your name in the boy's bathroom. Your kid isn't even in the same state. Think about it—you're pregnant already, so we can have delicious, forbidden, *unsafe* sex. Can you imagine how good that will be? God, I can't even remember the last time—"

Tory started making definite movements to get vertical. Alvarez gave up and opened his eyes. "Okay, what was it I said that was wrong?"

Tory pushed him away. "I'm sorry, I'm really sorry—" she said.

"What is it?" He didn't mean to sound so gruff, but damn it, he felt gruff, and that wasn't the least of it. "What's wrong?" He tried to use a gentler tone.

"I think I'm going to throw up," she said, and was gone. Alvarez rolled over onto his back, looked at the ceiling, and sighed. Then he followed Tory into the bathroom.

It was sad, the sight of an attractive woman in a sexy nightgown draped over a toilet, throwing up. Tory kept alternating between saying she was sorry and saying she thought she was going to throw up again. Alvarez got a blanket and draped it around her shoulders. Then he fetched two glasses of water and wet washcloths, talking steadily to distract them both. Sometimes Tory participated, and sometimes he had to carry on the conversation for long stretches by himself. Sometimes he could get her to lie down, but she refused to budge from her proximity to the toilet.

"Tory," he mused at some point past midnight, "do you think you have a phobia about sex, or maybe about me? I'm not paranoid or anything, but have you thought about the timing of these bouts of nausea? There's another advantage to marrying me. You'd be covered by my health insurance, and the police department is big on counseling—" Alvarez realized his words were falling on deaf ears. He looked down at Tory and saw that she'd fallen asleep, curled around the toilet. He sighed, got up, and fetched a pillow to tuck under her head and another blanket to put over her.

He took one longing look at the bed, grabbed the remaining

blankets and pillows and stretched out on the carpet next to the bathroom. From there he could reach out and touch one of Tory's feet if he craved physical contact.

Damn, but he still missed Cotton.

THIRTEEN

Trading Secrets
November, 1918. Rosewood, Florida

THE MAN AND HIS DADDY were home, just like everyone said they would be, and it was a happy time for the Carrier family. In the midst of all the celebrating and hugging and kissing, The Man took Lissy aside and specially thanked her for everything she'd done. Lissy was so proud that she thought her face must be shining like the fireball she'd seen that one night so long ago. But The Man wasn't done talking to her. He asked her to come back before suppertime in exactly one week. He told her he had a new secret to share with her.

So one week after The Man's return, Lissy sat on the steps of the Carrier porch in the late afternoon, when a chill was just starting to come up off the swamps outside town. She hugged her knees to her chest and waggled them back and forth as she waited. Sylvester's mother had told Lissy to wait right there because Sylvester had something he wanted to bring out to her. It wasn't long until The Man joined Lissy on the porch, back to wearing fancy black clothes again, carrying something in his hand.

"You got something for me?" Lissy asked breathlessly.

The Man made a big show of looking around. "I don't see no one else here 'bouts, do you?" He looked down at what he had in his hands. "Your name be Lissy Hodden?"

Part of Lissy wanted to remind The Man that her name was really Ruth Ann, but something told her it wouldn't be the thing to do right now. "Yes, Lissy Hodden be my name," Lissy said solemnly.

"Then I guess this be for you," The Man smiled, "'cause it

sure nuff have your name on it." Sylvester sat down beside her
and showed Lissy the most beautiful wooden box she had ever
seen. "I most had this finished afore I went away," he told her.
"It sure nuff got me riled, leaving afore I could give it to you."
The Man frowned. "It sure nuff got me riled, all that business,
and them mixing my daddy up in it to boot." Then he looked
at Lissy and smiled. "But it behind me now, and this box be
for you."

Lissy held the gift as though it might disappear at any moment. It was a big keepsake box, with a hinged cover that opened
and closed smoothly. It was this very lid that was the most wonderful part. Carved flowers spread over every inch except for a
corner at the bottom, where there were the words LISSY HODDEN,
ROSEWOOD, 1918.

"It's beautiful," breathed Lissy. She didn't even mind that
the box said Lissy instead of Ruth Ann. "I ain't never had nothing so beautiful."

"I glad you like it, Lissy-sister," said The Man. "It gave me
good reason to behave while I be gone. You know why?" Lissy
gave Sylvester a questioning look. "'Cause I ain't want to come
back and have to start all over, carve a different year on top, not
no way," laughed The Man.

Lissy didn't see anything funny about The Man being away
so long that the year almost changed before he returned home.
"I'd like it no matter what you carved on the top," she said.

"Well, you just be easy to please, 'cause I ain't even showed
you the best thing 'bout this box." Sylvester reached over,
swung the lid open and told Lissy to look inside. "What you
see?"

"Nothing."

"No, you be smarter than that," said The Man. "You look
real careful and tell me what you see."

Lissy looked carefully. "Well, there be these two little holes
on two sides," she said slowly. She hoped she wasn't pointing
out an imperfection in the craftsmanship. She'd love this box
even if the entire bottom was riddled with holes.

"Those be called notches," said The Man. "You put your

fingers just like this." He stuck his two hands in the box. "And you pull up and look—what you have now?" Sylvester was holding what Lissy had thought was the bottom of the box in his hand.

"Another bottom to the box," said Lissy.

"A secret place," corrected The Man. "You put regular stuff in the top part of this box."

"I ain't never going to put no regular stuff in it," protested Lissy.

"You put whatever pleases you in the box," amended The Man. "But this place, this secret place at the bottom, that where you keep your mostest secret stuff. This be a special secret box with a special secret place for my special secret sister."

Lissy's heart was so full she thought it would burst. The only thing spoiling the moment was that she didn't have anything to give The Man in return. Lissy put the false bottom back in the box and closed the lid, thinking hard. She set the box carefully down on the porch next to her. "I got a secret to show you, too," she said.

"What secret?"

"You gots to follow me," said Lissy. She stood up and walked around the side of the house to a huge oak tree. "Watch," she told The Man, and began to climb nimbly up until she disappeared from sight.

"Where you gone to?" asked The Man, craning his head toward the sky to look for her. "Your mamma'd boil me in oil if'n you fall out that tree and break your neck, girl."

"You gots to climb up and look," Lissy told him.

"You be joking me, girl."

"You gots to," Lissy insisted.

The Man gave a quick look around, as though to make sure that there would be no witnesses to his foolishness, sighed, and started to climb the tree as directed. He could only get a third of the way Lissy had gone, being so tall and big, but he got far enough up into the tree so that he could see where Lissy was sitting.

She was perched on a high twisted limb that had grown out

from an old lightning strike that had split the branch. The portion forming her lookout veered away from the tree horizontally for a foot or so until regaining its natural bent and turning again toward the sky. This formed a small seat for Lissy, not unlike the seat of a swing, and the heavy foliage sheltered her from view. The Man labored to climb higher until he could touch the base of the branch forming Lissy's perch. He reached up and tried to bounce the branch back and forth with one hand, but it wouldn't budge.

"That be some secret," he told Lissy admiringly. "Now I don't want to hear a single laugh out of you while I tries to get myself down. I ain't a boy no more, used to climbing trees and such foolishness." With an ease that belied his words, Sylvester returned to the ground. He looked up toward where Lissy sat. "I can't hardly see you from here," he said. "You come down now afore I get dizzy looking up at you, and tell me how you come to find this place."

Lissy was back on the ground in no time. "I came visiting like you done asked me," she told The Man. "I visited your mamma and your sisters, and sometimes I helped with the babies."

"What that got to do with climbing trees?"

Lissy drew small circles with her foot in the dirt under the tree. "Sometimes it gets tiresome," she said, "visiting with folks. Sometimes I runs out of words to say, and they be talking all the time and then waiting for me to say something. Days I couldn't think of nothing to say, and days they don't need no help with the babies, I came anyway—to watch over them."

The Man studied Lissy. "I be a lucky man to have a secret sister like you, Lissy Hodden, watching out for my family."

"What you being all serious and solemn for?" she asked, using the words he so often directed at her. "I gonna pull me a nice big leaf off this tree, be the first thing I put in my box so I always remember this day."

The Man swung Lissy high in the air to pull a leaf off the tree, and when he put her down he tickled her some. When they sat back down together on the porch for Lissy to put her leaf in her box, The Man said, "I got another secret to tell you, Lissy-sister, but you can't tell no one about it."

"I ain't never told nobody none of our secrets."

"Then listen close," said The Man. When Lissy complied, he whispered in her ear, "Gussie and I gonna get married."

Lissy looked at him, her eyes wide with wonder. "Really?" She'd seen lots of young men courting Gussie while Sylvester was gone. Lissy didn't think Gussie had missed him a bit.

"Really," said the Man firmly.

Lissy sensed a problem. "Why can't I tell nobody? Your daddy think you too young to be marrying Gussie?" The Man threw back his head and laughed long and loud. Lissy didn't understand what she had said that was so funny. "Maybe Gussie be too young?" she ventured.

The Man thought this was funny, too. "Gussy be old enough to be married three times over, if'n she had a mind to."

"Then why it be a secret, you and Gussie getting married?"

The Man gave her one of his widest grins. "'Cause I done asked her, and she said no."

Lissy was even more puzzled. "Then how you know you gonna be marrying Gussie?"

"Now that," said The Man, "is such a big secret even I don't know it yet. But soon's I figure it out, I tell you, baby sister."

Lissy smiled right along with The Man, but she thought to herself that no matter how old he got, or who he married, or how many children he had, he could sure still use someone to watch over him.

FOURTEEN

Conversational Skills
Monday

TOM WHEATLEY DIDN'T LOOK too bad for a man who had survived the wreck of his political and personal life, in addition to the car he'd been driving just three days ago. Except for the hospital setting, complete with wires, tubes, and monitors, and some stitched gashes, Tory thought her father looked capable of sitting up at any moment and gazing at her. It would likely be a look of resigned tolerance with an undercurrent of disapproval running too deep to disguise.

It could be worse. Tory could be sitting in an Ocala hospital, driving down Ocala streets, surrounded by Ocala horse farms, facing familiar scenes everywhere she looked. Gainesville was a good thirty-minute drive from where she and her brother grew up, and although it became a place to get into trouble as she got older, it wasn't really a place she'd ever called home. Tory should count herself lucky—here in Gainesville so far, she'd only encountered three individuals from her past: George Nelson, Rolland Reynolds, and of course, her own father.

"Talk to him to pass the time," Nurse Sosa suggested after Alvarez took off on his self-assigned research. Easier said than done. What was there to talk about? Shared childhood experiences? Hardly. Tory's earliest memories of her father were of someone always away or in a meeting. As she grew older, she was expected to be an extension of her parents' political ambitions, expected to fill out the portrait of a loving, picture-perfect family. When that didn't work out, there had been anger and recriminations on both sides, but Tommy had been the glue that held them all together. Once he was dead, on-going covert skirmishes became all-out war, with no quarter asked and no quarter given. After the final apocalyptic family battle, there had been a total breakup of relations. That had worked okay too.

But one could never totally discount those damned blood ties. Tom Wheatley coveted a connection to his only grandson and Cody was understandably curious about an extended family he had never known. This left Tory in the middle, in a place where truth seemed to be viewed as a reasonable sacrifice in the name of reconciliation. Tory searched for nonjudgmental words to speak to her unconscious father and found none.

One always remained a child in some fundamental sense when dealing with a parent. If Tory sat in judgment of her father, she also had to sit in judgment of herself. She could maintain her adult neutrality only when there was no contact. Even now, faced with his possible death, there was still an adolescent inside Tory, wanting her father to admit the truth, to side with her for once, to *apologize*. But as an adult she knew that her truth would never be his truth, and that her father was such a politician at heart that she wasn't even sure if the word "truth" meant the same thing to them both.

Tory stood up. Not only was she bereft of words for her father, she didn't want to be near him either. Turning away from him, the first thing she saw was Dana Halloran on the wrong side of the glass separating Tom Wheatley from those not allowed at his side.

Tory thought about the burden of spending endless hours at a hospital with a man to whom she had nothing to say. She thought about what Dana Halloran thought about her. She weighed these two in her mind, decided that a bargain could be struck. She might not be any good at reconciliation, but she had lots of practice in the art of negotiation.

Nurse Sosa had said, "Talk, just talk."

Tory walked away from her father's bedside. "Why don't we go get some coffee and talk?" she asked Dana Halloran.

DR. MARILYN MORTENSON didn't keep Alvarez waiting. Even better, she didn't take phone calls, fidget, or push papers around while meeting with him. Since Mortenson was black, Alvarez felt certain she had heard charges of favoritism during her academic career. After only a few minutes in her presence, he also felt certain that she had earned every position she ever held.

Mortenson heard him out completely, without interruption. Alvarez started by explaining his connections with both Amy Cooper and Wheatley's daughter; he expressed his condolences over Amy's death; and he described Reynolds's visit at the hospital to discuss Wheatley's purported plans to make a sizeable contribution to UF's history department. Then he closed his mouth and waited to see what she had to say.

"I can verify that Senator Wheatley intended to establish an eminent scholar chair in this department," said Mortenson. "There's not a lot more that I can tell you that isn't explained in these papers—perhaps overly explained," she added, using a pencil to push a large, sealed envelope across her desk toward Alvarez. Mortenson didn't seem anxious to pick up the packet, and Alvarez let it sit without touching it.

"I'm sure there's more you can tell me," he said. "You could explain the expression on your face when I described Reynolds visiting Wheatley's daughter at the hospital last night."

Mortenson stared at Alvarez a moment, then laughed. It was a nice laugh. "Guilty as charged, Mr. Alvarez. As much as I want funding for my department, I find it distasteful that a colleague would visit a hospital ICU to try to get the signature of a comatose man, should he regain consciousness."

"What's in it for Reynolds?"

"That's blunt and to the point."

"I'm just trying to understand. I'm wondering why he's pushing so hard if there's nothing in it for him. To hear him tell it, if this endowment goes through, it's got nothing to do with him and his Center for State Heritage Studies."

Mortenson leaned back in her chair. "Anyone in academia would tell you that's a very simplistic way of looking at things. You might call it half the story."

"Then what's the other half?"

"The endowment would fund the work of an eminent scholar, as you already know. It's true there's no direct benefit to Dr. Reynolds or the Center he heads. But the endowment would benefit our department, of which the Center is a part. Those who bring funding into the department are first and foremost in our minds when annual budgets are allocated. In the bigger picture, those who bring significant funding to the university, regardless of the funding's ultimate purpose or source, shall be as likely to be rewarded here on earth as in heaven."

Was she making a joke? Alvarez, with his Hispanic Catholic upbringing, did not have enough experience with Southern Baptist tradition to hazard a guess. "And two million is significant funding?" he asked, playing it straight.

"Very significant."

"So the payoff for landing money like that might not be direct, but it would be a pretty sure thing."

"Again, you have an interesting way of phrasing things. But your observation is essentially correct."

"What's your opinion of Reynolds?"

Mortenson studied Alvarez for a long moment. "What's your real interest in all of this?"

"I already explained, I'm a friend of the family."

"Making that statement and explaining are two different things," Mortenson said sharply, and Alvarez figured he'd just gotten a peek at her lecturing style. "I'm not interested in sharing my personal history with you, Mr. Alvarez, but I'd bet my tenure you're not an attorney. From the moment you walked in here, all my street smarts screamed 'cop.' So far, I've found no reason to change my mind."

Alvarez shrugged, noncommittal. "What can I do to get you to answer my question?"

"Tell me if you're an attorney."

"Okay, I'm not an attorney. I'm a cop—but I am a personal friend of Wheatley's daughter. I came here with her so she wouldn't have to face this alone. Besides, I'm in love with her and she's got more than enough to handle right now."

"Why didn't you say so from the beginning? An attorney I'd never trust. A cop in love, now that's something else. You repeat anything I tell you outside this room and I'll say you lied, understand? What's more, I'll make you sorry you ever said it."

"Understood," said Alvarez. Damned if Mortenson didn't resemble some of the nuns he'd grown up with.

"If it were up to me, I'd tell Senator Wheatley's daughter to stay as far away from Rolland Reynolds as she can get."

"That's blunt and to the point," Alvarez said, feeding Mortenson's words back to her.

"You want it prettied up?"

"Not prettied up. Fleshed out—there's a difference."

"The Center for State Heritage Studies was an initiative that was an outgrowth of the Rosewood Bill. You know about that?"

"Some."

Mortenson was nothing if not a teacher. "Rosewood was a predominantly black town, Sumner was a nearby predominantly white town. Strangely enough, many of the homes in Rosewood were nicer than the ones in Sumner, and the Rosewood residents were well off, generally speaking. On January first, 1923, a white woman in Sumner accused a black man of attacking her. A week of mob violence followed. At least eight people, six blacks and two whites were killed, and Rosewood was burned to the ground. That about sums up what we know about Rosewood. What we don't know would fill a library."

"Why wait seventy years to do something about it?"

"If you were black and a Southerner, you wouldn't ask that question. The silence of black victims of violence is a survival strategy. Some historians estimate that between 1880 and 1923, an African-American was lynched every two and a half days in this country. The Rosewood massacre was not an isolated incident; it was simply one of the most flagrant. In the 1980s a white reporter unearthed the tale as a human-interest story. About that same time, some survivors and their descendants started having annual reunions."

"How do you get from a human-interest story and annual reunions to a legislative bill and payouts?"

"You introduce an attorney into the mix." Mortenson gave a wry smile. "A highly respected legal firm took up the cause and a compensations claim was eventually filed. An investigation and hearing followed. The legislature found in favor of the claimants in a very politicized and controversial procedure. At virtually the last minute, the beneficiaries of the bill were limited to direct survivors of the violence and those who could prove that their families lost property as a result."

"Direct survivors being those who were actually there at the time?"

Mortenson nodded. "Obviously, the majority of the survivors had died off, leaving only descendants, so this last minute limitation excluded many who felt they were entitled to restitution. After a lot of controversy, allegations, in-fighting and bitterness, a handful of survivors were paid $150,000 each, and those who could prove that their families had lost property were paid anywhere from $100 to $5,000, depending on the claim and how it was split.''

Alvarez thought about payments of $150,000 to individuals who had survived a massacre, payments made over seventy years after its occurrence, when the recipients were approaching the end of their lives. ''Kind of like winning the lottery of hate crimes,'' he mused. ''Only a little late.''

Mortenson raised her eyebrows. ''Only a cop would put it like that, but you do have a point. The handful of people who were identified as bona fide survivors of the Rosewood incident came into a significant amount of cash in their old age. Other survivors of similar crimes were not similarly compensated. The rationale behind the Rosewood claim was that the events went on for so long and were so widespread that law enforcement authorities were remiss in failing to call for help to preserve order and bring an end to the violence.''

''A sticky business,'' said Alvarez. He could only begin to imagine the problems with trying to gather evidence for a seventy-year-old crime.

''A very sticky business,'' agreed Mortenson. ''The problem with reparations, damages, restitution, whatever you want to call it, is that the guilty are generally not the ones who end up paying. On the other side of the equation, monetary payments don't compensate for the damages sustained—damages to individuals, families, communities, an entire race.''

Alvarez decided not to comment. ''Amy Cooper mentioned that her cousin is the assistant director of the Center for State Heritage Studies. I got the impression that this woman obtained her position by identifying a Rosewood survivor and then marrying into the family.''

Mortenson frowned. ''Chloe Marshall was an outstanding student and she is a gifted historian. If she was human enough to fall in love as a consequence of her work, well, she certainly isn't the first one to do so.''

''Can you explain how she came to be in her position then?''

''Dr. Marshall, or Chloe Pitts, as she was then, went back to interview one of the survivors after everyone else had given up. A Mrs. Andrew Garner was the one survivor who had no interest in talking to the investigators, no interest in communicating with the other Rosewood families when they were trying to band together to get behind the bill. Mrs. Garner had no living relatives. She had her husband's railroad pension, and she didn't want any part of Rosewood, money or no money. But Chloe went back toward the end of the time period for identifying survivors, and asked her a question no one else had asked—if you don't want to talk about yourself and your experience, do you know of any other survivors, someone we may have missed?''

"A matter of asking the right question at the right time."

"Sure enough, Mrs. Garner knew everything there was to know about a two-year-old orphaned boy who survived Rosewood. He was adopted by Mrs. Garner's older sister afterwards, and Mrs. Garner had the recollections and the documents to back up her story."

"Why didn't this man come forward himself?"

Mortenson sighed. "Notification and search procedures are imperfect," she said. "I'm convinced there are survivors still out there who were missed. The boy, Homer Marshall, turned out to be a World War II veteran, an alcoholic who'd been in and out of treatment centers for years. He had one child, a son named Richard. Richard had recently lost his wife when he met Chloe through her work in identifying his father as a survivor. One thing led to another, and Richard and Chloe got married soon after Homer was declared a Rosewood survivor."

"What about the money?"

"It's complicated," Mortenson hedged. "Mrs. Garner lost touch with Homer after he went off to fight in World War II. Because of Chloe's work, Mrs. Garner met Homer's son Richard. Her friendship with Chloe and Richard gave the old woman a great deal of joy in the last few years of her life."

"The money," Alvarez insisted.

"The money," Mortenson sighed again. "Mrs. Garner was named a survivor, even though she didn't lift a finger for herself. Someone at the nursing home took an interest and filed the papers for her—so hold that thought in your cop-mind, that Chloe had nothing to do with Mrs. Garner receiving any money. Homer Marshall was named a survivor based on Mrs. Garner's testimony and the documents she'd kept. And before you ask, all the testimony and documents were independently authenticated by a group of people in charge of implementing the legislative bill, so it wasn't a case of a sole investigator fabricating a survivor and then marrying his son.''

''So Mrs. Garner and Homer Marshall each got a cool one hundred and fifty grand,'' Alvarez summarized.

''Right.''

''But that's not the end of the story.''

''Right again.'' Mortenson didn't look happy with having to continue. ''Both Homer Marshall and Mrs. Garner died within two years of receiving their payments.''

''And the son inherited from them both.'' Alvarez didn't make it a question. ''And by then, Chloe-the-historical-researcher was married to Richard Marshall. You have to admit, Dr. Mortenson, it's a hell of a story.''

''Who else would the two individuals leave their money to? Don't make judgments about Richard Marshall until you've met him. It's no wonder that Chloe fell in love with him. He's an outstanding individual—a real role model for what a black man can achieve in this country.''

''Unlike Rolland Reynolds.''

''I didn't say that.''

''Yes you did. You just didn't say it out loud. Why don't you like Reynolds, Dr. Mortenson?''

Alvarez had pushed too far and too fast. ''I'll answer that question, but then our discussion will be at an end.'' Mortenson said. ''You must be very good in your chosen profession.'' Alvarez barely nodded in acknowledgment of the compliment; he didn't want to interrupt. ''I don't like how Rolland treats Chloe. He never lets her forget that in the eyes of academia, she sullied her pristine record by mixing work and romance. It may be subtle, but it's always there. Just like I'm always aware that Rolland is standing just behind my shoulder, eyeing my position, or maybe something even better, off in the distance. Lots of people are like that, but most learn to cover it up better. Rolland uses people like stepping stones.''

''Is that how he used Senator Wheatley?''

Mortenson considered the question. ''I don't see it as one using another. I would say they treated each other more like wary contemporaries, but then, who am I to say?''

Probably his best source to date. ''Anything else?''

''You're going to laugh at this.''

''I doubt it.''

''It's silly—contradictory even, but it bothers me. Rolland brings in money all the time, from sources we've never even heard of before. That's what I don't like about him, Mr. Alvarez, although I'd become a laughingstock among my colleagues if I ever admitted it outside this room.'' Mortenson frowned again, thinking over what she'd just said. ''Rolland Reynolds just brings in too much damn money,'' she concluded.

ALVAREZ BELIEVED IN using any sources available as many times as was necessary, so before he headed back to the hospital, he called George Nelson from a pay phone on campus. While he waited for Nelson to pick up, he thumbed through the stack of papers Mortenson had given him; they would keep him busy for a while.

''I don't know why you're calling me again,'' grumbled Nelson when he picked up the phone. ''It's not even our case.''

''I'm calling because I have a feeling that a nice homeboy like you would know what's breaking whether it's your case or not.''

''Flattery will get you nowhere. They found what they think is the hit-and-run vehicle, abandoned off a dirt road two miles from the airport.''

''Get anything from that?''

Nelson sighed. ''Maybe criminals make it easier for cops in Texas. The car was torched.''

''No chance someone was careless, left a can of gasoline in the bushes, complete with some fingerprints?''

Nelson sighed again. "No chance, and before you ask, there's nothing new on Wheatley's accident, either."

"How about Cooper's lost luggage?"

"Nothing yet."

"Well, at least there's a consistency to all the developments."

"I hear the Gainesville PD notified Cooper's husband and he took it real cool, but then he's supposedly one of those engineer-type computer geeks. They're tossing her office, but if they've found anything, I don't know about it. What I'd like to hear is that you've decided to take my advice and dump Vicky Wheatley. I'd sleep better at night, knowing I'd saved you some trouble on down the road."

"Ah, but I wouldn't," said Alvarez. "And if she hears about you calling her Vicky Wheatley, she'll pull out her little George Nelson doll and start sticking pins in it again."

"Yeah? That's nothing compared to what the sheriff said when he heard she was back in town. You better hope she stays clear of him. He's someone who knows how to hold a grudge."

"I'll keep that in mind, try to make sure she adheres to curfew and all that. I noticed this morning that the front door to Wheatley's condo had already been repainted."

"Yeah, I hear they're real sticklers at a fancy place like the Seagle Building. One thing about traveling with Wheatley's daughter, I bet you travel first class."

"Sticklers like that," continued Alvarez, "they probably have some kind of top-rate security system. I just haven't had time to check into it yet."

There was silence on the other end for a while.

"Okay, Mr. Civilian, I'll give you this much, but you didn't get it from me. The security cameras got the back of a blond, skinny kid doing the door. Can't tell for sure, but looks like it could be a local Skinhead."

"What kind of Skinhead?"

"Skinheads, Hammerskins, KKK, Church of the Fucking God that Hates Black People, they're all the same to me. My partner keeps trying to explain the differences, but I'm too old a dog to learn stuff like that."

Yeah, I'll bet, thought Alvarez. "So this particular Skinhead is part of a white racist group?"

"I like how you Latino out-of-towners catch on real fast."

"I know where Tory keeps the doll and the pins."

"You'd be better off messing with a doll than with her, buddy."

"In El Paso, we say *ese* instead of buddy. So is someone looking for the Skinhead with his back to the camera, *ese*?"

"You could say so."

"Got a name?"

"Not from me, he don't. You already got your hands full, hanging around with Vicky."

"Okay, I'll give you a name instead, Richard Marshall."

"The black guy?"

"So I've heard."

"Nice guy. Worth a bundle, big pillar in the black community, does a lot of community work, makes a lot of contributions."

"Anything else interesting about him?"

"Well, he's married to a white woman."

"Amy Cooper told me Marshall's wife is assistant director where Amy worked, and she was her second cousin or something."

"Do tell," said Nelson.

"Anything else interesting about the Marshalls?" Alvarez probed.

Nelson took some time to think about it. "There was some hoopla a year or so ago, when Marshall and his wife moved into Haile Plantation."

"Haile *Plantation?*" Alvarez thought for sure he'd heard wrong.

"Keep cool, buddy. Haile Plantation is the name of a big upscale community, complete with golf course, club, pool, and some real fancy houses."

"So what was the hoopla?" Surely Nelson wasn't going to tell him that in this day and age, Marshall had been barred from playing on the golf course.

"Some black professor at UF made a statement about how it

wasn't right, a well known successful black man moving into a development built on land where there used to be slaves. It was kind of stupid, seeing how there's other blacks who live out there, but this guy decided to make a big deal out of it, single Marshall out, kind of call him an Oreo, if you know what that means."

"Even we burrito-eaters know what that means. What happened?"

"Not much. Marshall is a pretty cool dude. He said he couldn't think of anything more appropriate than a black man being able to build the home of his choice on the very same land where other blacks had worked as slaves. Said it was a sign of real progress, something that should be celebrated instead of criticized. Turned the whole thing around, gave it a different spin, real clever-like."

"You remember the name of the professor making the fuss?"

"I sure do. Rolland Reynolds. He's always making a fuss, and he's in charge of that center where Cooper worked. He's made a career out of claiming racial harassment. He gets so much press out of it sometimes we can't help but wonder if he's behind some of it himself. You didn't hear that from me, though." Nelson paused. "Never knew Mrs. Marshall worked there. Never heard any complaints from her. Wonder how Mrs. Marshall feels about working with the man who hassled her husband about where he wanted to live."

"Dr. Marshall," Alvarez corrected. "Anything else interesting about Dr. Marshall and her husband?"

"Yeah, there is, come to think of it. About six months ago they were off on a trip, forgot to set the burglar alarm, and their fancy new house in Haile Plantation was broken into. A neighbor noticed, but not before someone made off with some cash and a nice haul of jewelry." Alvarez whistled in appreciation at Nelson's estimate of the value of the stolen jewelry.

"What happened?"

"We took a statement, looked around, got nowhere. The stuff was gone, probably out of state or down in Miami within hours of the break-in. What're ya gonna do? The Marshalls were real nice about it, cooperated and thanked us for the shit-awful little bit we could do. They said everything was insured. The only thing even near a complaint was Mrs. Marshall saying there were things gone she couldn't ever replace, insurance or not, but that's how it usually goes.''

It was indeed. "Interesting," said Alvarez.

"You may think so. Me, I'm thinking I need to stop talking to you and go do some real work.''

"I'll be in touch.''

"Make sure the next time there's something in it for me.''

"I gave you something," Alvarez protested. "I told you that Cooper worked with Marshall's wife, and that they're related.''

"I want it to mean something, *ese.*''

IT WAS ALMOST worth sitting all afternoon in a hospital ICU to see Alvarez's expression when he walked up and saw her and Dana Halloran sitting on each side of Wheatley's bed. Tory slipped out to join him in the waiting area.

"Any change?" he asked, and Tory shook her head. *"Cara,"* he said, "has the pregnancy turned your brain to mush? I haven't had a chance to check out that woman yet. If she tried to hit me, a man with an arm in a sling, think what she could do to someone who's unconscious.''

Tory frowned to keep from showing relief at his return. Somehow things just seemed brighter, more positive when Alvarez was around. Of course, after an afternoon in the ICU, she'd probably feel the same way about Saturday morning cartoons. "Not to worry," she told Alvarez. "I've managed on my own just fine.''

"How do you know Halloran's not an escapee from a mental institution? How do you know she won't smother your father with a pillow the minute you turn your back?''

"I did a background check. I asked to see her driver's license to prove she's who she says she is. Then she gave me a business card. She's a realtor down in Ocala. I called her boss, and he verified that Dana and my father have been an item for the past couple of years.''

"So it's Dana now?"

"Yeah. Now I have someone else to share the load, someone who *wants* to be here. And she's so grateful. No matter how horrible a person she thinks I've been in the past, now she worships the ground I walk on." See if you can top that. Investigating was easy compared to finding someone to do ICU bedside shifts.

"I worship the ground you walk on, and look where it's gotten me."

Tory thought this over. "I'll buy you dinner. I took the afternoon shift, so Dana's going to stay with my father this evening."

"Does that mean we have other plans?"

Tory could almost see Sylvia's nightgown reflected in his dark eyes. Men were so transparent. "We're having company," she told him.

Alvarez groaned. "Tory, we don't know anyone here. Okay, we know *some* people, but all of them dislike you."

"This is someone we haven't met."

Alvarez frowned. "Don't tell me you've been contacted by a skinny blond kid who packs a can of red spray paint."

"What? No. Chloe Marshall called—the woman related to that poor Amy Cooper, the one who works with Rolland. She wants to see us because we were some of the last people to talk to Amy. And, get this, she wants to apologize for Rolland pitching the endowment papers to us last night."

"Any chance she's bringing her husband?" Alvarez asked.

Damn, the man was never satisfied.

FIFTEEN

Just Rewards
May, 1920. Rosewood, Florida

LISSY WAS REALLY CAREFUL walking home the last day of school. She had a prize from Mizz Mahulda all written out on fancy paper and she didn't want it getting dirty before she had a chance to show it to Aunt Sarah. Now that Lissy was older and more acquainted with the rest of the Carrier family, she called Sylvester's mother by the same name that many Rosewood residents used as a title of honor.

Lissy had won first place for her story, first place in the whole school. She had written about Git, about how having only three legs made him different and kind of ugly, but how he never seemed to mind, and how he was a really nice dog, smart and all, once someone took the time to get to know him. Mizz Mahulda made such a fuss over Lissy's story that she'd read it out loud to the whole school.

There wasn't much point in going home to show anyone. It seemed as though Lissy's daddy was gone more and more in order to find enough work to make ends meet. The Negro-owned turpentine company had shut its doors, and the cedar trees, whose pink wood had given Rosewood its name, had been cut down to make pencils years before. There was still work to be had at the sawmill in Sumner, but Lissy's father disliked Poly Wilkerson, who ran the work crews at the mill. There was even talk about how long the sawmill work could last, with timber worth harvesting getting scarce in the area.

Lissy's mamma wouldn't be home today either. She was making frequent visits to Archer, trying to keep Garland's spirits up. Garland wasn't happy and smiling any more. She wanted a baby, and no baby seemed in sight. A discussion of these puzzling circumstances had led to one of the rare occasions when Lissy had seen her mamma cry.

They'd been sitting at the dinner table, the three of them, and Lissy's mamma was talking about how unhappy Garland was and how she kept saying every single woman she knew who had been married going on three years had a baby by now, some even had two or three.

"I don't understand it neither," said Lissy's daddy, serving up the mashed potatoes. "All the Hoddens I ever knew, back home in Alabama where my family comes from, they had six, seven kids at least." Lissy had just dug her fork into her mashed potatoes when her mother burst into tears and fled the room. "Oh, hell," said Lissy's daddy.

The only other time she could remember hearing him say that was when he hit his thumb with a hammer, nailing shingles up on the roof with Lissy standing on a ladder handing them to him. Then Lissy's daddy got up and left, too. When Lissy figured out that neither were coming back any time soon, she got down from the table and went and got a piece of apple pie. No point in eating mashed potatoes when there was apple pie.

Lissy had been so wrapped up in her thoughts walking home from school that she'd almost run into a white man hurrying out of John Wright's store.

John Wright was one of the few white people living in Rosewood, and his house and grape arbors were something to behold, just like this white man standing in front of Lissy was something to behold. He wore a familiar yellow bandanna around his neck.

Lissy didn't take running into a white man lightly, especially not a road gang guard. She started stammering apologies, poised to run and looking to see who might be around to help should the man take her to task. But all her worries were in vain. The man with the yellow bandana fleetingly put a hand on Lissy's shoulder to steady her.

"It's okay, little girl. I was in such a hurry I wasn't looking where I was going neither. Are you all right?" Lissy nodded wordlessly. "What you got in your hand there?" the man asked. He had a nice, friendly smile.

"A prize," she said.

The man squatted down next to her to get a better look. "What's it a prize for?" he asked as though he really wanted to know.

"For writing the best story in the whole school," Lissy told him.

"Is that right?" The man took a careful look at the paper Lissy held, then stood up and gave her another smile. "You must be one smart little girl. You just make sure you're smart enough to watch where you're going, you hear me? You want to get home safe and sound, so you can show that prize to your mamma and daddy." Then the man with the yellow bandana took off down the road, whistling as he went, and Lissy looked after him a while, thinking.

After she showed her prize to Aunt Sarah, maybe she'd go next door and show it to Tressa Marshall. It didn't look to Lissy as though Tressa was going to have any problem having a baby, although Lissy's mamma told Lissy to be sure and wait until Tressa told her about the baby before she went on talking and asking questions about it.

After she showed the prize to Aunt Sarah and Tressa Marshall, Lissy would put it up to show her daddy and mamma later. She knew exactly where she would put it. The prize, along with her story about Git, was going into the box that The Man had made especially for Ruth Ann Hodden of Rosewood, Florida.

SIXTEEN

Boxed In
Monday Evening

TORY THOUGHT THAT sharing a condo in a strange city with David Alvarez was kind of like playing house with a friendly psychopath, and that was without taking into account the weighty issues of sex and pregnancy. She couldn't afford to think about those things right now, just like she couldn't afford to consider the choices she would confront if her father failed to regain consciousness. Instead, she thought about what it was like to spend time with Alvarez, in a place free from the constraints of home and during a time when he wasn't investigating a case.

Not officially, Tory amended. She knew it bothered him, having a young woman die before his eyes while the killer got away. But thinking about that led to thinking about Alvarez being a cop, which led to considering those other things she wasn't going to think about.

If she didn't think about those other things, it was kind of fun being with Alvarez. He was funny, smart, and unfailingly considerate, not counting the times he lost his temper. But just when Tory started to get comfortable with enjoying herself, there would be a sudden jolt, an awareness of how her life was starting to mesh with his.

When they were riding back to the condo, it was unnerving to discover he had purchased a tape of Tom Petty and The Heartbreakers, one of Tory's favorite groups.

Alvarez told Tory about talking to George Nelson and Marilyn Mortenson, with The Heartbreakers providing a steady rock beat as backup to the tale. Suddenly he cocked his head and stopped mid-sentence.

"What is it?" Tory asked.

"The whole Rosewood thing," he said. "It's like the Tom Petty song."

"What song?"

"The one playing a little while ago—'Even the Losers.' It says something about even losers getting lucky sometimes. Makes you wonder, doesn't it?"

"Makes you wonder what?"

"Makes you wonder what a loser is, once a loser gets lucky. Still a loser, or a winner?" Alvarez cruised through five o'clock traffic at precisely the legal speed limit. "And if a lucky loser becomes a winner, I wonder how the winners feel about that."

After arriving at the condo and seeing no new words spray-painted on the door, Tory called Cody, then went to take a shower and change her clothes. She managed not to think too much about the encroachment of Alvarez's toiletries set on the sink next to hers. There were two bathrooms and two bedrooms, but it seemed petty to insist that he move his things now.

The next jolt came over shared pizza. Sitting at the breakfast bar, knees bumping casually, Alvarez was teasing Tory about liking anchovies on pizza. "Cody thinks it's pretty weird, too," Tory conceded. There was just the barest pause, a stillness that hadn't been there a moment before, and she knew, she absolutely knew what Alvarez was thinking. "Cody doesn't need a step-father," she said.

Alvarez continued to chew, swallowed. "I'd like Cody even if he wasn't your son," he said.

Tory put down her slice of pizza. "You're always so cool; you always know what to say."

Alvarez raised one eyebrow. "Cool? Cool? I am so un-cool. Come over here, I'll show you."

"I'm too old," countered Tory.

"You're thirty-six years old," replied Alvarez. "Not too old," he added for emphasis. Then he paused and said, "There is something, though, something we need to talk about."

His voice wavered. Tory held her breath—she'd come to depend on the fact that he'd never wavered. Then the doorbell rang.

THERE WAS A TOUCH of grief underlying Alvarez's realization that Chloe Marshall looked nothing like her cousin, and that Amy Cooper was gone and lost forever.

Marshall was blond. She was tall and thin and awkward-looking, and older than Alvarez had expected, probably in her late thirties. She got through the exercise of introductions with an economy of emotion and expression. By the time the three of them were seated in the living room, Alvarez was willing to bet that whatever emotions Chloe Marshall might be feeling, this would not be a tearful encounter.

"I understand you were the one closest to her when it happened, the one who stayed with her until help came," Marshall said to Alvarez, turning light gray eyes on him.

So much for small talk. "I did what I could," Alvarez said, "which wasn't much. You should know that she died very quickly—I doubt that Amy even realized what was happening."

"Thank you," said Marshall. Alvarez waited, but she didn't say anything else. Her tone seemed as colorless as her eyes.

"I'm sure the police asked you this question already, but do you know of anyone who might have wanted to harm Amy?" Alvarez asked.

"I didn't really know her all that well," Marshall said instead of answering the question. "We're only distantly related. When Amy came to work at the Center, I was careful to keep our relationship professional."

That sounded a little cold. "What about your professional relationship, then?"

"Amy was very good at what she did." Dr. Marshall certainly didn't seem to be one to expand on her answers.

"Which was what, exactly?"

"Detailed research—she did a lot of genealogy, fact checking, review of historical documents."

"She was good at this?"

A small smile, finally. "She was very good—dedicated, resourceful, and organized. Amy never lost or misplaced a single piece of documentation. She took copious notes on everything. For a historian, that's not too unusual, but the thing about Amy was, she could always put her hands on what she needed."

"What about her husband?" Tory asked.

"What about her husband?" Marshall echoed.

"I spoke to Amy after we got off the plane," Tory said. "She talked about staying in Tallahassee a little longer to give herself some space. She said her husband had been offered a position in Atlanta, but she needed to stay here to finish her degree."

Marshall looked at Tory blankly. "Todd? Are you asking me if she was having problems with Todd because—" Marshall decided not to complete her sentence. "That's ridiculous. We weren't exactly close, but I know that Todd worshipped Amy. He's one of those engineer types. That's all he had in life, work and Amy. That's all he wanted."

"Then it might have been a problem to choose between work and Amy," observed Alvarez. Everything in his experience told him that Dr. Marshall wanted to get up and leave right then and there. For some reason she didn't.

"The police need to look at some of the groups who've threatened the Center," she said. "It would be a good idea to track down the person who spray-painted Amy's car before asking whether she and Todd were having problems. All two-career marriages have those kind of problems."

"Does the Center get a lot of threats, then?" asked Alvarez.

"It's hard to quantify 'a lot.' The research we do is controversial to some, threatening to others. Then there's the added factor that two of us have mixed-race marriages. It's hard to separate the work-related threats from the personal ones when you're a target for racist groups."

"Amy told us that you met your husband as a result of the research you did on Rosewood," said Alvarez.

"And there are people who will be happy to tell you that was unethical on my part," Marshall replied.

"That's ridiculous." This from Tory, who'd married a professor twenty years her senior when she was a sophomore in college. "Who you marry isn't anyone else's business."

Oh God, thought Alvarez, don't let Tory bond with this woman before I have a chance to figure out what she's up to.

"Thank you for that," Marshall told Tory. "It's true that I met Richard while doing the research that led to his father being identified as a Rosewood survivor, but that had nothing to do with anything else. My husband is a wonderful man. His wife died shortly before we met, and he was totally lost without her. For me, I had never met anyone like him—kind, wise, dependable. And the rest, as they say, is history."

"What does your husband do professionally, Dr. Marshall?" Alvarez tried to use just the right tone of polite interest.

"He started a business in his twenties—a janitorial service. Richard expanded into doing things that business owners never have time to take care of—small repairs, maintenance, things like that. It's been very successful."

A cash infusion of $300,000 was bound to make almost any business successful.

"Enough about me," said Marshall, turning to Tory. "I've been remiss in not expressing *my* sympathies. I'm so very sorry about your father's accident. How is he doing?"

"We're trying to remain optimistic," said Tory.

"Have they identified the other driver?"

Tory shook her head, and in spite of himself, Alvarez felt responsible.

"It's horrible," said Marshall, "sitting here and talking about these things as if they make sense. When I heard that Rolland went to the hospital last night to talk to you about the endowment, I knew I had to come over here and apologize."

"You don't have anything to apologize for," said Tory.

"Well, someone needs to apologize, and it sure won't be Rolland," said Marshall.

Tory nodded. "I grew up with Rolland. I can remember a lot of things about him, but him apologizing isn't one of them."

"That's right. You grew up around here, didn't you?"

"Near Ocala," said Tory, "but I've been gone a long time. How about you?"

"I'm from Micanopy."

"That's between Gainesville and Ocala," Tory said for Alvarez's benefit.

"Not horse farm country," said Marshall, which struck Alvarez as a strange thing to say. She must have noticed his confusion. "I grew up dirt poor in a family proud to call themselves Crackers. It took me a long time and a lot of hard work to get through school, get to where I am today. That's why it's so sad about Amy. I would look at her and think she'd have some chances I didn't."

Amy Cooper didn't have a chance to marry a cool $300,000. For some reason, Alvarez didn't want Tory and this woman to start sharing their Florida heritages. He didn't want Tory and this woman to start sharing anything. "It seems strange, you coming here to apologize for your boss," he interjected.

"Just because he's my boss doesn't mean I always agree with him," Marshall replied. "Rolland is very good at what he was hired to do, which is to raise funds so that our research and information dissemination can continue. But he's so enthusiastic, so tunnel-visioned, that sometimes he oversteps his bounds. I'd say this is one of those times, and so I wanted to apologize."

"Let's just hope my father recovers and can speak for himself," Tory said. "Then none of us will have to worry about figuring out what he would want us to do."

"That's the ideal solution," said Marshall. "But I don't want either you or your father to feel like you're under any added pressure. Even if——when——the Senator regains consciousness, the endowment can wait. It's not the type of thing that should be waved in his face the moment he opens his eyes. He should take all the time he needs to recover, get his bearings, think things over."

"Next you'll be telling us you think he should keep his two million dollars to himself," said Alvarez.

"Maybe I am saying that," Marshall told him, surprising the hell out of him. "It's not such a bad thing for people to learn that there are limits to what is considered acceptable behavior, Mr. Alvarez."

This last sounded so arch that Alvarez had an overwhelming urge to tell Dr. Marshall that it was Detective Alvarez to her, but Tory interceded.

"I understand that you met with my father the evening of his accident. How was he?"

"Charming, as usual, but you just reminded me that I wanted to ask you for something." Alvarez refrained from saying "ah ha" out loud. "The night I brought the papers over," continued Marshall, "we got to talking and the time just disappeared. Your father wanted to show me some things he collects, and we were looking at the items in his display case in the entry hall when I realized that I was looking at an heirloom from Richard's family. It's a carved wooden box, one that disappeared when our house was broken into a few months ago."

"What a coincidence," Alvarez deadpanned.

Chloe Marshall didn't turn a hair. "Yes, isn't it," she said, then turned back to Tory. "Your father told me that he had recently bought the box at an antique store. In Micanopy, of all places." Marshall gave a wry smile that looked as though it had been rehearsed. "He was anxious to return it to me, but he'd misplaced the key to the case. He told me he was going back to Ocala over the weekend and had a spare key there. He asked me to come back—this evening, actually. He was going to give me the box, and I was going to pick up the executed papers."

Alvarez's every instinct was screaming that there was something wrong with this picture. "I suppose the box was listed on the police report of stolen items," he said.

Marshall looked at him with thinly disguised distaste. "I believe so, although there were so many things stolen, we may have inadvertently left some out." She's covering, and she's good, thought Alvarez. "I used this particular box to store certain pieces of jewelry," Marshall continued. "The Senator told me it was empty when he bought it, and I'm not surprised. Even so, just finding the box is a miracle. Richard was so excited when I told him. It was a present from his great aunt, and it's very special to him. I can describe it to you in great detail, if that will help, or I suppose I could get documentation that it really does belong to us—"

"You don't need to do that," said Tory, standing up. "Just point it out and we'll make sure it goes home with you tonight."

"Well, only if you're certain," said Marshall, with just the right amount of hesitation.

"Oh darn," said Alvarez. "What about the missing key to the display case? We certainly don't know where it is."

Tory gave him a level look. "I'm sure a lock on a display case won't be any problem for you."

Then there really wasn't any choice after that, was there? Alvarez followed the two women out to the entry hall, where he picked the lock on the glass case. "How interesting, to carry lock picks with you," Marshall said as he lifted an ornately carved wooden box down from the shelf.

"It's beautiful," Tory said.

"It's from Rosewood," Alvarez observed, studying the words carved on the box. "Who is Lissy Hodden?"

"The younger sister of the woman who adopted Richard's father, the same woman who identified him as a Rosewood survivor. Her married name was Garner, but her maiden name was Hodden and her nickname was Lissy."

"That's interesting," was all that Tory said.

Alvarez thought it was more than interesting. "Hodden," he repeated, watching Marshall closely. "Didn't you tell me that was your mother's maiden name, Tory?"

Marshall seemed genuinely surprised. "Your mother's name was really Hodden? How strange. I've never heard of any other

Hoddens before—I know for a fact that Lissy was the last of her line. Where is your mother's family from?"

"Alabama," said Tory. She glared at Alvarez as he opened the lid of the box and peered inside to make sure the box was empty.

"See how smoothly it's hinged," he murmured to appease her. Then he had no choice but to hand it over to Dr. Marshall.

"Thank you," she said to Tory. "Thank you for everything. I'll be thinking good thoughts for your father, and I'll check back to see if there's anything I can do." She turned to Alvarez. "And thank you, too, for picking the lock."

"Let me walk you down to your car," he said.

"You don't need to do that," she replied.

He smiled at her. "Oh, yes I do."

ALVAREZ AND DR. MARSHALL stood side by side in the elevator, Marshall clutching the wooden box, reminding Alvarez of Amy and her computer. "Something I forgot to ask you," he said. "Did Amy's luggage turn up?"

Marshall kept her eyes straight ahead, as though counting the seconds until the elevator doors would open. "Yes. The airline claims that somehow her bags didn't get unloaded that night, then they got shuttled back to Atlanta."

"Sounds strange to me."

"Strange things happen to luggage on airplanes."

Alvarez couldn't argue with that. "Amy was carrying her computer when she was killed. I wonder if anything can be retrieved from it." Marshall shuddered at his words. "Would Amy be likely to carry duplicate files of her work, hard copies, in her luggage?"

"I don't know. What a strange question to ask. It's not like she was in Tallahassee doing top secret research."

"What was she doing, then?

Marshall turned to face him in exasperation as the elevator doors slid open. "She was doing research for me. You don't like me, Mr. Alvarez. Since I've never met you before, I'm curious. Why?"

If Marshall thought that Alvarez was going to be embarrassed by some plain speech on her part, well, others had tried, and with plainer speech than that. He stepped out of the elevator and held open the door to the parking lot. "You strike me as being someone like Reynolds, someone who wants something," he told her. "I know what Reynolds wants—two million dollars. I haven't figured out what you want. Not yet."

Marshall frowned and countered, "You strike me as someone who wants something, too. Someone who wants to cause trouble."

Marshall might be tall, but Alvarez was taller. "What kind of car do you drive?" he asked, looking over her head.

"A white Lincoln sedan," she said, surprised into a quick and forthright answer.

"Figures," Alvarez said to himself as he set off across the parking lot toward a dark-coated figure squatting down beside her car. Alvarez had the advantage of speed and surprise, and it didn't take a lot of skill to knock what turned out to be a skinny blond kid to the ground and sit on him. A can of red spray paint went rolling under the car. "Go inside and call the police," Alvarez told Marshall. She did as she was told.

"Kid," Alvarez said conversationally to the young man with his face scrunched into the asphalt, "what's your name?"

"Sledge," the kid grunted.

"Figures," said Alvarez again.

"I SUPPOSE IT'S NOT a black nightgown type of night," Alvarez said.

This was after waiting for the police, reassuring the neighbors, explaining to Tory what had happened, and giving statements. It was after eleven when Chloe Marshall and the last police officer took their leave, although Sledge had been hauled off much earlier to account for both his artistic efforts and his whereabouts the night Amy Cooper was killed. Sledge left in handcuffs; Dr. Marshall left with the wooden box clutched to her breast and the police following behind her car to ensure her safe return home.

And now here was Tory, ready for bed in a pair of leggings

and a long T-shirt. "What can I say? Rhinestones just aren't my style," she told him.

Alvarez pulled her down onto his lap. "How are you feeling?" he asked, stroking her hair.

She relaxed against his chest, a good sign. "Pretty good," she said. "Especially considering everything going on. I've been thinking."

Alvarez braced himself. Tory thinking was not always a good thing. "About what?"

"About you saying that I get to choose. For tonight, I choose to be held. Just held."

"I can do that," he said. He tried to sound obliging. He tried to remember that Tory was dealing with a comatose father, an unplanned pregnancy, and confronting pieces of her past. It didn't work. He kept remembering the rhinestone nightgown instead.

"And I choose for you to wear some clothes when you come to bed," she added.

Alvarez sighed. "I can do that, too. Keep in mind I wouldn't do it for just anyone."

"I will," she said, and then she surprised him by turning her face up to kiss him—a real grown-up, sexy, clothes—coming-off type of kiss.

"I'm getting mixed messages here," Alvarez told Tory when he came up for air. "What is it that you're trying to tell me?"

"I'm just making sure," she said.

"Making sure of what? That I'm still alive and breathing? If that's the case, you're doing a good job."

"No, I'm making sure that I can still keep you interested without finding dead bodies."

"I'm still interested," said Alvarez. "The last thing we need is for you to start finding dead bodies—I hear the sheriff hereabouts isn't too fond of you, little lady."

"You don't do country nearly as good as you swear in Spanish. Why don't you like her?"

"Who?"

Tory frowned at him impatiently. "You know who. Chloe Marshall."

"Who says I don't like her?" Tory punched him in the ribs. "Okay, okay. The whole thing tonight felt like a set-up. She strikes me as someone who has an agenda."

"Everyone has an agenda." Alvarez could feel Tory start thinking again. He pushed her up and off his lap. Given enough time, Tory would remember that he had told her there was something they needed to talk about, back when they were eating pizza for dinner, and it was a subject he didn't want to broach now. "Enough," he told her. "I get to choose some things, too."

"Like what?" she asked warily.

"Like which side of the bed I sleep on. I don't need you getting carried away and rolling over my injured arm in the middle of the night."

She looked at him, horrified. "Do I do that?"

He smiled up at her. "Lighten up, *querida*. You can roll over any part of my body, any time." She rolled her eyes and headed toward the bedroom.

Later, as he held her and listened to the even breathing of her sleep, he whispered against her ear. "You were right, *cara*, when you said that everyone has an agenda." She didn't stir, so he decided that he could speak the truth. "When I said that you could choose, I lied."

SEVENTEEN

Grown Up Times
August, 1922. Rosewood, Florida

AT TWELVE, Lissy was still considered strange by her contemporaries. This was mainly because she would rather steal off and write stories on the endless supply of paper provided by Mizz Mahulda from the Rosewood school, rather than engage in activities with the other children. Only the stories that she considered to be the very best were saved to go into the carved keepsake box.

But Lissy couldn't spend all her time watching and dreaming and writing. She had grown-up duties and responsibilities, especially now that she had two adopted brothers instead of one. The Man was married with children of his own, and these days Lissy was busy helping her mother take care of her neighbor's boy, little Homer Marshall. This was more grown-up responsibility than it might have been had things been different with Garland. It seemed that every time Lissy turned around, her mother was off to visit her sister, who continued to struggle to come to terms with her still-childless state.

Fertile but of fragile health, Tressa Marshall seemed to exhaust the last of her meager life force in bringing forth Homer, an amazingly hale and hearty son. Tressa lingered only a few weeks to admire the fruit of her labors, then slipped from life as quietly as she had lived it. John Marshall was half mad with grief over the death of his young wife, and so it seemed only natural that little Homer found a haven at the Hodden residence, or at the Carriers when Lissy and the little boy were sent to stay over there.

It hadn't taken long for Sarah Carrier to recognize Lissy's natural abilities with younger children, for there were always children needing minding at the Carrier house, where extended family filled every room on every occasion. It was a trade-off of sorts for Lissy, deciding which place she liked best. At home, she was free to spoil the chubby toddler as much as she liked, but she filled only the role of junior caregiver in deference to the superior knowledge and experience of her mother. When Lissy stayed at the Carriers, not only was she likely to see The Man, but Aunt Sarah surrendered the children in the household to Lissy's sole care for hours at a time.

The risk of this heady autonomy was the danger that Sarah Carrier might discover Lissy favoring Homer in some way, letting him get by with something another child wouldn't be allowed to do, or finagling the largest portion of some treat for him. Then Aunt Sarah would light into Lissy something fierce, telling her how she was spoiling Homer rotten and that no good would come of it.

But one thing Aunt Sarah acknowledged for sure was that Lissy was the very best child-minder to take with her to Sumner on her frequent trips to do laundry and other chores for some of the white women who lived there. Lissy would put Homer on her back and walk two miles to the mill town with Aunt Sarah and the other children. At sunup the men went off to work, so the mill-provided housing held only women and children during most of the daylight hours. Aunt Sarah could get her work done more easily with someone like Lissy along, someone who could invent endless games and stories to keep the children occupied and out of mischief.

Fannie Taylor was the one who hired Aunt Sarah the most regular. She was a thin, dark young woman who already had two children of her own. Lissy had heard talk that Fannie married her husband, a millwright, when she was just fourteen, and there Lissy's own daddy had thought Garland too young to marry at seventeen.

After Lissy had been going to Sumner with Aunt Sarah on a regular basis, Fannie asked Lissy to watch her children for a while. Two more wasn't really any trouble, and besides, Fannie always paid Lissy a little bit for her efforts, which meant that she and Homer could buy treats at John Wright's store when the other children were safely back at the Carrier house and wouldn't be clamoring for a share.

Lissy didn't know what to think about Fannie at first—she always seemed disapproving, and she pursed her lips in a sour-looking way when she listened to other people talk. Lissy had spent enough time around the mill quarters to know that some of Fannie's neighbors called her "peculiar." Fannie didn't seem to have friends the way the other women did. She didn't allow children to run through her yard in pursuit of their rough games, and her neighbors took her to task behind her back for keeping her floors spotless, bleaching them until the color was burned from the wood and the planks looked as leached and white as old bones.

When Fannie first asked Lissy to watch her children, she would turn up every fifteen minutes or so, as though to see i she could catch Lissy letting the children do something they shouldn't. But as time went on, Fannie grew more trusting of Lissy's child-minding abilities, and she would leave her children with Lissy for longer periods of time without checking up. She grew almost friendly with Lissy, giving her a shy smile as well as payment, and sometimes taking the time to ask after Lissy's parents or her schoolwork or something like that. Lissy didn't get the feeling that Fannie ever paid much interest to her answers, but since she didn't feel at ease making conversation with the woman, that was just fine.

One summer day was different than most, in that Sarah Carrier had other chores, and didn't start on Fannie Taylor's laundry until well after they had all stopped to eat the lunch they had brought with them. Lissy sat the children down and told them a long story about a little lost dog trying to escape a swamp 'gator until their eyes drooped with the heat and the stupor of heavy food. Then she had them lie down in a heap of white and dark children all mixed up together like a litter of puppies.

It wasn't long until they were dozing in the shade of a huge oak tree like the one that grew beside the Carrier house. Homer had brought a little rag doll with him and it was missing, so Lissy kept one eye on the huddle of children while she retraced their steps to the back stoop of the Taylor house, where Fannie had handed out cool water for everyone after lunch.

The back door was open, as was natural in the heat. What wasn't so natural was to hear a man's voice drifting out into the hazy afternoon air. "Fannie, Fannie," the man said, a hint of laughter in his voice. "What am I going to do with you? We didn't even make it to the bed. Proper neat little Fannie, and here you like it hard and rough, don't you?"

There were some rustling sounds and then Lissy heard Fannie Taylor say, "I don't know what I like—I never had a chance to figure it out. Maybe I was better off that way. Being with you is like a sickness. I can't get enough of it, and I've become a shameful woman. I don't know what's to become of us."

Now the male voice was husky, with no trace of laughter left in it. "There ain't no shame in a woman wanting a man to act like a man. You don't worry about what's to become of us, Fannie. You just think about what's happening right now. About how you feel when I do this—'' There was silence, then a sharp intake of breath, followed by the amazing sound of Fannie Taylor moaning.

Lissy knew without a doubt that she was courting trouble, but she could see Homer's rag baby by the side of the stoop. Everyone told her she had a talent for sneaking up on people quiet-like, so she relied on this talent now as she made a silent rush for the rag baby. Right as she grabbed it, before she turned to put some distance between her and the house, there was just a moment when she could see inside the door into Fannie Taylor's cool dark kitchen.

On the floor, almost out of sight, was a yellow bandana.

Lissy was old enough to know what could get her into trouble, and what could get other people into trouble. She had been born old enough to know how to keep her own counsel. She was rather surprised, however, to discover that she was old enough to find all of this quite exciting in an unsettling kind of way. Lissy put all these thoughts behind her and headed back to the sleeping children so that Homer would have his rag baby when he woke up.

EIGHTEEN

Equal Opportunity
Tuesday Morning

A UNEVENTFUL NIGHT—well, uneventful after the police and various parties departed—and a night free from bouts of nausea had enabled Tory, after the prerequisite call to Cody, to arrive at the hospital early for the first time. Of course, an early start meant even more time to spend watching, waiting, and worrying.

Dana Halloran was already bedside, impeccably dressed. She greeted Tory with a smile. ''There you are, dear. I tried calling but you must have already left. Tom has been making some movements and sounds this morning—almost as though he's muttering to himself. The doctor said not to get our hopes up too high, but that it's definitely a positive sign.'' Tory was stunned when Dana hugged her and started crying at the same time.

"I'll go get everyone coffee," said Alvarez and was gone.

Tory sat down and considered her father while Dana chattered about the positive change in his condition. To Tory, he looked just as he had the last time she saw him.

Good job, Dad. Show a little life when I'm away, then revert to a comatose state when I show up. Maybe you'd recover quicker if I'd stayed in New Mexico. Why the hell did you name me as your next of kin, you sly old trickster? You may live to regret it. If I tell you that I'm pregnant out of wedlock, will that infuriate you so much that you'll have to wake up to tell me how I've let you down once again?

"Tory." Alvarez was standing next to her, looking down at her, holding out a paper cup with steam coming off the top. "Are you okay?"

"I'm fine," she said, and took the cup.

"There's someone here who wants to talk to you," said Alvarez. Tory looked up in surprise through the glass separating the waiting area from ICU. Sure enough, there was a middle-aged man standing in there, dressed in slacks and a sports shirt, holding a briefcase. He was big and hefty, with a large nose and a thick head of gray hair. Tory was getting more visitors here in ICU than her father.

"Who is he?"

"His name's Frank Paxton," said Alvarez. "You could say that he's Rolland's opposition," he added.

"Rolland's opposition? What do you mean?"

"Mr. Paxton heads a group called Rip Tide." Tory looked at him blankly. "*White* Rip Tide."

"Don't tell me my father promised a contribution to some sports team. We're going to have to start telling these people we gave at the office or something."

Alvarez shook his head. "He's not with a sports team, Tory, but maybe you could think of it like this—that guy standing out there is Rolland's opposition from the professional league. Remember Sledge from last night? He was from the minors.''

Dana Halloran was watching them, looking confused.

"Rip Tide strongly opposes the work done by the Center for State Heritage Studies," Alvarez added.

Tory took another look at the man standing in the waiting area. He didn't look anything like she expected. He looked, well, like he could be a high school teacher or something. "You're kidding," she said. "Where's his white hood?"

Dana Halloran's mouth fell open, but she didn't say anything.

"They've traded in their white hoods and burning crosses for the Internet and cyberspace," said Alvarez. "I think Mr. Paxton is determined to talk to you one way or another. It would be better to get it out of the way now, while I'm around."

Tory bristled. "Around for what? Will you hit him with your sling if he gets out of line? Remember, we're not on your turf anymore. You can't just whip out your handcuffs whenever you feel like it."

"Handcuffs?" Dana squeaked.

"She's overwrought," Alvarez told Dana. He dropped his voice. "I never use the handcuffs in public."

Tory wanted to kill him. Dana took a step away from Alvarez and towards Tory. "Maybe you should go talk to this man, if he's determined to see you," she whispered. She had actually been reduced to whispering. "I'm happy to stay with Tom this morning. I was hoping you might be able to cover the afternoon—I have an appointment with a potential client, and life does go on…" Dana sounded apologetic and beseeching at the same time.

"If you're sure you don't mind," Tory said.

"You watch out for her, you hear?" Dana called belatedly to Alvarez as they walked out of the ICU.

"I'D REALLY PREFER to talk to you alone," said Frank Paxton. After introductions, they had decamped to the solitude of the mid-morning hospital cafeteria. Feeling secretly perverse, Tory selected the same table where they'd sat with Rolland Reynolds only two days ago—or was that one day ago?

"As I explained earlier, I'm here to advise Mrs. Travers." Alvarez said, ignoring the look that Tory was giving him. "Whatever you have to discuss with her can be discussed in front of me."

Tory watched Paxton study Alvarez for a moment, then shrug his acquiescence. A cop voice sure did come in handy. She might have to think about developing one for future confrontations on construction sites. Of course, it would be easier and quicker to just pull out a gun or a pair of handcuffs when something didn't pass inspection... Tory pulled herself up short and tried to focus.

"Travers, that's a good Anglo-Saxon name," said Paxton. Was that a jab at Alvarez?

"I can't take credit for it—it was my husband's name."

"It's good to know you did the traditional thing, took your husband's name," said Paxton, seeming determined to salvage a compliment from his statement.

"Paxton, now that's a peaceful-sounding name," Tory replied. She was beginning to think her father had the best of it, lying unconscious in a bed while other people took care of everything.

"We certainly try to achieve our aims peacefully," Paxton said.

"And just what are your aims?" she asked.

"The promotion and preservation of the White Race," said Paxton without hesitation. Tory could hear the capital letters in how he said it.

"So Rip Tide is some kind of racist group?" asked Tory, groping for words that sounded accurate but not insulting.

"We prefer the term racialist," said Paxton. "Racist has such a negative connotation. Unfortunately for us today, anything that can be construed as an expression of White Pride is considered to be a form of prejudice, or even worse, a form of hatred. Don't you see that as a problem, Mrs. Travers, living in a society where pride in your own race is seen as something to be detested?"

"It hasn't been a major problem for me so far," said Tory honestly.

"Then maybe I can open your eyes," said Paxton, placing his briefcase on the table.

Tory gave Paxton her very best contract negotiation smile and said, "Maybe it would be a good idea to tell me what it is you want. Then we can see about having my eyes opened."

"Very well," said Paxton. "I like someone who comes to the point. I'm here to try to convince you to reconsider your father's planned endowment to the history department at the university here."

"It's his money," said Tory.

"But you're the one acting in his interest right now," countered Paxton.

"Why should you care about any of this?"

"Two words. Rolland Reynolds. We started watching him years ago, long before he came to Florida. He's been busy accumulating a power base, and we believe that he has political ambitions, with an agenda to support more reparation payments to supposedly oppressed people. Are you familiar with the Rosewood Bill?"

"A little, yes."

Paxton leaned forward intently. A detached part of Tory's mind noted that he wore a very nice aftershave, something she wouldn't have associated with a member of a group called Rip Tide. "That's all anyone has about Rosewood, a little knowledge. I'm sure you heard the version about a white woman claiming a black man raped her, and the mob violence that followed."

"That's pretty close," admitted Tory.

"Well, I'll bet you haven't heard this version—the black rapist went back to Rosewood to claim sanctuary. The blacks knew there would be retaliation, so they decided to strike first. They sent word to a member of the white community that they had captured the rapist and were ready to surrender him. A group of whites went to Rosewood to take the man into custody. It was an ambush. The blacks opened fire on a group of unprepared men."

"But not unarmed," Alvarez said.

"Of course they weren't unarmed," Paxton said. "Would you go unarmed to apprehend a violent criminal?" He didn't wait for an answer. "Innocent white men died as a result of this treacherous subterfuge, and then seventy years later, our sick government hands out payments to the very people who were responsible for these crimes—payments taken from the wages of the hard-working taxpayers of this state. It has to stop somewhere. Preventing Reynolds from building his power base is a first step."

Tory tried to chose her words carefully. "I'm no fan of Rolland Reynolds, Mr. Paxton, but the money you're talking about is my father's, and I have every hope that he's going to recover and make these decisions for himself."

"I hope so, too," said Paxton. "Your father is a fine man. He took some difficult stands in his time, stands that I admire and respect. That's why it's so hard to understand this action on his part. The only possible explanation is that he doesn't understand how this endowment, benevolent as it might appear, will help Reynolds to further his own agenda. I'm hoping that if your father does recover, you'll urge him to talk to me before he does something that can't be undone. And, should it turn out that he's not able to act in his own interests, God forbid, I'm hoping that you'll consider what I've told you."

"I'll keep it in mind." A veteran of numerous negotiations, Tory had stored up a veritable wealth of noncommittal remarks that came in handy on occasions like this.

But Paxton wasn't falling for it. "Don't brush me off without the same consideration you'd give any group considered to be politically correct."

"Okay," said Tory. What else could she say? She certainly didn't want this man branding her as prejudiced. Paxton whipped a notebook out of his briefcase and put it in front of her.

"Read some of these press clippings," he urged. Tory started scanning the pages, becoming interested in spite of herself. There

were newspaper stories describing the work of various white
supremacist groups, in surprisingly factual text, free of profanity
and derogatory racial slurs. Rip Tide figured predominantly as a
high-tech supremacist group with an established Internet presence. There was even an article on a company that had been
formed exclusively to design web pages for "racialist" groups.

Interspersed amongst these clippings were various articles that
supported Paxton's premise of a government gone wrong,
skewed too sharply in the direction of making amends for past
racial wrongs. There were stories questioning why a violent
crime perpetrated by white on black was termed a hate crime,
while the converse was not. There were stories about criminal
charges being brought against individuals accused of denying the
Holocaust.

The strangest story was about two black employees suing a
government law enforcement agency for discrimination. They
claimed that racial harassment had occurred because the job interview took place in a room with a Nazi flag displayed prominently on the wall. A spokeswoman for the agency stated that
the vacant positions were for a gang control unit, and that the
room had been filled with gang-related insignia to demonstrate
to the applicants the wide range of knowledge required for the
job. The spokeswoman went on to state that the two plaintiffs
were unqualified for the positions because of a lack of prior
experience.

"This is interesting," said Tory, returning the notebook to
Paxton.

"I hope you'll think about it, and decide it's more than merely
interesting," said Paxton. "Blacks can join civil rights groups,
and Hispanics can be activists without fear of being branded as
racist. But White Pride has become a dirty word."

Actually, two words.

"I assume that your organization opposes racial mixing," Alvarez said.

"It certainly does. We also vehemently oppose homosexual-
ity," said Paxton.

"I'm curious. What about someone like me? Of mixed heritage, I mean."

"You would never be allowed to join Rip Tide, or any of our affiliated groups," said Paxton.

"Ah, but I've never been much of a joiner," Alvarez replied. "My father was Mexican, but my mother was of good white Midwestern stock, mainly German in origin. Not much I can do about that now, is there? But if I married, my marriage would by definition be racially mixed, regardless of whom I married. The same thing for any children."

"We would encourage you not to reproduce," said Paxton.

What would Frank Paxton say if Tory told him that she was carrying a racially mixed child, right now, even while she sat here letting him try to recruit her to his cause? Maybe she could join Rip Tide first and confess later.

"But what if I wanted to embrace my white heritage?" Alvarez persisted.

"You should remain childless, support the White Race from the sidelines." Paxton looked uncomfortable as though he had to improvise these free-lance guidelines at the drop of a hat.

"Thank you for clarifying that," said Alvarez gravely. "Is a blond kid, nickname of Sledge, with an affinity for spray paint, associated with your group?"

Paxton shook his head. "Rip Tide and our affiliated groups have no desire to be connected with people wielding cans of spray paint. Our strategies and methodologies are more sophisticated, and hopefully, more effective. Before you even ask about that unfortunate woman's death at the airport, no, I don't know anything about who did it, and yes, I can account for my whereabouts at the time of the accident."

Efficient man, this Frank Paxton.

"You keep talking about affiliated groups," continued Alvarez without a pause. "Is Rip Tide associated with the more familiar Ku Klux Klan?"

"We share many of the same goals and philosophies."

That sounded like a hedge to Tory.

"Isn't it true that the supremacist groups have splintered due to the successful civil damages suits brought against the Klan in the last decade?'' Alvarez persisted.

"It's harder to kill a snake with many heads," replied Paxton.

"One more question then," said Alvarez, "just out of curiosity. Why do you call your group Rip Tide?"

Paxton smiled then. "Because when you get caught in a riptide, Mr. Alvarez, it overwhelms you. And it doesn't matter how hard you try to swim for shore.''

After that, there didn't seem to be a lot more left to say. Paxton asked Tory once more to consider what he'd told her, wished her the best for her father, and took his leave.

She and Alvarez sat for a moment of shared silence. "Are you okay?" he asked. "I kept getting this strange feeling that you were trying not to laugh.''

"It's not funny," Tory said. "but I like Frank Paxton a hell of a lot more than Rolland Reynolds."

"You know," said Alvarez thoughtfully, "so do I."

NINETEEN

Mixed Messages
November, 1922. Rosewood, Florida

ONE FRIDAY EVENING, Aunt Sarah took to bed with a cough and a fever. The following gray Saturday morning, she asked Lissy to take some clothes that she'd mended to Fannie Taylor, and to tell her that Aunt Sarah wouldn't be coming to do the laundry. Lissy left Homer with her mother, for she didn't want him slowing her down on this particular errand.

As she approached the stoop where Homer had dropped his rag baby all those months ago, she heard a male voice through Fannie Taylor's window, the same male voice she'd heard before. Lissy froze right where she stood, holding a bundle of clothing about as large as Homer himself.

"You don't mean it," the man said. "You don't mean a word of it."

"It's over," Lissy heard Fannie say. "You can't come here any more."

"Somewhere else then."

"No. We can't see each other any more. It has to stop before my husband finds out."

"I'm here two more months. You think we can be in the same county and not see each other?"

"I'm telling you it's over."

"If that's what you're telling me, how come you sent the kids off somewhere so we'd be in an empty house together?"

"Because they can't see you here, that's why." Fannie sounded tired of having to make explanations.

"You could of written a note, told me this. But no, you send for me to come here and then I find you all alone, with your next door neighbor gone to visit her sick mother. I'll tell you what I think, Fannie. I think this will be over when I tell you it's over." Lissy heard the sound of flesh striking flesh, an answering sound, then scuffling and heavy breathing. "Watcha gonna do, Fannie, scream? Call the other next door neighbor? I don't think so, do you?" The sounds that followed this last question were barely discernible to Lissy's sharp ears.

She decided right there and then that Fannie Taylor might be white, she might have a husband who got to boss around other white men, and she might have a rent-free house, but Lissy wouldn't trade places with Fannie Taylor for the world.

She quietly put the mended clothes down on the stoop and left as silently as she had come. She figured Fannie Taylor would know without being told that there wasn't going to be any dirty laundry getting washed this particular winter morning.

TWENTY

Lunch Break
Tuesday

ALVAREZ WAS TAKING a break, roaming the halls, thinking about calling George Nelson again when a huge black man, in his late

fifties or early sixties, lumbered down the hall toward the ICU.
He was wearing khaki pants and a casual black pullover, but
there was a sense of purpose to his step. This was no maintenance person. "Excuse me, sir," the man said to him. "I'm
looking for Tom Wheatley."

"He's in there," Alvarez pointed through the glass separating
the ICU from the waiting area to a name plate labeled WHEAT-
LEY on the foot of the Senator's bed, right above a hanging file
folder containing thick reams of medical information. "You a
friend of the Senator's?" he asked.

"No," said the man, quietly studying the patient and the two
women sitting on either side of him. "He doesn't look too bad,
does he? Lord willing, he'll be fine, given enough time."

"You looking for someone in particular?" Alvarez pressed.

"The daughter—"

"You're looking for Tory Travers?"

"The man with her—David Alvarez."

"I'm Alvarez."

This earned a smile and a handshake of such enthusiasm that
Alvarez almost winced. "I'm happy to meet you, sir. I'm Richard Marshall. I'd like to take you to lunch, say thank you for
looking out for my Chloe last night."

Well, sometimes the mountain comes to you. "No thanks necessary," Alvarez said. "I just did what I could. Sorry it happened, but I'm glad I was there. Let me get Tory—I know she'd
want to meet you."

Richard Marshall was as enthusiastic about meeting Tory as
he'd been about meeting Alvarez, but Alvarez noted that he
shook her hand gently, almost reverentially. "I want to thank
you for giving my great aunt's box back to Chloe. She's worried
and fretted over that box ever since the robbery. I just kept telling
her to be grateful it was only things we'd lost." Marshall paused,
grimaced. "Not like that little Amy Cooper, now. Isn't that
something just too terrible for words? Her poor husband, he just
doted on that girl, and now she's gone, here one minute, gone
the next." Marshall shook his head.

"I'm glad we could return the box," said Tory. "My father would be happy to know that it's back with the original owner."

Marshall smiled. "Well, the original owner's dead and gone, but she lived a long and bountiful life. That box belonged to my great-aunt Lissy, sister to the woman who raised my daddy. Aunt Lissy was amazing, full of knowledge about the past, and I wouldn't have never even known about her, if it hadn't been for Chloe. Whatever your father paid for that box, I'll be glad to pay him back, double."

"No, no—" protested Tory. "He'd be glad to know it's back where it belongs."

"The least you can do is let me take you and Mr. Alvarez to lunch. I know this isn't an easy time with your daddy in the hospital and all, but a person's got to eat, and sometimes the waiting goes easier for taking a break."

"I appreciate it, but I just took a break. My father's been making some small movements, and we're hopeful he'll wake up soon. I want to be here if that happens."

"And I'll pray it does. How about you, Mr. Alvarez? If Mrs. Travers needs to stay here, what do you say that you and me go get a bite to eat somewhere? It's the least I can do, and it would make me proud to buy you lunch. I've got a phone with me— I'll leave the number so Mrs. Travers can call if there's any good news to report."

Alvarez figured this man could make a career out of visiting hospital wards—natural optimism flowed out of him. Tory gave Marshall one of her real smiles, the kind that made her face light up all over, then turned to Alvarez. "Go ahead," she told him. "Go to lunch with Mr. Marshall."

"Richard," the big man said firmly.

"Richard," said Tory. "I'll get some lunch with Dana. I think she'd like that."

"I have customers all over this county," said Marshall, "so don't repeat this, but the best lunch to be had in Gainesville is at this little deli—"

Alvarez remembered a cold winter night, Tory hovering over the phone in a motel room with a secure line, waiting to get in touch with Cody and tell him to lay low. "The 43rd Street Deli?" he asked.

"How'd you know that?" Marshall looked surprised.

"The Senator brought Tory's son to Gainesville on a visit. He mentioned going to this deli where the owner was some kind of a barbecue champion or something."

"That's a fact. Still, it's a wonder you'd remember something like that. So, Mr. Alvarez, are we on for lunch?" Marshall favored Alvarez with another wide smile.

"We're on," said Alvarez, "as long as you drop the mister. Just call me Alvarez."

THE 43RD STREET DELI was jam-packed with all sorts of people—construction workers, mothers with small children, business people, and kids in baggy pants and shirts who didn't look old enough to drive, much less have lunch on their own. Marshall and Alvarez didn't stand in the crush of people waiting for tables more than a few minutes before a dark-haired man in a chef's apron came over and greeted them. "Richard, my man, long time no see. What are you doing hiding out back here? Let me show you to your table."

Marshall's smile faded into a look of discomfort. "No, Paul, no need for that. We'll wait our turn, just like everyone else."

"Isn't he great?" the dark-haired man asked Alvarez and didn't wait for an answer. "Richard is The Man."

"This is David Alvarez," said Marshall, "a friend of mine."

"Any friend of Richard's is a friend of mine. I'm Paul Cakmis—welcome to my deli. I was ordering supplies at the back table. Come on, I'll clear it for you. No one was eating there, so you can clear your conscience as well, Richard." Cakmis led Alvarez and Marshall to a table in the back of the lunchroom. He seated them as though he were the maitre d' at a fancy restaurant, then produced two laminated menus for their perusal. "Voilà," he said. "You stay away long enough, things change. We've got new menus."

Marshall didn't look pleased at the news. "Still got the old favorites?" he asked.

Cakmis shrugged. "Some old, some new. Important thing is that we updated all the prices; I'll have a waitress right over. What can I get you to drink, gentlemen?"

Before Cakmis could turn away to put the order in for two iced teas, Alvarez got in a question. "Are you one of Richard's customers?"

"Not any more," said Cakmis. "Hard to believe, but before I started this place, I was a homebuilder. Richard used to do construction cleanup for me. He bailed me out quite a few times, when I was down to the wire trying to get a model home ready for the parade."

"Parade?" asked Alvarez. The idea of parading homes was surely more than a cultural difference between Florida and Texas.

"Parade of Homes, a bunch of open houses, something the homebuilders here put on, draws quite a crowd. If Richard here hadn't been willing to clean my models in the wee hours of the morning, I'd have been screwed."

"You would have managed," said Marshall.

"See, he never sings his own praises, does he? I'll tell you, Mr. Alvarez, if you're looking to do business with someone, this is the man to do it with. Richard does a good job, treats his employees right, and he never signs a contract before he's had a chance to sleep on it."

"You don't go away and stop embarrassing me, we're going to have to go buy lunch somewhere else," Marshall told Cakmis.

"Never let it be said that I got between a customer and my cash register," said Cakmis. He no sooner vanished than a waitress appeared as though by magic. Marshall might be a good businessman, but Cakmis seemed to run his deli tighter than a ship's captain.

"What's good?" Alvarez asked, scanning the menu.

"Everything's good," said Marshall.

When in Rome and all of that, thought Alvarez. "I'll have the Cuban sandwich," he told the waitress.

"Make it two," said Marshall.

Alvarez turned his attention back to Marshall. "How's your

wife holding up? It must've been hard, losing a staff member, then finding someone vandalizing her car.''

Marshall frowned as though these topics brought him physical pain. ''Chloe never talks about her feelings much, but I know she's upset. Amy wasn't only a coworker, she was Chloe's second cousin.''

''That's what I understand.''

''Then there was that ugliness last night. I'm really grateful to you for what you did. I hate to think of Chloe walking into something like that by herself.''

Alvarez shrugged. ''I just hope things get better for her.''

''Well, maybe bad things come in threes, because I talked to her this morning, and she'd just had another disappointment.'' Marshall looked pained. ''Chloe's boss decided to pull her off the stuff she's been working on, switch her over to something else.''

''What's she being switched to?''

''Seminole studies. Chloe's specialty is Florida black history, but now that Amy's gone, Reynolds wants to switch Chloe over to the Seminoles full-time and take over the black studies himself.''

Alvarez examined this statement, found nothing of interest there, and decided to cast his line somewhere else. ''I understand that you and Chloe met as a result of her historical research.''

''Yes, sir,'' said Marshall, ''Chloe found out about my grandfather's lynching, and how my father was orphaned. Because of her work, I got a whole new extended family I never knew anything about, and a wife, to boot.''

''And some money,'' added Alvarez, watching for the smile to disappear.

It did disappear, but it died a natural death. ''The money's nothing, compared to the other stuff,'' said Marshall.

A new waitress appeared out of nowhere bearing two Cuban sandwiches, amazingly quick service.

''Tell me about the wooden box that belonged to your great aunt,'' said Alvarez. ''Was it listed on the police report as a stolen item?''

Alvarez's questions weren't affecting Marshall's appetite. The man took a huge bite of his sandwich and washed it down with iced tea before answering. "I think so. Chloe made the lists for the police and the insurance company. Most the stuff that went missing belonged to her, and my Chloe's good at making lists— that's one of the things that makes her a good historian. Now me, I'd be lost if I had to sit around all day, reading little bitty tiny print and writing down stuff." Marshall flashed another disarming smile before redirecting the conversation. "But that's enough about me. Compared to my Aunt Lissy, I'm downright boring. Let me tell you about the woman first owned that box. Let me tell you about Lissy Hodden Garner."

TWENTY-ONE

Falling from Grace
January 1, 1923. Rosewood, Florida

LISSY WAS FEELING uncharacteristically truculent. It wasn't a good way to start a brand new year, but she just didn't care. She was angry, angry with her parents who had left the day after Christmas on their self-appointed mission to console Garland in her misery.

Lissy didn't care that her mamma and daddy had tried to compromise and take her feelings into consideration. Her parents had wanted all of them to go to Archer before Christmas, but Lissy dug in her heels. She didn't want to, especially not at Christmas-time. She wanted no part of her parents' plans to cheer up her older sister—Lissy wanted to stay at home in Rosewood, and she wanted things to stay just the way they were.

Some compromise. Her parents postponed the trip until after Christmas, but Lissy still refused to go, even though they were to be gone for two weeks. Along with everything else, Lissy's father had found some temporary work replacing an injured friend at a meat-packaging plant in Archer, and it had been decided that Garland would benefit from some of the mothering she missed out on after marrying and moving away.

In spite of the length of the trip, finally even Lissy's mamma lost patience and gave in. "Stay then," she said to Lissy in frustration, "you so all fired set on having your own way, being selfish and not thinking 'bout anyone else. You be sure you mind Aunt Sarah, and you be sure you help out 'round there." As though Lissy had ever acted in any other way.

Some New Year's Day this was. There was no haven of comfort to be found at school since it was closed for the holidays, and except for that, it was just another regular workday. The men were already up and gone to their jobs like any other Monday, and Aunt Sarah was heading into Sumner and expecting Lissy to come along as usual to mind the children. About the only thing different was the weather. There was frost on the ground, it was so cold, and Lissy had hardly ever seen that before.

At least, that was the only thing that was different until they got to Sumner.

There were men milling around the living quarters, which was a surprise, considering it was already late in the morning. There were white men with hunting hounds, a lot of white men. Looking closer, there were women there too, but they were harder to see because they were at the center of the group of men. And at the very center of the group of women, inside the group of men, was Fannie Taylor.

Lissy could see Fannie because the group seemed to part of its own volition upon their arrival. For a moment, before the group closed ranks again, it looked as though Fannie Taylor was standing there all alone in the bitter cold. She had tears running down her cheeks, her hair looked as if it hadn't seen a comb in days, and there were bruises and scratches on her face. She was hugging herself tightly and making little sobbing noises as though it hurt to breathe.

One of the men, Poly Wilkerson, the man Lissy's daddy disliked so much, raised his voice and shouted, "You go on home, old slave woman. We don't want none of your kind 'round here today."

It was true that Aunt Sarah had been born a slave, the only one in Rosewood who could claim with impunity to remember what slavery was *really* like, and sometimes she was called Slave Woman to pay homage to her store of historical knowledge. But the way Poly Wilkerson said slave woman didn't sound like homage to Lissy.

Aunt Sarah just smiled and said, "I be back some other day, then," and turned around and walked off just as she did at the end of any other workday. But as soon as they were out of sight of the mill quarters, Aunt Sarah turned on Lissy and grabbed her by the front of her coat. There was no smile and no easy manner in her behavior then.

"You take these children," she told Lissy, "and you get them back to my house soon's you can, 'cause your young feet goes lots faster than mine. Soon's you done that, you go straight to Aaron Carrier's house, 'cause I hear he be home sick today. You tell him there be white men coming, trouble coming."

Aaron Carrier was related to Aunt Sarah, but he didn't live in the two-story Carrier house. He was married to Mizz Mahulda, Lissy's beloved schoolteacher, and he and his wife lived in their own house in Rosewood. Lissy nodded her understanding and turned to herd the children toward home, but Aunt Sarah wasn't done with her yet. She grabbed the sleeve of Lissy's coat to pull her back once more.

"You gets these children to my house quick's you can, Lissy Hodden, every single one of them. This ain't no time to be thinking 'bout anything other'n what I told you, you hear? No favorites—you treat each and every one these children just like they was Homer Marshall."

Lissy nodded her understanding and took off, taking care to keep all the children moving quickly and in front of her, not daring to turn around and look back.

TWENTY-TWO

The Threat
Tuesday Afternoon

THE FIRST MISTAKE that Tory made was assuming that it would save time and effort if she just gave in and talked to Rolland Reynolds when he showed up a second time, right after her hurried lunch with Dana Halloran. The second mistake she made was telling Nurse Randy Sosa that it was okay for Rolland to join her at her father's bedside, where Tory was keeping sole vigil after Dana left for her afternoon meeting. And the third mistake, the one she would tell herself afterwards that Alvarez would never have made, was not looking up to read Rolland's face before he grabbed a chair, pulled it next to her and dropped into it.

She didn't look up because she was engrossed at that moment with studying her father. Maybe Dana could see some change she couldn't. Or could it be that her father simply refused to make the minor movements that he seemed to make when anyone else—Dana, Randy, his doctor—was around? Right before she left, Dana said, "Look, Tory, he moved his left hand—did you see?" No, she hadn't. Every time she looked, Tom Wheatley was lying motionless and unchanged on his hospital bed. It was driving her crazy.

"Do you think he looks any different, Rolland?" she asked. Maybe her father would respond with Rolland here, and if she watched really closely, she wouldn't miss it.

"Why? Are you afraid he'll wake up and do the things he wanted to do?"

Tory finally looked then, really looked, at her new companion in the ICU. If Rolland Reynolds wasn't furious, he was sure putting on a good act.

"What's wrong?" asked Tory. "You look like you just lost your funding or something." It was the wrong thing to say.

"I know that Chloe Marshall came to see you last night," hissed Reynolds, keeping his voice low in deference to their surroundings. "And I know what you talked about."

Tory was giving Rolland her full attention now—his temper was veering out of control. If her father decided to sit up now and recite the Pledge of Allegiance, he would have to do it without her watching. "Dr. Marshall came to thank David for trying to help Amy Cooper," she told Rolland.

"Dr. Marshall came to tell you that she thought I was out of line in talking to you at the hospital, and that you shouldn't worry about trying to follow through on your father's wishes about the endowment. She told you that she thought the whole idea of the contribution should be reconsidered, because maybe that would teach me how to behave appropriately. You don't need to bother lying about it, Vicky, she already told me herself.''

"I'm not going to lie about it, and my name's not Vicky."

"You'll always be Vicky to me. You can't change the past, no matter how much you try to pretend that you're someone different now."

Tory took a deep breath. This man and his petty problems were not worth losing her temper over. Good God, she was pregnant with David Alvarez's child, she had a comatose father and a teenaged son in love. How important could Rolland Reynolds really be in this scheme of things?

"Calm down, Rolland. So what if Dr. Marshall doesn't approve of your fund-raising methods? She's been under a lot of strain, too. You weren't the only topic of conversation by any means. She told us about a wooden box that belonged to her husband's family, something that had been stolen, then bought by my father in an antique store. He wanted to return the box to her, so we did. That should make you feel better—I followed through on something my father wanted to do."

Rolland's lips were turning white around the edges. "You gave Chloe Marshall the Rosewood box? And you thought your father would want you to do that? You think that should make me feel *better?*"

"Rolland, none of this is about me. I think my father is going to pull through, and if he does, then anything he wants to do as far as the endowment is just fine and dandy with me. If he doesn't, it's a whole new ball game, and I'd be just as happy to be out of it. I don't have an agenda here. You trying to browbeat me into agreeing that the endowment is a good idea is about as meaningful as Frank Paxton and the whole membership of Rip Tide trying to convince me that it's not."

"You know about Rip Tide?" Rolland exclaimed. Tory nodded. "You talked to Frank Paxton? About me?" Tory nodded again. Then Rolland lowered his voice again, which just made his furious words sound more sinister. "You listen to me, Vicky, and you listen good. I know things about your family, ugly things, things you'd rather keep the lid on.''

Tory was getting angry, too. ''Here's a news flash for you, Rolland. I know some pretty ugly things about my family, too. Why do you think I left and never came back? Surely you don't think it had anything to do with you? Or do you remember, that fine spring day on our back porch when you came over and no one else was around? Your comprehension skills weren't too good then either, were they? I kept telling you no, but you didn't understand. Then when you were doubled up grabbing your crotch and moaning in pain, it seemed like you got the message.''

''You were always such a slut, Vicky,'' Rolland shot back.

''Yeah, me and the whole football team. Or was it the whole basketball team? I forget.''

''But such a particular little slut,'' Rolland continued as though she hadn't spoken. ''Only white boys were good enough for you. But then you worked your way up. Up from white boys to white men—married white men, right?''

''Old story,'' said Tory. ''I think you should leave now.''

''Not when I have so much more to tell you. It really pained Tommy, you know, the way you turned out.''

''Leave my brother out of this.'' Tory tried to keep the fury out of her voice. She didn't want Rolland to know that he'd picked the one target where she might still be vulnerable.

''Okay, we'll talk about the other members of your family. How about your father there? He became such a martyr, didn't he? Losing his son, disgraced by his daughter, abandoned by his wife. What people don't remember is that Senator Wheatley got where he did by keeping score. That old man lying there is the same wheeler-dealer he ever was.''

''Do you understand English, Rolland? Leave, go tell your stories to someone else. I don't care.''

''He came to me, not the other way around.''

This brought Tory up short. ''What do you mean?'' she was surprised into asking.

''He found that stupid box at an antique store. He didn't know shit about Rosewood, didn't know that Lissy Hodden Garner was one of the survivors, didn't know she had a connection to Richard and Chloe Marshall. All he saw were the words 'Rosewood' and 'Hodden' and that was enough for him.''

"You're not making any sense." Even as she spoke the words, Tory was afraid that maybe he was.

"Your father told me that there had always been rumors about your mother's family—the great political Hodden clan of Alabama," said Rolland. "Rumors that back when they'd owned slaves, there were some awfully brown Hodden babies. It's all the trend now, ever since the Thomas Jefferson thing, looking for the real truth about the heritage of renowned southern families. How many years have you been gone—eighteen? Then your mother's been gone seventeen. How does it feel to know that the man lying there, your father, was willing to pay *two million dollars* in return for me finding evidence to discredit your mother's family?"

At least this speech, distasteful as it was, had given Tory a chance to get control of her feelings. All of this had nothing to do with her, who she had been, or who she was. It really didn't even have anything to do with who people thought she had been, or who they thought she was. "You want to know how I feel?" She repeated the question, giving herself time to phrase her answer precisely right. "I feel like anyone with two million dollars to spend should get his money's worth."

It was the wrong thing to say—it was like throwing gasoline on a fire—a fire in a library, perhaps, since they were forced into hushed tones, made vicious by the implied intimacy. "If you don't care about that, then try this one on for size," snarled Rolland. "Do you know why Tommy died?"

"Gosh, I don't know, Rolland," Tory replied, her temper out of control again. "That's a really *big* family secret. Do you think maybe it's because he joined the Marines and got shipped off to Vietnam and got in the way of a bunch of bullets? Am I getting warm here? Are you going to tell me that he was really court-martialed in the field and executed for cowardice? It doesn't matter, because I wouldn't care."

"No, you wouldn't, would you? You worshipped the ground your brother walked on. Sweet, sensitive Tommy. The one who was always around when a buddy needed a friend. The one who chose to study English literature. The one who didn't play sports, didn't ever have a steady girlfriend. Maybe you'd be interested in the rumors that he was gay."

Tory projected fast-forward footage of family films in her head. Everything Rolland said about her brother was true. Everything but the last thing. She would have *known*. "He wasn't gay," she said automatically.

"But I thought you didn't care, loving sister that you are. It doesn't really matter though, does it? All that mattered to your father was the *possibility* that his son was gay. Didn't you ever wonder why your brother enlisted, Vicky? Didn't that seem just a little strange to you?"

"He thought it was the right thing to do." Even though she'd told herself this for years and years, when spoken out loud, she had to admit that it didn't quite ring true. But you had to tell yourself something to make sense of the fact that your only brother died in a foreign land, on the very day before the order came to pull out all US troops.

"No, he didn't think it was the right thing to do," Rolland taunted.

Tory had had enough. She stood up. "Get out. I should have had you thrown out a long time ago."

Rolland stood up too. "Your father asked him to do it, to put to rest any rumors that might affect future campaigns."

"I said get out."

"But it backfired. Tommy wasn't like your old man. He didn't want to take advantage of any of the favors offered to him. So he ended up like any other poor sucker, in the front lines, then home again in a body bag. The pieces of him that they could find."

"Get out!" Tory yelled.

Rolland took that as permission to yell too. "How does it feel to know what your father is *really* like, Victoria? Do you feel so goddamned high and mighty now?"

If Rolland didn't get out of her sight now, Tory was going to hit him. "Why couldn't someone run over you with a car instead of that poor girl? Get out, get out now, before I—" Tory was surprised to feel something wet hit one of her clenched fists, and she realized that tears were running down her face.

A male voice came to Tory's rescue. "You need to leave now. Immediately. You're upsetting the patient."

Rolland snorted. "Upsetting the patient? That's rich. How do you upset someone in a coma?"

"Leave now, unless you want me to call security and have you forcibly removed."

Rolland seemed to consider the reemphasized message, made a decision, turned on his heel and left.

Tory had spent most of her life *not* looking toward the horizon in hopes of seeing a knight in shining white armor. She was therefore immensely thankful to whatever power had seen fit to send someone to her rescue. Tory let herself collapse into Randy Sosa's arms.

He did everything right. He held her, patted her back, asked no questions, and most importantly, provided a steady supply of tissues from the box on the table by her father's bed. Of course, the welcomed silence couldn't last forever.

Wiping her nose one last time in preparation for abandoning Sosa's comforting hug, Tory heard someone clear his throat. Peering around Sosa's nicely defined biceps, Tory saw Alvarez standing in the doorway. How like him, to arrive just in time for the interrogation.

"Have I missed something?"

TWENTY-THREE

The Threat
January 1, 1923. Rosewood, Florida

LISSY GOT ALL the children safely to the Carrier house and under the supervision of adults worthy of the weighty responsibility of caring for someone as special as Homer Marshall, so there was really no excuse for her to avoid the second task with which she'd been charged. But as quick as Lissy was making her way from Sumner to Rosewood, she wasn't quick enough to bring

Aunt Sarah's message to Aaron Carrier before someone else beat her to it.

The door to Aaron's house was standing half-opened, unusual in this cold weather. Even more unusual was the familiar male voice that Lissy could hear coming from inside the house, underscored with an unmistakable tone of fear. "You know who I am, doncha?"

There was unintelligible muttering in reply.

"Don't speak my name, boy. Don't even think of speaking it. You know who I am, and you know what I do, and that's enough, isn't it? I'm in trouble, and I need you to help me get out of here, that's all. Then you forget you ever seen me, you hear?"

This time Lissy could hear the words that Aaron Carrier spoke in reply, words that were tinged with fear. "Can't you see I be home all alone, sick in my bed?"

There was a pause. "Then find me Sam Carter," was the reply. "He's got a wagon and he's been in the system, just like old Sylvester and Haywood. Carter knows what I can do if the two of you ever speak my name. You go fetch Sam Carter, boy, and have him bring his wagon over here. He can take me a ways down the road and that'll be the end of it. It will be like I've never been here, like you've never seen me. You understand me, Aaron Carrier? I know you, and I know where you've got kin working road gangs, so you tell me you understand, boy."

Aaron's voice sounded as though it came from a man twice his age. "I be understanding every word."

Lissy silently turned and went back the way she'd come. There was no point in telling Aaron Carrier that white men were coming, that trouble was coming. He already knew.

TWENTY-FOUR

Picking up the Pieces
Tuesday

ALVAREZ WATCHED TORY remove herself from Sosa's embrace. She looked like shit—a red runny nose, tear-streaked cheeks and dark circles under her eyes. "Nobody died, right?" he asked, slanting a look toward Wheatley.

"There's been no change in the Senator's condition," said Sosa calmly. Alvarez liked how the man didn't get flustered and try to disentangle himself from Tory in a hurry. At least, he halfway liked it. "There was a visitor—"

"That damned asshole Reynolds," clarified Tory.

"That damned asshole Reynolds," Sosa corrected himself. Alvarez was going to have to keep an eye on this guy. "He got into a heated discussion with Mrs. Travers," continued Sosa. "I could tell that it was quite upsetting to her. By the end, we could hear shouting all the way out at the nurses' station."

"I told him that I wished someone had run over him with a car instead of poor Amy Cooper," sniffed Tory.

"Indeed you did," agreed Sosa. "In fact, I think those were your very words."

"Then what?" asked Alvarez, mentally backtracking. There had been at least five people gathered at the nurses' station watching Sosa comfort Tory when Alvarez arrived, and he was wondering how much damage control was in order. "What happened after Mrs. Travers told Reynolds that she wished someone would run over him with a car?"

"What happened then?" Sosa sounded insulted, as though Alvarez had asked a stupid question. "Well, then I told him to leave, of course."

"Atta boy," Alvarez said. Sosa ignored Alvarez while he made sure Tory was steady on her feet without his support, then retreated to the nurse's station. "Three things," Alvarez said to Tory as soon as they were left alone together. "First, sit down. You look like you're about to keel over." Tory dropped into a chair without a comment. She must be feeling worse than he thought. "Second thing—you eat lunch?"

"Don't turn all solicitous on me," she said. "It's not your style. And I hate it when you stand over me and ask questions—it's such a cop thing. I don't know whether you do it without realizing it or whether you do it on purpose." She glared at him. "I don't know which is worse."

Alvarez dropped into a chair next to her, but he refused to be derailed. "You've got to eat, *querida,* if you want to go the distance." Tory continued to glare at him. "Third thing, what the hell is going on here?"

"I don't want to talk about it."

"*Cara,* if all the spies in the world were like you, we wouldn't have to worry about security leaks. We wouldn't have to worry about getting any information, either. Tell me what went on with you and Reynolds, or I'll go interview everyone at the nurses' station out there."

"You would, wouldn't you?"

He nodded.

So she told him and wasn't too far into her tale before Alvarez felt like finding Reynolds and punching him. He could hear raw pain in Tory's voice when she told him about her father's purported role in her brother's enlistment and death. He tried to tread carefully.

"*Cara,* whatever your father may have said or done, surely your brother was old enough to make up his own mind after finishing college."

"He never finished college. He enlisted after his first year."

So what if background investigations weren't one hundred percent accurate? It was a good time to change the subject. "Tell me again what Reynolds said about the box. Tell me exactly."

Out of the whole story, the thing that interested Alvarez as a detective was the information about the Rosewood box. If Wheatley saw the box as some link to a hidden part of his wife's heritage, would he return it to the Marshalls? More to the point, if Wheatley was aware of Richard Marshall's connection to the box, wouldn't he try to pump Marshall for details about the box's original owner?

Before Alvarez had time to fully consider these questions, there was another visitor. This one walked in as though he had a right to be there, but he came respectfully, holding his hat in his hand. It was Deputy Nelson.

"Hey, Mr. Alvarez, Vicky. How's the Senator doing?" asked Nelson.

"No change," said Tory.

"I'm sorry to hear that."

"Why are you here?" Alvarez asked. He doubted Reynolds would file a complaint, but you never knew, and he remembered Nelson's warning about keeping Tory out of trouble. "Any progress in finding the person who ran down Amy Cooper?"

"Maybe, maybe not," said Nelson. "I thought I'd come over and give you a head's up, you being somewhat helpful to me and all."

"Helpful with what?" asked Tory.

Nelson looked at Tory. "You went and growed up all right, but didn't you learn any manners, Vicky? You gonna ask someone to tell you something, it'd be nice to invite him to sit down."

Alvarez hooked a vacant chair with his foot and pulled it over to where he and Tory were sitting. "Please, Deputy Nelson, sit down."

"Don't mind if I do," said Nelson, reaching in his pocket for a toothpick to chew.

"What did he help you with?" Tory asked Nelson doggedly.

Nelson had his own version of what Tory called a cop-voice. "You worried we were talking about you? Relax. Mr. Alvarez here pointed out how Amy Cooper was related to Chloe Marshall, who just happens to be the assistant director of the center where Ms. Cooper worked."

"So, what does that mean?"

"Doesn't mean a thing," said Nelson placidly. "Not that I know of at the moment. But I passed it on, and it got someone in the GPD to thinking, which is always good. Turns out our friend with the spray paint is related to Chloe Marshall, too."

"Sledge?" asked Alvarez.

"The one and only. Turns out he's a second cousin to Mrs. Marshall on the other side of the family. Can't see where that means anything yet either, but still, it's good to know."

"Can you make him for Amy's car and Wheatley's condo?" asked Alvarez.

"Probably. But I wouldn't go out celebrating right yet." Nelson sighed. "Hitch is, our friend Sledge has a watertight alibi for the night Amy was killed. He says he did her car the night before. The night Cooper got killed, Sledge was up in Jacksonville. Twenty-five Hammerskins will vouch for him."

"Hammerskins?"

"More serious, more organized than Skinheads. We're talking about a group that thinks the Ku Klux Klan is out of style. Groups like the Klan, you can just sign up, pass the look-see test, send in your money, and bingo—you're a member. Hammerskins, they're more serious. You have to earn your way in. Maybe that's what old Sledge has been doing down here in Gainesville lately, stepping up his activities in hopes of getting to play with the big boys."

"Where does Rip Tide fit into the scheme of things?" asked Tory. For an intelligent woman, Alvarez sure wished she'd keep her mouth shut sometimes.

"What do you know about Rip Tide?"

"Someone named Frank Paxton came to see Tory this morning," Alvarez said. "He wanted to convince her to change her dad's mind about his contribution to UF's history department."

"Why would Paxton care about that?" It seemed that no one needed to explain who Frank Paxton was.

"This specific contribution is being solicited by Rolland Reynolds," said Alvarez. "All two million dollars of it." This was more than he'd told Nelson during their first meeting at the airport, and Alvarez watched the man closely. He didn't believe the rural-deputy-act for a moment. Sure enough, the information seemed to make sense to Nelson.

"What did you tell Paxton?" Nelson asked Tory.

"The same thing I told Rolland Reynolds, that it didn't matter what I thought, the money belongs to my father, and if he recovers, he'll be the one deciding what to do with it."

"So both these guys, Reynolds and Paxton, contacted you about this contribution?"

"That's right," Tory said.

"Two people come to the hospital to talk to you about two million dollars, right after your dad's in a hit-and-run accident. One heads the place where Cooper worked, one hates the place where Cooper worked. Might bear keeping in mind," mused Nelson.

"Sounds like we're feeding you information," said Alvarez. "What's the heads-up you were talking about?"

"Might be a break in the Cooper case. Thought you'd like to know, you trying to do the decent thing by her and being a detective yourself. GPD tossed Cooper's office out at this Center where she worked, found some copies of some pretty hot letters from her to her boss. Not employee-boss kind of letters, if you know what I mean. These are the kind of letters where you describe who's done what to whom, exactly how good it felt, and what you have in mind for next time."

Alvarez examined this and found two things wrong with it, even while noting that Nelson could use impeccable grammar when he chose to. "You told me that GPD was tossing Amy Cooper's office first thing after the accident. I can understand luggage getting lost, and her laptop getting smashed, but what took so long to turn this stuff up?"

Nelson shook his head. "Another one of those human oversights. The letters were filed in a neat little folder labeled 'DIRECTOR,' along with a bunch of administrative stuff. Cooper must have thought it was real clever, and come to think of it, it was. Like hiding something in plain sight, you know? Took a while for someone to think of looking through everything in the folders. Can't be perfect, then again, we're talking the GPD."

"They found copies of letters to Reynolds?"

Nelson nodded. "Yeah, turns out Cooper was compulsive about keeping records—she must have been a natural for historical research. There's copies of everything imaginable in that office, hard copies and computer copies both. Everything's filed away neat as a pin, but there's reams of information, most of it boring as shit. Got to cut the GPD guys some slack on this one."

"But that doesn't really prove anything, does it?" This from Tory.

"Got a point there," said Nelson. "Could be she just wrote the letters, saved them in a file, never delivered them. Wonder if that'll be the story we hear. Heard stranger stories in my time, but I'm a big believer in the simple explanation. Maybe because not too many of the strange stories I hear turn out to be true. Anyway, gives us someone to look at, the boss and the husband."

"Rolland Reynolds was just here," said Tory.

Nelson looked at her with new interest. "You're kidding. I walk in, that's all they're talking about at the nurses' station, Wheatley's daughter getting into some yelling match with someone bedside in ICU. You don't change much, do you, Vicky? Trouble seems to follow you everywhere you go."

"This isn't my trouble," said Tory.

"Hope not. Sheriff here, he still remembers you, not favorably, I can tell you that. Still, it's interesting, Reynolds being here just a little while ago. Wonder if that means GPD missed him at his office. Maybe I'll get called out to go talk to him later. I'd like to hear if he claims Vicky's defense, that he never saw none of the letters in that file."

"Why would you be called out to talk to Reynolds?" Alvarez asked before Tory had a chance to comment on the phrase, "Vicky's defense."

"Reynolds lives out in the county if I remember right. Once GPD goes outside the city limits, they're civilians, just like you, Mr. Alvarez. They gotta take along a deputy if there's even a remote possibility of an arrest."

"You find out something, I'd like to know," said Alvarez.

Nelson nodded, put his toothpick back in his pocket. "I'll keep that in mind." He turned back to Tory. "Vicky, you don't look so good. Matter of fact, I been sitting here thinking how you look worse than the Senator there. Might be a good idea for you to call it a day, get some rest. What do you think?"

"I think that's an excellent idea," said Alvarez.

Tory shook her head. "I told Dana I'd stay here this afternoon. She saw some movement this morning, and I was hoping—"

"I know what you mean," said Nelson. "I just saw him move his head a little bit a moment ago—didn't you see it?" Tory stared at Nelson. "I bet your daddy's gonna wake up any time now. Thing is, you want to look all healthy and happy when he does." Nelson gave Tory a grin she didn't return.

"Go back to the condo," Alvarez urged. "Eat something, get some rest, and it will give you a chance to call home for the millionth time today. Didn't you say that Dana was coming back this evening? I'll stay here until she does."

"What about the car—"

"No problem." Nelson stood up. "I'll give you a ride. Least I can do, it'll be—" Nelson stopped himself, and Alvarez was almost certain that he had been going to say, "it'll be just like old times..."

"Giving you a ride is the least I can do, for old times sake and all," the Deputy amended.

Alvarez stood up, too. "I'll stay 'til Dana gets here, then I'll pick up some groceries, head back, cook you dinner."

Tory was on her feet now, being smoothly turned toward the doorway by the affable but efficient Nelson. "You're going to get groceries and cook dinner?" she asked Alvarez.

"Yeah, men do it all the time now, getting in touch with their feminine side," said Nelson. "Where have you been all these years? You and me got some catching up to do, Vicky."

Tory shot a look over her shoulder at Alvarez, but she was already being ushered out as efficiently as a collar being escorted off the street. "You and Deputy Nelson take all the time you want, getting caught up," Alvarez called after her. "Just think, every moment you spend in his company gives you an alibi if you need it later."

It was a remark he would come to regret.

TWENTY-FIVE

First Blood
January 2, 1923. Rosewood, Florida

BY TUESDAY, there were two groups of people in Rosewood. Those who thought the worst was over, and those who didn't. As a temporary member of the Carrier household, Lissy was firmly allied with the second group.

Even before Lissy returned from Aaron Carrier's house yesterday morning, it was as though the women in Rosewood could smell trouble coming. They were all calling their children in, keeping them under close watch and off the streets, drawing the curtains aside to peer out through the windows. Those who lived near Aaron Carrier's house would live the rest of their lives regretting that they looked out.

When the white men from Sumner arrived in Rosewood, they were no longer a group milling around in search of a purpose. They had become a mob, and armed with both liquor and guns, this mob followed the hunting dogs down the railroad track from Fannie Taylor's house straight to Aaron Carrier's. The men burst through the door, pulled Aaron out of bed, and started asking their questions. To which, Aaron said, "I don't know nothing 'bout what you be saying." That was not the answer that they wanted to hear.

There was always Someone in a mob.

Someone had a rope, and Someone else tied it around Aaron's wrists. The rope was attached to the bumper of a car, and Aaron was dragged down the road until the driver of the car yelled that he was tired of wasting gas for the little results they were getting.

When the car stopped, Someone said, "Kill him."

Then Aaron Carrier said, "I don't know nothing 'cept Sam Carter took a man out of here in his wagon, a man looking to be gone in a hurry."

A few men stayed with Aaron while the rest roamed the streets of Rosewood, looking for their next suspect. At dusk, when Sam Carter pulled his wagon up in front of his house, they'd found one.

This was about the same time that rumors of trouble at home found Sylvester deep in the woods where he had been hunting. The rest of the story was his, and he was telling it to arm the people in the Carrier house.

The Man had glimpsed the mob as he came out of the woods. Tying a rope around Aaron Carrier's wrists had been practice—the rope they used on Sam Carter was tied around his neck. Someone threw the end over a thick limb of an oak tree, and they hoisted Sam Carter off the ground. Sometimes they'd let him down just enough to let his toes touch the ground, so he could get his breath and they could ask their questions. Who was it? Where'd you take him? Sam Carter gave the same answers as Aaron Carrier, and then he was hoisted in the air once more.

As she listened, Lissy felt conflicted. On one hand she was proud to be included as an adult. But such a privilege came with a heavy price—she had to listen to The Man's story. The house was silent as he continued.

Upon seeing Sam Carter, Sylvester circled back toward the road, hoping that even on a workday, by some miracle he would find others who could help. What he found was Levy County's Deputy Sheriff, Clarence Williams, leaning against the bumper of his car with a limp and bloodied Aaron Carrier collapsed in front of him in the dirt road.

"You got to do something," Sylvester told Williams. "They got Sam Carter strung up over there in those woods, and they gonna kill him."

Williams took in The Man and his hunting rifle with one glance. "I know, boy, but what's happening over there, it's bigger than both of us put together."

"How you know, you not even gonna try?" asked The Man. He was desperate. Then they heard a shotgun blast. Williams and The Man just looked at each other, each refusing to acknowledge the reality of the sound they had just heard.

Williams pushed himself off the car. "Ain't nothing more can be done for Carter, boy. You help me get this other nigger in my car, in the backseat where nobody can see him. Then you go on home and you ain't seen nothing, you hear?"

It didn't seem right, standing on the road while Sam Carter was in the woods being lynched by a white mob, but there was an immediacy to what Williams was saying. Sylvester helped the deputy lift the half conscious Aaron Carrier into the back seat of the car. Williams threw a blanket over him. Then the deputy took off down the road away from where the mob had Sam Carter, and he never looked back.

Sylvester heard the men coming out of the woods, and he heard one of them say, "Damn it, you fool. Why'd you go and kill him? Now we'll never know who done it."

The Man turned and melted back into the woods and made his way home. He hadn't left the house since, not even when the other Rosewood men started to trickle back into town, done with their day's work, shocked to find what had transpired during their absence. Not even when some of these same men went out into the woods and found what was left of Sam Carter. His face was gone, blown off by the shotgun. Other parts of his body, ears and fingers and toes, were also missing. No one knew for certain if they had been cut off before or after his death.

No, The Man hadn't stepped out of the house for any of this. Not until this evening, when he was explaining to the adults what he was planning to do.

"It ain't over," he said, "'cause they ain't found what they was lookin' for. They be studying on it, and they be back. I plan to give 'em somethin' to find when they come back. Anyone here wants to leave, say so now."

No one spoke.

Lissy thought that with the responsibility of so many people in the house, and with the horror of the story The Man had just told, maybe he had forgotten about her. But he hadn't.

Sylvester cocked his head toward Lissy. "How 'bout you, little sister? I be going out now, do what I need to do. I can put you on the train to Archer. What you say?"

Lissy had never been so scared in her whole life. "I'm gonna stay," she said without hesitation.

TWENTY-SIX

No Alibi
Tuesday Evening

IT WAS SEVEN P.M. by the time Dana Halloran arrived at the hospital to relieve Alvarez from his vigil at Tom Wheatley's bedside. Although there was little to report at the changing of the guard, it was eight o'clock by the time he finished buying groceries and returned to the condo. The grocery shopping hadn't gone as quickly as he would have liked, but then Alvarez had planned whole investigations with less thought than he'd given to this particular dinner.

Cooking with seduction in mind was one thing, cooking to persuade an edgy pregnant engineer to marry you was another. Alvarez selected salmon steaks, wild rice, and broccoli. He picked up some milk for Tory, a bottle of Champagne for himself, and a lushly decadent chocolate cake. In the bakery department of the grocery store, it suddenly struck him that he wanted to marry Tory, and he didn't even know how she felt about chocolate.

Life was strange sometimes.

Alvarez stepped out of the elevator with his bag of groceries and knocked on Wheatley's door. Getting no response, there was one bad moment when he had the horrible idea that Tory wasn't inside. He fumbled for the duplicate key provided by the building manager.

Once inside the condo, Alvarez saw Tory asleep in the bedroom, fully dressed, curled up in the middle of the bed with her jacket pulled over her for a cover. God forbid she should actually crawl into bed or get a blanket out for herself and take a real nap.

Alvarez left the bag of groceries in the kitchen, returned to the bedroom, sat down on the bed, pulled off his shoes, and quietly stretched out beside her. He seldom had the uninterrupted chance to study something that fascinated him—the light sprinkle of freckles on her white skin, marching over the bridge of her nose to disperse themselves high on her cheekbones, right under dark eyelashes. Those eyelashes fluttered and Tory's eyes halfway opened, focused on him, then opened completely. Gone was the relaxed abandon of unawareness, replaced by a serious frown.

"My God, you could get shot, sneaking up on a person like that," she said without moving, her face inches from his.

"I try to be selective who I sneak up on, and how," he told her, reaching out to stroke her hair. "So far it hasn't backfired."

It was the wrong thing to say. "So far," she repeated, rolled onto her back, and stared at the ceiling. "Any change?"

"Dana Halloran is there now. She'll call if anything happens."

"What time is it?"

"After eight." Alvarez circled the base of her neck with his hand. He could feel a strong, steady pulse, and he pressed his lips against her temple. "We need to talk." He moved his hand down to where her shirt was tucked into her jeans. It was one of those silky, solid-colored shirts that Tory seemed to favor, this one a deep rose. All day long he'd looked at her shirt and hadn't really noticed the color; for some reason it now filled him with optimism.

"Why?" she asked, her voice cool.

"Because it's what people do, that's why. People talk about issues, relationships, decisions; they work things out." He had enough of her shirt untucked so that he could place his hand against her bare stomach. He found it exhilarating to think of the possibilities that lay beneath his splayed fingers.

"Is that right?" Tory asked. She didn't sound so cool now.

"That's right," he told her. "I don't want it to be like the first time."

She closed her eyes as he kissed the side of her neck. "No kidding. This time we're actually on a bed."

Alvarez stopped kissing her. "That's not what I mean. I don't want it to be like the first time I finally got you to talk to me—remember, I had to rescue you from someone shooting at you."

Tory's opened her eyes. "You—" she reached blindly for a pillow. "That's not all that happened." Alvarez barely managed to grab her wrist before she could arm herself. "You're the one who ended up getting held at gunpoint," she said as he pulled her towards him. Tory suddenly used the momentum to roll on top of him. She looked down at him, dark hair falling forward, skimming his face.

"Some men, all they want to do is talk, talk, talk."

"I could do a better job with both arms."

"That's what you keep telling me. More talk. I rest my case."

Alvarez rolled her off and under him in one smooth movement, and sat up just enough to start discarding his clothing. His jacket was the first thing to go. The sling was the second. "Don't do anything rash on my account," she said. He started to unbutton his shirt. "This doesn't really mean anything," Tory told him; Alvarez didn't let it discourage him. He shrugged his shirt off, started unbuttoning hers. That seemed to be as much as Tory could tolerate with her eyes opened; as he reached the last button she clenched them closed. "I mean, how do you know that I'm not just using you to distract myself—"

Alvarez laid a finger at her lips. "Shhhhh," he said. "You don't need to be nervous."

"Right." Her voice sounded brittle. "Tell me something I can believe, something I can understand."

"You are smart and beautiful and clever. And bilingual to boot. You always understand me when I speak Spanish." She opened her eyes then as Alvarez eased her shirt off her shoulders.

"Not always," she said, a stickler for details. "Not all of the things you say."

Alvarez kissed his way from the tip of her nose down to the zipper on her jeans. "Listen," he said, "and I'll tell you things that you can understand." He told her in flowing Spanish how beautiful she was, how fascinating he found the light scattering of freckles across her nose and over her cheekbones, and how her eyes looked so startlingly blue, fringed with lush dark lashes against her pale skin. He told her exactly how he felt about the rose-colored lace panties he discovered when he removed her jeans, the ones that matched the rose-colored lace bra.

"It's because Sylvia packed for me," Tory said. "I don't usually do half as good a job—"

Alvarez got his pants off and pulled Tory back under him, using one of his knees to nudge her legs apart so that his could slip in between. He told her how good it was to feel her skin next to his. Then he turned his attention to her breasts, the warm-up exercises over, and he told her what he wanted to do with her. He had forgotten how literally Tory took everything; he had also forgotten that while she might claim she couldn't understand everything he said, her familiarity with Spanish slang and profanity had startled him in the past.

"Wait," she said.

"What?" He was just being polite, keeping up his end of the conversation. He had no intention of waiting.

"Did you really just say that you want to 'do me till my ears leak?'" She sounded as though she couldn't decide whether to be alarmed or insulted.

"Wrong idiom," he said.

"Wrong idiom, hell." Predictably, she was going for the insult. "What a cop thing to say. You never stop, never turn it off, do you?"

Alvarez kissed her hard enough that further conversation was impossible. It silenced Tory, but it didn't have any effect on the knocking sound coming from the front door. Alvarez started cursing in such trite, profane Spanish he knew for sure that Tory could follow every word. The knocking didn't go away. Then someone yelled, "Police, open up."

Alvarez opened his eyes and stared into Tory's—wide, blue, questioning. She lay perfectly still. "God is punishing me," she whispered. "I told you so."

"That's ridiculous." He scrambled off the bed, pulled on his pants, raked his good hand through his hair, and stalked off to confront the agents of law and order knocking on the front door. When he pulled the door opened, hard enough to let them know just how he felt about this intrusion, two deputies and one policeman stood there. One of the deputies was George Nelson.

Nelson took in Alvarez's appearance without missing a beat in chewing his toothpick. "Sorry to disturb you, Mr. Alvarez, but we need to talk to Vicky."

Alvarez stepped into the hall and closed the door behind him. He spoke only to Nelson, because he figured that Nelson was the one who really mattered. "I don't know what kind of game this is, but you're playing it with the wrong person," he said. His voice sounded ugly even to himself.

Nelson didn't make a move toward the door, but he didn't back up an inch, either. "Sorry to tell you, but it's not a game, Mr. Alvarez. I dropped Vicky off close to five. When did you get here?"

Nelson could check when he'd left the hospital. "A little after eight," Alvarez paused. "What happened?"

"Reynolds is dead."

The words hung in the air. Alvarez opened his mouth to reply, but the seriousness of Nelson's stare made him think better of it. Instead he turned, and opened the door to the condo. The policemen followed.

As soon as they were all inside, the bedroom door swung open, and out walked Tory, fully clothed.

"What were you doing before Mr. Alvarez came back to the condo?" Nelson asked immediately.

"I took a nap." Tory made the four words sound like a curse.

"Any witnesses?"

"None. Is that something I'll come to regret?"

Nelson sighed. "Sit down, Vicky, and let me tell you what's what."

Tory dropped into the nearest chair. "How's that, George? I sit upon command. What comes next? You can always hit me with a rolled up newspaper if I don't behave." Alvarez closed his eyes.

"It's Deputy Nelson," he said, but his voice lacked any personal stake in the comment. "Rolland Reynolds was found dead at his house this afternoon. Our best guess right now is that he was killed sometime between five and seven. You know anything about that, Vicky?"

Tory's eyes never left Nelson's. "No. You dropped me off here, I took a nap, end of story."

"I happen to believe you," said Nelson. "But I was on the scene when we found Reynolds, and believe me, this whole thing's a mess. You may be one of the last people to have seen him alive. When your name came up, one thing led to another, and there's just no way the Sheriff is going to let this go down without hauling your butt in for questioning. You come with us now, cooperate, and it will go a long way toward making this the end of it."

Tory raised her chin, looked at Alvarez. "What do you think?" she asked. Was there just the barest quiver in her voice?

"If he's giving it to us straight, it would be best to go with them," Alvarez admitted. "You don't have to, but they can probably make things difficult for you if you don't." Alvarez was afraid that if Tory refused to cooperate, it would goad the officers into arresting her. It wouldn't be hard for Nelson to turn up a couple witnesses who would swear to hearing Senator Wheatley's daughter threaten Reynolds shortly before he was killed. It might not mean anything of substance, but it would give the police leverage to do whatever they wished in the short term.

"Just don't say anything stupid," he felt compelled to add.

Tory gave him the kind of look his lame remark deserved, then turned to Nelson. "It's going to take a long time, isn't it?"

"They're not going to make it easy for you."

"I need to be able to call my son later."

"That can be arranged," said the cop. Tory ignored him, kept her eyes on Nelson.

"Can I make a phone call now?"

Nelson considered. "If you tell me who you're calling, and you do it out here, maybe."

"Here I was thinking of asking you if I could go down the street and use the pay phone," Tory snapped. "Dana Halloran," she said. "She's a friend of my father's; she's sitting with him this evening. She'll be expecting me to call, and more to the point, she'll wonder what's happened if I don't show up bright and early tomorrow morning."

"Go ahead," said Nelson.

It took a few minutes for Tory to get through to ICU and then to Halloran. "Something's come up," she said into the phone, turning away from the four men for a modicum of privacy. "I'm sorry—I don't have any choice." She listened for a moment, then obviously decided on full disclosure. "I don't want you to worry, but I don't want you to think I'm running out on my responsibilities, either. Two deputies and a policeman are here. Someone who came to see my father this afternoon has been killed, and they want me to go with them to answer some questions. I'm sure it's just a formality, but there's no way of knowing how long it will take." There was another silence while Tory listened. "Yes, it's the same man that Randy told you about, and no, I don't need you to do anything. I'll call you as soon as I can." There was another pause. "Goodnight then. Thanks." Tory turned to Nelson. "I'm ready to go," she said.

"Get a jacket." Nelson and Alvarez said it in unison. Tory gave them both a look, but she went into the bedroom and got her jacket.

"Handcuffs?" she asked Nelson when she returned.

"I think these two will be able to cope without handcuffs." Nelson said mildly.

"You're not coming?"

"No, I'm going to stay and talk with Mr. Alvarez, fill him in on some things, maybe pick his brain."

"Try to leave some for later on," said Tory, and she walked out the door with none of the assurances she'd given Dana Halloran about calling as soon as she was able, and not a single goodbye. That probably was the price for being able to exit on her own terms, but it didn't make Alvarez feel any better.

Nelson turned to him as soon as the others were gone. "You look like a man who wants to punch a hole through a wall," he observed.

"She's pregnant," said Alvarez. He didn't know if he was soliciting an ally or divulging a strategic weakness to an enemy.

Nelson nodded his head. "Kinda has that look to her, now that I think about it." He turned and headed toward the kitchen. "Man with one good arm shouldn't go around punching walls," he said as he left the room. "'Specially not if he wants to hear about a murder scene."

TWENTY-SEVEN

Suspects
Tuesday Evening

SINCE NELSON HAD wandered specifically into the kitchen, Alvarez assumed it wasn't a random action. "Would you like a drink?" he asked, trailing after the deputy, keeping his voice polite as he began to put up the ingredients for the dinner that wasn't to be.

"Don't think so. A piece of that chocolate cake would be

nice, though," Nelson said, "unless you're saving it for some special occasion or something."

Or something. Alvarez cut a large piece of cake, thought what the hell, and cut a second. He got out plates, napkins, forks, and poured two glasses of milk before joining Nelson at the breakfast bar. "Just why would you be willing to tell me about the murder scene?" he asked, pushing Nelson's piece of cake toward him.

"Couple reasons," said Nelson as he began to dig into the cake. Whatever the deputy had found at Reynolds's house, no matter how messy he said it was, it certainly hadn't impaired his appetite. "I don't see how Vicky could be involved. She'd have to get her hands on a gun, and from what I can tell, she's had a full plate ever since she got here. Reynolds lives in a subdivision northwest of town, so she'd have to take a taxi or rent a car to get out there. Those things are easy enough to check."

"There's always hitchhiking, accomplices," said Alvarez automatically, and could have kicked himself.

Nelson eyed Alvarez dubiously. "You been hanging around with Vicky too long, son, if you've taken to shooting your mouth off like that."

Alvarez couldn't argue. "You said there were two reasons you're willing to talk to me. What's the second one?"

"I checked you out, morning after you came in."

"Why?"

Nelson shrugged. "One or two strange things happen, you think maybe it's just a strange night. Three strange things happen, then you think maybe you better check up on things."

"I'm not following you."

"You're not eating your cake, either," Nelson pointed out. "Nothing to lose your appetite over. First, a young woman dies in a mysterious hit-and-run. Second, the man at the scene turns out to be a Texas police detective. Third, there was Vicky."

"What about Vicky—Tory, I mean?" Alvarez asked, irritated with himself for getting tripped up.

"Well, there was little Vicky Wheatley, after all these years, all growed up, and traveling with a police detective. It was enough to make anyone wonder.''

"Wonder what?''

"What she was doing with you, if she wasn't in custody.''

"That's what you decided to check on?'' There was a warning undertone to the question in spite of Alvarez's best efforts.

Nelson looked at him, surprised. "Hell, no. I tried to warn you once. After that, the company you keep, I figure it's your business. I called to check on you. Turns out you're one of the good guys, a real hot shot, they say.''

Alvarez used only the barest moment to wonder who Nelson talked to. "Too bad I haven't had a chance to return the favor,'' he said evenly.

"Me?'' Nelson laughed, swiping up the last of the cake crumbs with his fork. "I may not be a hot shot, but I'm one of the good guys. Anyhow, I figure with your reputation, and you being personally involved and all, you'd run around tomorrow and start digging. Thought I'd save you some time, tell you what's going on, get your take on things.''

"I appreciate that.'' Alvarez wondered if the time would come when he would have to pay for this favor.

"Besides,'' continued Nelson, "I always did have a soft spot for Vicky in spite of myself, but you ever tell her so, all bets are off between us, buddy.''

"She's not exactly what she seems.''

"Who is?'' replied Nelson. "You want to hear about what went down with Reynolds or do you want to talk about more touchy feely stuff?''

"Why do you think I sacrificed a perfectly good virgin chocolate cake?'' asked Alvarez.

"TAYLOR, HE'S GPD, but not the same uniform who was here tonight,'' explained Nelson. The kitchen had lost its appeal after the cake break, and Alvarez followed Nelson back out to the living room, where the deputy made himself comfortable on the couch. "Taylor's a tad lazy, not one to take initiative, you might say. Anyhow, he was pulled up outside Reynolds's house, waiting in his car for me and Doogan—that's the other deputy—to come and make everything kosher for talking to Reynolds all official-like. Only problem is, the time Taylor spent sitting in his car, he coulda maybe looked up, seen that Reynolds's door wasn't closed all the way.'' Nelson paused, shook his head. ''All water under the bridge now. Doogan and I roll up a little bit after seven, get Taylor, and we go up to the front door together. Ring the doorbell, no answer, and there's the door standing cracked open maybe six inches.''

''So you go inside,'' said Alvarez.

''Yeah, and we didn't get far. A little ways into the entry hall, there's Reynolds lying in a pool of blood, took a big one right in the chest. 'Rahowa' is spray-painted in black on the wall beside him.''

''Sounds like someone wanted to leave a major clue.''

Nelson reached in his pocket, took out a toothpick. ''Thing is, Sledge tells us how it's important to make sure 'Rahowa' is written in red spray paint. Says it's a problem when he has to do a red car, but hey, what job doesn't have its problems?''

''Interesting. Maybe Sledge told you that to throw you off?''

''Maybe, but I don't think Sledge is that bright. And then what's the point of writing the damn thing there anyhow, he don't want it to lead back to him and his groups?''

''You've got me there,'' admitted Alvarez.

''Anyhow,'' continued Nelson, ''we scope out the rest of the house, make sure no one's there, then Taylor gets all upset. He wants to start talking to me about who's gonna be in charge, since it was his interview and his case, but now we've got a homicide outside city limits. I'm trying to get him to tell me how long he's been sitting out front, and things maybe get a little heated in our conversation, so I tell Doogan to call it in. Doogan goes back out to our car, I'm standing there having my discussion with Taylor, and next thing I know someone pushes open the front door and comes in with a gun yelling, 'Where are you, Reynolds, you son of a bitch?' ''

''A guy walks into the house to kill Reynolds with two cop

cars sitting outside?'' Alvarez asked in amazement. This was the very definition of *cojones*.

"What can I say? He was more than just a little unhinged. You know, like he'd worked himself all up to do something, and now he was gonna do it by God, no matter how many people tried to get in his way.''

"Anyone we know?''

"I thought I said. It was Todd Cooper, Amy Cooper's husband.''

"Of course," said Alvarez, as though this made perfect sense.

"Anyhow, Cooper's standing there with a gun in his hand, but holding it loose down at his side like he doesn't really know what to do with it. Taylor pulls out his piece and I think he's gonna cap Cooper, so I get between them and I tell Cooper to drop the gun and he looks at me and tells me that he's come to kill Reynolds and nobody's gonna stop him, that Reynolds killed his wife and so now he has to die. I figure the thing to do is point out how Reynolds is on the floor behind Taylor, already dead. Then Cooper really flips out and starts yelling at Taylor, asking why he killed the son of a bitch Reynolds when it was his wife got killed, not Taylor's. Dumb fuck doesn't even know Taylor hasn't got a wife, since number three wised up and left him about a year ago.'' The memory of flailing guns and testosterone-laden yelling had brought out a fine sheen of perspiration on Nelson's forehead. He paused to wipe it before going on.

"Then Taylor starts yelling at Cooper that he's gonna shoot if Cooper doesn't put his piece down, and I figure with me standing in the middle, I'm gonna get shot by both of them. Doogan's at the front door now asking me what I want him to do, and I say get the gun, so he tackles Taylor.''

"Taylor was the only one pointing a firearm at someone?'' Alvarez needed some clarification. Nelson nodded. "Good man, Doogan,'' said Alvarez. Nelson nodded again.

"While Taylor and Doogan are wrestling on the floor, I walk over and take the gun away from Cooper. Then the guy sits down on the floor and starts bawling like a baby.''

"What kind of gun did Cooper have?"

"Little bitty thing—not the same gun that plugged Reynolds, that's for sure."

"So test Cooper to see if he's fired a gun."

Nelson sighed. "I wish it was that simple. Turns out Cooper's never shot a gun before. He tells us that he made up some story about feeling threatened after his wife's accident, then borrowed the gun from a buddy. He says he went out in the country today and practiced shooting it."

"So Cooper may be an inept, grief-stricken individual, prevented from committing an act of violence by the timely appearance of law enforcement officers."

"That would play a lot better if our timely appearance had stopped Reynolds from getting capped." Nelson shook his head. "Cooper may be a really devious, clever individual, who shot Reynolds, figured he'd be fingered as a suspect, ditched the murder weapon and came up with the second gun and the hysterical act to draw suspicion away from himself."

"Pretty effective," Alvarez observed. "Be kind of hard to come up with all that on the spur of the moment."

"Yeah, but he's one of those engineer nerd types. Those kind, sometimes you can't hardly tell the difference, them being really brilliant and being really devious."

"There is that," agreed Alvarez. "So what set Cooper off? GPD asking about the letters they found in Amy's office?"

Nelson shook his head. "GPD couldn't find Cooper this afternoon to question him. That fits with his story about going out to practice shooting."

"So why did Cooper go after Reynolds now? Did he find some letters at home? Maybe letters from Reynolds to his wife?"

"He's being real coy about that," said Nelson. "Tells us he knew his wife was having an affair with Reynolds, but he was willing to put up with it, wait it out. Kept saying if he'd only gotten her to move to Atlanta with him, things would have been okay."

"Why does Cooper think Reynolds killed Amy?"

"He says his wife knew things about stuff Reynolds was doing, stuff Reynolds didn't want anyone to know. Stuff Cooper can't define, of course. You got any idea what he might be talking about?''

Alvarez shook his head. "There's bad blood between Tory and Reynolds, but it's old grudge type of stuff, not anything that I can tie to Amy Cooper. If Cooper thought Reynolds killed his wife, why wait three days to do something? Did something set him off, or was he just working up his nerve all this time?''

"Something set him off, okay. He says he has proof that Reynolds killed his wife.''

"What?''

"You're not going to believe this when I tell you, but Cooper's telling us some story about the kind of work he does in this field office for a traffic engineering company. Says they're monitoring traffic patterns on 39th Avenue, the street that runs out to the airport. Cooper says the Department of Transportation paid for cameras to be mounted in the traffic signals on 39th.'' Nelson shook his head in disgust.

"Cooper has pictures of Reynolds driving the hit-and-run vehicle out to the airport?''

Nelson shook his head. "Cooper says he was analyzing data at the office today, first day that he'd been into work, and he started looking at stuff from the traffic light at 39th and Waldo Road, the last light between town and the airport. Cooper says there were pictures of Reynolds heading toward the airport a little while before Amy was killed, and pictures of him driving back, with someone in the passenger seat, thirty minutes later. He took the pictures home, thought about it, decided that Reynolds had to die.''

"Cooper thinks Reynolds hired out the hit and then went out to pick up the driver after the killer torched the hit-and-run car?'' Nelson nodded. "That's pretty circumstantial. Can you ID the passenger?''

"We'll never know,'' said Nelson. "I told you this was messy. GPD sent a unit over to Cooper's house. They couldn't get there because the street was blocked. Cooper's house burned to the ground this afternoon.''

"Arson?"

"We don't know yet, but I'll give you any odds you want."

Alvarez shook his head. "So either Cooper is very clever—"

"Or whoever was supposed to make sure that Amy Cooper never told anyone what she knew about Reynolds, dead or alive, that person completed the job this afternoon by torching the house," Nelson finished for him. "We asked Cooper about it, and according to him, between neighbors and other people coming over to be helpful after his wife's death, there was always someone in the house until this afternoon when he went off to practice shooting."

"Then this might be the first chance someone had to finish the job," mused Alvarez. "Why not torch Amy's office, too?"

Nelson shrugged. "Who knows? Not enough time, or someone knew her well enough to know that the really incriminating stuff would be at her house. Or, Cooper set the fire himself. Photos, letters, any references to this shady stuff Reynolds was doing, poof, it all goes up in smoke. Wish there was someone we could talk to, find out whether this stuff he's telling us about Big Brother in stoplights is true or not."

"Why not talk to his coworkers?"

"Only one other guy here in the office with Cooper."

"Talk to him, then."

"Turns out he's the guy who lent Cooper the gun. They're college roommates, go back a long ways."

"Bummer," said Alvarez. Nelson looked glum.

"We'll call the home office in Atlanta in the morning. See if we can get them to cooperate, or if engineers have developed some kind of client privilege shit like every other type of professional we talk to these days. If that's the case, we'll have to get fucking DOT to sign off on them talking to us." Nelson frowned. "If we have to subpoena those DOT assholes, maybe we can work out a deal where they have to share all the stuff from their Peeping Tom stoplights. No one wants to help the police these days, and I bet fucking DOT won't be any exception."

"You could ask Tory about it," Alvarez suggested.

Nelson blinked. "Why would I want to ask Vicky about Cooper's tale of Big Brother in the stoplights?"

"She's an engineer."

"No shit?" Nelson thought about this. "Think she'd be willing to talk to me?"

"I don't know, I guess it depends on how it goes for her tonight. I'm just hoping she doesn't stop talking to me because of guilt by association." A phone rang. Alvarez started to look around to answer it, then realized it was Nelson's.

"Yeah? You sure?" Nelson said into his cell phone. "She agreed to that? Anybody ask her why she didn't think of it before? Well, shit, don't that beat all? So you're taking her out now? Tell Vicky I'm waiting to talk to her when she gets back here." Alvarez was ashamed to find that he was relieved Nelson was going to stick around for Tory's return. "Tell her that her friend Mr. Alvarez has a real nice chocolate cake—maybe that will cheer her up and make her feel like chatting." When hell freezes over. "Yeah." Nelson spoke that one last word into his phone and hung up. "Turns out our Vicky came up with an alibi after all."

So it was "our Vicky," now that Nelson thought Tory might be able to help him.

"What alibi?" Alvarez asked.

"A woman named Dana Halloran turned up, that ring a bell for you? Seems she was mad as a wet hen, and swore up and down that she'd called Tory from a pay phone this afternoon, right at six o'clock, and Tory answered."

"What did Tory say?"

"My guys say that she looked as surprised as they were, then she played right along and said that was what happened. Said she was napping and the call woke her up and she couldn't really remember the time, but if Halloran said it was six p.m., then that must be when it was. Convenient, her claiming not to remember the exact time after Halloran told our guys she made the call at six p.m." Nelson cocked his head at Alvarez. "Think our Vicky would forget something like that?"

"Did your guys ask the two women what they discussed—

ask them separately, I mean?'' Alvarez asked, sidestepping Nelson's question.

"Of course they asked them. We may not be from the big city here, compared to El Paso, but we're not stupid.''

"So what did they say?''

"They both said that they talked about who would sit with Wheatley tomorrow.''

Of course. Alvarez didn't want to discuss his opinion of the veracity of this alibi any further. "So, with Tory out of the picture, who does that leave?''

"Cooper, for one. And the guy who did the hit-and-run, if that turns out to be the case. He may have decided to collect his money and clean up the loose ends all at the same time.''

Alvarez shook his head. "That doesn't play for me.''

"Me either,'' said Nelson, "but we'll have to look at it. We'll have to look at Sledge and Frank Paxton and all their buddies, and anyone else who hassled Reynolds over the type of work they did at this Center for State Heritage Studies. We'll have to look at Reynolds's wife.''

"I thought she was in Puerto Rico.''

"That's what we think, too. Thing is, her father is tied to organized crime over there. Those kind of people don't take too well to their son-in-laws running around with the hired help.''

"Sounds like Reynolds was into a little bit of everything.''

"Doesn't it just. Then there's the phantom stuff that Cooper claims his wife knew about. If it was worth killing one person over, then maybe it's worth killing two.''

"Chloe Marshall,'' said Alvarez suddenly. "I think you should look at her.''

"What for?''

"She came over here one night, apologized for Reynolds chasing a contribution from Tory's father at ICU, thought it was tacky. She didn't approve of the way Reynolds went around doing things.''

"Still not a reason to kill him.''

Alvarez thought about the Rosewood box. "Did you know

that Dr. Marshall did the research that resulted in her husband being named a Rosewood survivor?''

''I remember something about that,'' said Nelson. ''So what?''

''So her husband's father was a winner in the Florida hate crime lottery,'' said Alvarez.

Nelson raised an eyebrow. ''I'm pretty sure that what you just said isn't politically correct.''

Alvarez didn't let himself get sidetracked. ''To the tune of $150,000,'' he continued, ''which he left to his son, Richard Marshall, now married to Chloe Marshall, who works with Reynolds. Then there was an adoptive great-aunt who was named as a survivor. She didn't have any relatives, so she left her $150,000 to Richard Marshall, too.''

''Where are you going with this?'' asked Nelson.

''I'm adding $150,000 and $150,000 and coming up with $300,000. What if the authenticity of these two supposed survivors was rigged, and Reynolds was in on it somehow?''

Nelson stared at Alvarez. ''Have you ever heard of JanitorAll?'' he asked.

''Janitorial?''

''No,'' said Nelson, and he spelled it for Alvarez.

''I don't care how you spell it,'' replied Alvarez. ''I still haven't heard of it, and what does it have to do with $300,000?''

''JanitorAll is the business Richard Marshall started twenty years ago. About five years back, he franchised it, hit the jackpot. It was real sad, he and his wife had built the business up from a two-person deal into this big outfit, then she up and dies—had some kind of chronic heart disease. That's when Marshall met the second Mrs. Marshall, when she was doing the Rosewood research you're so all fired up about.''

''What are you trying to tell me?'' asked Alvarez.

''Remember when I told you about the hullabaloo over Marshall buying a house in Haile Plantation?'' Alvarez nodded. ''Well, Marshall didn't buy just any house. He bought the biggest, fanciest house out there. Richard Marshall is probably worth every bit as much as Vicky's old man.''

Alvarez shook his head in surrender. Never overlook the obvious, he reminded himself. Everyone kept telling him that Marshall was loaded, but he had just assumed that was post-inheriting $300,000.

Nelson might call him a hot shot, but Alvarez knew enough to know that he was playing blind, without the home team advantage.

TWENTY-EIGHT

Herky-Jerky
Tuesday Evening

DEPUTY DOOGAN delivered Tory to the front door and Nelson asked him to wait in the car. The young deputy left with a relieved expression on his face.

Tory walked in the door, took off her jacket and took a good look at the two men sitting in the living room of her father's condo. Damned if they didn't look like they wanted something. Alvarez wanting something she could understand all right, but why was Nelson hanging around? "Have a nice heart-to-heart while I was gone?" she asked them.

They looked at each other as though trying to decide who would field the question. "Nelson told me about the Reynolds case," said Alvarez finally. "There may be some engineering aspects involved. He hoped you might be able to answer some basic questions."

Tory stared at him. "You've got to be kidding. I go from having to account for my whereabouts to being asked to help out with the investigation? It's enough to give a person whiplash."

"Why don't you sit down, have something to eat first?" asked Nelson. "Someone in your condition—" His words faltered as both Tory and Alvarez stared at him.

Tory looked at Alvarez. "You *told* him?"

"All I'm saying is that there's some mighty good chocolate cake in the kitchen," said Nelson, looking back and forth between Tory and Alvarez, backpedaling fast.

"I *know* you," Tory told Nelson, "and I *know* him. He told you I was pregnant, didn't he?"

Nelson got to his feet. "Listen, this is between the two of you. If you're going to have a fight—"

"You're not going to stay to provide backup?" she asked.

"Tory—" said Alvarez warningly, but she didn't listen.

"Aren't you going to threaten me with something?" she asked Nelson. "Use some kind of leverage to get my cooperation? Isn't that how it usually works?"

"There's the alibi," interjected Alvarez. Now he stood up, too. "If they really wanted to, they could probably check—"

Tory didn't give him a chance to finish telling her what "they" could probably check. "Just exactly what do you think I should have done instead, *Detective* Alvarez? Leave that poor, well-intentioned woman out on a limb, lying through her teeth to the nice policemen?"

"I'm not hearing this," Nelson declared.

Alvarez said in his cop voice, "That's enough, Tory." He gave her a warning look as though he could will her into silence, and she gave him a warning look right back.

Nelson put a hand on Alvarez's shoulder. "I think she's saying that she's tired of having people tell her what to do."

"Sounds to me like she's telling us she wants to be locked up somewhere, the stuff she's saying," replied Alvarez, shrugging off Nelson's hand. He was pissed, so now the two men were no longer united in a common cause. Tory felt a childish sense of elation.

Nelson spoke to Tory. "Mr. Alvarez here told me that you're an engineer. I thought, good for you, little Vicky going off and doing something like that, something that doesn't have anything to do with her daddy's connections or her daddy's money. Hell, from what it looks like to me, you don't even go around getting into trouble regularly anymore."

"Don't jump to conclusions," threw in Alvarez, but Nelson ignored him.

"So your friend here, he's right. I have some questions I thought maybe you could answer, but only if you want to."

"Technical questions," added Alvarez, as though she couldn't figure that out. "But Deputy Nelson's questions aren't in your area of expertise. I didn't want to get his hopes up. I knew you wouldn't want to lead him on, have him think he could get something out of you if you weren't going to be able to deliver."

"If I commit to something, I'll come through, don't worry about that," she replied.

"It's not the commitment part that bothers me—I worry about you going off half-cocked, doing something self-destructive."

George Nelson gave an exaggerated sigh and sat down again, looking distinctly uncomfortable. "Look, I just wanted to ask you about some stuff Cooper's husband told us, has to do with his job. I can probably get my answers somewhere else—"

Tory shifted her focus to Nelson, took a deep breath and asked, "What kind of engineering questions?"

"Traffic," Alvarez answered for him.

"Maybe we could all have a piece of cake while we're talking about it," said Nelson, and Alvarez stood up.

"I'll get it," said Alvarez.

"I hope you can manage okay, with your injured arm and all," Tory said. Then she turned her attention to George Nelson's tale. By the time Alvarez returned with refreshments, she had the gist of the story. "It sounds plausible," she told Nelson. "This Todd Cooper told you he was looking at pictures, not video?"

"I can't remember," said Nelson, splitting his attention between Tory and his slice of chocolate cake. "Why? Does it mean something?"

"I'm not a traffic engineer," she told him, "so what I'm telling you is just off the top of my head. But if he doesn't claim to be using continuous video, that makes the whole thing sound more credible to me."

"Why?"

"It has to do with the way you collect and transmit information. Sophisticated video systems generally require fiber optics, and it costs a lot of money to wire for fiber. You might find a system like that in a city where they're doing traffic enforcement through surveillance cameras. You don't have that here, do you?"

Nelson shook his head. "I've heard about those systems. Private companies install equipment to photograph people running red lights. They send out the citations, get a take of the revenues. But not here—the way Gainesville is, with the university and all the academic liberals, it would take an act of God for us to get a system like that. That's why I have a hard time buying Cooper's claims."

"Academic liberals?" inquired Alvarez. "And you told me I wasn't being politically correct."

Nelson ignored him. "I can understand the concept of surveillance at intersections for law enforcement purposes. What I can't understand is how DOT could get away with doing something we'd have our butts kicked for, especially if we did it without proper notification and permission of the voters and all."

"DOT can do things you've never imagined." said Tory. "What Cooper is describing sounds like a preliminary study of some kind. For something like that you'd probably use telephone lines, generate time-elapse images instead of continuous video." She paused a moment, trying to retrieve someone else's jargon. "There's something that traffic engineers call it. I remember— herky-jerky."

"Herky-jerky?" asked Nelson, tentatively enough that Tory wondered if the term had other meanings.

"Pictures taken at timed intervals. A study of traffic patterns— origin and destination studies—only requires data about when and how many vehicles are on the road. A system like that doesn't have to be able to identify the make of a car or who's driving it."

Nelson frowned. "So maybe it's all jive then, Cooper telling us he could place Reynolds's vehicle at a specific intersection the night of his wife's death?"

"No," said Tory, thinking about it, trying to retrieve more information from long-term memory. "That's not what I'm saying. If Cooper knew what kind of car Reynolds drove, he might be able to identify it from a herky-jerky system. He could verify by checking the license plate number."

"Wait," said Alvarez. "I thought you just said that these

kinds of studies aren't concerned with identifying individual vehicles."

"Well, they are and they aren't," Tory hedged. "It depends on the type of study. Sometimes license plate numbers are recorded in case that's needed later."

Nelson looked indignant. "So while we're out patrolling the streets, trying to keep people safe from crime, DOT may have records of every single damn vehicle that goes up and down 39th Avenue and the time they were there?"

"Maybe," said Tory. "If what Todd Cooper is describing turns out to be true."

"Fucking DOT," muttered Nelson, sounding downright jealous. "What the hell do *they* need license plate numbers for?"

"I'm trying to recall," said Tory. "I think that sometimes they do follow-up studies. Some places started doing follow-ups on origin and destination studies in the sixties, I think." She grimaced at Nelson. "I'm trying to remember this stuff from back when I was in school, and that was a while ago."

"It's okay," said Nelson. "You're doing fine."

"They'd write down license plate numbers at a certain intersection, look up the registration, and send out a questionnaire asking the owner where he or she was going and how often he or she made this particular trip."

"What happened then?"

"I think they stopped pretty soon," Tory admitted. "I think there were lots of calls from irate people wanting to know what was going on—they knew perfectly well their spouse or kid or whoever was out of town or at work, and not at some particular intersection across town."

"So how can Cooper's outfit be doing this kind of stuff for DOT, and nobody knows about it?" asked Nelson. "Just let us set up DUI checkpoints on New Year's Eve, and we get blasted for invasion of privacy."

Tory had never thought about it like that. "I guess they have their studies set up so they don't have to ask anyone questions anymore," she theorized. "They just go out and collect the information, and unless you're in DOT or traffic engineering, no one knows about it."

Nelson considered what she had to say. "Fucking DOT," he said again.

"So it's possible that what Cooper's saying could be true?" asked Alvarez.

"It's possible," she said. "If the images were transmitted somehow, there should be a way to retrieve them. But if they were collected from a device installed in the traffic signal itself, your only proof burned up in the fire you say happened at his house."

"They have a bigger budget than we do," said Nelson. "Least they could do is take duplicate pictures."

"Let it go," said Alvarez. "That's all you're going to get for tonight." Nelson looked at Alvarez, seemed to remember where he was and that he could take a hint. Before he left, he thanked Tory for her help and told them both that he had really enjoyed the chocolate cake.

Alvarez closed the door behind Nelson and turned back to Tory. "You okay?" he asked.

"Everyone keeps asking me that."

"Last time I asked, Reynolds wasn't dead."

He had a point. "I mainly feel numb," Tory said. "I couldn't stand Rolland, I thought he was a horrible person, but it's strange knowing someone walked up to his door and shot him, just hours after I felt like killing him myself." She hurried to explain. "I just felt like it, I wouldn't have actually killed him. I don't think," she added.

"I hope you put it a little differently when you talked to the detectives," said Alvarez. "Two different methods supports the supposition that there are two different killers. But both victims worked at the same place, and both of them had contact with you shortly before they died. I wouldn't want to see things get blown out of proportion, the idea that these deaths are somehow connected to you."

Tory waved away his concerns. "You worry too much. Now I'll never get a chance to get to the bottom of the things Rolland was telling me. I'll never get a chance to figure out if what he was saying is true."

"Maybe it's best not to know," Alvarez replied. "Kind of like that song says."

"What song?"

"The one we talked about earlier, 'Even the Losers.' It says something about how life's a drag if you're living in the past."

"I think you've been spending too much time listening to that tape."

"We could spend time doing something else. We could pick up where we left off."

"I don't think so," said Tory. But Alvarez did look appealing, appearing fully capable of handling anything that might come along in spite of having an arm back in a sling again. He was leaning against the door and studying her in that intense way he had, as though she were the only thing that mattered. The problem was, she knew what it was like to be the object of that gaze when it wasn't tinged with passion.

"Last thing you said, before we had visitors, was that God was punishing you. Then you get back here and all of a sudden, I'm one of the enemy. I think I preferred the God version. Seems like I might have had a chance of convincing you you're not being punished."

Tory considered this, decided it had definite appeal, but rejected it anyhow. "The problem is, if I sleep with you tonight, I'll be sleeping with a cop."

"Define sleep," said Alvarez.

"Define cop," she shot back.

"Define hard-to-get."

That was hitting below the belt. "You told me I could choose."

He frowned. "I want to make sure you make the right choice." All of a sudden, he didn't look like a cop any more. He looked like a man who was tired and frustrated. It unexpectedly pulled at her heartstrings, but Tory had already made her decision.

"How's your arm?" she asked.

"Getting better all the time." It sounded like an automatic response.

"Would you tell me if it wasn't?"

Alvarez frowned again, considering. "I'd have to think about it," he admitted.

"At least that's a start."

He looked surprised at having given the right answer for once. "A start at what?"

"Not being a cop all the time."

He grinned. "Insults will get you nowhere. I could still throw you over my shoulder, injured arm and all, and carry you off to bed. And you'd like it. No handcuffs, no Kevlar underwear, and I won't even refer to the bedroom as the pokey, just for you."

His unexpected humor was her undoing. Even after an evening in which she'd been detained and questioned in a murder investigation, he could still make her smile. Suddenly all of her carefully thought-out conclusions seemed questionable. "I need a shower," she said. Those were the only words that came to mind.

His grin widened. "That's doable," he told her.

"That wasn't a yes," she said, alarmed at how quickly both her feelings and the conversation had taken another turn.

"It wasn't a no," he replied, already across the room.

Only a cop took the absence of a no to mean yes. "Cop, cop, cop," she called him, but it lacked conviction. Then he actually had her over his shoulder and was heading for the bedroom. Tory-the-engineer noted that she had been accurately forewarned about exactly how she'd get carried away.

IT QUICKLY BECAME APPARENT to Tory that David Alvarez was going to make love to her in the shower. "This isn't easy for me," she told him as he removed her shirt for the second time that day.

"You're doing just fine," he assured her. He sat her up on the counter by the sink and started removing her shoes. "What's the problem?"

"I'm embarrassed."

"We could turn out the lights."

"No." Tory said it more emphatically than she had intended. "If you get injured in front of me one more time, I'll know it's me."

"There is that," he agreed. Her shoes and socks discarded, he lifted her down from the vanity and started taking off her jeans. "Think of it this way—if you start to feel nauseated, we're in close proximity to the toilet."

He started shedding his clothes and she squeezed her eyes shut. "Is that a problem you encounter often?" she asked.

"Nausea during lovemaking?" She could hear the smile in his voice. "Not unless I start referring to my big night stick, or stop to ask my partner how fast she's going."

Maybe talking dirty in another language was less mortifying, but Tory remembered they'd tried that already. She heard the water start, then Alvarez removed her bra. "Partner, now there's an interesting term," she said. How stupid did she look, standing in the bathroom half naked, having a conversation with her eyes closed? "Have you done this with many women?"

Alvarez went very still. She could almost hear him thinking— cop think—have I made love to another woman in the bathroom of this condo? "Never," he said emphatically.

At least one of them should be perfectly honest. "This isn't a package deal," she told him as he guided her through stepping out of her underwear. "It doesn't mean anything about the baby, and it doesn't mean I'll marry you."

He took her hand and led her into the steamy shower. "Well damn," he said, his voice having taken on a husky tone she remembered so well. "I'll have to stop then. I can't make love to you if you're not going to marry me. I don't happen to believe in irresponsible sex," he added, and Tory realized that he was feeding back the same words she'd told him on a previous occasion. Did the man ever forget anything?

She opened her eyes. "Are you serious?" she asked.

He looked down at her, water running off his dark wet hair and down his face. His smile was totally self-assured, which was good, since it meant one of them was. "About stopping, *querida?* Never."

And then Tory lost track of the conversation and her questions and his answers. He told the truth about one thing. Awkward, shy, and self-conscious, she still liked being carried away. She liked it very much indeed. Her engineering mind filed that away as another thing to worry about at a later date.

TWENTY-NINE

The Calm
January 3, 1923. Rosewood, Florida

LISSY MIGHT BE old enough to be included in the adult conversations at the Carrier household, but she was no longer considered old enough to mind the children. As more and more adults gathered at the house, there were plenty of women to take care of the growing group of children, who were impatient and unruly from staying inside day after day.

Haywood Carrier, Sylvester's father, was still away on a hunting trip, but the rest of the Carriers gathered at the two-story house in response to The Man's call to collect and unite together. Aaron Carrier's parents, Emma and James, came, and with them more children and grandchildren. Aaron's parents had no idea where their son was, and there was only The Man's account to give them hope that maybe, somehow, he had avoided the same fate as Sam Carter.

Lissy heard Emma Carrier tell Aunt Sarah how the white men, desperate for new direction in their manhunt, had gone back to Aaron's and this time found his wife, confused at having returned to an empty house. Emma Carrier said the mob dragged Mizz Mahulda off into the woods, screaming that she didn't know anything, that her husband had been home sick, and where was he now? No one knew any more about Mizz Mahulda's fate than they knew about Aaron's.

Other people gathered at the Carrier house too, people Lissy didn't know, people who weren't related to the Carriers. Men, mainly, coming in from Otter Creek, Cedar Key, and places too small to have a name other than a reference to the distance from the nearest town. These men mostly brought rifles with them instead of families. They talked about how they'd already fought in one white man's war and it was time to put to use the lessons they had learned.

Aunt Sarah wasn't happy with what was happening in her house. Her husband might be gone, but she was the one in charge. Lissy happened to be following hard on her heels, hoping to find something useful to do, when Aunt Sarah was descending the stairs and her son was on his way up. Aunt Sarah stopped so suddenly that Lissy almost ran into her.

"I don' like this," Lissy heard Aunt Sarah tell her son in a voice that wouldn't carry any farther than where they stood, eyeing each other on the staircase. "You maybe think this the right thing to do, but you just giving them white mens more to drink and worry over. No way all these niggers be coming here to this house, coming with guns, talking 'bout a war that's done and over with, and nobody take notice. You give a care, boy, there be babies here."

"I know there be babies here," Sylvester replied. "Gussie and my babies here, you think I be such a fool I don' know that? Sam Carter never had no chance when they come for him, Mamma. You think on that."

"Don' talk at me like I be a fool, son. I know what happened to Sam Carter, and I don' want no more happening here."

Sylvester sighed. "I know you no fool, Mamma. Those same men that killed Sam, they got a taste for it now. They know we be ready, we be willing to fight back, then they think twice afore they start up again. There be safety in numbers, safety in being ready. There be no safety in anything else," he added.

"Syl, you gonna promise me that with all this you be doing, nobody gonna get hurt?" Lissy had never heard anyone, not even Gussie, call The Man "Syl" before.

There was a brief silence before The Man replied. "I promise you," he said finally, "that we not gonna give up anything we have here, not without a fight."

Aunt Sarah shook her head, went on downstairs into the kitchen and started giving directions to the women cooking in there. This left Lissy and The Man standing on the staircase staring at each other. Sylvester gave her a quick grin. "How you be doing, Lissy Hodden?"

There had never been room for lies between them. "I be scared," said Lissy. "When I gots something to do, it's not so bad. But your sisters, your aunts, they taking care of the children, and there's nothing for me to do."

The Man looked at Lissy hard this time, considering. "I gots something you can do, Lissy Hodden, but it be a big thing, a thing you need to think on afore you say you'll do it." Lissy nodded solemnly to indicate that she understood the seriousness of his words. "You know it's not safe, Negro men be out on the street right now." Lissy nodded again. She knew what Sylvester was talking about. Unexpectedly, at any time of the day, small groups of armed white men would show up, walking the streets of Rosewood, looking, looking. So far, that was all they did, walk the streets and look.

"I know that," she said. She fervently hoped that whatever The Man asked, her quaking heart would be brave enough to do it.

"I wants you to go to John Wright's store," said The Man.

"What's so big about that?" she asked, the words rushing out of her mouth before she knew it, she was so relieved at this request. But The Man didn't smile, if anything, he looked even more serious.

"I wants you to go there, and wait 'til there be nobody in the store but you and John Wright. Then you tell him Sylvester sent you, that Sylvester says there's gonna be trouble, and that Sylvester Carrier be asking him to do the right thing. You think you could do that, baby, tell him those very words?"

"Sylvester sent me, Sylvester says there's gonna be trouble, and Sylvester Carrier be asking him to do the right thing," repeated Lissy flawlessly. "I can go to Mr. Wright's store and do that."

The Man gave her one of his brilliant smiles, the serious look gone from his face. "Thank you, baby," he said, and kissed her forehead. "You be careful. You make sure you go when there's no men out on the street, you hear? And you gets back here soon's you can." Then Sylvester headed on up the stairs and Lissy headed on down. No one seemed to notice when she slipped outside.

It was a cold, clear day, and everything seemed normal except for the fact that there wasn't a soul to be seen on the streets of Rosewood. Lissy made her way to John Wright's store without seeing a single other person, and she delivered Sylvester's words without a single mistake.

John Wright was a short, good-tempered man with a wide mustache that always seemed to frame a smile, but he wasn't smiling today. "You go stand over by the door," he told her sharply, "and if anyone comes in you go away and come back later. You understand that, missy?"

Lissy nodded her understanding and went to stand by the door as she was told. John Wright disappeared from sight and Lissy wondered how long she was going to have to stand there. She wondered where he had gone, what he was doing, and what she would do if he came back and ignored her. She resolved that for today, she would not be ignored. She would repeat Sylvester's words again and again as many times as she needed to.

She didn't have to wait long. John Wright came back with a flour sack that was full of something a lot bumpier than flour. It was heavy when he handed it to Lissy.

"Anyone ever asks about this, I never gave it to you, you understand?" Lissy nodded, but that wasn't enough. "I mean it," he warned her. "Anyone ever tells, I'll say Sylvester came over here and held a gun on me, made me give him this. You understand that, little girl?" Lissy nodded again. Secret upon secret seemed to pile up on her slight shoulders, heavier than the sack she was now holding. "Then what are you doing still standing here, girl? You get out of here, get on home, and don't be coming back."

Lissy ran all the way back to the Carrier house. She never even stopped to peek into the sack John Wright had given her until she reached the Carriers' back door.

The sack was full of boxes and boxes of bullets. Lissy knew that they were bullets for the guns those strange men were bringing to Rosewood. And they were bringing themselves and their guns in response to a promise made by The Man.

THIRTY

Research
Wednesday Morning

ALVAREZ WOKE EARLY. Tory was sprawled on her stomach next to him, sleeping the sleep of the truly exhausted. She was wearing one of his shirts, which was the closest thing handy for him to grab when he finally carried her to bed last night, and he thought it looked damned good on her. All that creamy skin with scatterings of freckles where they were least expected. She had been surprisingly shy and reticent for someone who could be so in-your-face at other times. Dormant passions waiting to be mined. He started to ease the shirt off Tory's shoulder, and she woke up.

Her eyes, inches from his, widened and were immediately alert. "Oh my God," she said, giving equal emphasis to each word.

"It's still okay to call me David," he assured her, still focused on the task of getting his shirt off her.

She pushed his hand away. "Don't be ridiculous. I'm late—I need to get to the hospital."

Alvarez hoisted himself up on his good elbow so he could look down at her. "I thought we could try something new, *querida*—making love in bed. Reliable sources say it can be quite pleasurable."

She reddened, wouldn't look at him any more. "I'll bet you didn't need any reliable sources," she muttered. "I mean it, David, I told Dana I would be there first thing—"

"And the least you can do for someone who lies through their teeth for you is be punctual," he finished for her, kissing her nose. "A rain check then, but one that's good in any kind of weather. So if you're in such a hurry, what are we waiting for?"

Tory studied his collarbone. "I'm waiting for you to leave."

"Ah," he nodded. "Still shy. If you're in such a hurry, it's a good thing you don't have to take a shower. I tried to be diligent—I don't think I missed anywhere last night." Tory went from slightly red to scarlet. Alvarez had mercy on her, scrambled out of bed, started to get dressed.

"You have your sling on again," she said suddenly.

"Yeah," he answered, shrugging into a clean shirt. "I put it back on last night, after you went to sleep. The arm is bothering me some, no big deal."

"I'm sorry—" she started.

"I thought you were too shy to look," he interrupted, turning around. Tory pulled the covers over her head and Alvarez laughed. "Okay, I won't tease you any more, at least not right now. What would you like for breakfast, *cara*?"

Her answer was muffled, coming from under the covers. "Something quick. Something easy. How about chocolate cake?"

THERE WAS A SMALL GROUP gathered around Wheatley's bed when Tory and Alvarez arrived at ICU. Dana Halloran turned to Tory, a bright smile on her face, and said "They think we can be optimistic now, dear. Tom may have woken up for just a bit late last night—he seemed to mutter something. The night nurse thinks he was asking where he was."

Alvarez looked at the man lying on the bed. Was it just the power of suggestion, or did Wheatley appear more like someone in a light sleep than he had the day before? One of two men in white coats standing bedside with Dana Halloran and Randy Sosa made it official.

"There's definitely some movement, more activity on his part. I think we can be optimistic that he's going to regain consciousness."

"When?" Tory asked.

The doctor shrugged. "I can't say. My best guess would be today or tomorrow. But keep in mind that's just the first step. When your father wakes up, he's bound to be confused, disoriented. There will probably be short-term memory loss, maybe some long term. There's always the chance of—" The doctor seemed to remember that he was giving a message of optimism and stopped himself from further elaboration, which was good, for neither Dana Halloran or Tory were listening anymore.

Tory turned to Alvarez. "That's really good news, isn't it?"

He pulled her close, gave her a hug, noted Sosa's raised eyebrows. "That's very good news," he told her. "Will you be okay here for a while? There's some things I want to check on."

Tory went on alert. "What kind of things?"

"Stuff I need to take care of," he said, inwardly cursing himself for such a stupid answer. Thankfully, Tory chose to let it go, letting herself be drawn into sitting down with Dana Halloran, a mood of celebration now bravely surrounding that one small part of ICU.

By the time Alvarez left to find a pay phone, the two women were engaged in animated conversation. Maybe they were getting the fine points of their stories straight, and that might be a good thing. Unless he was losing his touch, Alvarez was certain that an unmarked patrol car had picked them up at the condo and followed them to the hospital.

GEORGE NELSON came on the line so quickly it surprised Alvarez. "Don't you ever go home?" he asked.

"Got five kids," said Nelson, "all grown up, and my wife, she's used to me working all the time. Says it might upset things now if I started coming home at regular times, paying a lot of attention to her and all."

"Hope you don't have any good-looking retired neighbors."

"Retired neighbors, hell. She says if she trades me in, she wants three twenty-year-olds in return. Besides, I pay attention to the important stuff. How else do you think we ended up with five kids?"

"I don't think you want me to answer that. Got anything new on the Reynolds case?"

"Any particular reason you're asking, short of curiosity and all?"

"When we left the condo this morning, it seemed to me we had company."

There was silence on the other end. "It don't mean anything," said Nelson finally.

"What do you mean, 'it don't mean anything?' You guys really that hard up for something to do?"

"Okay, it's stupid. What do you want me to say? It's Vicky paying dues for some of the hell she raised in the past. It didn't go down too good with some people, her getting sprung with an alibi so nice and neat and all. They're just keeping an eye on her to make sure she walks the straight and narrow, stays in line. You do your part, make sure she has stuff to do to keep her out of trouble, and it will all work itself out."

Alvarez looked at the phone in his hand, thought of three different replies and made himself discard them all. "So, back to where we started," he said evenly. "Any new developments in the Reynolds case?"

There was a pause on the other end. "Yeah, there's new developments. Know how we were talking about Reynolds maybe having lots of enemies? Well, seems we were talking about the tip of the iceberg."

Tip of the iceberg, interesting reference for a Florida cop. "What do you mean?"

"Listen, I'm going out on a limb telling you this, buddy. What I want in return is anything you can think of, anything that might have to do with this, what with Reynolds's connection to Tory's dad and all."

"Agreed." Alvarez had no idea what he was agreeing to.

"Reynolds's wife was notified, and she's on her way home with the kids. We've got someone verifying her whereabouts in Puerto Rico, just to cover that base. What's interesting is what turned up when we tossed the house—lots and lots of detailed historical research."

"What's so interesting about that? The guy was a historian."

"This was real specific research—having to do with the historical background of very specific people—people like Frank Paxton, for example."

"What do you mean?" This must be the third time he'd asked Nelson the same question.

"We're not sure what we mean, not yet, not completely. But it looks pretty certain that Reynolds used his connections and his position to go a little bit beyond what might be expected for his job description. The file on Paxton shows that Reynolds was in the process of getting documentation to prove that Paxton's maternal great-grandmother was Jewish.''

"Bet that wouldn't go over too well with Rip Tide's members, not to mention their associated organizations.''

"No kidding. And it looks like Reynolds was an equal opportunity researcher. There are files on some black separatists operating in Florida. Some of this stuff, it wouldn't be a real reach to go from research to real creative fund-raising.''

"You mean blackmail.'' Alvarez remembered Marilyn Morenson telling him her misgivings over Reynolds's unprecedented ability to obtain contributions.

"I doubt that's what Reynolds called it.''

"Is there a file on Sledge?'' asked Alvarez.

"We haven't turned one up, but that doesn't mean anything. We're bringing him in for questioning anyhow. Then we'll have to decide who else to add to the list, based on this new stuff.'' Nelson didn't sound as though he thought it would be a short list.

"Any file on a family named Hodden?'' asked Alvarez.

"I don't know off the top of my head,'' said Nelson. "Why?'' Alvarez told him about Chloe Marshall, Senator Wheatley, the rosewood box, and the claims about researching the Hoddens that Reynolds had made to Tory the afternoon before he was killed. "I'll look into it,'' said Nelson. "I kinda hope it doesn't put more heat on Vicky, you telling me this.''

"Get real, Nelson. Even with what you know about Tory being ancient history, so to speak, could you really see her killing somebody to *protect* her family's reputation?''

Nelson thought that over, grunted. "You got a point there.''

"I still think you should look at Chloe Marshall.''

"For what?''

"Just a feeling.''

"Can't arrest people based on feelings. If that was the case, our Vicky'd be behind bars now.''

"The sheriff has that much of a grudge against her?''

"You buy me a beer sometime, I'll tell you stories that would raise the hair on the back of your neck. She gave that man some terrible grief, she did."

Alvarez looked temptation in the face and resisted it. "Maybe I'd be happier not knowing. Tell you what I'd like to know instead—a couple things about Chloe Marshall."

"You're pushing it, buddy. Your two questions better be simple and quick."

"Was a carved wooden box, like the one I told you about, on the list of stolen items reported from the burglary? Does her name turn up in your records in any other context?"

Nelson gave a grievous sigh, but he didn't hang up. "Hold on a minute. I'll see what I can do."

"Should I call back?"

"Hell, no. We're computerized now, just like everyone else. The Sheriff's Office has entered the age of instant information dissemination. I don't do this now, I'll get caught up in doing some real work."

It wasn't instant by any means, but it wasn't a long wait, either. "No box is on the report of stolen items," Nelson said, "but you told me that Mrs. Marshall herself claimed she didn't remember whether she listed it, and there's a whole shit load of stuff listed here, mostly jewelry, worth a lot more than any wooden box I've ever seen. Could be an honest oversight."

"Could be. Anything else come up?"

"Like does Mrs. Marshall have a record of hit-and-run accidents, vehicular homicide, and plugging her previous bosses at close range? She doesn't even show a parking ticket, buddy. But you're in luck. I did a whole system search, and her name turned up. Doesn't mean much, so don't go getting all excited."

"What is it?"

"She's listed as one of five witnesses to an attempted robbery at a pawnshop. Seems she was in the store when someone came in, high on crack, pulled a gun and tried a hold-up. One of the owners came up behind the guy, stuck a gun in his ribs, and called the police. It turned out to be a simple collar. They took the guy down, got statements on the spot."

"Was this before or after her house was burglarized?"

There was a pause. "About a week after. Maybe Mrs. Marshall was looking for her stuff. Dumb thing to do; look for stolen stuff at a pawnshop. Those guys have more regulations than escort services; they're even plugged into our system now—they have to log their stuff in with us on a daily basis.''

"Maybe Dr. Marshall has lived a life sheltered from the realities of pawnshops." Alvarez thought about what he'd just said. Chloe Marshall had told Tory that she grew up poor, but not all poor people frequented pawnshops, and besides, she'd said she grew up in a small town. Pawnshops generally needed larger communities to thrive.

"Yeah, probably so," said Nelson.

"You know if any of the other stolen items were recovered?"

"Not that we show. You got your answers to your two questions."

"I have another question."

"You said two, buddy."

"This question doesn't have to do with Chloe Marshall, not exactly. What's the address of the pawnshop?"

Nelson sighed and gave him the address. "You're barking up the wrong tree, buddy, but I guess it's your time to burn. Thought from looking at you the night we picked up Vicky, maybe you had other things to do, but I guess that's not any of my business."

"Good guess," said Alvarez. "Guesses like that, maybe they'll promote you."

"Just don't make waves with anyone, so I don't end up sorry I told you this stuff. And you come across something, you let me know, pronto."

"You're supposed to say, you let me know pronto, *ese*. I find out anything, I'll let you know. Good luck with your list of suspects."

"Wait," said Nelson. "There's something else you should know. Preliminary report came in on Cooper's place—they can't show it's arson."

"Bummer."

"Looks like the fire started from a faulty electrical circuit." There was a pause. "This case just keeps getting worse and worse. Who would know about faulty circuits better than an engineer?"

"That's exactly what I was thinking," Alvarez told him. "I'm sure you'll figure out something. Thanks for the help."

"Yeah," said Nelson. "You know what they say. We're paid to respond."

MARILYN MORTENSON wasn't too anxious to talk to Alvarez a second time, especially since she'd been interviewed by detectives just before he called. Alvarez told her the same thing he'd told Tory after his phone call—that he was working on something with George Nelson. It sounded good and it was almost true. Mortenson capitulated not too ungraciously, assuming Alvarez could make it to her office in the next twenty minutes. She informed him that she needed to do some real work after their meeting. At the rate she was losing staff, Alvarez could understand the problem.

He told Tory that he needed to run an errand and reminded her not to skip lunch. Dana Halloran assured him that she would make sure Tory ate to keep her strength up. Tory looked at Halloran in a bemused fashion, and it occurred to Alvarez that this was probably the closest Tory had ever come to being mothered.

His next thought was that it was too bad the man in the unmarked unit showed no interest in following the rental car if Tory wasn't on board; after last night, in spite of some lingering pain in his injured arm, Alvarez felt up to meeting just about any challenge.

"What is it you've come to ask me this time?" Marilyn Mortenson met him with the same undiluted attention and impeccable manners as the last time, but she looked tired and worried; there were lines in her face that he could swear hadn't been there before.

"I'm curious about Chloe Marshall," he said. "Two out of three people staffing a research center die violently, mere days apart. You have to start wondering about it."

"Maybe what we should wonder about is whether Dr. Marshall is in danger," said Mortenson coolly.

"Maybe so. But I'm wondering whether Dr. Marshall might have been mixed up in what Reynolds was doing."

This earned a severe frown from Mortenson. "I have no reservations about either the caliber of Dr. Marshall's work or her moral character."

"Sometimes people get caught up in things without meaning to," said Alvarez. He told Mortenson about Chloe's visit to the condo, her criticisms of Reynolds, her claim to the Rosewood box, and Reynolds's claims that the box had to do with research requested by Tory's father to discredit her mother's family. Mortenson, as before, listened without interruption, but her face showed distaste.

"Not a single thing you're telling me has to do with the death of Amy Cooper or Rolland Reynolds," she said flatly. "Unless it's related to Rolland doing research for the Senator like you've described. That line of thought would seem to implicate the Senator, and he's lying in a hospital in a coma. If you think that Chloe," Alvarez noted that they were back to "Chloe" now, "had anything to do with the things you're telling me Rolland was involved with, why on earth would she have any reservations about the Senator's planned contribution to the history department?"

The problem with educated women was that they often made sense. Alvarez refused to admit the logic of her question; he had a feeling that there was something here, something right in front of him, just barely out of reach. "How did Chloe Marshall feel about Reynolds?" he asked instead. "You said you didn't like how he treated Chloe. Reynolds openly criticized her husband about choosing to live in Haile Plantation. That has to be a problem, working for someone who criticizes your husband."

Mortenson sighed. "Rolland is always making statements about this and that; we've all come to accept it as part of who he is. I don't think Chloe ever took the whole Haile Plantation thing personally, but I do think she's been unhappy since Rolland came here. She was acting director in the beginning, and she was understandably disappointed when we brought in someone else to head it up." Mortenson shook her head. "If it had been up to me, we wouldn't have done that, and then we wouldn't be in this mess. I think Rolland kept Chloe on a short leash, didn't let her pursue the things she wanted to study, but she never complained. On the other hand, Rolland probably resented not being able to name his own assistant director. He may have seen Chloe as someone who was grandfathered in, someone he was stuck with."

"And she got the position specifically because of her work on the Rosewood study?"

"No one would come out and say it like that, but yes. Without the work she did on Rosewood, Chloe would never have been considered for her position."

"What if that work was flawed?"

Mortenson frowned. "Are you still pursuing the money angle, Mr. Alvarez?"

"No, someone wised me up about that. But how about academic reputation, standing, all of that?"

"Those are pretty petty things to murder someone over, although there are people on my staff who I swear might be capable of it." Mortenson seemed to hear what she'd just said and stopped herself from elaborating. "It's not like Chloe was out there on her own, fabricating stories and manufacturing documents. The identification of all Rosewood survivors was subject to review by numerous individuals."

"So this Lissy Hodden—"

"Lissy Hodden Garner," Mortenson corrected.

"This survivor who didn't want to talk about it, didn't want to put in a claim—how was she identified?"

"That's easy. Other survivors remembered her, had kept in touch with her sister, who, by the way, was living in Archer at the time of the Rosewood incident. The sister is the one who took in Richard Marshall's father, Homer, and ended up adopting him. Lissy was very close to the child, but she was just thirteen in 1923."

Alvarez held up his hand. She was going too fast for him. "Wait a moment. So Lissy was identified based on the testimony of other survivors?"

"Initially. Then when the woman at the nursing home filed her claim for her, it turned out that Lissy had Hodden family documents from Rosewood—the deed to her family's land, marriage and baptismal records, things like that. It wasn't a case of her not being able to prove that she was a Rosewood survivor, it was a case of her not wanting to have anything to do with it. Remember, she was Mrs. Garner by the time people showed up, talking to her about Rosewood. As far as she was concerned, Lissy Garner had no connection with Lissy Hodden of Rosewood.''

"But she made an exception for Homer Marshall.''

"After Chloe went back to talk to her, yes.''

"And Homer was adopted by Lissy's older sister, who was dead by the time people started looking for survivors.''

"That's right. Her name was Garland Grant. She was living with her husband in Archer, and Lissy's parents were visiting them at the time of the Rosewood Massacre. Lissy was left behind; she was staying with neighbors.''

Alvarez had to acknowledge that this must have been a nightmare, a child left on her own, without her family, when her whole world went spiraling out of control. But he needed to concentrate. "If this Garland Grant and her husband adopted Homer Marshall, why isn't his name Grant?''

Mortenson shrugged. "We're talking about poor black people in 1923. Adoption was seldom a legal process back then, and who knows? They may have wanted the child to retain something of his own family heritage.''

"So Homer Marshall was identified on the basis of Lissy's testimony? How old was he in 1923?''

"He was two years old," replied Mortenson gravely.

Alvarez forged on regardless. "So he was two. Then he couldn't be expected to have any memories of Rosewood, could he?''

"I see where you're going with this, Mr. Alvarez, and it's a dead end. Other Rosewood survivors remembered Homer's father, and remembered the little boy. The Hoddens and the Marshalls were next door neighbors. Homer's mother died when he was an infant, so the child often stayed with the Hoddens. It's only natural that Lissy would have the strongest memories of the boy, what happened to him and how he ended up with her sister, who, by the way, was never able to have children of her own. But in addition to her memories, Lissy also had Homer's baptismal certificate and the Marshall family Bible, showing the date and place of Homer's birth. Not easy to falsify records like that."

"I never said it was." Alvarez just wanted her to go on talking.

"Lissy gathered all those records right before a white mob burned Rosewood to the ground. For a thirteen-year-old girl whose parents were somewhere else, who had seen neighbors killed before her very eyes, and who was in charge of the safety of other children, I think she did an admirable job. Don't you?"

Alvarez nodded his agreement. "Something like that, it would change you. You'd never get over it."

Mortenson looked at him as though he were a slow student who was finally starting to catch on. "It changed them all. Some lived in fear the rest of their lives. Later, when they started to come together to talk about it, a few decided to try to tell the story. Lissy wasn't afraid, but she never wanted any part of discussing Rosewood."

"If Homer Marshall's mother died when he was an infant, what happened to his father?"

"That, Mr. Alvarez, like so many other things concerning Rosewood, is a mystery. My theory is that he was probably killed by the mob. If not, if he was part of the blacks who fought back, he may have thought that the best thing he could do for his child would be to disappear and never come back."

"You said six blacks and two whites were killed at Rosewood. So Marshall's father wasn't identified as one of the blacks?"

"What an excellent memory you have. If you quit law enforcement, maybe you should consider a career in history. Homer's father is not documented as one of the blacks that died in the violence at Rosewood. On the other hand, Sylvester Carrier is, yet there are people to this day who will tell you that Sylvester Carrier lived out his life in Texas and died a peaceful death decades after the Rosewood massacre."

"Who is Sylvester Carrier?"

"He's the man who led the black resistance to the mob—the

man who was responsible, so they say, for the two white men who died. There are people in this very town who will swear to you that by the time everything was done, three hundred white men were killed and buried in a mass grave.''

"Three hundred white men? I thought the rumors were the other way around—that untold numbers of blacks were killed.''

Mortenson shook her head. "Depends on who's telling the story. For every tale that there were scores of blacks killed and that's the reason the violence was covered up, there is someone else to claim that by the time the blacks finished fighting back, there were too many dead white men to count, and that's the reason no one talks about what happened at Rosewood. Damned inconvenient, wouldn't it be, to have a father and three uncles disappear with a group of their friends one day, with their corn liquor and their rifles, never to come back? That might take some explaining to the children and the neighbors.'' Mortenson leaned back in her chair and regarded Alvarez. "You look as though I've given you something to think about.''

"Three hundred men—white or black—slaughtered?'' he asked. "With no follow-up, no investigation? That's hard to believe.''

"My personal estimate,'' said Mortenson quietly, "is that it was somewhere around fifty. Rosewood not being my personal specialty.''

This was hard to swallow. "And the official record says that only two white men died?''

"And the official record says two,'' she answered him. "History is neither as cut-and-dried nor as simple as we would all like to believe. If you want to look at money as a motive for crime, look at the families of the survivors. Amazing things have happened to some of them. Brother pitted against brother, family against family. Arguments that what was done to someone's ancestor wasn't quite as horrible and violent as what was done to someone else's. Claims that some of the people who pushed the Rosewood Bill through the legislature turned around and preyed on the old and feeble who reaped the financial benefits. Black or white, there's one thing history shows us, that basic human nature remains the same.''

Alvarez considered the woman sitting across the desk from him. "You ever want to change careers, you might consider law enforcement," he said. This earned a brief smile.

"Have I answered your questions for today?" asked Mortenson, discreetly glancing at her watch. "I can recommend some good books on Rosewood."

"I'm almost finished. Can you tell me the name of the nursing home where Lissy Hodden Garner lived?"

"It's in Lake City, about forty-five minutes north of here. But you're wasting your time, Mr. Alvarez."

"I can understand your respect for a colleague," said Alvarez.

"Let me make myself perfectly clear," replied Mortenson. "Put aside the fact that I've known and respected Chloe Marshall for several years. If you think there's something suspect about the work she did regarding Rosewood, then Richard Marshall would have to be involved. I've known Richard for over twenty years, Mr. Alvarez, and I can say there is no one more unlikely to be involved with anything, and I mean anything, that would be morally or ethically questionable."

Damn, thought Alvarez as he got up to go. There was that.

THIRTY-ONE

Fireball
January 4, 1923. Rosewood, Florida

ANOTHER TENSE, claustrophobic day. Night fell, bitterly cold but brilliantly moonlit. A little before nine, one of the men who had shown up at the Carrier house the day before slipped inside the back door, looked at Sylvester and said, "They're coming." Aunt Sarah turned to the women gathered in the kitchen and told them to take the children upstairs. Lissy heard a dog start to bark out in the yard.

"What about the dogs?" she asked in a panic. She should have thought about it—*someone* should have thought about it; if there was going to be a siege, they should have called in the dogs.

"Lord, child, I can't be worried 'bout no dogs," said Aunt Sarah. "You gets yourself on up the stairs."

Lissy looked to Sylvester for direction, but he was already busy dousing lights. There was nothing Lissy could do to help ensure the safety of Homer Marshall or any of the other children. Adults had taken on those responsibilities, but Lissy couldn't bear to be herded upstairs with the children.

She looked out and saw Git limping along behind the dog that was barking. Lissy made a split second decision. Her coat was hanging by the back door, the same coat she had worn just three days before, back when Aunt Sarah had entrusted Lissy with the task of getting the children safely to Rosewood. She grabbed her coat and darted out the door to scoop up Git and bring him to safety.

But the little dog thought Lissy was playing and ran into the bushes. She headed after him, engaged in a desperate game of silent pursuit, for she didn't dare call his name out loud. In that single moment of running after a dog, albeit a little three-legged dog that couldn't even run very fast, Lissy's path back to the Carrier house closed forever.

As Lissy stepped into the bushes, a Model-T drove up and came to a screeching stop in front of the house. Poly Wilkerson and six other men spilled out, guns and bottles alike shining in the moonlight. Lissy caught up to Git, made a well-aimed grab, and held him close, horrified at the scene that was unfolding in front of her, the scene that couldn't really be happening, not with her outside while those she knew and cared about were in the silent Carrier house.

"We're gonna get that nigger, the one attacked ole Frannie, get him tonight," said one of the men with relish. Lissy had never seen the man before. Was he drunk, or did he really not know Fannie Taylor's name?

"Damn right," replied Poly Wilkerson, his words slightly slurred. "Four whole days gone by without us stringing up the bastard, them other niggers gonna think they can do whatever they want."

There was a great deal of cursing in agreement with Wilkerson's statement. Lissy stood perfectly still in the bushes, thinking what it would be like to tell these men who was responsible for Fannie Taylor's troubles. She thought about what had happened to Aaron Carrier and Sam Carter and Mizz Mahulda, and she wondered what these men would do to a skinny thirteen-year-old girl clutching a three-legged dog, even if that girl had the information they sought. Little three-legged Git was half white, half black, but Lissy knew with deadly certainty, standing frozen with fear in the bushes, that she was all nigger.

"Damn, but it's cold," said one of the men, rubbing his hands together. "Where the hell are the others?"

"They'll get here," replied Wilkerson. "They're coming from Otter Creek, probably on foot. All we gotta do is wait."

"Hope we don't freeze in the meantime."

"Well, if we gotta wait, oughta make ourselves comfortable," said Wilkerson, and kicked at the picket fence surrounding the Carrier front yard with his big work boots, then started pulling the fence to pieces with his hands. "We can use this here nigger kindling."

The rest of the men busied themselves tearing apart the fence. Emboldened by the noise they were making, Lissy took off her coat and tied the two sleeves together to make a primitive sling. She transferred Git into her coat and waited, her breath puffing out in little white wisps, her heart beating in her ears. When all the men seemed to have their attention focused on tearing down the fence, Lissy made her move. She crossed the ten feet between the bushes and the oak tree at the side of the Carrier house, and she began to climb, up and up and up, never looking down.

About the time she made it to the saddle branch, a dog rounded the corner of the house, stopping a moment in surprise to see the group of men kicking down the fence. Then it advanced, barking, growling. Lissy heard a shot, a high scream, then another shot. "Got the nigger dog that time," someone exclaimed, then there was another dog barking and another shot. Lissy closed her eyes, but she couldn't put her hands over her ears. She needed to hold onto the tree limb tightly to secure their precarious perch in the oak tree, especially with Git scrambling around in the coat, tied against her chest.

After six dead dogs lay in the Carrier yard, no more came to question the destruction of the fence. Through it all, the Carrier house sat still and dark, no sign of life inside.

With no more dogs to shoot, the white men turned their attention to building a bonfire by the railroad tracks. As the fire grew, more men came to join those who had arrived with Wilkerson. Lissy recognized Henry Andrews from the sawmill at Otter Creek, and she recognized several of the men who came with him. But still others kept coming, some in twos and threes, some by themselves. They swelled the number of men gathered outside the Carrier house as though they were drawn by the bonfire to materialize there from the dark swamp, men Lissy had never seen before, some with liquor, all with guns.

Lissy had no idea how long she had been sitting there, hanging onto the tree with fingers lifeless from the cold. She thanked Jesus that Git had finally stopped his panicked scrambling, seemed to sense the danger surrounding them, and lay still against Lissy's heart, his small body helping to combat the piercing cold.

Nothing had happened since the death of the six dogs, and Lissy began to allow herself to hope that the men would grow bored with their bonfire and their drinking, that they would become tired of watching a house that was dark and silent, and would go home. That was when Poly Wilkerson broke apart from the group, took two steps toward the house, and yelled, "We want Sylvester Carrier. We think he done been hiding the nigger attacked Fannie Taylor. If Sylvester comes out here, talks to us, we won't hurt none of the rest of you."

For the very first time, a sound came from inside the Carrier house. "Yeah, you bastard," yelled a male voice that Lissy did not recognize. "We seen how you done talk to Sam Carter."

Wilkerson turned back to the group surrounding the bonfire. "Did you hear what that nigger called me?" he asked the others.

Before any of them had a chance to answer, Lissy saw Aunt Sarah throw open the living room window and lean out. "Y'all just go on home now," she said, in the same tone she used to send children playing in her yard home to dinner. Lissy saw a fleeting movement in the group of men by the fire as one of them shouldered his rifle. A shot rang out, then Aunt Sarah was no longer at the window.

"Mamma—they done shot Mamma," a voice wailed from inside. Lissy knew it was one of The Man's sisters, but she didn't know which one.

The group of men surged forward without further conversation, as though they were an animal of one single accord, Wilkerson and Andrews in the lead. The front door of the Carrier house swung open, and shots flashed from inside. The group of men surged back again toward the bonfire, but Wilkerson and Andrews remained sprawled on the Carrier porch; neither one was moving. Another shot rang out and a man by the bonfire clasped his shoulder in surprise. "Get away from the damn fire," someone yelled, and they dispersed into the bushes.

From that point on, it was like a bad dream, and how does one measure the duration of a nightmare? Attacks were mounted on the house, shots rang out, screams were heard, then the white men would fall back and regroup. Other bodies fell on the porch and in the yard. From her vantage point, sometimes Lissy thought she could see groups of dark shadows vanish from the back of the house into the swamps. How many attacks, shots, screams, bodies—how many shadows escaping from the back of the house, she had no way of knowing. There was just her and the dog and the cold and the tree, and the primal knowledge that no matter what happened, no matter how long it took, she must never let go.

As the bonfire burned down the mob began to disperse, looking for other, easier targets in its wake. One by one various houses of Rosewood were substituted for the now-defunct bonfire, but there was a belated emptiness to these acts of random destruction. During the assault on the Carrier house, the rest of the residents of Rosewood must have melted away into the swamp. Lissy thought she heard one single scream as the mob departed, burning and destroying whatever it found in its way, but she'd heard so many screams that night that maybe she was mistaken.

One by one the fires burned out, the night was nearly over, and everyone was gone. And then Lissy discovered that even though she could finally force her frozen fingers to relax their grip on the tree limb, even though she could finally shift her numb arms and legs in tiny movements without immediate fear of being discovered, she could not make herself climb down the tree into the yard, where dead men and dead dogs lay mingled together.

THIRTY-TWO

Tazzled
Wednesday

ALVAREZ FOUND A PAY PHONE outside the university bookstore where he'd picked up a Rosewood book recommended by Dr. Mortenson. He admired the steady flow of young female students as he made his calls, first to directory assistance, then to the nursing home in Lake City where Marilyn Mortenson said that Lissy Hodden Garner had met the future Mrs. Richard Marshall and lived out her days. He told the person who answered the phone that he was a police detective working on a case.

Alvarez said he would like to talk to anyone who had known Lissy Hodden Garner, but most especially, he would like to talk to the woman who helped Mrs. Garner file her claim as a Rosewood survivor. "You mean Tazzy," said the voice on the other end. "Not here."

"Tazzy?"

"That's her name. Think I could go and make up a name like that? You're talking about Tazzy Martin."

"And when will Tazzy Martin be back?"

There was a pause, a long, suffering pause. "I had to look that up," said the voice on the other end. "Tazzy's supposed to pull the afternoon shift. She'd better, since we're short-handed as it is."

"Would I be able to talk to her, if I came there early this afternoon?"

Another pause. "Guess so. Long's you don't get between her and her work." The line went dead.

Alvarez meant to head back to the hospital, check in, maybe

even let Tory know what he was doing. But he remembered an interchange a little ways beyond the hospital. This particular one had a sign that boasted I-75 NORTH: Lake City. Alvarez cruised by the hospital and turned north onto the interstate.

He admitted to himself he was putting off the possibility of spending extensive downtime with Tory, sitting with her father, waiting, time when she would have nothing to do but sit and think. Tory thinking about some technical issue related to an investigation could be a good thing—well, it could be a good thing if she wasn't out chasing down answers by herself. At least her father's accident was keeping her tied down. But Tory thinking about her personal life, that tended to take her down roads where no man had gone before, and should probably never go.

Of course there were problems to discuss, issues to resolve, and Alvarez would not have chosen an unexpected pregnancy as the way to push her into considering them. But he knew how he felt about Tory, so the rest was a foregone conclusion. The issues at hand were the kind that could be discussed forever, but were really no-brainers in the end. Unfortunately, Tory was quite good at discussion when she had a mind to be.

Alvarez's partner had once told him that there were two theories about arguing with a woman, and neither one of them worked. Therefore it was only reasonable to postpone as many discussions with Tory as he could, until such discussions were held at a time and place where Alvarez could use passion as an ally to strengthen his arguments. After all, timing was awfully important in the outcome of any rain dance.

A hint of a doubt clouded his mind as Alvarez continued north past the turnoff for a town called Alachua. Did his present course of action have something to do with Tory's repeated claims about him always acting like a cop? How his first instinct was to operate independently? Her accusations that he saw people as being on a need-to-know basis, merely obstacles between him and the answers he was seeking? Could those very questions have anything to do with the fact that he was driving to Lake City, leaving Tory under the watchful eyes of the local law enforcement?

No. It was merely a matter of efficiency, each person doing

what was required at the moment, doing what they did best. Tory could firm up her alibi with Dana Halloran and play the dutiful daughter should her father regain consciousness. And Alvarez would do what he did best, follow the trail of pieces that didn't seem to fit, doggedly gathering information until he could fit the pieces together to form a complete and unified picture. With Nelson and GPD covering the obvious leads, it left Alvarez free to follow his gut instincts, and his gut instincts were sure there was more to Chloe Marshall than met the eye.

The black Ford pickup that cut in front of Alvarez had a gun rack, a Confederate flag in the back window, and a bumper sticker that said HONK IF YOU'VE NEVER SEEN AN ASSAULT RIFLE FIRED FROM A CAR WINDOW. Alvarez figured he could back-end the truck quietly should there be a pile-up on the interstate, no matter how much he might be tempted to lean on the horn.

THE NURSING HOME in Lake City had an air of genteel shabbiness and relaxed procedures regarding visitation. No one asked Alvarez who he was, or why he was there. He could probably have kidnapped as many of the residents as he could fit into the rental car, and no one would report it for days, or maybe ever.

When Alvarez asked for Tazzy Martin, the plump, pimply teenaged boy at the front desk said vaguely, "I think she's supposed to be cutting Mrs. Tilbarten's toenails."

"And where would I find Mrs. Tilbarten?"

"Down there, end of the hall," said the boy, turning his attention back to the *Nintendo Magazine* he had been studying before Alvarez's first question. He gestured to his right, leaving Alvarez to wonder if maybe room numbers were considered too formal in Lake City.

Alvarez walked down the hall, starting to look into rooms after he was halfway to the end. He was in luck—in the second room he saw a young black woman with a white uniform and shocking pink hair, kneeling on the floor in front of a shriveled old woman in a wheelchair. The one on the floor looked to be doing something with the old woman's feet, so Alvarez asked, "Tazzy Martin?" from the doorway.

She didn't even look around. The woman in the wheelchair

was rocking and crooning to herself, so it appeared as though cutting her toenails might be a job requiring full attention.

"I'm Tazzy. You the guy called earlier?"

"How'd you know?"

"It's not like we get many calls here that don't have to do with providing care. We're not on the regular newsbeat, in case you hadn't guessed. Mrs. Garner, she was about the closest we've ever come to our fifteen minutes of fame."

Alvarez stepped into the room and around the kneeling woman so that he was in her line of vision. She had a number of interesting snake tattoos crawling up her arms and numerous gold hoops through her ears. "I'm David Alvarez," he said. "Want me to hold one of her feet for you?"

Tazzy Martin looked up then, gave him an appraising once-over with large brown eyes. "Can you do it gentle-like, without riling her up?"

Alvarez was affronted. "Do I look like someone who manhandles old people?"

"They said you were with the police."

"So?"

"So I thought I'd ask," replied Tazzy. "If you're gonna help, you're wasting time standing there. Don't make any sudden movements, either, it will upset her."

Alvarez slowly knelt down by Tazzy and gently took one of Mrs. Tilbarten's feet in his hand. He could see now why this pedicure might be a time-consuming task—the old woman had several ingrown toenails that Tazzy was clipping a little at a time with the utmost care. "Are you the one who filed the Rosewood survivor claim for Mrs. Garner?" he asked the pedicurist.

"That would be me. And I've got to wonder what you're doing here asking me questions."

"And I've got to wonder why you have a problem with it, when you haven't even heard the questions yet, and the person I'm asking about is dead."

Tazzy looked up again from her task then, shot him a hard look. "Just because someone's old or dead doesn't mean they don't deserve respect."

"Granted. And I don't mean any disrespect. Why don't you

give me the benefit of the doubt, wait to hear my questions before you decide?''

This didn't rate another look up. "I'm not too partial to policemen in general, particularly not white policemen," Tazzy told Mrs. Tilbarten's toes.

"I'm not white," he countered.

She glanced up again, fleetingly. "There is that," she admitted. "Other foot."

Alvarez put down Mrs. Tilbarten's foot and Tazzy drew a sock over it. He gently took the other foot in hand, decided to press on. "When did you find out that Mrs. Garner was a Rosewood survivor?"

"Not 'til they came looking for her, that's for sure. Even then, I didn't know much about it, just the stuff those people told me and the things I read in the paper. Lissy didn't want to talk about it, she asked me to send them away, so I did. But then that mousy woman, Chloe Pitts, started coming around, and after a while Lissy started talking to her—mainly about the little boy she'd brought out of Rosewood, the one her sister adopted.''

"Homer Marshall."

"That's the one."

"So what prompted you to file for Mrs. Garner, if she wasn't interested in doing it herself?"

"Homer's son Richard started coming around. It really perked Lissy up—sometimes they'd sit and talk for hours. Later on, him and Chloe got married, and that tickled Lissy to no end."

"So did the Marshalls suggest that you file for Mrs. Garner?"

Tazzy looked up, eyes narrowed, shook her head. "We're gonna do the hands now. You sit on the bed, real quiet like, and hold one of her hands on your knee for me, spread the fingers if you can."

Alvarez complied, feeling faintly ridiculous, as though he were taking unwarranted liberties on a first date. It didn't help when Mrs. Tilbarten stopped rocking and crooning and said, "Henry, how nice to see you. How are the twins?"

"They're fine," replied Alvarez, and Mrs. Tilbarten looked confused.

"I thought they had the measles," she said.

"That's what I meant, they're getting better. The spots are fading—you can hardly even see them anymore." He thought about it, added, "Thought we were seeing double there for a while—all those spots before our eyes." Tazzy flashed him a grin and turned her attention to Mrs. Tilbarten's hand.

"It wasn't anybody's idea for me to file for Lissy, it was mine," she said. "She got out the stuff she'd saved, stuff she needed for Homer Marshall's application, and there was all this other stuff having to do with her and her family, things she'd carried out of Rosewood in a keepsake box." Tazzy sounded almost reverent.

"A wooden keepsake box? With flowers and her name carved on top?"

Tazzy looked up. "How'd you know that?"

"Dr. Marshall showed it to me." Which wasn't too far from the truth.

"Well, then." His revelation seemed to make Tazzy feel better about talking to him. "It seemed like a shame," she continued, "Lissy providing all the documentation and testimony for Richard Marshall's father, and there she was a survivor herself. Homer Marshall might very well never have come out of Rosewood if it hadn't been for Lissy."

This echoed the tone of something Marilyn Mortenson had said, and Alvarez was struck with a sudden surprising regret that he would never have the chance to meet the woman they were discussing. "So what happened?" he prodded.

"I kept on her about it, gentle-like, telling her that it was a shame not to be named with the others, and that if she gave me permission, I would take care of all the paperwork for her. Finally she told me to go ahead and please myself. With her credentials, it was just a matter of filling out the form and sending it in. It wasn't any big deal on my part. Other hand."

Alvarez waited to see what Tazzy had to say on the other hand, then realized that she was giving him a command, not changing subjects. "What was in it for you?" he asked as he put Mrs. Tilbarten's hand back in her lap and gently but firmly placed the other one on his knee. He had to ask that question; it was his job.

But somewhere in his head he heard Tory, inquiring sarcastically, "*What* job?"

"Everyone asked that, afterwards," said Tazzy, smiling to herself. "Can you believe I didn't even think about it? Well, it doesn't matter whether you believe it or not. You're a policeman, you could find out. Lissy left me $20,000 when she passed. I'm using it to go to school. That's why I'm only working part-time."

"Why work at all?"

"The old people here, they like me, and I like them. That's not often the case with people who work in nursing homes," said Tazzy. "Seemed like the least I could do to say thank you to Lissy was to stay here part-time, help take care of them. There, Mrs. Tilbarten." Tazzy returned the woman's hand to her lap, patted it gently. "Besides," she added defiantly, almost as though daring him to mock, "I'm studying to be a nurse. The kind with a four-year degree."

"Good for you," Alvarez told her. "I assume that Mrs. Garner left everything else to Richard Marshall?"

"Yeah. It was sad. Lissy really wanted to see him at the end, but it was only his wife who came that last time. When I looked in a little while afterwards, Lissy had passed."

This sounded horribly coincidental to Alvarez. "Was there an autopsy?"

Tazzy looked at him as though he were stupid. "We never expected Lissy to last as long as she did. She had massive congestive heart failure at the end, all swollen up with retained fluids, couldn't hardly even catch her breath enough to say anything. Not a good way to continue, if you get my drift. We don't consider it particularly mysterious when someone like that passes on."

Alvarez was struck with another thought. "Did you give Dr. Marshall the Rosewood box?"

Tazzy shook her head. "These may be old people here, but they're entitled to the full protection of the law. Once someone dies, the belongings here have to be held until the legal heir is determined, then we turn everything over, all proper like, with receipts and everything."

"So Mrs. Garner's possessions, the ones she kept here, were turned over to Richard Marshall?"

"That's what I've been trying to tell you. And if you're grateful for me answering your questions, you'll do something for me."

The cost of information was getting higher all the time. "More nails?"

"No, I'm running behind today—I can't stay and visit, but you could." Tazzy Martin stood up and Alvarez could see then just what a big, strapping young woman she was.

"Yes, ma'am," he said, and stayed to talk with Mrs. Tilbarten about the twins and the measles, and about other people she thought he should know. Just when he was thinking this would be a good exercise for undercover cops, she fell asleep, and he was free to go. The boy at the front desk didn't look up as he walked out the door.

All the way back to Gainesville Alvarez tried to make some sense out of it, with no success. Maybe George Nelson was right, and Alvarez *was* barking up the wrong tree. If there was something odd going on with Chloe Marshall, and if that something had to do with Lissy Hodden Garner and her Rosewood heritage, that meant that Richard Marshall had to be in on it. That was a piece that even cynical Alvarez couldn't make fit.

THIRTY-THREE

Coming Down
January 5, 1923. Rosewood, Florida

"LISSY, YOU GOTTA climb down outta that damn tree now," someone called softly from the bushes. "I know you up there, so don't you be pretending you don't hear me calling you."

The voice, the words, they sounded almost normal. Lissy blinked, looked down—not toward the yard and its bodies, but toward the bushes, the bushes where Git had run when Lissy went to save him, when she'd slipped out of the Carrier house so long ago.

She should have known that The Man wouldn't forget her.

Sylvester Carrier had come back for Lissy, before the dawn broke through the winter sky and brought daylight and reinforcements to finally and irrevocably complete the destruction of Rosewood.

"I be stuck," Lissy said softly into the cold dawn air. Sitting in the tree, after everyone left, she had finally done what she had resolved not to do. She had looked down and counted. Lissy knew that below her were the bodies of exactly seventeen white men and six dogs of varying colors.

"You *not* be stuck," The Man said firmly. "You think 'bout all the people loves you—your mamma and daddy and sister, and little Homer Marshall. They be needing you down from that tree, so if you be stuck, you gets yourself unstuck right now."

There didn't seem to be any answer to that other than to climb down. Lissy was as careful and quiet as her stiff arms and legs allowed her to be. She mustn't fall out of the tree now, not after everything that had happened. When Lissy's feet touched the ground, she could see Mr. Herrington lying by the base of the tree. She remembered him from the times she drove into Sumner with her daddy when she was just a little girl. Lissy walked right on by him and into the bushes to join The Man.

He took her hand and they walked away from the house. Sylvester smelled like sweat and blood and gunpowder, and one arm was bleeding, soaking the side of his shirt although she could see no tear in the fabric. A detached part of Lissy's mind registered the fact that it was strange to see The Man wearing a blue flannel shirt, because everyone knew that Sylvester Carrier always wore black. But Lissy didn't say anything as The Man took her hand and led her away from the Carrier house, away from the seventeen dead white men and six dead dogs.

"They killed Aunt Sarah," he told her. "And they done killed Lexie Gordon, too."

"Lexie Gordon?" Lissy asked, surprised that she could still be surprised. What did the siege at the Carrier house have to do with Lexie Gordon, Lissy wondered. The Gordons lived a good ways from the Carrier house.

"Lexie was sick, told her family to go on without her," explained Sylvester. "She ran out when they set fire to her house, and they shot her in the back."

Lissy filed this away to think about at a later time. "What about—" she started to phrase her question; couldn't quite manage to finish it.

"All the children got out of the house," Sylvester told her. "They hiding at John Wright's, and that's where you need to go. He's gonna help you get out of here, you and the other children."

Lissy didn't like the sound of this. She stopped walking. "Where are you going?"

"I gotta leave, gotta disappear from 'round here. It be the only thing left to help Gussie and my babies. I came back for you, Lissy, 'cause I knew you be up in that tree. Now I needs you to keep my secret."

Lissy stared wordlessly at The Man, too tired and too numb to respond. Was there really to be *another* secret? When would it all end? How could she ever live with them all? But Sylvester didn't wait for her answer, he went on hurriedly, as though they were running out of time. "Gussie, my babies, my sisters, they can't know, Lissy. Nobody can know, not even my daddy. Gussie ever think I be alive, she'd move heaven and earth to find me. The only thing's gonna satisfy those white bastards be a dead nigger, so that's what I gotta be from now on." Lissy looked at him wonderingly, not understanding this new secret. "I changed clothes with someone back at the house," he told her.

"Who?" she asked without thinking, as though it mattered.

She saw a muscle clench in The Man's jaw. "A good man, that's who. You don't know him."

Lissy still didn't understand, not completely. "How they gonna be thinking someone else is you?" she asked. Everyone recognized The Man, there was none other like him, not in all of Levy County.

Sylvester Carrier looked down at her. "There not be a whole lot left to be looking at," he said, and then Lissy understood. She understood way too much.

"There gots to be another way," she whispered. All she'd

been through without a single whimper, and now she was going to cry.

"Ain't no other way," said The Man. "You gots to go to John Wright's house, and I be dead back there." He looked steadily at Lissy, and she couldn't think of a single word to say. "Give me a hug, baby," he told her. She didn't want to, because she knew that would mean the end of their time together, but she did as she was told. Sylvester kissed the top of her head and hugged her tight, but then pushed her away almost immediately. "What you got there in your coat, girl?" he asked. It was amazing that something could still astonish him.

Git. Lissy had Git, and she'd forgotten all about him. The Man stared at the little dog peeking out from her coat. "Lissy Hodden, you can be sure I ain't never gonna forget you, not all the days of my life." Then The Man gave Lissy a smile just like one of his smiles on any other day, any other day Before.

It was the very last present he ever gave her. Before she could say another word, he turned and disappeared into the swamp.

THIRTY-FOUR

Otherwise Engaged
Wednesday

THE MORNING HAD BEEN an exercise in more waiting. In spite of everyone's optimism, Tom Wheatley showed no signs of waking up on this, the fifth day after his accident. Dana was holding up far better than Tory; she apparently had more ability to patiently sit and watch without brooding and worrying.

Tory, on the other hand, had more than enough to occupy an idle mind. How Cody and Sylvia and Jazz were getting along. Whether her son's visits with his girlfriend were adequately supervised. How things were going at the office. Whether her father would ever regain consciousness, and whether he had requested the sleazy research Rolland Reynolds claimed. What it would mean if Tory's mother was somehow related to the Rosewood Hoddens, and what her father would do with such information. Who killed Amy Cooper and Reynolds, and why. How in God's name she had ended up pregnant and sleeping with David Alvarez, and what in God's name she was going to do about it.

By eleven a.m. Tory was wondering where Alvarez had gone and what was taking him so long. By lunchtime, she would have almost welcomed a visit from someone like Reynolds or Paxton to liven things up. By one p.m. she was seriously worried. By two p.m. she was furious.

It was two forty-five and Tory was trying to pretend she was listening to Dana talk about the Ocala real estate market when Alvarez appeared.

Tory excused herself in the middle of one of Dana's house descriptions and moved swiftly to intercept Alvarez. "Where have you been?" she asked, catching up with him by the nurses' station. She sounded like an irate wife, furious mother, and indignant kindergarten teacher all rolled into one, and that didn't even begin to encompass how she felt.

She saw a flash of surprise in his eyes, and he glanced quickly in her father's direction. "What's the matter?" Alvarez asked. How like a cop to answer a question with a question. "Has something happened?"

"How would I know?" she asked, and tried glaring at him. The words were dripping with sarcasm, but Tory fell short with the follow-up glare. Surprising no one quite as much as herself, her eyes filled with tears and they began to run down her cheeks. She was mortified.

Alvarez looked really worried now. "What's happened?" he asked. Randy Sosa stepped out from behind the nurses' station to pull Tory to him, patting her back and making soothing sounds. This must look very much like a soap opera, Tory thought. If there was ever a time for her father to sit up and awaken, this would be it, but she could see him out of the corner of her eye, and it looked as though he was going to miss his cue.

"Mrs. Travers has been under a lot of strain," Sosa told Alvarez. "She's been worried about you. She kept checking at the desk to see if you'd left any message, but of course, I had to tell her that you hadn't."

"Hell, Tory, I'm sorry," said Alvarez.

"I wasn't worried," sniffed Tory, peering around Sosa. "I was mad. I didn't know where you'd gone."

"I told you I had to run some errands."

"What errands? You have errands here in this town where you know *no one,* errands that take *four and a half hours?*" The tears were a thing of the past; outrage had taken their place.

"You know how it is," said Alvarez.

"No, I don't know how it is," Tory snapped.

"Maybe it would be better if you discussed this later," contributed Sosa.

"Don't you have patients to attend to?" asked Alvarez. "The way you go around hugging people all the time, you must have really excelled at the Heimlich maneuver in nursing school."

"I can't believe you said that," Tory said.

"I can't believe you're making such a big deal out of nothing," replied Alvarez.

"Two people are dead. You were with both of them shortly before they died. You've been gone four and a half hours. You think that's nothing?" Tory heard someone shouting, realized it was her. "And it's not like I don't have enough to worry about. There's Cody and Sylvia and Jazz and all kinds of other things—" She ran out of words as her eyes overflowed again. "You told me I could depend on you," she concluded forlornly, thinking that had to be one of the lamest things she had ever said.

Alvarez reached out with his good hand, pried Tory and Sosa apart. "Thanks," he told the nurse, holding Tory firmly by one arm. "I'll take over from here." Sosa hesitated a moment, then grabbed some tissues from the nurses' station, handed them to Alvarez, and walked off. Alvarez led Tory over to the chairs in the waiting area.

"Long morning?" he asked, handing her some tissues. She nodded, wiping her eyes, wondering how she had turned into someone who could break into tears without the slightest warning. "No change with your dad?" Tory shook her head, dabbed at her eyes again. "Listen," said Alvarez. "I'm really sorry if you were worried. I get going on something, I don't like to be slowed down." There was a silence while they both thought about this. "I mean," he said, starting over, "I'm not used to checking in with anyone, unless it's Scott."

"Don't mess up a perfectly good apology with an excuse."

Alvarez thought this over, nodded. "I shouldn't have left you like that, not telling you where I was going or when I'd be back. I can do better."

"Yeah, right," said Tory.

"Would it help if I told you what I've been doing?" Alvarez asked. Tory had no idea how this would help, but she was curious, so she nodded and he told her about his conversations with George Nelson, Marilyn Mortenson, and Tazzy Martin.

Tory was not impressed by the results of his four and a half hour absence. "I don't see what any of this has to do with the deaths of either Amy Cooper or Rolland Reynolds," she told him.

"I don't either," he admitted. "But I feel like I'm on the trail of something. I want to follow it through."

"Follow it where?"

"The pawnshop would be my next choice."

"Then take me with you," said Tory impulsively. "I've never been to a pawnshop, and if I have to stay here one more minute, I'm going to start screaming."

"And I'll bet if you started screaming, Randy Sosa would think he needed to embrace you. Once is understandable, twice is coincidence, but three times, I might have to punch him."

"Not a good idea for someone with an arm in a sling."

"True. Okay, I'll take you with me. But there's one condition."

"I have to shut up and let you do all the talking once we get to the pawnshop."

"I hadn't thought it out that far," Alvarez said. "Let's take it one step at a time. For now, I want you to shut up and let me do all the talking to Dana Halloran."

"What do you need to talk to Dana about?"

Alvarez shook his head at her. "Are you in or out?"

Tory thought about her alternatives. "In."

"Then shut up," said Alvarez. "Starting now."

He hadn't said anything about her staying put, so Tory followed Alvarez back to her father's bedside. She didn't know which astonished her the most—Alvarez asking Dana to switch coats with Tory and drive their rental car around the block while lending them her own vehicle, or Dana agreeing without the slightest hesitation.

"WHEN WERE YOU going to get around to telling me that I was under surveillance?"

"I thought it might take your mind off things to figure it out for yourself," replied Alvarez. He steered Dana Halloran's sedan past the university toward the northeast side of Gainesville.

"Isn't this kind of childish, ditching the officer who was supposed to keep tabs on me?" Tory heard her question, couldn't believe that she had asked it. Was she actually siding with the police now?

"Maybe," Alvarez admitted. "But it pissed me off, them putting a tail on just to hassle you, then having the guy be complacent to boot. Losing you will serve him well some time in the future. Sometime when he's tailing someone who matters."

"I'll bet he'll think it matters when he has to tell someone that he has no idea where I've gone."

"Good judgment comes from bad experience and a lot of that comes from bad judgment," said Alvarez. They stopped at a stoplight, and he leaned over and kissed Tory. It was not a casual kiss. As a matter of fact, it was about as X-rated a kiss as Tory had ever experienced at a stoplight. "What was that for?" she asked in astonishment, pushing him away, pulling his good hand out from under her sweater where it had insinuated itself.

"For the camera."

"What camera?"

"Up there." Alvarez pointed to a small piece of equipment mounted on the traffic light. "That's so obvious, even I can tell what it is. I'm amazed they don't get more complaints."

"That's an annunciator," said Tory.

Alvarez took his eyes off the road long enough to look at her curiously. "What the hell is an annunciator?"

"A piece of equipment that picks up the signals given off by the sirens of emergency vehicles. It automatically overrides the traffic signal timing system to give the emergency vehicle a green light.''

''Damn,'' said Alvarez. ''The things you miss out on, being an investigator.''

''So that little display was all for naught,'' Tory told him.

''Can *you* tell which traffic signals are rigged like the ones Cooper was describing?''

''No,'' admitted Tory.

''Then I rest my case.''

Tory decided it was time to change the subject. ''Where are we headed?''

''King's Ransom Pawn & Loan, Waldo Road,'' replied Alvarez.

Tory knew where Waldo Road was, but how did he know? ''How do you know where you're going?''

''Looked it up on the map before I went to the hospital. It's always good to have a plan, know the next step to take.''

Tory suddenly wondered if Alvarez had stopped at the hospital because he'd planned to take her with him to the pawnshop all along, decided not to ask, that she didn't want to know. ''King's Ransom, that's an interesting name for a pawnshop,'' she said.

''Yeah, it's one of the more up-scale ones.''

''There's such a thing as up-scale pawnshops?''

''Yeah. Pawnshops tend to specialize—some are really big into guns, some into electronics, like VCRs, computers and stuff.''

''I suppose you've already checked out what this shop specializes in?''

''That's right. Gold, jewelry, and collectibles.''

''What do you hope to find out by going to this pawnshop?''

''Don't know. I'll ask some questions, see where it takes me. Good to have a plan, not anticipate the outcome. Anticipating the outcome screws up your judgment something royal.''

Tory tried applying this statement to their relationship, decided it was more of a challenge than she was up for, and opted for discussing the task at hand. ''I don't see what's so unusual about Chloe Marshall going to a pawnshop.''

"You said you'd never been to one."

"I've never had my house broken into."

Alvarez smiled, his eyes still on the road. "It tends to be an exclusive-type deal. Either you're someone who does the B and E, or someone who has it done to you. You're in the first group, remember?"

Tory ignored this. "It makes sense to me to go to a pawnshop to look for stolen items," she insisted.

"That shows what you know about pawnshops. They're generally not a good place to look for stolen items, unless the stuff is coming in from out of the area."

"My father bought the Rosewood box from an antique dealer," said Tory. "It was stolen and it was local."

"Which proves my point. Pawnshops are regulated like you wouldn't believe. They're really a lending institution, not necessarily a conduit for stolen goods."

"I always thought that pawnshops were, well, shady," Tory said.

"That's what most civilians think. Pawnshops provide a valuable service for people who could never get a bank loan. They're often seen as a community resource—lots of times pawnshops are immune from vandalism and burglary because nobody wants the local source of loans closing up and shutting down."

"What's to keep them from taking stolen goods?"

"More regulations and procedures than you could even begin to imagine."

"Like what?"

"The pawnshops here are computerized, tied into the law enforcement computer system. That means they have to enter a description of every item they take in pawn so it can be compared with descriptions of stolen items. In Texas, pawning an item requires an ID and here it's even more stringent. You want to pawn something in Florida, you furnish ID and a fingerprint. Not exactly procedures your career criminal seeks out."

Alvarez was nothing if not thorough. "Then what does it mean to you, that Chloe Marshall went to a pawnshop?" Tory asked, trying to think it through.

"She was trying to find the stuff that had been stolen on her own, without consulting the police."

"And what does that mean?"

"I don't know, but I think we're on the right track."

"Why?" For the life of her, Tory couldn't follow his reasoning.

"Because of the bumper sticker on the car in front of us. Look."

Tory looked at the blue Mustang in front of them. On the bumper it said, FEEL SAFE TONIGHT. SLEEP WITH A COP.

"WHAT DO I DO?" asked Tory. She wanted to get her role straight before she entered a pawnshop for the first time.

"Go in, look around, see if there's anything you like."

"You're kidding."

"You might be pleasantly surprised. Pawnshops are where all the discriminating criminal attorneys buy their jewelry and electronic equipment."

"What about their guns?"

"They don't need guns," said Alvarez as he got out of the car. "At least not the discriminating criminal attorneys."

"Which ones are those?"

"The ones who sleep with cops." Alvarez held open the pawnshop door.

Tory paused a moment to look at the signs posted on the front window. They said things like, IF YOU'RE ON DRUGS, DON'T EVEN THINK ABOUT COMING IN HERE and THESE PREMISES UNDER 24-HOUR VIDEO SURVEILLANCE. Her favorite was the one that said WE ONLY KEEP $20 IN CHANGE—THE REST WE SPEND ON AMMUNITION.

She walked through the door into a warehouse-like space. There were things everywhere. Glass display cases surrounded three sides of the room, and the interior had crowded rows of shelves. There were TVs, computers, boom boxes, small electrical appliances and an endless variety of other items piled onto the shelves. Even the walls were covered with items hung for display: guns, power tools, a fur stole.

A ceiling-high chain-link fence separated a back area from the rest of the room, and three signs were posted there, facing toward the front door. In descending order and size of letters the signs said: ABSOLUTELY NO ADMITTANCE, ARMED AND WILLING TO SHOOT and JEWELRY REPAIR WHILE YOU WAIT. People waiting for jewelry repair probably didn't complain that it was taking too long.

An older, dark-haired man seated at a workbench behind the chain-link barrier looked up briefly. A short, stocky man with long reddish hair pulled back into a ponytail came out through the gate, a ready smile on his face. "Hi folks. My name's Danny. Anything I can help you with?" he asked.

"We're just looking," said Tory automatically.

Danny all but ignored her, his gaze tracking Alvarez's. "We got all our licenses in order—you're welcome to look. There's nothing here that ain't been entered into the system, 'cept for stuff we took in this morning, and we've got 'til closing on that."

Alvarez looked at him. "I walk in here and you start giving me explanations. What do you take me for?"

"A cop."

"I haven't even started asking questions."

"But you're gonna, right?"

Tory interrupted with, "If you think he's a cop, what does that make me?"

Danny studied her. "A cop's girlfriend?" he suggested.

Tory felt belittled. "Why not a cop?"

"You just don't have the look, babe. You know, like you're checking out who's where, who's carrying, that sort of thing."

"I noticed that you have reinforced steel plating on the bottom half of your chain link fence," Tory replied. "What's that for?"

"To stop bullets."

Tory didn't flinch. "It's supposed to stop bullets?" she asked. "You realize you've got it attached with duct tape?"

The man at the workbench looked up. "Duct tape is like The Force," he said. "It has its light side and its dark side and it holds the universe together." He nodded as though agreeing with his own statement. "Besides, that plating's stopped bullets before, and the tape's never been a problem."

"Oh," said Tory. She could think of several reasons why using duct tape to attach steel plating intended to stop bullets wasn't a good idea, but she decided to let it go. "I think I'll go look at your jewelry now, if that's okay."

Danny smiled his approval. "It's okay by me, babe. Your buddy here gets twenty percent off the top, being who he is and all."

It all came down to the company you kept. Tory walked over to study the items in one of the display cases. She could see a Doberman Pinscher lying at the feet of the man doing jewelry repair. The dog wagged its tail, but didn't get up. Maybe even the dog could tell that she was just a cop's babe.

"You had an attempted robbery a few months ago," said Alvarez.

"The crackhead, you mean?" Alvarez nodded.

"Do you have robberies often?" Tory asked. She couldn't help it, she was curious.

"Not too often," said Danny. "Someone suspicious-looking comes in, Mike over there gets down the shotgun, then we usually don't have no problem. The bad ones are the ones we don't see coming." Danny turned toward Mike. "Remember that lady, came in with a baby, gave us a sob story about her man running off on her, then whips her piece outta the diaper bag? Now, that was a bummer."

Mike grunted his agreement without looking up.

"What did you do?" Tory asked, fascinated.

"We talked her down. She didn't really want to go through with it, standing there holding the kid and all."

"What would you have done if you couldn't talk her down?"

Mike looked up then. "If you can't dazzle them with brilliance, riddle them with bullets," he said to Tory with a big smile. Several of his teeth were missing.

It occurred to Tory that this was the man within reach of the reported shotgun. She glanced at Danny, who looked at her and shrugged. "Takes a special kind of person to work in a pawnshop," he said.

"About the crackhead," Alvarez reminded him.

"Oh yeah, him. Good thing about crackheads, they don't think things through too good. Not like a gang hit, now that's the thing makes you piss your pants, four or five guys come in all at once, armed to the teeth.'' Danny shook his head just thinking about it.

"The crackhead," said Alvarez for the third time. Tory could swear he was grinding his teeth.

"This guy, he comes in dressed nice, no tell-tale bulges anywhere. We got several people in the store, so we don't notice that he's sweating like a pig. Turns out he has the gun in his pocket. He pulls it on Mike and tells us to empty out the cash register. Guy don't notice I'm over across the room, showing someone this VCR. He musta thought I was just another dude browsing the store. So I whip out a gun, stick it in his ribs, and that's the end of that."

"What gun, from where?" asked Tory.

"We have them concealed all over the store, strategic places." Tory couldn't help herself; she started to try to figure out where the strategic places were.

"The people in the store when this went down—" started Alvarez.

"They didn't have nothing to do with it," Danny said. "Believe me, we could tell."

"That's not what I'm after. There was a tall, thin woman, dishwater blond, late thirties maybe, mouth that looks like she's just eaten a pickle." Tory winced at this description of Chloe Marshall, but Danny picked up on it right away.

"Oh, you mean the pawn cherry."

"What's a pawn cherry?" asked Tory.

"Someone who doesn't frequent pawnshops," said Alvarez. "Like you. Go check out the jewelry. I'll ask the questions."

"Maybe you'd rather I go somewhere and powder my nose?"

Danny turned to Tory. "That case over there to your right, it has a nice sapphire solitaire ring, would match your eyes real good. Mike, go show the nice lady the sapphire ring." Mike sighed, got up from his workbench and came out through the gate. Mike, go keep the nice lady out of the way. Maybe she'd ask to look at the shotguns in stock just to keep everyone on their toes.

"So what's a pawn cherry doing in your pawnshop?" Alvarez asked as Mike selected a key from his chain, opened the display case, and pulled out a square-cut sapphire flanked by three small diamonds on each side.

"What all pawn cherries do in pawnshops, look for lost items like Wendy in Peter Pan looked for the Lost Boys," said Danny.

Tory shook her head at Mike.

"Family problems?" asked Alvarez.

Mike reached out, took Tory's right hand, and tried to slide the ring on her third finger. It wouldn't quite go over the last knuckle.

"I didn't get the feeling she was looking for the loot her teenaged son lifted from grandma to feed a habit. Probably had something stolen, was my guess."

"Then what was she looking for?" Alvarez asked.

Mike took Tory's other hand, slid the ring onto her third finger. It was a perfect fit.

"Maybe I don't remember. What's in it for me?"

Tory held up her hand to look at the ring.

"I'll take that ring off your hands," said Alvarez without a single glance in her direction.

"No, really," said Tory. She put her hand down, started taking off the ring.

"Yes, really," said Alvarez, never taking his eyes off Danny. "What did the pawn cherry want?" Mike took the ring from Tory and closed and locked the display case without putting it back.

Danny wrinkled his forehead, thinking. "Some antique family thing—a wooden keepsake box. That's really all I can remember. Since we didn't have nothing like that, we didn't have no long, drawn-out discussion about it." Mike returned to his place at the workbench.

"What did you tell her?" Alvarez asked.

"That we didn't normally take stuff like that. That it would be better to look at antique stores. That we don't take nothing that's hot."

"And what did she say?"

"She said it wasn't hot, that it was lost. She said if I came across a box like that, or if I heard of anyone who did, she'd make it worth my while."

"Then what happened?"

"Then the crackhead pulled his gun, I pulled mine, the police came, and we all had to tell our stories. She just kinda melted away after all that went down. Never gave me no name or phone number or anything. Wouldn't be surprised, that kind of thing, shaking up someone like her."

Mike looked up from his work. "Hell, that kind of thing shakes me up too."

Alvarez ignored him, concentrating on Danny. "She didn't ask about any jewelry, just the box?"

"Just the box, man. Is that it? Anything else you want to know?"

Alvarez appeared to consider the question. "How about thirty percent off on the ring?"

THIRTY-FIVE

Going Home
January 5, 1923. Rosewood, Florida

LISSY WALKED ACROSS the deserted town in the twilight of dawn, some detached part of her noting the randomness with which some houses had burned and some stood untouched. It didn't really make any difference. With the town deserted, the remaining buildings would surely be fodder for fires to follow. As it turned out, she was right, and not one single building belonging to the Negroes of Rosewood survived the next forty-eight hours. Not a house, not a school, not a church, not a shed. Not anything.

But that last clear cold morning, the Hodden house stood untouched, just the way her family had left it a lifetime ago. Not so the Marshall house—there were only smoldering ashes where Jim and Tressa Marshall once lived, once made a baby together. That baby was now a toddler, nearer and dearer to Lissy's heart even more since The Man was dead to her now. And it was The

Man himself who had told Lissy that she needed to go on living for those who loved and needed her, no matter how great the burden of her secrets. Lissy kept reminding herself of that as she carried the little three-legged dog to her home, as the sun began to light up the sky of yet another day.

It didn't matter that the Marshall house had been one of the first to burn. John Marshall had signed the deed over to Lissy's daddy the day before he left for Perry, looking for a better job, hoping to send for his son once he got settled. When it became apparent that Homer's father was never coming back, Lissy's parents removed everything of value from the Marshall house. That task had taken little enough time, as Lissy remembered it. Her father had been thinking about renting out the Marshall house and the land it stood on, or maybe selling it. Well, that was surely one thing he wouldn't have to worry about now.

Daybreak was coming, and with it increased danger for any Negro walking the streets of Rosewood. But she didn't hurry as she went about her self-appointed tasks. She felt no fear, no sense of urgency, just a great determination to get done what needed to be done. Fear would never again alter her priorities.

Upon arriving at her house, the first thing Lissy did was go into her father's tool shed and cut a length of good strong rope. After all that she and Git had been through together, it wouldn't do to have him run off now. Once the little dog was tied to a post on the porch, Lissy went into her bedroom and got her wooden box out from under her bed. She needed to make room for the important papers her mother kept in her dresser, the Marshall family Bible that her father had brought over from next door, pictures of Lissy and Garland together as children, and her mother's few pieces of jewelry.

The only way Lissy could fit all this in the box was to get rid of the stories she had written over the years. That suited Lissy just fine, as she never intended to write another story. From now on, the only things she would collect would be things written by other people. She sat on her bed and pulled story after story out of the box, dropping them one by one on the floor of her bedroom, to be committed to the fire with the rest of Rosewood.

After gathering and carefully placing the chosen objects into her box, Lissy walked outside, untied the rope from the porch and started down the street in the direction of the Wright house. She held the box in one hand and led the dog with the other.

She did not look back.

THIRTY-SIX

Visitation Rites
Wednesday

AS ALVAREZ PULLED OUT of the pawnshop parking lot, Tory regarded the ring on her finger as though her hand belonged to someone else. She felt railroaded, embarrassed, and just a tiny bit ungrateful. She thought of and discarded several statements, then settled on saying, "You buying me this ring is ridiculous."

Alvarez glanced over, picked up her hand and looked at it for a moment, studying the ring as though it were a piece of evidence. "I think it looks good," he said, returning her hand to her custody. "You have to admit, it was a great price."

Tory stole another look at the ring on her finger. It was beautiful, much more tasteful than anything she would have imagined coming from a pawnshop. "It doesn't mean anything," she said. Things were moving much too quickly.

"Yes, it does," Alvarez told her. "It means that Chloe Marshall was looking exclusively for the Rosewood box, not her stolen jewelry. That's damned strange."

It was difficult to have an argument with someone who didn't stick to the subject. "I'm talking about the ring. You tell me that I get to choose, then you keep making choices for me."

"I try to influence your choices. It's not the same thing."

"So if I'd walked out of the pawnshop, you wouldn't have bought the ring."

Alvarez looked at her as though she were stupid. "No, I would have still bought the ring."

"So what I do, what I choose, doesn't affect what you do."

Alvarez glanced at her again, smiled this time. "I think I can say that if you'd walked out of the bathroom last night, it would have affected what I did.''

Tory could feel herself flush. "Let me get this straight. To you this means, what—that we went and picked out a ring together?" She could imagine an innovative article for one of those magazines for brides: How to Get the Best Bargain on Your Ring By Interrogating a Pawnshop Owner.

Alvarez shrugged. ''I've never been much for shopping.''

Tory couldn't leave it alone. "Just what do you think you got for your money?''

''Other than the fact that you have ambivalent feelings about commitment?'' Alvarez didn't give her time to answer. "I found out that my instincts are right. There's something fishy going on with Chloe Marshall.''

''Just because she went into a pawnshop and asked about a stolen item?''

''No, because she didn't ask about any of the jewelry that went missing. Doesn't that seem just a little bit odd to you, logical problem-solver that you are?''

''Maybe the jewelry was recovered.''

Alvarez sighed. "We detectives are trained to check these things. None of it has been recovered to date, not according to George Nelson.''

''Maybe the jewelry wasn't that important to her,'' Tory said after a pause.

Alvarez snorted. ''Not likely.''

''How do you know?''

Alvarez told her the estimated value of the stolen jewelry. ''Oh,'' said Tory, for lack of a better response. The sapphire ring on her hand appeared to be a bargain indeed.

When they got back to the hospital, they learned that Tom Wheatley, with his usual sense of impeccable paternal timing, had regained consciousness about the time that Tory and Alvarez left in Dana Halloran's car for the pawnshop. Wheatley was weak but clearly lucid. He remembered leaving his condo the night of the accident, but had no memory of anything after that.

Since there had been a steady flow of people, including doctors, policemen, and Dana Halloran, with Wheatley since his awakening, Tory was allowed only a few minutes with her father. They were told that if they went to dinner and let the patient rest, they could come back and see him before bedtime, which the nurse said would be early.

It was as gleeful as a dinner in a hospital cafeteria could be, if one counted Dana Halloran's demeanor. Alvarez wondered at Tory's subdued behavior, which turned downright morose when Dana took her leave, claiming exhaustion and promising to return early in the morning, saying that Tory would surely want some private time with her father.

"What's wrong?" Alvarez asked as soon as the older woman left. "Are you worried about all the other stuff you'll have to face, now that the crisis with your father is past?"

Tory looked up from her plate, where she had been making creative designs in her mashed potatoes. "No, it's not that. It's the thought of confronting my father. Somehow it's easier to deal with him when he's unconscious. Now I'll have to talk to him, try to figure out what's real."

"Tell me what that means," said Alvarez.

Tory ignored his suggestion, continuing to trace designs in her mashed potatoes. "Doesn't it strike you as strange that I never knew about Dana Halloran?"

Knowing what little he did know about Tory's past, Alvarez had never been a big fan of Tom Wheatley, but he tried to be fair. "Maybe your father was waiting for the right time to tell you."

"If that's the case, doesn't it strike you as strange that Dana thinks I'm the one who broke up our family?"

Alvarez knew that he was treading on thin ice here. Tory's son was the one who had informed his grandfather that it was not his mother who was caught having an affair with Wheatley's top aide. As far as Alvarez knew, Tory and her father had never discussed the subject since the day she left home, taking the blame for someone else's misdoing. "Maybe he thinks it's better to let the past lie," Alvarez said carefully.

"And how willing are you to let the past lie?" asked Tory, as though by trying to be fair to her father, Alvarez had somehow become the enemy. "Don't tell me that you don't want to know whether my father's story about Chloe Marshall's visit jibed with the version she told us."

"Okay, I won't tell you that." Alvarez was having a hard time seeing the connection between Wheatley family history and the current murder investigations. "What's the big deal about me asking your father some questions?"

Tory was looking straight at him, but he could have sworn she was someplace else. "The big deal about asking my father any questions," she said softly, "is that you never know when he's telling the truth."

"FIFTEEN MINUTES," the ICU nurse told them.

Tory walked to her father's bedside and gave him a kiss on the cheek. "I'm so glad you're going to be okay."

"Senator Wheatley," said Alvarez formally, shaking the man's hand. He would give no sign that what he knew about the Wheatley family made his own upbringing—living in poverty with a mentally retarded sister, a grandmother who spoke no English, and a mother who had been abandoned by both husband and family—look good.

"No one knew where you were." Those were the first words Wheatley had for his daughter.

"I took Tory out for a while," said Alvarez. "She's been here four days, most of it at your bedside. She needed a break."

"Of course," said Wheatley. "Thank you for coming."

"I don't know if they told you when you talked to the police earlier, but Rolland Reynolds is dead," Tory told her father. That was certainly coming to the point. Tory must be taking the fifteen-minute time limitation seriously. She explained Rolland's visit to the hospital and his concern about Wheatley's planned contribution to the history department.

"That's horrible," Wheatley said when Tory was done. "I'm sorry to hear about Rolland's death. But you know, there always was something sly about him. There was talk about his wife, something about her family being tied to organized crime. I wonder if the police are looking into it.''

"That's being covered," said Alvarez, impressed with how smoothly Wheatley had transitioned from condolences to focusing potential blame on someone. He hoped that if he ever came out of a coma, he would awaken as fully functioning.

"Rolland was unhappy when I wouldn't give him the assurances he wanted about the endowment," said Tory, not looking at her father, pleating a fold of his bed sheet between her fingers as she spoke. Alvarez liked how the sapphire ring looked on her hand, liked the fact that she hadn't taken it off.

Wheatley frowned. "You never liked Rolland, did you? Did the two of you have words?" Wheatley paused. "Good God, Vicky, don't tell me that you came down here to see about me and got yourself mixed up in a murder investigation."

"Okay, she won't tell you that," said Alvarez. Wheatley and Tory ignored him.

"Rolland got angry, said some disturbing things," Tory continued doggedly. "He said Tommy enlisted in the Marines because you asked him to."

"That's ridiculous. Why would you repeat something like that to me?"

Tory didn't answer his question. "There was a box in the display case at your condo," she said. "It had the name Hodden and Rosewood carved on it. Rolland said that you asked him to investigate whether my mother's family had any ties to Rosewood—blood ties. He said that's what the endowment money was really about, him finding something you could use to discredit my mother's family."

"It seems that Reynolds was doing a lot of unauthorized historical research," interjected Alvarez. "Digging up things that some people would pay to know, things other people would pay to keep quiet. Last I checked, they didn't know whether he was researching the Hoddens or not. Be interesting to see if a file turns up on them."

Of course, a file on the Hoddens might turn up from bona fide Rosewood research, but Alvarez wondered if Wheatley, in his weakened state, would be quick enough to think this through. The man didn't disappoint him, even if he did disappoint his daughter.

"If I asked Rolland to do some research, it wouldn't have been to discredit anyone. I might have expressed some interest in the Rosewood connection after I saw the name on the box, but all I can say right now is that I don't remember. The doctors say that there may be some things I never remember," he added.

Alvarez found himself almost holding his breath. He felt certain Tory knew that her father had given way too much explanation. But she came through; just like a cop, she moved on.

"Do you remember meeting with Chloe Marshall the night of your accident?" she asked.

"Yes, I remember that. She brought over the endowment papers." Did Wheatley sound weary or wary now?

"Why didn't you sign the papers for her then?" asked Tory. "Did you really decide that you needed more time to look them over?"

Tory's father looked genuinely puzzled now. "Why should I need to look the papers over again? The time to look over an agreement is before someone brings you the final version. I already knew what those papers had to say—I didn't sign Friday evening because my signature required a notary."

"Dr. Marshall says that she talked to you about the Rosewood box being a family heirloom that was stolen in a burglary," interjected Alvarez. "She said you wanted to return it to her, but you'd misplaced the key to the display case."

"That's right," said Wheatley. "It was a beautiful box, and of course it got my attention, having the Hodden name carved on it. But Dr. Marshall was quite convinced that the box belonged to her husband, so it needed to be returned."

Alvarez was dumbfounded. So Chloe Marshall's lame story about the lost key to the display box was true after all?

"But you don't remember anything about how finding the box in an antique store prompted an interest in having Rolland look for ties between my mother's family and Rosewood?" Tory persisted.

Alvarez wondered if Wheatley had tried to pump Chloe about the box's history, or if he'd decided to leave that to Rolland. Still, Alvarez couldn't see what it had to do with the two murder investigations, and knowing the answer might cause Tory more pain.

"I already answered that question," said Wheatley, almost echoing Alvarez's thoughts. "It's not very pleasant to have you at my bedside if you're going to badger me. I don't want to discuss this subject ever again."

Alvarez knew the sound of truth when he heard it.

"Time's up," said the nurse.

TORY ASKED ALVAREZ to wait for her in the parking lot. Thinking she might need some time to recover her composure after the conversation with her father, he didn't argue. She came out the front door of the hospital ten minutes later and asked him for the keys to the rental car. "What?" he asked. "I had plans for tonight. Salmon steaks, wild rice, a little music, a perfectly good king-sized bed—"

"There are lots of things more important than sex," Tory told him.

"Sex is like air," he replied. "It's only important when you're not getting any."

"Truth is important. Let's go find some."

"And how do you suggest we go about doing that?"

"The good old-fashioned way, by arranging to talk to someone. I looked up Richard Marshall in the phone book and called him. It's so much easier than breaking in, planting recording devices. I told him about my father waking up, about the possibility that Reynolds was researching the Hoddens."

She just wasn't going to let this go. "What did he say?"

"He said that his wife was at a faculty meeting, but to come on over, and he'd answer any questions we had."

This was what you got, hanging around with an overachiever. "I'll drive, you navigate," he said.

THIRTY-SEVEN

End of the Line
January 6, 1923. Rosewood, Florida

LISSY SAW THE anxious faces of her family as the train pulled into the station at Archer. Many of her neighbors on board were weeping; many of them had been hiding out in the swamp. Lissy and the contingent from the Carrier house were fortunate to have found shelter at John Wright's house, although nothing could shelter them from news of the growing death toll.

Before the sun set the previous day, the mob found James Carrier wandering around the deserted town. They took him to the graveyard, tortured him, and killed him there. Lissy learned later that Mingo Williams, a Negro man from a neighboring town, was found out on the road by the mob and shot dead on that same day.

Finally, on this evening five days after New Year's, the train that had sped past the Rosewood depot for the last few days stopped and took on passengers. Lissy learned that this was only because of the intervention of two wealthy, eccentric brothers who liked to play at the job of train conductor. The train they commandeered made numerous additional stops along the tracks leading out of town, taking on Negro passengers coming out of the swamp at each juncture. Even so, the gesture of rescue was not extended to everyone; Lissy heard the conductor say regretfully to more than one person who tried to get on board, "I'm sorry, son. We're only taking women and children. We can't run the risk of the posse finding Negro men on this train. God bless you, and good luck."

Most of the passengers on this train of sorrow continued on into Gainesville, but Lissy saw her family waiting for her at the Archer depot and she climbed off there, making sure she took with her everything that she had determined to bring out of Rosewood. Many of the passengers called after her, sending her blessings and telling her that they would be in touch. Lissy didn't say anything in return; she had already said all her goodbyes, and as for staying in touch, what was the use of neighbors from a town that no longer existed?

As her family closed around her, Lissy knew that she and Homer and Git would always have one thing in common—an inability to discuss the last days of Rosewood.

THIRTY-EIGHT

Touching the Past
Wednesday

NAVIGATING HAILE Plantation was a nightmare. The place must have been designed by someone who hated straight lines; the various neighborhoods merged seamlessly into one another. The area had undergone such rapid development that much of it was not reflected on the map, and after they'd passed the small neighborhood commercial center several times, Tory began to make remarks about men who wouldn't ask for directions. Alvarez replied that he'd never been bested by a subdivision yet, and didn't plan to start with a Florida one. Fifteen minutes later, mostly by trial and error, they pulled to the curb in front of an imposing three-story brick structure.

"Wow," Alvarez said, looking at the house. "My old *abuela* used to tell me that if I didn't straighten out, I'd end up being a janitor. I wonder if this is what she had in mind."

"Let's go," said Tory, unbuckling her seat belt. Alvarez reached over, caught her hand. "What?" she asked.

"I'm not sure this is such a good idea."

"Why wouldn't this be a good idea? You've been saying all along that you think there's something funny going on with Chloe Marshall and that keepsake box. Here's a chance to get those questions answered, and you're saying that you're not sure it's a good idea?"

"Doesn't this remind you of one of those cop shows?" Alvarez asked. "The made-for-TV movies where the main character figures out who did it and goes after the bad guy all by himself?"

"What bad guy? It turns out that everything Chloe Marshall told us about the keepsake box was true. Richard Marshall is a respected businessman. You had lunch with him, remember? He's invited us to his house to ask any questions we want. What's the problem?" Alvarez just sat and looked at her, not saying anything.

Alvarez sighed. "Have you thought about why you're so set on this, *querida?*" he asked finally.

"I want some answers."

"I don't think Richard Marshall can give you the answers you want to hear." Tory shrugged. "Listen," said Alvarez. "You're an intelligent woman. You're an engineer. You own a business, you've raised a son. If we go inside and talk to Richard Marshall, no matter what he tells you, you'll still never get any straight answers out of your father."

"What happened to you thinking all this had something to do with the murder investigations?"

"What if it does? If we go inside and talk to Richard Marshall, and somehow, based on that conversation, or based on something else, you manage to figure out who killed Amy Cooper and Rolland Reynolds all by yourself, it still won't change things between you and your father."

Tory stared at him. "Let me make sure I get this straight. It's okay for you to go chasing off, messing with a murder investigation a thousand miles out of your jurisdiction, but when I do the same thing, I have ulterior motives?"

"I'm a cop," said Alvarez.

"And I'm what? Some bimbo with the IQ of celery?"

"You're a woman in a difficult situation who's not thinking clearly. I'm a cop. That's what I do—pressure people into things, figure stuff out, exert authority to make things go my way. How can you forget this, *cara,* when you accuse me of it at least ten times a day?"

"What does that have to do with anything?"

"You drop this bombshell on me," Alvarez continued calmly, "you tell me that you're pregnant. Then you keep insisting that you want to be free to choose what happens next. How do you expect me to react? When I'm around you, I want to make you do things my way—marry me, have the baby, the hell with everything else. I go chasing somebody else's murder investigation to keep my hands off you, keep from shaking you 'til you give me a written statement saying you'll do what I want."

Tory looked at the empty street ahead of them. "I don't know what to think," she said after a moment. "It's too many changes all at once. Too many to keep track of. I try to think about us together—" she faltered. "Maybe you're just trying to do the decent thing."

Alvarez resisted the urge to bang his head against the steering wheel. "I know what I don't want. I don't want to walk away from this, walk away from you." He stopped, trying to think how to explain. "It's like the first time you put on your gun, fresh out of the police academy, and go out and walk a beat. Nobody who's sane wants to do that. But there's a bigger part of you that wants to give it a try."

"God, that's romantic. An analogy that equates marrying me to the possibility of being shot dead on the street."

"You should be grateful to be with someone who's been fire-tested," Alvarez suggested, but Tory didn't go for the humor.

"You have no idea what being married, what being a father would be like," she said.

"No, I don't," he admitted, "but I'm willing to give it my best shot, no pun intended. Besides, you're hardly one to talk about romance. I ask you to marry me and you throw up."

Tory continued to look out on the street. "That first day at the condo," she said. "You told me there was something that we needed to talk about. Then you never said anything else about it."

"And you thought all this time I was having second thoughts? How about all the other times I've told you that I want you to marry me, have the baby?"

Tory shrugged, still not looking at him. "You were trying to get me into bed," she said. "When you said that there was something we needed to talk about, we were sitting down, eating."

"Give me a break, Tory. Even when I was undercover, I

didn't ask women to marry me to get them into bed." He knew this was a mistake the instant the words were out of his mouth.

"What did you do instead?" she asked immediately, looking straight at him now.

"Maybe," said Alvarez carefully, "when we've been married oh, twenty years or so, I'll be willing to discuss that. For now, let's get back on topic. When I told you there was something we needed to think about, I meant my sister Anna. We need to talk about Anna. You know that she's mentally retarded. I was told it was congenital, that there were problems at birth, but now that I really think about it, I realize I have no proof."

"That's all?" Every time he thought he had her figured out, she surprised him.

"Isn't that enough?"

Tory shrugged again. "I've always had to live with the knowledge that any child of mine carries my family's genetic heritage, and that's not something to be taken lightly. Sometimes it's pretty scary."

Alvarez grinned. "You think there's a chance you might wake up someday, decide to run for office?"

Tory shook her head. "I don't think so, but there are no guarantees."

"No," said Alvarez. "There are no guarantees. It doesn't matter how smart you are, or what you achieve. Your father is never going to change, Tory. He's never going to be the person you want him to be, and he's never going to explain to you why things were the way they were."

Tory looked out again for a while, then she turned back to look at him. "Okay. Maybe you're right. Let's go talk to Richard Marshall anyhow. Let's see if you're as good as you think you are."

Alvarez still hadn't gotten the answer he wanted, but at least Tory had sat still for the conversation. "There are other ways to find that out," he told her.

She shook her head. "You've been saying all along that there is something funny going on with Chloe Marshall. I think you're dead wrong. Here's our chance to find out."

Alvarez winced at her choice of words, then glanced in the

rearview mirror. "You're prepared to be my back-up?" he asked. Not that he expected any problems, not that he didn't have his bets covered.

"I have a miniature calculator in my wallet," Tory told him.

"Then what are we waiting for?"

RICHARD MARSHALL answered the doorbell immediately, as though he'd been standing behind the door waiting for them to ring. He ushered them into a lavish entry hall with a white wooden staircase spiraling upward out of sight. He took their coats and hung them in a closet by the front door.

"It's a beautiful house," said Tory.

Marshall smiled. "It is, isn't it? It's all Chloe's doing," he said. "Come this way, I have a study off the hall to the right." The study was dark and masculine, paneled and furnished in leather and mahogany. There were no papers on the desk, and few books in the bookcases. Instead, there were numerous photographs of various people posing in front of various businesses. Alvarez assumed that these were pictures of JanitorAll clients. Tory and Alvarez sat on a large leather couch. Marshall sat in a chair opposite them and leaned forward.

"I'll be happy to answer any questions you have," he said. "It worries me, Chloe's two coworkers getting killed within days of each other. It makes you realize how useless money really is. I'd hire someone to follow Chloe around, but she won't hear of it, says the deaths have nothing to do with her. But she's like that, not wanting to cause any trouble, Chloe is. It's the way she was raised."

"What do you mean?" asked Tory.

"I don't mean to speak badly of anyone, but I figure you want honest answers. Chloe's people, they're dirt poor, mainly, and ignorant. She's the only one in her family to go to college, make something out of herself. Everyone talks about how Chloe and Amy Cooper were related, but it's through marriage, not blood. Chloe's family disowned her, marrying a black man. Sometimes I think we built this house just to show them, but if it's what Chloe wants, it's fine with me. My first wife, she worked her fingers to the bone helping me build my business, then she never lived to see how it turned out. I figure that should tell me something about how to live the rest of my life. If Chloe wants something and it's within my power to get it for her, I do.''

Alvarez filed this statement away to consider at another time. "What about your family?" he asked.

"My family? I haven't got any family left. It was just me and my mamma for most of my growing up, and my mamma died when I was twenty.''

"What about your father's side of the family?"

"Daddy was an orphan, taken in by neighbors." Marshall shrugged. "Most everything I learned about my daddy, I learned from other people. He walked out on us when I was just a little boy. He'd come around sometimes, give us some money once in a while, but mostly he was just a drunk. Truth is, I'd lost track of him until all this business started up about Rosewood.'

"Did your father ever talk about Rosewood, about coming out of there with Lissy Hodden Garner?"

"I told you, he left when I was just a little thing."

"What about after you found him again, when your wife tracked him down as part of the Rosewood investigation?" Marshall shifted his large frame in the chair as though he found the question uncomfortable.

"When Chloe found my daddy, he was in a veteran's hospital. You ever seen someone in the last stages of alcoholism? Besides, he was too little to remember anything about Rosewood.''

"Were you surprised to find out that your father was a Rosewood survivor?"

"Well, yes and no. My mamma always told me that my daddy had a hard time, losing his parents so young and losing his home too. The way I was brought up, you listened to what you were told, and you didn't ask questions. I knew my daddy's family came from Rosewood, and I had a pretty good idea what happened there, but it wasn't something that we talked about much, if you know what I mean. I thought my mamma cut him too much slack, myself. I thought he was damn lucky to have family willing to take him in and raise him.''

"So you grew up knowing that your father was from Rosewood.''

"I knew my granddaddy was lynched there, but I didn't think too much on it. There wasn't much point, and I was busy trying to help my mamma out and get on with my own life."

As jaded as Alvarez thought he was, it shocked him to hear Marshall refer to having a relative lynched in such a matter-of-fact way. Regardless, his detective's mind noted that this was a different version of the story Dr. Mortenson told. "Everything you knew about Rosewood was from what your mother told you?"

"Until the stories started making the news, and until I met up with Aunt Lissy. It was amazing, finding someone who could tell me about my father as a little boy, before he started drinking and getting into trouble."

"Your father and Lissy Hodden Garner were both named Rosewood survivors, they both got reparation payments of $150,000, and they both named you as their heir," said Alvarez. He wasn't interested in nostalgic trips down memory lane.

"Is that what you wanted to ask about?" Marshall sounded surprised. "You think these deaths might have something to do with Rosewood money? Lord, some of that's a mess for sure, and there's tales to be told about it, but no Richard Marshall tales, I can tell you that. My father lived for only two years after the settlement. I moved him out of the veteran's hospital. After two years in the best treatment center I could find, there wasn't all that much of the $150,000 left."

"But there was still Lissy Hodden Garner's money," Alvarez said doggedly. There was something here, but until he figured out what it was, he had no choice but to keep on asking the same kind of questions. Tory was looking at him in disbelief, as though he was so stupid that he didn't realize all his questions led to the same dead end.

"Yeah," said Marshall without rancor, "there was Aunt Lissy's money. She didn't have any relatives, and she wasn't the kind to be duped into anything, not like some of the other folks who got payments. Aunt Lissy didn't want to go anywhere, either. The Rosewood business didn't make much difference to her. She just wanted to live out her life on her terms, right where she was."

"And part of living out her life on her terms was bequeathing her estate to you." Surely if Marshall kept talking, he would say something that Alvarez could use to his benefit.

"Aunt Lissy left some money to an aide she liked—the same one who filed her papers for her. But you're right, she left everything else to me."

"So she left you about $130,000," said Alvarez, hoping to startle the man with his knowledge that Tazzy had gotten twenty thousand.

Marshall blinked. "Oh no," he said. "It was more like $200,000. Aunt Lissy, she didn't just let money lie around. She hired herself an accountant, had most of it invested."

Alvarez couldn't think of what to say to this. "What did you do with the $200,000, then?" asked Tory.

"Well," said Marshall, "that was hard. I ended up donating the money to the scholarship fund for Rosewood survivors. Aunt Lissy never liked to talk about what happened at Rosewood, but still, it seemed like the right thing to do."

"You donated the money," repeated Alvarez, trying to buy time, trying to think what his next question would be.

"The important thing she left me was her papers," continued Marshall as though Alvarez hadn't spoken. "Papers she hadn't ever shown anyone except me."

"Papers she kept in her wooden keepsake box?" asked Alvarez, taking a leap of faith.

"That's right," said Marshall. "Sylvester Carrier made Aunt Lissy that box when she was a little girl. They had a special relationship, like brother and sister. Aunt Lissy would never talk about what happened to him, but she had to have been there when he was killed."

"What did you do with the papers?"

"Well, that was the thing, wasn't it?" asked Marshall, as though Tory and Alvarez should have an answer to his rhetorical question. "Some of them, they weren't so nice, having to do with lynchings and all. So I showed them to Chloe and we talked about it. Those papers were all I had to connect me to the things my family lived through. Still, they weren't something you'd want to frame and hang on the wall, or leave lying around. We finally decided that those papers should stay right where they'd been all these years.''

Alvarez was too slow; Tory beat him to the punch. "And where was that?" she asked.

"Why, in the bottom of Aunt Lissy's box, of course. When Chloe went to talk to you that night, didn't she tell you that the box has a false bottom, one you can pull out if you know just where to put your fingers?"

Alvarez recovered first this time. "No, she didn't tell us that," he told Richard Marshall.

"Would you like me to show you?"

"Yes," said Alvarez. "We'd like that very much."

"I'll go get it then," said Marshall. "You'll have to wait a minute. We used to keep the box in the bedroom—Chloe kept jewelry in it. But ever since the burglary, and since we got it back against all odds, Chloe decided it would be a good idea to keep Aunt Lissy's box in our safe."

"We'll wait," Alvarez assured him. When Richard Marshall left the room, he looked at Tory. "Am I on drugs?" he asked her. "Have I been drinking? Do I have a search warrant in my hand and I just don't know it?"

Tory looked as puzzled as he felt. "Maybe he's going to show us some old pictures and locks of hair," she said.

"Like hell. There's something going on here, I can feel it."

"And you're never wrong?"

"Not often. Not about things that matter. But right now I'm wondering if I turned off the lights in that damned rental car. Wouldn't want to be set to make a quick departure and find ourselves stuck here with a dead battery." Before Tory could point out how all the new cars had warning systems—bells and whistles, even conversational voices to prevent operator error, Alvarez got up. He walked out of the room, retraced their steps back to the front door, and slipped outside, leaving the door slightly ajar behind him so he could return without ringing the doorbell.

When Alvarez walked back into the study a few minutes later, Richard Marshall was sitting next to Tory on the couch, the Rosewood box on his lap. Alvarez sat down on the other side of Marshall. Their host then showed them how the bottom of the box could be lifted out to expose a second storage space about an inch in depth. Marshall took the contents from the concealed space and spread them on the coffee table in front of them for inspection. There was a letter and a few newspaper clippings, but none of the baptismal certificates or property deeds that Alvarez had come to expect from his conversations with Marilyn Mortenson.

"These are things that have to do with the killings at Rosewood," said Marshall.

Alvarez could see immediately that one of the yellowed newspaper clippings now spread before them showed two dead black men hanging from ropes around their necks. He selected the faded letter to start with. It was addressed to a Miss Lissy Hodden in Rosewood, Florida, from a Mrs. Garland Grant in Archer, Florida. It was postmarked December 28, 1922. Only three days before the violence started in Rosewood, Alvarez noted automatically.

"You see, there's two lines of thought about things like this," said Marshall, looking solemnly at the items in front of them. "Dr. Reynolds, he wanted stuff like this put on display, out in museums and in schools, right in people's faces. Chloe, she thinks differently, and that caused some problems between the two of them. She thought that historical records should be made as accurate as possible, but that using people's personal belongings for shock value was wrong. Rosewood wasn't all that long ago, you know. A lot of people could still be hurt, if they knew everything that happened there."

Tory was sitting as still as a statue on the other side of Richard Marshall. "What is shocking about this letter?" Alvarez asked Marshall, finding himself reluctant to read the contents of the envelope and thus violate the privacy of the earnest man sitting next to him.

"That's a letter from Garland Grant," Marshall said. "Garland was Aunt Lissy's older sister, and it was Garland and her husband who took in my daddy. That letter tells about what happened to Aunt Lissy in Rosewood, and how my grandfather was killed by the mob."

"Do you mind?" asked Alvarez, hand poised to extract the paper from inside the envelope.

Marshall shook his head. "Like I told you, I want this stuff figured out before anything else happens. You helped my wife when that man was out there, vandalizing her car. You look at whatever you want, ask me whatever you want."

Alvarez took the letter out, spread it on his knee and began to read. Garland Grant had a nice, even handwriting. The letter told how the arrival of Homer Marshall at the Grant household had been the best Christmas present ever, even if the little boy had come the day after Christmas. Garland's letter went on to assure Lissy that Homer coming to live with the Grants was the best thing for everyone involved, even if it wasn't what Lissy wanted, and that Lissy was welcome to come and visit whenever she wanted. Garland acknowledged how much Lissy cared for Homer, and that she understood Lissy was angry about having to part from him. The letter ended by saying that everyone missed Lissy, but they were sure she was in good hands staying with the Carriers.

Alvarez had to admire Garland Grant; she had obviously gotten what she wanted at the expense of her younger sister's desires, but the letter had neither a pleading nor apologetic tone. It sounded just like what an older sister would say while waiting for a younger sibling to get over a grievance and come to her senses.

Tory held out her hand and Alvarez gave her the letter, raising an eyebrow as he did so. He doubted that the date on the postmark would mean much to her, but he was sure if she merely skimmed the handwritten lines, she would discover that the content of the letter differed quite drastically from what Richard Marshall described.

Alvarez reached out and picked up the clipping showing the two lynched black men. "That's what ran in the newspaper before anyone even knew who they were," explained Marshall.

Someone had written the date December 11, 1922 along the side of the clipping. The handwriting was not Garland Grant's. Alvarez looked at the brief text under the grisly photograph:

In a second wave of violence resulting from the murder of a white schoolteacher, two unidentified Negro men were found lynched on the outskirts of Perry early yesterday morning. The accused Negro murderer was burned to death on December ninth. A Negro church, school, Masonic Lodge, and meeting hall were also burned. The names of the two dead men and their connection to the victim are still being sought. Anyone with pertinent information is asked to contact the sheriff.

Not a single request for information regarding the identities of those responsible for three executions. Alvarez put the clipping back down on the table, hoping that Tory wouldn't pick it up, but his hopes were in vain. He picked up the next yellowed newspaper clipping. This one was just a small bit of paper, with no picture and no date anywhere on it.

"That's where they printed my grandfather's name," said Richard Marshall with something between pride and regret.

It didn't take long to read this clipping, either.

According to reliable sources, one of the dead Negro men discovered five days ago on the outskirts of Perry was John Marshall of Rosewood, Florida, aged twenty-nine. Marshall reportedly came to Perry seeking work. He reportedly had no history of violence or criminal record. Marshall's connection to the murdered woman and the identity of the other man hanged with him is still being sought.

Alvarez put this clipping back down on the table, and Tory immediately picked it up. Marshall handed him the last item, almost half a page of newsprint.

This one had a printed masthead and date line proclaiming *The Tampa Morning Tribune*, February 14, 1923. The headline spread across five columns of newsprint and announced WE REMEMBER HATE AND INJUSTICE ON VALENTINE'S DAY.

"Most of the Florida newspapers, they just went along with the things that were happening back then," Marshall explained.

"Chloe knows about all that stuff. She says the *Tampa Morning Tribune* was one of the few papers to denounce hate crimes. While the newspaper here in Gainesville was writing about how lynchings were to be expected whenever a white woman was threatened, the *Tribune* called for law and order." Marshall paused. "The Rosewood Massacre was the first week in January, 1923," he said. "Less than two weeks later, a black boy was accused of stealing cattle in Newberry. Y'all know where Newberry is?"

"About fifteen miles west of Gainesville," said Tory.

Marshall nodded. "They took that poor kid out of his cell and lynched him," he continued. Marshall wasn't reading anything; he was obviously reciting facts long since committed to memory. "The *Tribune* ran this editorial while a Grand Jury was investigating Rosewood. The very next day, the same Grand Jury announced that there was insufficient evidence to prosecute anyone for anything related to what happened at Rosewood." Marshall paused again. "Chloe has spent years researching Rosewood, and she says the only public record showing that anything happened is a receipt for the sheriff using someone's bloodhounds that week."

Alvarez pointed to the *Tampa Morning Tribune* clipping. "What does this article mean to you?"

"It has my grandfather's name in it, and my father's name, too," said Marshall, with that same tone of solemn mixed emotions. Marshall pointed to a place in the middle of the article, and Alvarez read the paragraph silently.

John Marshall, a Rosewood man seeking work in Perry, was lynched outside that town in December of last year, victim of a mob reacting mindlessly to the murder of a white schoolteacher. Marshall had arrived in Perry only days earlier, and had no known contact with the murdered woman. He left behind an orphaned son, Homer Marshall, who through fortunate coincidence, was taken to Archer by neighbors just days before the massacre at Rosewood. Though saved from physical harm at Rosewood, this child lost his one surviving parent to a mob at Perry and any

*material belongings to another mob at Rosewood, in the
space of less than a month. How long will Negro children
continue to claim loss from mob violence as their heritage
in the State of Florida? How long will our elected officials
continue to condone justice meted out not by judges and
juries, but by groups of violent men fueled with hate and
liquor, armed with ropes and guns?*

The language might be more flowery than currently accepted
standards, but the message was loud and clear. Alvarez held onto
this newspaper clipping, thinking about some of the episodes
from the past few days.

There was Marshall at the hospital, asking where Wheatley
was when all along, his name was on his bed. There was the
restaurant owner, telling Alvarez how Marshall was known to
be someone who always took a contract home to sleep on it
before signing it. And then there was Marshall himself, looking
uncomfortable upon finding the menu had been changed, letting
Alvarez order first, quickly telling the waitress to double the
order.

Alvarez considered the man sitting beside him on the couch,
while Tory wore a puzzled expression, as though waiting for a
cue as to how to proceed. Alvarez considered their surroundings,
a spacious three-story house in which it seemed no expense had
been spared. Well, he had come across stranger things. He just
couldn't remember one at the moment. No wonder Richard Marshall had married so soon after his first wife's death. It had been
an alliance with significant benefits to both parties.

"Mr. Marshall," he said politely. "You told us you'd do anything, answer any of our questions to try to get to the bottom of
what's been going on with the recent deaths of your wife's coworkers."

"That's right," said Marshall, coming out of his reverie.

Alvarez reached down and picked up the smallest newspaper
clipping, the one that was only a paragraph in length. "Could
you read this to us?" he asked.

There was only silence in the room, making it easy to hear
the click of high heels in the hall approaching the study. Chloe

Marshall's tall form suddenly filled the doorway. She took in the gathered group, the Rosewood box, and the spread artifacts with one glance, then had eyes only for Alvarez. Two scarlet spots of anger stood out high on her very pale cheeks.

"How dare you?" she asked, breathing quickly through her mouth as though she had just crossed the finish line at a race. "How dare you come into our house and ask my husband a question like that?"

THIRTY-NINE

Reading Between the Lines
Wednesday

RICHARD MARSHALL and Tory sat immobile, side by side on the couch, but Alvarez was up and moving before the first question was out of Chloe Marshall's mouth. He wanted to put some distance between him and the others and get closer to the woman standing in the doorway.

"So we've figured out that your husband doesn't know how to read," he said conversationally, drifting away from the couch and closer to the door. "It's not something to be ashamed of, and it's a problem that can be fixed. There are lots of adults who are illiterate. It only makes what he's achieved that much more admirable."

Chloe reached one gloved hand into her coat pocket, pulled out a gun, and pointed it at Alvarez. He immediately knew the gun would outclass any calculator in Tory's wallet. "If you're so smart, then you can figure out how to sit down on the couch by your girlfriend and shut up," said Chloe.

"I'm not his girlfriend," said Tory. Of all the times for her to turn out to be predictable.

"Chloe, what are you doing?" asked Marshall, visibly stunned by his wife's actions. Alvarez wondered where Marshall's allegiance would lie if things went to hell fast.

"I'm sorry, Richard." Chloe might be speaking to her husband, but she never took her eyes off Alvarez, motioning him back toward the couch with the gun. "If this man had just left well enough alone, everything would have been okay. Richard, I want you to stand up slowly. Don't get between me and the others, but go sit in the chair."

"Chloe—" Marshall started.

"Just do it!" his wife yelled, which scared Alvarez more than anything else that had happened. "Please," she added in a shaky voice.

Chloe Marshall looked close to losing it, and if she lost it with a loaded gun in hand, none of Alvarez's back-up plans were going to help them. Also, she was waving the gun around with one hand instead of holding it with two, which did nothing for Alvarez's comfort level.

He sat down on the couch. Richard Marshall got up slowly and crossed over to the chair he'd been sitting in before fetching the Rosewood box.

"He can't help it, you know," Tory said to Chloe. "He's a police detective with this hot-shot department back in Texas, so when he came out here with me, he was at loose ends, then people kept turning up dead..." Tory's words came to a stop, as though she couldn't remember where she was going with that thought. "He even investigated me once," she added, "so it isn't anything personal. It's just what he does."

"Sweetheart," said Alvarez through clenched teeth. "Please shut up."

"Are you calling me sweetheart?" Tory asked. At least he'd gotten her attention. "Why should I shut up? You're the one who asked the questions that got everyone all upset." Tory glared at Alvarez and scooted as far away from him on the couch as she could get.

Good for her, he thought, keeping his eyes fixed on Chloe and the gun. Trust Tory to realize that it was harder to shoot people who weren't close together.

"Chloe," said Marshall, "I don't understand what's going on. These people didn't come here to hurt me. They've found out that I can't read, so what? It's a secret that I've kept too long. It'll be okay, honey, believe me."

"You don't understand. I'm trying to protect you."

"From what, sweetheart?" Chloe just shook her head, as though explaining was too much of an effort.

Alvarez decided to go for broke, hoping that if things went badly, Marshall would throw in with them. "It's true, I'm a police detective," he told Chloe, keeping his voice low and steady. "I know that we surprised you, being here, talking to your husband, and I can understand that. But if you think it through, you'll realize that you don't want to be doing what you're doing."

"You're so smart that you think you know the answers to everything?"

"No, I don't know the answers to everything. I'm still trying to figure out whether you killed one, two, or three people."

Marshall and Tory weren't looking at Chloe now, they were staring at him. Even Chloe looked incredulous.

"I have no idea what you're talking about," she said.

"I know one thing for sure," he told her. "I know that guns are really heavy, especially for women, who don't have the upper body strength that men have." He heard Tory's hissed intake of breath, knew that she would go on being judgmental to the bitter end. "Guns are also very heavy for people who aren't used to using them," he amended. God knew that if he got blown away in this room, he didn't want to die in the act of being politically incorrect. "People who are under a great deal of stress and who get tired at the same time often make mistakes. Serious mistakes they regret later."

Chloe seemed to consider what he had just said. "How do I know you don't have a gun?" she asked.

"I'm on medical leave—that's why my arm is in a sling. I'm also traveling outside my jurisdiction. Do you have any idea how much paperwork is involved in getting a permit to carry outside your state of residence? I never anticipated any of this, believe me."

"He doesn't have a gun," Tory chimed in. "He's got a really short temper, and if he had a gun, he would have done something stupid by now. Trust me." This from the woman wearing a ring he'd bought.

"Think about it," said Alvarez, ignoring Tory. "Remember

the night I walked you to your car, found the guy with the can of spray paint? If I'd had a gun, don't you think I would have used it then?''

Alvarez watched Chloe think this over. "Okay," she said slowly. "So what?"

"So I suggest you sit down, hold the gun with two hands, and rest it on your knees. That way you can still keep it pointed at me, still keep control of the situation, but you'll be able to sit down and talk to us, think about what you're doing."

"Listen to what the man's saying," Marshall pleaded. "Chloe, you look ready to fall over where you stand. Your hand is shaking, sweetheart."

Chloe looked for a hidden trap in the suggestions and found none. "Don't move," she told Alvarez.

"All I plan to do," he said sincerely, "is keep breathing in and out."

Chloe kept the gun pointed at him as she slowly sat down in the doorway, pulled her knees to her chest, and balanced the gun with two hands on top of her knees. "Now what?" Chloe asked Alvarez. "You're going to come up with some story about how I can get out of this okay, and I'll believe you and hand over the gun?"

"Maybe," said Alvarez. "It depends on what you've done and why you did it." Chloe regarded him steadily, not saying a word, not helping out a bit. "Did you kill Amy Cooper?" he asked.

Chloe made a disgusted sound. "No, I didn't kill her. Why would I?"

"Do you know who did?"

Chloe shook her head. "Todd's story about Rolland hiring someone to kill her sounds good to me," she said. "I'd like to believe it, because that would lend some poetic justice to the whole sordid affair. But I don't know. Todd's a clever boy, and he knew about Amy and Rolland. Amy was playing with fire. I tried to warn her, but she wouldn't listen."

"Did you kill Lissy Hodden Garner?"

Chloe narrowed her eyes and frowned at Alvarez. "You really don't think much of me, do you?"

"I had to ask," he said evenly. "She wanted to talk to your husband, but she died before she was able to, died right after seeing you."

"She died of natural causes. You're right, though. She wanted to see Richard, tell him the truth before she died. You don't know how often I've wished she had told him."

"Told me what?" asked Marshall desperately. "I don't understand any of this."

"I don't understand all of it," said Alvarez. "But I think I understand enough to be able to piece most of it together. Mr. Marshall, the papers you just showed us tell how your grandfather was lynched outside of a town called Perry a month before the violence at Rosewood. I don't know if it will make you feel better or worse, but it seems that he was as innocent as the blacks who died at Rosewood."

"I don't believe it," said Marshall.

"It's true," said Tory quietly.

"So your father was orphaned in December, 1922," continued Alvarez. "The Hoddens took him to live with Garland and her husband in Archer the day after Christmas. That's why their younger daughter was staying with the Carriers when the violence broke out. The woman you call Aunt Lissy appears to have had a peculiar sense of humor. She didn't care about being identified as a Rosewood survivor. For some reason, she lived her whole life avoiding anything having to do with the memories and the other survivors, but when her identity caught up with her, she decided to tell people that your father was with her in Rosewood. The other survivors were mainly children themselves, younger than Lissy when the massacre happened. There was no one around to contradict her."

"Why would she do that?" Marshall asked.

Chloe answered her husband's question. "She said that Homer turned out to be a drunk, in spite of how much everyone cared for him. She said she'd lost track of him, but that she'd heard he had a son somewhere. She decided that if anyone was going to get money out of what had happened at Rosewood, it might as well be Homer Marshall's son. She told me that she thought it was real funny when you turned up all successful and not needing any money. But at the end, she decided that you deserved to know the truth before it died with her."

"I can't believe this," said Marshall. "Even if it's true, what does it have to do with you, Chloe?"

"Your wife's early academic success hinged on the work she'd done in identifying Lissy and your father," explained Alvarez. "She must have thought that if no one else had found the truth in all this time, why would anyone now?"

"Then the damned box turned up," said Chloe, "your heritage from your beloved Aunt Lissy. And you could look at the pictures and pick out your family name, so you knew it had something to do with you. Lissy made it easy for me to decide what to do—instead of reading to you what was really there, I just told you the same stories you'd been told all along."

"I wondered about that," said Alvarez. "Why didn't you get rid of the papers after you got the box back, tell your husband someone figured out the secret to the box and that the papers were gone?

"I thought about it," said Chloe, as though the subject pained her. "But it all meant so much to him, and finding the box, getting it back again, that was like a miracle. What were the chances that it would fall into the wrong hands twice?"

"What were the chances that someone would find out your secret without the box?" Alvarez countered, asking a question that had been bothering him all along. "You killed Reynolds in spite of the fact that you had the box and its contents back safe and sound."

"*You* killed Rolland Reynolds?" asked Marshall in an agonized tone. "My God, Chloe, tell me it isn't true."

"The day your husband took me to lunch," continued Alvarez calmly, "he told me that you were upset with Reynolds, that you'd been assigned to research Seminole history. That was the day that you decided to kill him, wasn't it?"

Chloe nodded, her face pale. "He was an awful, horrible man. I knew what he was doing, blackmailing people, but I couldn't prove it. That's why I went to Amy, to try to get her to help me, but it was too late. She told me she was in love with him, that maybe she was even going to ask him to leave his wife and children for her. Then Amy died. I was really scared that she died because of what she knew about Rolland, but then I realized her death might be a blessing. God only knows what references she might turn up. There was just one *Tribune* article that said Homer Marshall left Rosewood before 1923. One single article with one single paragraph, and if I stayed in charge of the black heritage research, I was certain it would stay buried. But when Rolland pulled me off, I had to do something to stop him. Rolland was smart. If he found out about the *Tribune* article, he'd figure out that Richard couldn't read. Then he'd blackmail Richard, too. There would never be an end to it.''

"Chloe, honey," said Marshall, "I would never have let that happen. Put the gun down, baby. It's okay. I'll stand by you, we'll get the best lawyers that money can buy."

Interesting, the possibility of Reynolds blackmailing Richard Marshall. Alvarez still thought the things at stake had been Chloe Marshall's reputation and her new way of life, but he was willing to let others argue that point some other day, some other place. "You knew Reynolds's wife and kids were out of town," he said, ignoring Marshall's interruption, and Chloe nodded. "You drove up to his house—"

"No, I parked several streets away," she corrected him. "I walked to his house."

"You walked to his house, rang the doorbell. It was only natural that he would ask you inside. You shot him, spray-painted 'Rahowa' on the wall to make it look like a hate crime. That didn't work so well, you know. You should have used red spray paint, not black."

There was an exasperated sound from Tory.

"I did the best I could. I'd never killed anyone before."

Alvarez reminded himself that the whole point of this exercise was to prevent her from getting any more practice. "The spray paint was a good thought," he told her. "I can understand the rest of it, but why didn't you get rid of the gun? Hanging onto the gun is like hanging onto the box, Chloe. Why didn't you get rid of it?"

"This gun belongs to a member of Blood and Honor," she said. Alvarez didn't ask what Blood and Honor was; George

Nelson would fill him in. "I have a cousin, lives in a trailer out in Micanopy," Chloe said. "She's just had a baby. I stopped by when her husband wasn't there, took her a baby gift. She was so grateful that she burst into tears, had to go into the bathroom to get herself pulled together. I walked into the bedroom, reached under the bed, and got this." Chloe nodded at the gun resting on her knees. "They all keep a gun under the bed," she added disdainfully, "like that's not the first place a kid is going to go."

Did the woman realize that she'd just admitted premeditation? "Still a risk, keeping the gun," Alvarez said.

"I've been careful," Chloe replied. "It doesn't have my prints on it. Remember Sledge? Did you know he's actually related to me? With everything that's happened, I figured that if suspicion ever fell on me, I'd discover the gun in some obvious place, claim it was planted to frame me."

"That's pretty good," Alvarez admitted. "But it has to end here. What are you going to do, shoot all of us?"

"Of course not," said Chloe, sounding genuinely shocked.

"Your husband isn't going to stand by and watch you shoot Ms. Travers and me."

"I'm certainly not," said Marshall, right on cue. "Put down the gun, Chloe."

Chloe looked as though she were starting to panic. "I've worked hard for everything I have," she said, "harder than Reynolds, harder than Wheatley's daughter over there, harder than either of them ever thought about working." So this must have been what set off Alvarez's inner alarms about Chloe Marshall, a disdain toward Tory cloaked with solicitousness in order to get the Rosewood box.

"You haven't worked any harder than I have," said Marshall quietly. "If you hurt someone else, you'll be hurting both of us."

Marshall's wife started crying. "I kept the box because of you," she said. "I wanted you to be happy."

"I know," said Marshall. "I love you, Chloe. I know what a good person you are, and I'm going to be here for you every step of the way. Everyone makes mistakes. But I'm asking you to do one more thing for me, honey. Put down the gun."

If they were on TV, this would be a long, drawn-out moment. But this was reality, which was often anticlimactic. With no more suspense, no sudden movements, and not one more word, Chloe Marshall put the gun down on the floor. Alvarez exhaled on the way to grab it, not realizing until then that he had actually been holding his breath. As quickly as Alvarez scooped up the gun, Richard Marshall was on the floor, gathering his sobbing wife into his arms. Alvarez turned to Tory, sitting pale and still on the couch.

"You okay?" he asked. She nodded. "I still remember the part where you said I would have done something stupid if I'd had a gun."

"It's not like I ever had any training in these things," she told him. "I thought you said some things that were pretty dumb, too—so what do you want me to do?"

"What do I want you to do?" he repeated, thinking about salmon steaks in the refrigerator and the king-sized bed back at the condo. The doorbell rang and Alvarez sighed. "I want you to let the nice deputy in before he panics and kicks down the door."

The look on Tory's face was almost worth the horror of the last twenty minutes. "It's one of the few advantages of hanging out with someone who rates a tail," he told her, then added for good measure, "sweetheart."

FORTY

Side Trips
Friday

ALVAREZ'S ROSEWOOD REFERENCE said that the only remaining remnants of the town were John Wright's house and a road sign. That reference, like the street map that didn't show all the new neighborhoods in Haile Plantation, would soon be out of date, since there were signs of development in the Rosewood area. So much could happen in a short time. Or, alternatively, so many things could remain the same.

After the excitement at the Marshall house wound down two

nights ago, Alvarez suggested to Tory that they return to the condo for a long-overdue dinner and relaxation. She looked at him for a moment, as though considering all the untidy pieces, past and future, left strewn around them, then simply said, "Okay."

Police work had taught Alvarez to value current results over future potential ones. Tory had never said that she loved him, that she would marry him, or that she was going to have the baby. But Alvarez was patient, he was used to waiting to get what he wanted, and in the case of someone like Tory, he figured her current silence on these subjects was progress in the right direction. After all, it had been quite a week for everyone involved.

George Nelson told Alvarez that although the investigation of Amy Cooper's murder would remain active for a while, they currently had little hope of conclusively determining the identity of the person who ran her down, or whether in fact that person had been hired by Rolland Reynolds. Nelson didn't volunteer whether a research file on the Hodden family had surfaced, and Alvarez didn't ask.

This was one of the many subjects that Tory remained silent on, and as far as Alvarez was concerned, it was just as well to let that particular sleeping dog lie.

Nelson did, however, offer to see Alvarez and Tory off at the airport, so Alvarez told him the time their flight would be departing from the Gainesville airport tomorrow. He figured George Nelson wanted to see Tory get on the plane with his own eyes.

The last two days, in spite of issues remaining to be resolved, had passed with a seeming normalcy that filled Alvarez with something resembling optimism. Instead of asking her father more questions, Tory had slowly stepped back from the role of dutiful daughter to leave Wheatley more and more to the enthusiastic ministrations of Dana Halloran. Of course, not everything progressed smoothly, and there were at least two tense moments that Alvarez witnessed between father and daughter.

The first occurred when Wheatley asked Tory to remain long enough to visit him at her childhood home, the second when he explained that although he had kept company with Dana for several years, he wouldn't quite describe their status as an engagement. Tory responded to the invitation with polite but firm excuses about needing to return home. She met the explanation about Dana with simple silence, refusing to either ask questions or sanction Wheatley's explanation. It never occurred to the man to question the sapphire ring on his own daughter's finger, but then, after all, he was in the hospital recovering from a serious accident.

Richard Marshall had been as good as his word, standing steadfastly by his wife, doing everything in his power to help her. He refused to request an investigation into the death of Lissy Hodden Garner, so it appeared that he was willing to take Chloe's word that she had no part in the old woman's demise. When Alvarez went to see Marshall to thank him for his help both before and after his wife's confession, the man was still unwilling to place blame on anyone but himself. He told Alvarez that in addition to seeking the best legal help he could find for his wife, he had engaged a reading tutor. He was determined to be at Chloe's side as someone who could read any document put in front of him.

So far the newspaper had reported only the arrest of Chloe Marshall on suspicion of murdering her supervisor over work-related issues. Alvarez had no idea how many details would be uncovered and aired by the press, or how the issue of Rosewood compensations paid in error would be addressed. He simply assumed that he would be long gone by the time that was all sorted out. Alvarez hoped that if anyone were to draw a parallel between Fannie Taylor and Chloe Marshall, that someone would be wise enough to also recognize in Richard Marshall the true spirit of reconciliation.

Marilyn Mortenson told Alvarez that with no one to staff it, the Center for State Heritage Studies would be shutting down, at least temporarily. She said that in light of recent developments, the Center's mission might be incorporated into the history department at large instead of existing as a separate entity, and that might be a good thing. She was the one who suggested that Tory and Alvarez visit Rosewood before they left Florida. She went on to say that after losing three members of her staff during the week they had been in town, she was ready to suggest anything that would keep Alvarez away from her department. She sounded halfway serious.

Alvarez and Tory drove from Gainesville to Rosewood on this mild winter afternoon, planning to continue on to the coast and Cedar Key for dinner. They saw the green-and-white road sign and the white, wooden two-story house that had once been John Wright's home, the same house that once provided shelter for Lissy Hodden and others while the rest of Rosewood burned to the ground.

In addition to these two landmarks, there were the earmarks of new construction—dirt roads leading off from the highway and a sign advertising lots in a new subdivision. Regardless of what happened in the past, life went on.

Mortenson told Alvarez that the old Rosewood cemetery was on private land, and having had enough excitement in the last few days, he and Tory didn't go looking for it. They found the Sumner graveyard at the end of a dirt road with a sign proclaiming the place to be Shiloh Cemetery. It was quiet and peaceful, with large moss-draped oaks gracefully bending over the graves, many of which were covered with mounds made of earth and oyster shells. There was everything from small unkempt, unmarked graves to large ornate monuments, complete with marble benches for visitors to sit on and contemplate the final resting place of those before them. John Wright himself was supposedly buried here in an unmarked grave.

Tory sat on one of the marble benches and considered the monument in front of her. "I wonder how many black people are buried here," she said.

Alvarez stood behind her, his hands resting lightly on her shoulders. This casual gesture felt good, felt right, and he resolved to remember moments like this in order to get through the times when Tory would throw up obstacles between them. He thought about the Confederate flag prominently displayed at a trailer park they'd passed. "Probably not any," he replied.

"I've been thinking about what to do after we leave here. I'm not sure that me getting pregnant is a good reason for us to get married." Tory paused. "I mean, I'm hopelessly out of date about all of this, but isn't that what a professional woman in my situation is supposed to say?"

It was too beautiful an afternoon to be bothered with doubts like this. "People have gotten married for worse reasons," Alvarez said. "And we'll never know how it's going to work out until we try."

Tory wasn't convinced. "I keep trying to imagine explaining this to people," she said. "To Cody, Sylvia, Jazz." There was a pause. "To Lonnie."

"Explain it to Sylvia," Alvarez suggested, "and let her explain it to everyone else."

"That might work," said Tory thoughtfully. "Except for Cody."

"Cody has other things on his mind."

Tory turned around to face him then. "What?"

"I said that Cody has other things on his mind."

"What a strange remark to make. How would you know?"

"Because I've called to check on him every day."

"You called to check on my son? After all the times you told me I was calling too often?"

"Yeah, and I called Sylvia and Jazz, too. Not only to check on them, but to let them know how you're doing. You're not the only responsible person in the world, Tory."

Tory raised an expressive eyebrow. "What other things does my son have on his mind?"

"Stuff between the two of us. Things he didn't want to bother you with. Things he wanted to ask me."

"If this has to do with how you got women to go to bed with you when you were working undercover—"

"If I won't discuss that with you, I sure as hell won't discuss it with Cody." Tory wouldn't let him off the hook with that little of an explanation; she continued to look expectantly at him. "I guess it's okay to tell you now—Cody wanted to know how to go about doing a background check on someone, how to figure out if they're really who they say they are."

"He wants to find out if we're really blood-related to my parents? He's found evidence that I'm adopted?"

Alvarez smiled. "No such luck. It seems that someone has contacted Kohli's parents, claiming to be Kohli's birth mother."

"And she wants her back?" Tory asked hopefully. Alvarez shook his head, knowing full well it wasn't Kohli Tory disliked, but the knowledge that her son was growing into a man. "I should have known it would have to do with that girl. I liked her much better when I thought she was a boy named Cole."

"If it wasn't Kohli, it would be someone else. She's a perfectly nice girl. It's obvious that they're crazy about each other, so you might as well go along with it."

"That's what you say about everything." Tory paused, thinking. "If you learned so much working undercover, surely you could figure out a way to make her disappear."

Alvarez raised an eyebrow of his own

"Just for five years or so," Tory added.

"Well, you know what they say."

"No, I don't know. What do they say?"

He pulled Tory up off the bench and into his arms. "They say that everyone has their price," he whispered into her ear. "And I can spend a nice long time, telling you exactly what my price is. Better yet, I could show you."

Tory was such a practical, literal person. "When are you going to start?" she asked.

"Right now," he said.

EPILOGUE

IN CHATHAM, Connecticut, Louise Herrington frowned where she sat at a writing desk built into a nook in the large country kitchen that had once accommodated a bustling, busy family of six. The children were all grown now, married and moved away, leaving behind a family of two, but a busy family nonetheless.

Louise's husband was an international banker who thrived on exchange rate fluctuations and stress. He would probably drop dead one day at his desk, not able to think of a happier way to go. Louise had long ago recognized that the very characteristics that made her husband successful in his chosen field were the same ones that she loved in a different context—his intellect, drive, and willingness to take risks. She considered her husband's workaholism to be part of the package deal, and had no intention of pressuring him into an unhappy retirement. Of course, it didn't hurt that he traveled extensively to very interesting places and never failed to invite Louise along.

Louise had devoted her life to raising her children, but now that they were grown, she had her own projects and interests to occupy her. Five years ago she presented a detailed summary of her family heritage to each of their children as a Christmas gift, and she intended to follow up with a matching bound volume documenting their paternal family tree. Blood ties were important, Louise felt, and long after she was gone, she wanted her descendants to have a tangible record of the family members that had lived before them.

However, researching her husband's family history had proven to be much more difficult than she anticipated. The Herringtons did not come from Connecticut, as Louise's ancestors did. She had to make most of her inquiries via long distance, and she encountered problems tracing the family line through the first half of the 1900s. She was therefore excited to find documents indicating that her husband's family had moved from Jacksonville, Florida, to the Cedar Key area in 1900, apparently to work in the sawmills that thrived in that part of the state at the turn of the century.

Louise's painstaking efforts had finally yielded no less than three Herringtons listed as employees of the Cummer sawmill in 1923, located a few miles inland from Cedar Key at a place called Sumner. But after finding payroll records, Louise could discover no further evidence of any Herrington in Levy County, Florida. It was as though they had moved from Jacksonville to Cedar Key, and then twenty-three years later, vanished from the face of the earth.

Louise talked to one of the volunteer workers at the Cedar Key Historical Museum, after her searches through various newspapers, school records, and personal papers could show no evidence of Herringtons in residence at Cedar Key post-1923.

"If they disappeared about that time," the woman on the other end of the line said slowly, hesitantly, "you might want to consider the possibility that it had something to do with Rosewood."

"What's Rosewood?" Louise asked. "And what could it have to do with my husband's family?"

"That's something you need to decide for yourself. I'll put together some information and send it to you."

Louise thanked the woman and then forgot about their conversation. Until today. Until the large envelope came in the mail, containing story after story about the destruction of Rosewood, the fear that had been the heritage of the survivors, and the legislative battle that had resulted seventy years later.

Louise frowned some more, looking at the material spread out over her desk. Then she carefully picked up each piece of paper and put it back in the envelope. She didn't throw the envelope away in the kitchen trashcan; she took it out to the garage and put it in the very bottom of the garbage bin.

Louise Herrington had lived over thirty-five years with the same man, and he was a good man, a decent, loyal, and law-abiding man. She and her husband might be old and set in their ways, without many of the outward trappings of passion so evident in younger couples, but her husband was a man for whom she would give her life, unquestionably. Louise decided right then and there that blood ties were vastly overrated in importance, and that besides, she had always meant to learn to quilt.

Maybe now was the time, while Christmas was still a good ways off.

AFTERWORD

Rosewood,
Haile Plantation and Miscellaneous Items

ROSEWOOD: On January 1, 1923, a white woman named Fannie Taylor living in Sumner, Florida, claimed that a black man had attacked her in the early morning. A group of white men gathered and followed hunting dogs down the railroad track to Rosewood, a nearby predominantly black community. They tortured a black resident named Aaron Carrier in an effort to obtain information about the attack, then tortured and killed another black resident named Samuel Carter to the same ends. During the next five to six days, mob violence continued to break out, purportedly as a result of the ongoing search for the attacker. These events culminated in a shoot-out at the residence of Sylvester Carrier and the burning of every black-owned building in Rosewood. The surviving black residents of Rosewood fled the area, leaving behind their property, never to return.

In the 1980s, some of the surviving Rosewood residents and their descendants started to gather and discuss the events that had led to loss of life and property. With growing interest in the Rosewood incident as both a human-interest and human rights story, a Florida law firm drafted a legislative bill requesting reparation payments to those who had suffered damages. These efforts, and the legal and personal maneuverings that eventually resulted in the controversial payments, are detailed in a book titled *Rosewood Like Judgment Day* by Michael D'Orso. The human-interest aspect of the story resulted in a movie titled *Rosewood*.

Qualified Rosewood survivors were identified through three separate mechanisms—the efforts of the survivors and the descendants themselves, the findings of a team charged with investigating the historical events, and the proceedings of the Attorney General's Office of Civil Rights in Hollywood, Florida. This latter group was charged with implementing the legislative bill, and was responsible for both notifying and authenticating potential claimants. For the purposes of my story, I have combined these three separate groups and activities, and added two fictional survivors to the nine who were authenticated by required procedures. The Hodden and Marshall families of Rosewood are fictional creations; other Rosewood residents mentioned in the story are historical figures.

The versions of events told by various characters in this book are all claims made by various individuals regarding what really happened at Rosewood during the first week in January, 1923. There exist to this day rumors of numerous, unreported deaths of both whites and blacks, and related claims of undiscovered mass graves.

The mystery of who attacked Fannie Taylor remains unsolved. The claim that it was a black man raises the question of whether one would be foolhardy enough to venture into the housing area of a predominantly white town, where the buildings were close together and the presence of a black male would be immediately suspect. Various blacks have long claimed that Fannie Taylor had a white lover who fled to Rosewood and demanded assistance by invoking his Masonic brotherhood with black Masons. The problem with this claim is that although there were black Masonic lodges at the time, historical records indicate that the Masonic lodges of that period and place were as segregated as other groups. Even if a white individual prevailed upon Aaron Carrier and Samuel Carter to help him leave the area, what is the likelihood that these two individuals would protect his identity, even to the point of death, as was the case with Carter?

The story seems to require that the individual who attacked Fannie Taylor have both a reason to head to Rosewood for assistance, and leverage to ensure the silence of those who helped him. Since the Florida prison system operated road gangs in the area, since various black Rosewood residents including Sam Carter and Sylvester Carrier are documented as having served prison time, and since the power of the men in charge of the road gangs was virtually absolute, I made the individual responsible for the attack on Fannie Taylor a road gang guard. This person and this conclusion are entirely fictional creations for the purpose of presenting a potential solution to this real-life mystery. I have been told that the correct term for the people in charge of the road gangs is "correctional officer." Again, for purposes of the story, I have used the more widely accepted term "guard."

Similarly, the version of events related by the fictional Lissy Hodden is a version that might be true, more or less, based on the recollections of various parties. No disrespect is intended to those who believe differently about what happened in Rosewood in January of 1923. The complete truth about what happened at Rosewood during that specific week is now hidden forever in history. The best that we can hope is to understand the essence of these events and try to learn what individual lessons we care to take from it.

HAILE PLANTATION: Haile Plantation is the name of a large development in Alachua County. The area was once a 1500-acre cotton plantation owned by Thomas and Serena Haile. According to the 1860 tax roll, Thomas Haile owned 79 slaves and his son, John Haile, owned 63. The 7000-square-foot plantation home has been restored to its original appearance on a forty-acre remnant of the original property. It is maintained by Historic Haile Homestead, Inc., and is opened for tours on special occasions and upon request.

MISCELLANEOUS MATTERS: The Seagle Building is a historical structure in downtown Gainesville, and its history is as described by Alvarez. Tom Petty and certain members of the original Heartbreakers grew up in Gainesville. Rip Tide is a fictional group, created for plot purposes. However, groups similar to Rip Tide exist, and remain controversial in the ongoing definition of First Amendment rights as applied to the Internet. Racist Skinhead groups, Hammerskins, and Blood and Honor are not fictional, although certain geographic locations of these groups have been altered for plot purposes. The lynchings in Perry and Newberry, as recounted by Richard Marshall, are factual, except for the inclusion of his fictional grandfather.

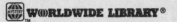

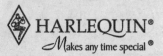